# SONG
## OF
## THE
## *F*IREFLIES

## ALSO BY J. A. REDMERSKI

*The Edge of Never*
*The Edge of Always*

*Killing Sarai*
*Reviving Izabel*
*The Swan and the Jackal*
*Dirty Eden*

*The Mayfair Moon*
*Kindred*
*The Ballad of Aramei*

## Acclaim for J. A. Redmerski's Novels
## *SONG OF THE FIREFLIES*

"Flawlessly and compellingly written, this is a story that made me live every page, every emotion, every unconventional facet of this truly epic romance." —NatashaisaBookJunkie.com

"A stunning and heart-wrenching novel...Redmerski captures the intensity of love so beautifully in each book she writes...[This book is] fantastic, fast-paced...It will keep you on your toes until the last page!" —GutterGirlsBookReviews.com

"I adored *The Edge of Never* and *The Edge of Always*...[This book is] equally amazing...I love Redmerski's style! It's so easy to read, flawless, and addicting. She has amazing talent."
—ReviewingRomance.com

## *THE EDGE OF ALWAYS*

"This was so good!...This book certainly throws its characters quite a few curveballs. Stuff that had my adrenaline racing, and my heart skipping beats." —Maryse's Book Blog

"Another fabulous journey with Camryn and Andrew...This series will take you on a ride down roads you never thought to travel, and when you return you'll be nothing like you were before you started." —MyBookAddiction.com

"I was blown away by this book in so many ways...The perfect closure to one of the most emotional and deep love stories I've ever read...*The Edge of Always* is a must read. All you'll want to do is read it and re-read it again." —BookishTemptations.com

"The Andrew and Camryn love story is epic and one I will never forget…very profound and heartwarming…a wonderful story and a beautiful ending to Camryn and Andrew's story."

—DarkFaerieTales.com

## *THE EDGE OF NEVER*

"Addictive and fast paced. Readers will be drawn to Camryn, a smart girl who has become emotionally numb. Her partner in crime, the mysterious, spontaneous, and sweet Andrew is the real highlight…Readers will quickly get wrapped up in the adventure."

—*RT Book Reviews*

"This was a beautiful, *beautiful* story. Amazingly detailed, poignant, eloquently written, and the characters' voices were so… honest. Emotion, thoughts, and fear down to their purest form."

—Maryse's Book Blog

"I found their blooming romance to be slow-burning and sensual, making for a real connection that gets lost in other books…All-consuming and riveting…Redmerski pours passion into this book and I know it will not fail in touching readers' hearts."

—FreshFiction.com

"5 stars! WOW! What an unexpected journey and an amazing read! This book tells a beautiful story about friendship and love, of living in the moment, living life to the fullest, being true to yourself and not being afraid to reach for your dreams…I totally loved this and would highly recommend adding it to your TBRs!"

—Aestas Book Blog

# SONG
# OF
# THE
# FIREFLIES

## J. A. REDMERSKI

FOREVER

NEW YORK    BOSTON

Copyright © 2014 by Jessica Redmerski
Excerpt from *The Edge of Never* copyright © 2012 by Jessica Redmerski
Excerpt from *The Edge of Always* copyright © 2013 by Jessica Redmerski

Forever
Hachette Book Group
237 Park Avenue,
New York, NY 10017

www.HachetteBookGroup.com

Printed in the United States of America

RRD-C

Originally published as an ebook
First trade paperback edition: September 2014
10 9 8 7 6 5 4 3 2 1

Forever is an imprint of Grand Central Publishing.
The Forever name and logo are trademarks of Hachette Book Group, Inc.

The publisher is not responsible for websites (or their content) that are not owned by the publisher.

The Hachette Speakers Bureau provides a wide range of authors for speaking events. To find out more, go to www.hachettespeakersbureau.com or call (866) 376-6591.

Library of Congress Cataloging-in-Publication Data
Redmerski, J. A.
    Song of the fireflies / J. A. Redmerski. — First trade paperback edition.
        pages cm
    ISBN 978-1-4555-5506-2 (trade pbk.) — ISBN 978-1-4789-5484-2 (audio download)
I. Title.
    PS3618.E4344S66 2014
    813'.6—dc23
                                                                2014002798

*For Michael N. and Alexander D.*

# SONG OF THE FIREFLIES

# ONE

## Elias

*T*hey say you never forget your first love, and I have to say that they are right. I met the girl of my dreams when we were both still fans of tree houses and dirt cakes—she made the best dirt cakes in Georgia—and today, seventeen years later, I still see her smile in everything good.

But Bray's life has always been…complicated. Mine, well, I guess the same can be said for me, but as much as she and I are alike, there are just as many things that make us so very different.

I never thought that a relationship with her, other than being the best of friends, sometimes with benefits, could ever work. Neither did she. I guess in the beginning, we were both right. But by the end—and damn, the end sure as hell blindsided us—we were proven wrong. I admit a few dozen mistakes along the way are what led us here to this moment, holed up in the back of a convenience store with cops surrounding the building.

But wait. Let me start from the beginning.

*Fourth of July—Seventeen Years Ago...*

The kind of crush a nine-year-old boy has on an eight-year-old girl is almost always innocent. And cruel. The first time I saw Brayelle Bates flitting toward me through the wide-open field by Mr. Parson's pond, she was marked my victim. She wore a white sundress and a pair of flip-flops with little purple flowers made of fabric sewn to the tops. Her long, dark hair had been pulled neatly into ponytails on each side of her head and tied with purple ribbons. I loved her. OK, so I didn't really "love" her, but she sure was pretty.

So, naturally I gave her a hard time.

"What's that on your face?" I asked, as she started to walk by.

She stopped and crossed her arms and looked down at me sitting on my blanket beside my mother, pursing her lips at me disapprovingly.

"There's nothing on my face," she said with a smirk.

"Yes there is." I pointed up at her. "Right there. It's really gross."

Instinctively, she reached up and began touching her face all over with her fingertips. "Well, what is it? What does it look like?"

"It's everywhere. And I told you it's gross, that's what it looks like."

She propped both hands on her hips and chewed on the inside of her mouth. "You're lying."

"No, I'm not. Your whole face, it's really ugly. You should go to the doctor and get that checked out."

The tip of her flip-flop and her big toe jabbed me in the back of my hip.

"*Owww!* What was *that* for?" I reached around and rubbed the spot with my fingertips.

I noticed my mother shake her head at us, but she went back to her conversation with my aunt Janice.

Bray crossed her arms and snarled down at me. "If anyone out here is gross, it's you. Your face looks just like my dog's ass."

Upon hearing that, my mom snapped her head around, and she glared at *me* as if I was the one who had cursed.

I shrugged.

Bray turned on her heel, sauntered away with her chin held high, and caught up with her parents, who were already many feet out ahead of her. I watched her go, the throbbing in my hip a reminder that if I was going to mess with that girl again, there would be more pain and abuse where that came from.

Of course, it only made me want to do it again.

As the pasture filled up with Athens's residents, come to see the yearly fireworks display, I watched Bray do cartwheels in the grass with her friend. Every now and then I saw her look over at me, showing off and taunting me. She did get the best of me, after all, and it was only natural for her to gloat about it. I got bored fast sitting with my mom, especially since Bray seemed to be having so much fun over there.

"Where are you going, Elias?" my mom asked, as I got up from the blanket.

"Just right over there," I said, pointing in Bray's direction.

"OK, but please stay in my sight."

I sighed and rolled my eyes; Mom was always worried I would get kidnapped or lost or hurt or wet or dirty or any number of things.

"I will," I said and walked away.

I weaved my way through the few families sitting in the space between us in lawn chairs and on blankets, ice chests filled with beer and soda next to them, until I was standing in front of that abusive girl I couldn't get enough of.

"You really shouldn't do cartwheels in a dress, you know that, right?" I asked.

Bray's mouth fell open. Her pale-skinned friend, Lissa, who had long, curly, white-blonde hair, and who I knew from school, smiled up at me. I think she liked me.

"I have shorts on under my dress thank-you-very-much," Bray snapped. "Why were you looking, anyway?"

"I wasn't *looking*, I just…"

Bray and Lissa burst into laughter.

My face flushed hot.

Bray had only just moved here from Atlanta a week ago, and it hadn't taken long for her to fit in. Or rather to pretty much own the place as far as the kids went. She was the kind of girl so damn mean and intimidating and pretty that the other girls knew they had better befriend her or else end up her enemy. She wasn't a bully; she just had this way about her that demanded respect.

"Want to go sit by the pond?" I asked. "The fireworks look cool reflected off the water."

Bray shrugged. "I guess so." Then she got to her feet; Lissa was already standing up, ready to go, before Bray had even made up her mind.

Lissa was a nice girl but clingy at times, and I admit I was the one who started a rumor about her being albino because of her white hair and sheet-white skin. I felt bad afterward. I hadn't expected the whole school to call her that every single day. When Bray moved to town, she told a group of girls off on her first day for making fun of Lissa. Afterward, Lissa naturally clung to Bray like Velcro.

And just like that, as if I'd never called Bray ugly and she had never kicked me, we walked side by side toward the pond and sat together for the next two hours. My friend Mitchell joined us eventually, and the four of us lay on our backs on the grass and watched the fireworks explode in an array of colors in the clear black sky. And although Lissa and Mitchell were there with us, Bray and I carried on with each other as if we were alone. We laughed at stupid jokes and made fun of people walking by. It was the best night of my life, and it was only just beginning.

Shortly after the fireworks ended and the darkness settled across the pasture again, most of the town had already packed up and gone home.

My mom found me with Bray, Lissa, and Mitchell.

"Time to go," she said, standing over me.

Bray was lying next to me, her head pressed against the side of my shoulder. I hadn't really noticed it much, but my mom sure did. I saw a look in her eye—upside down, since she was standing behind us, which made that look all the more scary—that I'd never seen before. I raised myself up from the grass and turned around to face her.

"Can't I stay and hang out a while longer?"

"No, Elias, I have to work in the morning. It's already late." She gestured with her free hand for me to get up and follow.

Reluctantly, I did as I was told.

"Oh come on, please, Ms. Kline?" Mitchell said on the other side of me, looking goofy with a front tooth missing and a light brown mullet lying against the back of his T-shirt. "I'll walk home with him."

Mitchell was a year older than me, but I did *not* need him to walk me home. This made me mad, probably because it embarrassed me in front of Bray.

I glared at Mitchell, and he looked back at me with apologetic eyes.

"I'll see you guys later," I said.

I took the ice chest from my mom to relieve her of some of the load she was carrying, and I followed her through the pasture toward our truck parked along the dirt road. Aunt Janice waved good-bye and sputtered away in her old beat-up Corsica.

My mom went to bed right after we got home. She was the manager at a hotel and rarely got any time off. My dad lived in Savannah. They had divorced three years ago. But I had a great relationship with them both. I often stayed at my dad's in the summer, except this year he had to go to Michigan for his job, so I was staying with my mom all summer for the first time since their divorce.

I think it was fate. Bray never would've ended up outside my bedroom window that night, tapping on the glass with the tip of her finger, if my dad hadn't gone to Michigan. I wondered how she knew where I lived but I never asked, figuring Mitchell or Lissa must've told her.

"You're already in bed?" Bray asked with mock disbelief as she looked up at me.

I raised the window the rest of the way, and the humid summer air rushed in past me.

"No. I'm just in my room. What are you doin' out here?"

A sly little grin crept up on the edges of Bray's lips. "Want to go swimming?" she asked.

"Swimming?"

"Yeah. Swimming." She crossed her arms and cocked her head to one side. "Or are you too chicken to sneak out?"

"I'm not afraid to sneak out."

*Actually, I kind of am. If my mom catches me she'll whip me with the fly swatter.*

"Then come on," she said, waving at me. "Prove it."

A challenge. Fly swatter or not, I couldn't back down from a challenge or she'd never let me live it down. She'd go to school and turn my friends against me. The whole town would think I was a chicken afraid of his mommy, and I'd grow up an outcast and never have a girlfriend. I'd end up homeless and die an old man living underneath a bridge—these are the things my mom told me would happen to me if I ever dropped out of school.

OK, so I was overthinking this whole sneaking-out thing.

I bit down on my bottom lip, thought about it for a moment. When I noticed Bray about to start running that mouth of hers again, I tossed one leg over the windowsill and hopped outside, landing in a smooth, crouched position, which I was quite proud of.

Bray grinned, grabbed my hand, and pulled me along with her away from my house.

Admittedly, I thought of the fly swatter all the way back to the pond in the pasture.

# TWO

## Elias

*B*ray was so free-spirited, she didn't seem to have a worry in the world. I noticed this about her the moment we reached the outskirts of the pasture and she broke away from me and ran out toward it. Her arms were raised high above her head, as if she was reaching for the stars. Her laughter was infectious, and I found myself laughing right along with her as I ran behind her. We jumped off the end of the little rickety dock and hit the water with a loud splash. She didn't even stop to take off her flip-flops, nor I my shirt, beforehand.

We swam for a while, and I splashed her in the face every chance I got, until she finally had enough and swam back to the dock.

"Have you ever kissed a girl before?" Bray asked, taking me by surprise.

I glanced nervously at her to my left; we both moved our feet back and forth in the water.

"No. Have you?"

Her shoulder bumped against mine hard, and she giggled and made a horrible face at me.

"No way. I wouldn't kiss a *girl*. Talk about gross."

I laughed, too. Really, I didn't realize what I had said until after she pointed it out; I was too blindsided by the kissing topic to notice. But I played it off smoothly as though I was just being weird.

"I've never kissed a boy," she said.

There was an awkward bout of silence. Mostly the awkwardness was coming from me, I was sure. I swallowed and looked out at the calm water. Every now and then I heard a random firework pop off in the distance somewhere. And the song of crickets and frogs surrounded us.

Not knowing what to say, or if I was supposed to say anything at all, I finally added, "Why not?"

"Why not what?"

"Why haven't you kissed a boy before?"

She looked at me suspiciously. "Why haven't you kissed a *girl* before?"

I shrugged. "I dunno. I just haven't."

"Well, maybe you should."

"Why?"

"I dunno."

Silence. We stared out at the water together, both of us with our hands braced against the dock's edge, our bodies slumped between our shoulders, our feet moving steadily in the water and pushing poetic ripples outward across the surface.

I leaned over and kissed her on the cheek, right next to the corner of her mouth.

She blushed and smiled, and I knew my face must've been bright red, but I didn't care and I didn't regret it.

I wanted to do it again.

Next thing I knew, Bray jumped up from the dock and ran back out into the pasture.

"Fireflies!" she shouted.

I stood up and watched her run away from me beneath the dark star-filled sky and she grew smaller and smaller. Hundreds of little green-yellow dots of light blinked off and on out in the wide-open space.

"Come on, Elias!" Her voice carried my name on the wind.

I knew I'd never forget this night. I couldn't have understood why back then, but something within me knew. I would never forget it.

I ran out after her.

"We should've brought a jar!" She kept reaching out her hands, trying to catch one of the fireflies, but she was always a second too late.

On my third try, I caught one and held it carefully in the hollow of both hands so that I wouldn't crush it.

"Oh, you got one! Let me see!"

I held my hands out slowly and Bray looked inside the tiny opening between my thumb and index finger. Every few seconds my hand would light up with a dull glow and then fade again.

"So pretty," she said, wide-eyed.

"Just like you," I said, though I had no idea what made me say that. Out loud, anyway.

Bray just smiled at me and looked back down into my hand.

"OK, let it go," she said. "I don't want it to die."

I opened my hands and held them up, but the firefly just stayed there crawling across the ball of my thumb. I leaned in to blow on it and its tiny black wings finally sprang to life and it flew away into the darkness.

Bray and I spent the whole night in the field chasing the fireflies and laying on the grass, staring up at the stars. She told me all about her sister, Rian, and how she was a snob and was always mean to Bray. I told her about my parents, because I didn't have any brothers or sisters. She said I was lucky. We talked forever, it seemed. We may have been young, but we connected deeply on that night. I knew we would be great friends, even better friends than Mitchell and I had been, and I had known him since first grade, when he had tried to con me out of my peach cup at lunch.

And before the night was over, we made a pact with each other that would later prove to see us through some very troubled times.

"Promise we'll always be best friends," Bray said, lying next to me. "No matter what. Even if you grow up ugly and I grow up mean."

I laughed. "You're *already* mean!"

She elbowed me.

"And *you're* already *ugly*," she said with a blush in her cheeks.

I gave in, though really I needed no convincing. "OK, I promise."

We gazed back up at the stars; her fingers were interlaced and her hands rested on her belly.

I had no idea what I was getting into with Brayelle Bates. I didn't know about such things when I was nine. I didn't know. But I would never regret a moment with her. Never.

Bray and I were found early the following morning, fast asleep in the grass. We were awoken by three cops; Mr. Parson, who owned the land; and my frantic mother, who thought I had been kidnapped from my room, stuffed in a suitcase, and thrown on the side of a highway somewhere.

"Elias! Oh dear God, I thought you were gone!" She scooped me into her arms and squeezed me so tight I thought my eyeballs were going to burst out of the sockets. She pulled away, kissed me on the forehead, embarrassing the crap out of me, and then squeezed me again.

Bray's mom and dad were there, too.

"Have you been out here all night with him?" Bray's dad asked with a sharp edge in his voice.

My mom immediately went into defensive mode. She stood up the rest of the way with me and wrapped one arm around the front of me, pressing my head against her stomach.

"That daughter of yours," my mom said, and already I was flinching before she finished, "she has a mouth on her. My son would never have snuck out unless he was influenced."

*Oh geez…*

I sighed and threw my head back against her.

"Mom, I—"

"Are you blaming this on my *daughter?*" Bray's mother said, stepping up front and center.

"As a matter of fact, I am," my mom said boldly.

Bray started to shrink behind her dad and every second that passed I felt even worse about her being blamed.

Before this got too out of hand, I broke away from my mom's arms. "Dammit, Mom—!" Her eyes grew wide and fierce, and I stopped midsentence.

"Watch your mouth, Elias!" Then she looked at Bray's mom again and added, "See, Elias never uses language like that."

"Stop it! Please! I snuck out on my own, so leave Bray out of it!"

I hated shouting. I hated that I had to put my mom in her place like that, but I spoke what I felt in my heart, and that was something my mom always taught me to do. *Take up for the bullied, Elias. Never stand back and watch someone take advantage of someone else, Elias. Always do and say what you know in your heart to be right, no matter what, Elias.*

I hoped she would remember those things when we were back at home.

My mom sighed deeply and I watched the anger deflate with her breath. "I apologize," she said to Bray's parents. "Really, I am sorry. I was just so scared something had happened to him."

Bray's mom nodded, accepting my mom's apology with sincerity. "I understand. I'm sorry, too. I'm just glad they're safe."

Bray's dad said nothing. I got the feeling he wasn't as forgiving as her mom had been.

I was grounded for the rest of the summer for that stunt I pulled. And yes, I met the fly swatter that day, after which I vowed never to sneak out of the house again. But whenever it came to Bray, from that time up until we graduated high school, I did sneak out. A lot. But I never got caught again after that first time.

I know you must be wondering why after so many years of being best friends, attending the same school, working together at the local Dairy Queen, even often sharing a bed, why we never became something more to each other.

Well, the truth is that we did.

# THREE

*Four years ago…*

I turned twenty-two on August 2, a week after I had moved into my first apartment. Bray, like she did every year, insisted that I not stay at home on my birthday. She wanted to drag me out to a party somewhere, get drunk, have some fun. And while I was never opposed to parties, drinking, and getting laid every now and then, the last party I went to with Bray landed me in jail and Bray in the emergency room of Athens Regional. It was a wild night, that's for sure.

"It won't be like last time," Bray said from the doorway, trying to convince me.

She closed the front door with her foot and practically danced her way into my living room. She plopped down on my oversized chair and draped her legs over the arm.

I closed the fridge and sat down on the ottoman next to her, bringing my Gatorade bottle to my lips and taking a swig.

"You mean you won't get roofied, and I won't overhear the douchebag who did it bragging to his friends and then beat the shit out of him?" I laughed and took another drink. "That's hardly something that can be predicted."

She leaned forward and swung her arms around my neck. The smell of her freshly washed hair and lightly perfumed skin intoxicated me.

"I won't drink anything unless you or Lissa give it to me," she said and then pressed her lips to the side of my face.

I always hated it when she did that. Best friend, so what, it made me hard.

"I guess I'll go," I said, giving in. "But you have to promise you'll be on your best behavior." I shook my finger at her playfully.

In all reality, asking Bray to be on her best behavior was a far-fetched request that was almost always met with disappointment. But nothing she could ever do would push me away from her.

She raised both of her hands up in the air, as if surrendering.

"I fucking promise," she laughed. "I'll be good. If I don't, you have my permission to bend me over your knee and spank the shit out of me."

*Oh Jesus Christ…seriously? That's worse than her innocent "best friend" kiss to my cheek.*

I inhaled a very deep breath, composed myself, and then got up from the ottoman, Gatorade bottle in hand.

"Where are you going?"

"To get dressed?" I looked at her like she'd just asked a stupid question.

"What you're wearing is fine," she said. "You're one hot piece of ass, as usual." She stuck her tongue out at me and then looked me over.

She did tend to look me over a lot in the years we'd known each other. I often wondered if she secretly had the same feelings for me that I'd always had for her, but I could never really be sure. I always knew she cared for me and was attracted to me, but regarding the two of us together, I was as confused as you probably are.

I ignored her and went into my bedroom to change my clothes. She followed.

While it was never anything unusual for her to see me naked, this time her following me did strike me as odd.

"Elias?"

I looked from the open top drawer of my dresser to her.

"There's something I want to talk to you about."

This was serious. I had only seen that thoughtful, intent look on her face a few times before, and it was always about something that would later prove to define our strange relationship even more, like adding colors to a black-and-white painting. So far only a quarter of that painting had been filled in. Once with her confession to me that she lost her virginity to Michael Pearson—that about fucking killed me. Once when I admitted I lost mine to Abigail Rutherford—I thought Bray was going to hate me forever after that. Apparently, Abigail Rutherford was Bray's worst enemy, though I never got that impression until *after* I slept with her. Then once when she gave me her first blowjob because she "needed the practice"—for days after that, I was in a haze. I couldn't get the image out of my head, not necessarily because of the act itself but because of the trust she had in me to want *me* to be the one. And once when I ate her out in my car underneath a bridge overpass, because she dared me to do it. Bray never ceased to shock the hell out of me. Always in a good way. Yeah, those were some colorful fucking brushstrokes.

As I stood at the dresser, new boxers in my hand, I could only wonder what color we would be adding to that painting today.

She sat down on the end of my bed. Her silky dark hair

framed her peach-colored face and fell down over both of her bare shoulders.

"What's up?" I asked, concealing my impatience.

She glanced toward the closet and then looked back at me. "Madelyn will be at this party."

I thought I knew where this was going, but I couldn't be sure. I was having a hard time reading Bray, which in itself was foreign to me.

"So?"

"So, I know you have a thing for her. I don't like her." Bray struggled with those words; I could see it in her face that she really wanted to say something else. She was hiding something. I was pretty sure I knew what it was, but I needed a bit more proof.

Giving up on changing clothes, I shut the top drawer and leaned against the edge of the dresser, crossing my arms over my chest.

"I don't have a thing for her," I said. *I wouldn't mind sleeping with her once, but that's not a "thing."* "Why don't you like her?"

"She's…well, she's just not right for you. She's a nice girl, but I get bad vibes from her." The more she tried to explain, the more uncomfortable she looked. "Just trust me on this, OK?" She swallowed nervously.

Bray never gets nervous around me.

I crouched down in front of her, forcing her blue-eyed gaze to connect with mine.

"Why don't you just say what you're really thinking?"

She looked stunned. "What do you mean?"

"You know what I mean."

"No, really I don't." Trying to avoid it, she stood up and moved to the other side of the bed, crossing her arms and putting her back to me.

"Don't do this," I said, rising to my feet, too. "We've been doing this for as long as I can remember. We have to stop."

I stepped up behind her. "Why don't we just try it, Bray?"

She swung her head around to face me, her eyes harboring confusion and shock and worry all at the same time. Only her confusion wasn't convincing. She knew exactly what I was talking about, but she wasn't masking it very well.

"Try what?"

I placed my hands on her upper arms. "Being together."

It was as if my words sucked all of the air and sound out of the room. For a long time she just stared at me, unblinking.

"I've wanted to be with you since we were kids in that pasture, Bray. You know this—you've *known* this. But anytime I ever tried to get closer to you, you pushed me away. Why don't we stop this, quit playing these games with each other, and just...*be together*."

Her big blue eyes fell away from mine. She took a step backward and sat down on the edge of the bed, letting her hands fall in between her thighs. She wouldn't look at me, and I was getting frustrated. I wanted her to say something, *anything*.

I crouched in front of her again and rested my hands on the tops of her bare knees. "Please look at me," I said softly. "Say something."

It seemed a struggle, but finally she met my gaze. I saw nothing but conflict in her eyes.

"I can't," she said.

"Why not? Are you not into me? If that's it, just say so. I can take it. I'll hate it, but at least I'll know—"

"That's not it at all," she said, shaking her head gently.

"Is it because of your dad?" I asked. "I know he's never really liked me much."

"No, Elias. It doesn't have anything to do with that. You should know that by now."

"Then what the hell is it?" The frustration began to show in my voice, probably in my face, too. "I don't get it. We've been close since we were kids. It's always been you and me, Bray and Elias, best friends forever, just like you used to scribble on your tablets. Shit, we've done everything together short of outright sex. You get pissed at me when I start to get too close to another girl."

"Are you saying I'm *jealous*?" she asked quickly.

"That's exactly what I'm saying," I answered truthfully, despite wanting to avoid offending her. She knew it was true as much as I did. "The only person you're fooling here is yourself."

Too much truth, I realized too late, would only shut her off.

She pushed me away from her and started to head for the door, but I caught her by the elbow and forced her back around to face me.

"It scares me!" she shouted, taking me by surprise. "You've been the only consistent thing in my life, Elias! I'm incapable of holding a relationship together. I always fuck it up!" She waved her hands out in front of her angrily. "What was my longest relationship?"

I didn't answer. I knew the answer, but I got the feeling it wasn't that kind of question.

"Two months," she said, holding up two fingers. "I get with a guy and two months is my record. Michael. Three weeks. Austin. Two weeks. Jack. One month. Hell, I went out with Avery for two days before I bailed on him! *Two days.* It's pathetic!"

"But what does that have to do with us?" I asked with almost as much intensity in my voice as hers. "We're not like everyone else. I'm not any of those guys. If anyone could hold a relationship together it's you and me."

"That's just it!" She was almost crying. "You're *not* like any of them! You're the only guy in this world that I *care* about!"

Tears streamed down her soft cheeks.

It was in this moment that I finally knew the truth. Bray was afraid of losing me, and taking our relationship any further than it had been was a risk that she wasn't willing to take.

"It's my worst fear," she confirmed it and her gaze dropped toward the floor. "Things between us changing. I know, Elias... I *feel* it...if we change the way things are, the way they have been, nothing will ever be the same again. We'll break up and grow apart and just thinking about not having you in my life hurts my heart." Tears shuddered through her chest.

I sat down fully on the floor and pulled her into my arms, wrapping them tightly around her body. I pressed my lips against her hair and did my best to hold back my own tears. Because I understood. Having known Bray practically all my life, I understood her more than anyone ever would or could.

Like I said, Bray was complicated.

She had always been a confident girl, the type that other girls in school looked up to and followed. She was wild and brazen and often too bold for her own good. When we were growing up, she got into more trouble than I thought one innocent, sweet girl could get into. She wasn't afraid of anything, even the occasional illegal stunt, which landed her in juvy once for a week when she was sixteen. Destruction of property—she got caught spray-painting the back of a grocery store building. But she wasn't a bad girl, just a little rebellious and reckless.

But her biggest flaw was her inability to form bonds with other people. Friend. Boyfriend. Even family. She had never really been close to anyone. The first time I saw her interact with her parents,

I thought that her family was very different from ours. My mom and dad always told me they loved me before I went anywhere or before we hung up the phone. Bray and her parents never said that to each other, at least not that I had ever heard. Bray's parents didn't seem to mind that she went where she wanted whenever she wanted. My parents were strict, and I had a crazy eight o'clock curfew up until I was fifteen years old. It took me a long time to truly understand why her parents treated her the way they did. And it wasn't until many years later that all of the pieces of the puzzle that was Brayelle Bates would fall into place and explain everything.

I was all that Bray ever really had.

Her attachment to me, her closeness to me, I knew all along was love. But she didn't know, because she had never really experienced love like that before. She grew up pushing people away from her, because it was all she had ever known. When someone started getting too close, she turned on them in an instant, as if a warning siren was going off inside her brain.

She wasn't a broken girl. She had never experienced abuse or had much of a hard life growing up. She was just cursed with the inability to recognize and filter and react to certain significant emotions.

Despite all of her flaws, all of her crazy antics and sometimes over-the-top personality, I loved her more than anything in this world.

And I knew that I always would.

But it was time I put my foot down.

"It won't be like this forever," I said, looking down into her glazed-over eyes. "We can't spend the rest of our lives being just friends and neither of us getting involved with other people."

Her tears shut off immediately and she froze. "What are you saying?" she asked.

I softened the look in my eyes, trying to be as delicate as possible with what I was about to say. My hands moved up her arms and rested against her cheeks. I brushed the bone under her eye with the pad of my thumb.

And then I lied to her.

"I can't do this with you forever," I said. "I want to be in love, to be loved back. I want to get married one day and maybe have a couple kids—call me old-fashioned, but whatever." She wanted to tear her eyes away from mine, but she couldn't; she was still frozen in place, her body rigid. "I've imagined that person being you. It's always been about you. But if you don't want to at least try to be her, then maybe we should stop being friends. This...*thing* we have, this...relationship, it's unhealthy."

She stepped back and away from me, still holding her unblinking gaze.

"Is this what you want?" she asked, her soft features appeared vacant, but her eyes held a profound amount of suppressed pain.

"What I want is to be with you. *That's* what I want. It's all I've *ever* wanted." My hands collapsed into half fists out in front of me. My whole body was consumed by emotion, a desperate need to make her understand how much I loved her without having to say the words. In the moment, they didn't seem right to speak aloud. I was afraid she'd run the other way.

I thought this was going to be the end. The end of us, the end of everything that we stood for. The last thing in the world that I wanted was for her to turn and walk out that door so I would never see her again. But that was what I expected. The truth is, I would've waited forever for her. I couldn't imagine myself in a serious relationship with any other girl. Sex? Sure. I'm a guy and I like sex. But to love someone other than Bray seemed eternally impossible.

So yes, I lied when I told her that it couldn't be the way it had been any longer. Because I would've waited for her forever. I would've stayed just like we were, unconventional best friends who shared a lot more than secrets and sleepovers. But with Bray, I knew I had to be harsh. I felt like I had to be the one to make her understand that our relationship might not be what she wanted. As much as it hurt me to do it, I had to let her know that it was OK to go our separate ways. I didn't want her to cling to the thought of us for the rest of her life and continue pushing people away because of me.

I just wanted her to be happy.

With her back to me, Bray's arms uncrossed and fell to her sides.

She turned around.

I waited, subconsciously holding my breath.

And just when I thought it was all going to be over, she said, "OK. I *do* want to be with you. I want to try with you."

That night after the party, we had sex for the first time since we'd known each other. But it wasn't what I had always hoped it would be. Bray changed. I noticed her change as I lay on top of her, peering down into her beautiful, blue eyes. It was as if she knew before it actually happened that if we had sex it would alter everything between us forever. And then as the days wore on, we grew further apart. We broke up after four months. Two months later, she moved away to South Carolina.

I was never the same.

# FOUR

## Bray

*I* know what you must be thinking: *What a bitch.* And you'll get no argument from me on that one. I was pretty messed up back then. I loved Elias with all my heart, and that scared the hell out of me.

But I should get something out of the way before I dive into the excuses of why I was the way I was. I'm sure Elias sugarcoated me with his bias and all, but if this story is going to be told, then it needs to be told in its truth and entirety, without Band-Aids and training wheels.

I was fucked up.

No, no one raped me or beat me or bullied me as a kid. My parents loved me. Maybe not as much as my sister, Rian, but I believed they loved me. They just showed it in different ways than Elias's parents did, usually with the best toys for Christmas and birthdays, a steady allowance, and the occasional pat on the back for doing a good deed. Sometimes. But every pat on the back I ever *did* get felt like an obligation, like they were being forced. I had issues. There's no doubt about that. And for much of my young life my parents did whatever they could to help me. They just gave up trying to fix me somewhere along the way. But I don't blame anyone for the way I was. A psychologist appointed by the State to evaluate me when I had my little run-in with the police and a stint in juvy called it bipolar disorder. I, on the other hand, called it just one of those things. We're all different. We all have our own quirks and flaws and dark secrets. All of us are fucked up on some level, whether or not we want to admit it to ourselves. And I like to believe that not every problem or issue that we deal with in our daily lives must be labeled with a fancy title.

I'll say it again: I was fucked up. It was as simple as that.

Well, just so you know, I didn't leave Elias and Georgia because I lost interest or fell out of love with him. Quite the opposite. I left because I fell even harder for him, which I didn't even know was possible. I've never really been scared of anything, except of Elias. I think that in the back of my mind I figured if I left him first, if *I* was the one who put a stop to any kind of relationship that we had, it might not hurt as much as it would have if he had ended it. It gave me a sense of control. At least, I fooled myself into believing that all the way to South Carolina. But once I got there—I moved with my friend, Lissa, who wanted to be closer to her brother—it didn't take long for me to see that I had made the biggest mistake of my life.

But instead of doing the right thing and following my heart by going back and hoping Elias would *take* me back, I did the opposite and pushed myself further away from him. Maybe it was my way of punishing myself for being the biggest idiot on the face of the Earth, I don't know, but whatever it was, it landed me in a year-long relationship with a guy I didn't love and never would.

I tried to go on with my life, but as time wore on I realized more every day that I really *had* no life without Elias. He *was* my life. He had been since that day we met by the pond.

I just wished I would've allowed myself to give in to that truth fully long before I finally did.

Because by then, it was too late.

Elias had a girlfriend, and according to our childhood friend Mitchell, Elias was serious about her and very much in love.

That was the time in my life when I didn't care about *anything* anymore. I pretty much gave up on life without actually committing suicide. That's the best way to describe it. I was completely dead inside. But no one else knew. Only Elias would ever have known that something was wrong with me deep down, that what I projected to the world was just a mask covering up the ugliness slowly eating away at my soul. But I never contacted him. I never tried to tell him how I felt, how much I was hurting, how much I missed and needed him. Because I wanted him to be happy. Even if it meant I wasn't part of that happiness. I ruined my happiness for myself. I wasn't about to waltz back into his life and ruin his, too.

Inevitably, I broke it off with my boyfriend and I told myself that I'd go back to being relationshipless, the way I had always been. Because relationships just weren't my thing. But—and here's some of where that "no Band-Aid" policy I was talking about comes into play—I went from a long-term relationship with one person to having sex with several different people. Call me a slut; say whatever you want. I never slept with anyone for the sheer pleasure of it—not in the beginning, anyway. I did it because I was trying to fill a void and I knew no other way. I was confused and I longed to feel loved the way I felt loved every moment I spent with Elias. I looked for that feeling in everything and everyone.

But I never found it.

And that's when I . . . no, I'm not ready to talk about that yet.

For now, let's just say when the dark secret I carried around behind that mask was out for the world to see, I had no other choice but to go back home.

Home to Elias. If he would have me. If he *could* have me...

I just never imagined that my homecoming would be met with *more* than I had ever hoped for... and, well, a lot more than I never could have possibly anticipated.

# Elias

*Two months ago...*

I hadn't seen nor heard from Bray in four years. As anyone would do, I went on with my life. I met a girl, Aline, at community college. She was beautiful. Dark hair. Bright blue eyes. Peach-colored skin. I loved her. But I wasn't *in love* with her, even though I tried really hard to be. I tried *so* hard that for a while I actually believed it. But after two years of dating, I realized it wasn't the kind of love I felt for Bray. And it never would be.

I heard from my friend Mitchell that Bray was engaged and in love with some guy in South Carolina. I felt like punching Mitchell for telling me this. I would have much rather gone on wondering about her, left clueless as to how she was carrying on with her life, instead of knowing the painful details.

I saw Bray in everything and everyone. Even in Aline—it wasn't until much later that I realized how they favored each other. Pathetic, I know, but love isn't always roses and rainbows and butterflies in your stomach. It's equally cruel and painful and the world's worst villain.

Aline dumped me. She knew I was in love with Bray. Not because I told her, but because women are smart like that. They have this weird fucking superpower that allows them to read a man's emotions and see straight through his lies. I had told Aline about Bray, my "best friend" since childhood, and apparently that was all the backstory Aline needed to know more about me than I knew about myself. It wasn't that I had tried to hide from Aline the fact that I was still in love with Bray, but that I had been trying to hide it from myself.

Aline was a great girl. She just wasn't *my* girl....

It was one day in April nearly two months ago when the landscape of my life changed forever. The colors on that black-and-white painting were finally starting to fill in.

I woke up Saturday morning to Mitchell rummaging through the cabinets in my kitchen. He had been my roommate since last year. A lot about both of us had changed since we were kids. Thankfully, his mullet was one thing. Somewhere along the years he traded that hairstyle for a short, stylish cut with longer bangs that framed his face.

"What the hell are you doing, man?" I asked as I entered the kitchen wearing only my boxers. My current one-night stand, Jana, was still asleep in my bed, tangled in the sheets.

I opened the fridge and drank down half a bottle of water.

Mitchell was standing on a chair pushed against the front of the oven and reaching into the cabinet high above the stove light. "Looking for my weed."

"Mitchell, man, seriously, you need to come down off that shit. Why would your weed be in the cabinet?"

"Come down off *what* shit? *Weed?*" His voice was muffled by the cabinet door.

"The meth."

"Fucking A, bro, I'm not on meth. What the hell is your problem?"

I sat down at the kitchen table, stretched my arms above me and yawned. "You haven't slept in three days," I said. "Last night I heard you going through boxes in your room. For three hours." I looked around the kitchen. "I haven't seen this place this clean since I moved in, and I sure as hell didn't clean it."

Mitchell's head finally came out of the cabinet, his bangs partially covering his dark brown eyes. He stepped down from the chair. His eyes were wide and feral and bloodshot, his pupils dilated. The corner of the left side of his mouth constantly twitched.

"Don't tell anyone," he said. He started to sit down but began pacing instead.

"I'm not going to tell anyone, but you're starting to worry me. That's some bad shit, bro. A month more and you'll be sucking guys off for a fix. It's no better than crack."

Mitchell's face went slack. "Dude, that's goin' too far."

I sipped my water. "Is it?" I asked and shook my head. "You know I'm far from Mr. Sober and Perfect, but I wouldn't touch that stuff if you paid me. You remember what it did to Paul Matthews."

Mitchell pushed air through his lips and rolled his eyes. "Paul got addicted. He was cooking the shit in his bathroom. You don't see me doing that."

"Not yet," I said.

I heard footsteps behind me, and Mitchell looked up.

"Do I get to fuck her next?" he asked.

I shut my eyes briefly and sighed. "Don't say stuff like that, Mitch."

"Fuck you," Jana said to him from behind me.

Her shoulder-length blonde hair was pulled into a sloppy ponytail that hung disheveled against her back. She had sun-kissed brown skin and she was skinny, with delicate wrists I could easily lock my fingers around. But her wrists and her frame were the only delicate things about her, really.

She leaned around the back of my chair and kissed me on the mouth. I noticed right away she was dressed only in a T-shirt and her panties. Mitchell may have been out of line with that comment, but she wasn't helping her case any, dressed like that in front of another guy.

Jana went to the fridge and opened it. I glimpsed her naked, tanned legs for only a moment. She was hot, but I was already regretting having slept with her.

"Whatever, man," Mitchell said and went back to the cabinet.

I got up and left the kitchen. I hopped in the shower and Jana joined me. I wasn't used to girls staying this late with me in the morning, certainly not inviting themselves into my shower. But I wasn't about to kick her out, especially when the first thing she did was get on her knees and give me a blowjob. But for some reason, I couldn't get off. I shut my eyes and gripped her head in both hands while she took the entire length of me into the back of her throat, but I couldn't get off no matter how hard either of us tried.

I was frustrated. Jana, I think, was worried about her technique.

She gave up on that method and rose to her feet, pressing her breasts against my chest. The hot water was beginning to run cool as it streamed down on us.

She had this crafty look in her eyes.

"I want you both to fuck me," she said and bit down gently on my chin.

Well, that definitely took me by surprise.

I don't know what made me go along with it, other than thinking with the wrong head, but a few minutes later I was on my knees behind her on the couch while she went to work on Mitchell in front of her—and he apparently didn't have the same problem I'd had with her minutes ago in the shower.

Despite sharing an apartment with a guy and both of us having our fair share of girls—girls who wanted a relationship as much as Mitchell or I did, I should add—threesomes definitely weren't the norm. The girls either of us usually brought home weren't as bold with their sexual desires as Jana was. And that was a good thing, really, because a threesome with another guy wasn't something I could ever really get accustomed to. I spent more time and effort trying to avoid crossing swords than actually enjoying myself. In the heat of the moment, I never cared about that much, but when it was all over, I was a little disgusted with myself. Every single time. Unfortunately, disgust rarely stopped me from doing it again.

After Jana left and Mitchell went on another cleaning spree in the apartment, I got another shower before I headed out to help my mom move the last of her stuff into her new house. Mom had bad credit, and when the rental house I had grown up in started going to shit, I took out a loan to get her a new house on the other side of town.

Her new boyfriend, James, was loading boxes into the moving van when I pulled up.

He man-hugged me and started his usual spiel, asking how I was doing and reminding me how good I was to my mom. It really wasn't necessary. I already liked him, and there wasn't any need for him to still be trying so hard. But I guess he just hadn't exhausted his efforts yet, and so I left it alone.

"This will be the last load," my mom said and handed James a box to put in the van. Then she enveloped me in a hug. "How's that new job going?"

"So far so good," I said. "I didn't think I'd like it as much as I do."

"That's great," James said, emerging from the back of the moving van. "I did construction for ten years. It's better than fast food or sitting behind a desk." He was a few inches shorter than my mom, with graying salt-and-pepper hair sprinkled above his temples. Physically, James wasn't my mom's usual type, but I think his personality made up for that.

I nodded.

"OK, I need you two to be very careful with my china cabinet," my mom said. "It was my mother's, and—"

"We've got this," James said, smiling over at me. "Don't you worry."

We followed my mom inside. She stayed close behind us every step of the way as we carried the massive china cabinet out the front door. Her face was as white as a sheet; she was worried we were going to drop it and shatter the glass doors along the top. We got it into the van and covered it with two thick blankets for extra cushioning. I stepped down from the ramp to see my mom staring out at the road. Her face was still white, but this time it seemed like she had seen a ghost. It took me a second longer than it should to turn around to see what she was looking at.

Bray stood at the end of the driveway, looking back at me.

# FIVE

## Elias

*M*y heart thumped so violently I felt light-headed for a moment. I think I gasped, but I couldn't be sure. I was too paralyzed to move or breathe, much less get my brain in working order again.

For the longest time Bray and I just stared across the driveway at each other. My first instinct was to walk straight over to her, lift her into my arms, and kiss her like I had never kissed anyone before, but I stopped a half a second before I acted upon it.

I had to play this cool. I had no idea what she was doing here after four years. Four fucking years! She could've been there just to see how I was doing after so long and to update me on her life, tell me that she was married and had a kid. I almost broke down. Right there in front of her and my mom and James. But I held my own, swallowed hard as emotion thickened my throat, and let out the breath I had been holding for the past few minutes.

"Bray?" I took a few steps forward.

Her smile was faint and shaky at first, but when I walked toward her those few steps her smile started to brighten.

"Hey," she said softly.

Her hands were folded loosely down in front of her like a delicate little basket near her belly. Her long, dark hair, soft as it always was, draped both shoulders and was tucked behind her ears. She looked exactly the way I had always remembered her: soft and fragile and beautiful, with the biggest blue eyes and the prettiest smile I had ever seen. I swear her eyes twinkled like they do in the cartoons whenever she'd smile. And I always found it funny that she looked so damn innocent, but whenever she opened that mouth of hers she would blow that innocent façade right out of the water.

But not on this day. She definitely wasn't herself. It was like she wasn't sure yet if she could be. Or if she wanted to be.

I looked back at the moving van and then at my mom.

"Honey, you go ahead," my mom said, waving me on. "James and I can move the rest."

Other than Mitchell and, even less so, Aline, my mom was the only other person who knew my history with Brayelle Bates. She knew how much I loved her, and over the past four years, she'd tried on several occasions to convince me to reach out to Bray, tell her how I felt.

Having an idea about the situation, James added, "No worries, Elias. I can move this stuff. You go do what you've gotta do." His smile was kind of goofy.

Bray stepped up then. "How about we all help?" she said to James and smiled at me.

*Take it slow. Feel each other out first. See what our boundaries are, if there are any.* It was the method Bray and I both used that day, without actually coming out and saying it.

We spent the next couple of hours helping my mom and James unload the van. After all of the heavy stuff was moved into the house, Bray and I left together in my gray Dodge Charger. We didn't talk much while moving boxes or even when we were finally alone in the car. We were both nervous, both worried about the same things: *Is she single? Does she have a family? Is this our last and final good-bye?*

I drove her to my apartment. Mitchell was as shocked as I was when he saw her. "Holy shit," he said when we walked through the front door. "Brayelle Bates. What are you doing here?"

"Hi, Mitch," she said and strolled over to give him a hug. "It's good to see you."

"You too, girl." He took a step back and looked her over, bringing one hand up to push his bangs away from his face. "Still smokin' hot, I see. You haven't answered my question."

"Mitch," I said dropping my keys on the coffee table, "do you mind going out for a while and—"

"Say no more." Mitchell put up both hands. "Privacy. I understand. I'm outta here in five seconds."

When he finally left, the silence that fell over the room between Bray and me was like the calm before the storm.

"Sit down," I encouraged her, taking her by the elbow and leading her to the oversized chair. She wore a pair of tight jean shorts and a white cotton top. A thin silver chain with a pink pendant hung from her neck. A mess of tan, black, and green hemp bracelets, some with beads, and others with intricate braided designs, were wrapped around both wrists.

I sat down on the ottoman, facing her, my hands folded together and hanging between my knees.

She broke my heart when she started to cry.

I could tell she was trying really hard to contain the tears in those final few seconds as I looked at her. But she couldn't. She buried her face in the palms of her hands and cried so hard, all I could do was reach out and grab her, try to pull her onto my lap. But she pushed my arms away gently.

"No, Elias, listen to me first before you give in to my shit this time. *Please!*" Tears choked her voice.

I was crying on the inside, my chest a twisted knot holding down a full-blown tear-fest with all the strength I could muster. I placed my hands on her bare knees instead.

"Why are you crying?" I reached up with one hand and tucked her hair back behind her ear. This was fucking killing me, to see her like this.

Sobs shuddered through her body, as if hearing my voice just made her cry worse. And for a moment I saw sitting in front of me that little girl I had met in the pasture that night.

"Bray, I'm here. You know that. I'll always be here for you."

I was beginning to lose hope, thinking maybe she just needed me for a shoulder to cry on. Maybe she'd just had a bad breakup with some guy and needed me to talk to about it. I hoped I was wrong.

Finally her sobs eased enough that she could look me in the eyes and she said, "I-I just wanted to say that...I've loved you all my life. I know I screwed up, Elias. I made the worst mistake of my life by leaving you and for staying away for so long." She began losing control again. So did I. "I know you'll probably never forgive me, but I had to come here to tell you how I felt! I *had* to!" Tears were shooting from her eyes again, her body was going rigid under my hands.

She went on:

"I was so afraid of you. I was afraid of losing you. I don't know what made me do the things I did. I-I was stupid and crazy and, and I don't know! But I was really messed up, Elias. I know I'm too late. Mitchell told me you fell in love and for the longest time I didn't want to come here because I didn't want to interfere with your life. I—"

"I'm not with anyone," I said softly.

She froze and I heard her breath catch. Her hands were trembling between her knees.

I scooted farther to the edge of the ottoman, closer to her, and held her face in my hands.

"Do you remember what I told you on my twenty-second birthday?" I paused, searching her beautiful blue eyes, which were glossed over with moisture. "I said it was always about you." I squeezed her face gently to add emphasis. "It's *always* been you, Bray. I could never love another girl the way that I've loved you since we were kids. *Never.*" I squeezed it again, my jaw grinding. "I've tried. Believe me, I tried to go on with my life—dating, relationships. But no matter what I did, no matter who I was with or how good they were to me, I couldn't stop thinking about you."

I was so intent on explaining these things to her—I had rehearsed them over and over in my mind for four years—that I hadn't even noticed her tears had changed. Instead of heartbreaking sobs rendering her weak, the tears streaming down her cheeks had become calmer, though heavier, laced with happiness even though there was still a bit of fear.

But I also hadn't noticed that *I'd* finally started crying, too.

"I love you so much, Bray. *So* fucking much!" Sobs rattled my chest briefly until I managed to calm myself.

Bray finally gave in and lunged forward, wrapping her arms around me. I scooped her up into them, squeezing the life out of her and into me. We shared that life. We always had. And from this day forth, we both knew that we always would.

Even if it killed us.

## Bray

It's the hardest thing in the world for me to describe, but when Elias held me in his arms like that, I literally felt whole again. Or maybe for the first time. Because things were different this time around. I *knew* that I wanted to be with him for the rest of my life. I *knew* I couldn't walk out that door without him. I *knew* that going forward, no matter what I did, I wanted Elias to be right there with me. Not just as best friends. But as lovers, girlfriend and boyfriend, husband and wife. I didn't care, as long as we were together and in love the way we were meant to be.

His lips covered mine and he kissed me deeply, passionately, stealing my breath away. My stomach fluttered and spun and did things it had never done before, not even the first time we had sex. And before I knew it, I was pulling his T-shirt over his raised arms and tossing it somewhere on the floor. He practically tore my shirt off me. We stood up and I wrapped my legs around his waist, and he carried me into his bedroom and threw me down on the bed.

He didn't wait even a minute before stripping off the rest of my clothes. And then his. I watched the muscles flex in his arms and in his chest as he crawled on top of me. He was so damn gorgeous to me, every muscle, every line, every curve in his sculpted, tanned body. His mouth hungry for mine, searching my breasts and my neck and the underside of my chin until he found my lips and kissed me ravenously. I speared my hands through his wavy, chin-length dark hair, and when I reached down and took his hard length into my hand he moaned against my mouth.

"I want you inside me, Elias," I said breathily against his mouth. "I've wanted this for so goddamn long." This time it felt real. It felt *right*. It felt the way it should have felt our first time. And I wanted to savor it as if it were.

His powerful hips rocked against mine before he reached down with me, and his strong fingers splayed around my hand as it held his cock firmly. He guided my hand, and I gasped and threw my head back against the pillow as I felt the head of his cock enter me. My eyelids fluttered and fell helplessly over my eyes. My lips parted and a sharp gasp escaped as he slid the rest of his length slowly into my wetness. I moaned with pleasure.

"I've missed you so much," he whispered hotly against my lips, and then slipped his tongue into my mouth, his hips thrusting relentlessly against mine. "I never want you to leave me again." He bit down on my bottom lip.

I wanted to cry hearing his words. And deep inside myself, I did. But they were tears of bliss. I wrapped my legs around his waist and pushed myself farther toward him, wanting him deeper.

"I'll never leave you again," I said, as those tears deep inside began to seep from the corners of my eyes.

I could hardly catch my breath.

"Promise me," he said, thrusting harder.

I looked up into his eyes and saw that they were as tearful as mine; the intensity in his face much greater. I knew in that moment that if I ever left him again, it would kill him. It would kill *me*.

"I promise. I'll never leave you."

"Swear it on your life," he said and rammed his cock into me so hard it took away what little breath I had left. My thighs trembled.

My stomach flip-flopped with pleasure and excitement. Elias stared down into my eyes.

"I fucking swear on my life," I said and meant every word. "I'll never leave you again."

His lips devoured mine and he fucked me harder than I had ever been fucked, until my fingers hurt from digging into the wooden headboard behind me and my legs were so weak I could hardly lift them. And when he came, he came hard on my stomach, his entire body trembling. I wrapped my arms around him, kissing the sweat from his temples and from his lips.

He rested only a few minutes before he was hard again, and then he made love to me slowly until I came.

We stayed in bed all day, tangled in the sheets, our arms and legs entwined. For a long time we didn't speak. We just stared up at the ceiling, his fingers combing through my hair, my head resting against his warm, hard chest.

"You promised," he whispered.

I raised my head and looked at him. "I did," I said and leaned over to kiss his lips.

He kissed me in return, but a worried look lingered in his eyes.

"I'm not going anywhere," I assured him. "I've lived for far too long away from you, Elias. I just wish that I had figured it out sooner."

His eyes smiled faintly and he moved a piece of hair away from my face with the tip of his finger.

"I'm glad you kicked me in the hip that night," he said and kissed my nose.

"Well, if you hadn't have called me ugly, I probably wouldn't have."

Elias smiled and pulled me back down, laying my head against his chest again.

"You've always been beautiful to me," he said, and then I felt his lips press against the top of my hair.

I was in heaven.

*We* were in heaven.

# SIX

## Elias

*I*t took us seventeen years to truly find each other. But now that we were together, neither of us was letting go.

The first two weeks of our newfound relationship was as I had always imagined it. We went everywhere together. I introduced her as my girlfriend to my new friends and she introduced us as a couple to our old friends. And it didn't seem to bother Bray when we'd run into an old girlfriend of mine—or a one-night stand. It didn't bother her *much* anyway. Bray took it all in stride.

"Elias Kline," Jana said, coming up behind me as I sat in a booth at the Denny's restaurant one day. Her blonde hair was pulled into a ponytail, and her eyes were painted with heavy, dark makeup that made her look somewhat like a raccoon to me.

"Hey, Jana," I said, setting my fork down. I looked at Bray and then back up at Jana, hovering beside our table, and said, "This is my girlfriend, Bray. Bray, this is Jana."

"Nice to meet you," Bray said with a smile at first I couldn't be sure was genuine or just for show.

Jana's darkly lined eyes skirted Bray, and I noticed their smiles seemed to match. I wondered if Bray could tell right off that I had slept with this girl before.

"Girlfriend, huh?" Jana said.

"Yes." Bray straightened her back and stretched her arms across the table in front of her. "And *you* are?" she said with a smirk.

OK, their matching smiles were definitely just for show. Suddenly I felt like a bear cub dangling between mother bear and an intruder.

"I'm just a friend of Elias and Mitchell," Jana said, and I felt a little relieved that was *all* she said. "There's a party goin' on Friday night on the river. Everybody'll be there. You two should come."

Bray looked over at me and relaxed her back against the cushioned booth seat again. She pursed her lips contemplatively.

"You want to go?" she asked me.

It felt like a dangerously loaded question that I wasn't sure I should answer, but Bray really seemed interested.

"Oh come on," Jana said, propping a hand on her hip. "We plan to spend the weekend out there. Bring a tent. Oh and it's BYOB. Allan will be there, too, so you know what that means." She glanced at me once, and Bray definitely noticed.

"We'll be there," Bray announced.

I just stayed quiet. Seemed like Bray had this secret duel going on with Jana and could handle herself. Besides, it felt safer to just stay quiet.

Women really do scare the shit out of me sometimes.

Jana smiled with teeth showing, and I briefly thought about my dick being in her mouth not long ago. I flinched inwardly as if Bray could read my mind or something.

"Awesome! I'll see you then." Jana smirked at me as she left our table.

"You definitely fucked her," Bray said and took a bite of her mashed potatoes.

I felt my face stiffen.

She wasn't angry or jealous, but she wasn't going to hold back, either. This was Bray, after all, and I'd be worried if she didn't say exactly what was on her mind.

I let out a small breath of laughter and picked my fork back up. "Yeah, though that's *all* it was."

"I know," she said, smiled at me, and washed her food down with a drink of tea.

"How would you know that?" I was truly baffled, but didn't doubt her for a second.

"Because that one was oozing *fuck-me*," she said and took another small bite. She added with her mouth full, pointing her fork at me, "Nothing wrong with that if that's what she wants to do. As long as she keeps her lips off you, we have no issue."

"I think we're good," I said. "She's kind of into Mitchell now, though I think it has more to do with him supplying her with drugs than with sex."

Bray cocked an eyebrow. "Mitchell's selling drugs?"

"Well, not exactly," I said, lowering my voice because of the topic. "He started doing meth about a month ago. The two of them have been spending a lot of time together since…" I hesitated because I didn't exactly want to bring up the fact that I'd slept with Jana the same day Bray came home. "Well, it's been about two weeks now."

"Why is this my first time seeing her?"

Bray was living with me in my apartment now. It took her five days to even let her family know she was back in Georgia. But that didn't surprise me. I would never say it to Bray, but I knew her parents wouldn't jump at the opportunity to bring her home to them.

"I kind of asked Mitchell to meet up with her somewhere other than my place."

"Because of me?" Bray smiled knowingly.

"Yeah," I admitted.

"Well, don't worry about it," she said, moving her hand underneath the table and rubbing it across my thigh. "I'm not going to freak out on you over old girlfriends or whatever. I never expected you to be celibate."

Was this her way of clearing a path for me before I found out who she had slept with since we had been apart? In a way it felt like that, but at the same time, I knew she was being sincere about it, too. I can't deny that I started wondering heavily about her sex life in that moment. Not that it would ever have made me love her less, but I still wanted to know.

"Who is Allan?" she asked.

Instinctively, I looked up and all around me to make sure no one was listening.

"*He's* the drug dealer," I whispered.

"Oh…" Bray looked at me warily. "And you know him *how?*"

"Everybody knows him," I said. "But don't get the wrong idea. I've only met him a few times."

"*Met* as in *bought from?*" She grinned.

"Yeah," I admitted. "Nothing too bad, just some weed here and there."

"Good," she said. "Because I don't deal with that meth stuff. Would hate to have to haul you off to the nearest rehab."

"Hell no," I said. "I'm with ya on that. I'm worried about Mitchell, though. I've tried to steer him clear of that shit, but he won't listen to me."

"I hate to say this, Elias, but if he doesn't get help now, you'll have to kick him out of your apartment. He'll end up blowing up your kitchen, or taking you down with him when he gets busted." She took a quick drink and set her glass back on the table. "Lissa's brother's friend in South Carolina was on meth pretty bad. They busted him before he blew his house up, but he was cooking that shit in his kitchen. It scares me."

She was right. I hadn't thought about it before, because Mitchell was my good friend and I never considered kicking him out. But when it comes to stuff like this, there were many more reasons not to have him living with me than there were to let him stay.

And I would never want to put Bray in any danger, either.

"I'll talk to him tonight," I said.

"Give him a chance, though," she said. "Don't just send him packing. He'll probably blame it on me if you do that."

And that was exactly what happened.

Later that night when Mitchell came home from wherever—I think he lost his job because of his habit, so I had no idea where he was spending his time during the day anymore—I tried talking to him.

"Mitch," I said, hitting the Power button on the television remote. "I need to talk to you about something."

His light-brown hair was dirty, thick with oil that kept his bangs from falling around his eyes like they naturally did. He was wearing the same Georgia Bulldogs T-shirt he had on yesterday. And the day before that.

I set the remote down on the coffee table and leaned forward in the recliner.

"Yeah, what's up?" He plopped down on the sofa, stretching his legs across the cushions and crossing his ankles.

"I think you need to get some help, man. You're really starting to worry me. You never sleep, and when you do it's for two days straight. Did you lose your job?"

He wasn't taking what I was saying seriously at first, or maybe he was just trying to brush it off, make it appear that it wasn't as bad as I was making it out to be. His head fell to the side so that he could see me and he reached out his hand. "Can you pass me the remote?"

I sighed, frustrated with him already. "No, Mitch, listen, I'm being serious here. You need to get some help. I'll do whatever I can to help you, just name it. I'll call around for a good rehab center, take you back and forth if you ever need me to. Whatever you need."

"*Rehab?*" Mitchell spun around on the sofa and sat upright in an instant. His expression distorted with insult. "What the fuck are you talking about, *rehab?* You can't be serious."

I put up both hands in a surrendering fashion, trying to defuse the situation before it started. "I'm just trying to help you. If not rehab, then—"

"I don't need your fucking help." He stood up. "I'm not addicted to meth," he lashed out, slashing his hand in the air in front of him. "I just do it every now and then. I can't believe you're even saying this shit to me. You're no fucking angel."

"I never claimed to be," I said, getting pissed but keeping it contained. "But Mitch, your 'every now and then' is *every day.*"

I stood up then, too. "Look, if you won't at least try to get some help, or get off that shit completely—drop it cold turkey if you're not addicted—then I'm sorry, man, but you're gonna have to find another place to live."

His eyes grew as wide as plates.

Bray walked in the front door at that very moment.

"Hi, baby," she said moving through the living room toward me and having no idea what was going on. She pushed up on her toes and pecked me on the lips.

Mitchell was glaring at us from behind her.

"Oh, I get it now," he said, and Bray turned upon hearing the anger in his voice. "This is because of her." He pointed at Bray once. "Little Miss Fucking Sunshine comes back to Georgia, moves in, and suddenly three's a crowd." His face contorted pathetically for a moment. "*Seriously*, man? You're picking a piece of ass over your best friend? The pussy way out, man, that's fucked up!"

I went toward him, both hands clenched into fists at my sides. Bray stepped in front of me and I stopped.

"Don't talk about her like that, Mitch." My jaw was clenched painfully and the blood rushed to my head. "You fucking know better. And besides, *she's* always been my best friend. Not you."

Mitchell smiled fiendishly and shook his head. He glanced back and forth between me and Bray. I was ready to knock him over the back of that sofa. One wrong word or syllable was all it was going to take. Bray knew it, too. She kept both hands pressed against my chest and her little body in my way, hoping it would be enough.

"Mitchell," she said before he had a chance to say whatever it was he was smiling so cunningly about, "I don't care if you stay here, and Elias knows this. This has nothing to do with me. We're just worried. Meth is some bad shit."

"You don't know shit about me," he said. "But I know about you. Ain't that right?"

The tips of my fingers were digging into the palms of my hands. But I waited, hoping he wasn't about to go the wrong way with this. I really didn't want to hit him.

Mitchell smirked and went on, "See, she and I talked while

she was living in South Carolina. Yeah. She told me all about that guy—" he snapped his fingers "—what was his name? Garrett? In fact, Bray called me *several* times. But she didn't call you, did she? Not once. Some best friend."

"I only called you to find out things about Elias!"

I still wanted to hit him, now more than before. But I also wanted to hear this.

Bray stepped away from me and started to go toward him, but I reached out and grabbed her hand, pulling her back before she got too far.

But that didn't stop her from shouting.

"You're such a prick!" she roared. "Don't you *ever* try to make what I did out to be something that it wasn't!"

Mitchell threw his head back and laughed.

"A game-playing little bitch," he said and before he could get the rest out, I was pushing Bray to the side and going toward him.

"Elias, don't hit him!" Bray shouted at me from behind. "You know it's the drugs!"

I shoved the coffee table out of my way and grabbed him by the front of his shirt and started pushing him toward the front door; his heels were partially dragging the carpet. By this time, I did want to hit him, more than anything, but I knew Bray was right.

"I can't even believe you took her back after what she did!" he screamed in my face, the smell of his meth-breath whirling cruelly up into my nostrils. "All that time, Elias! That hell she put you through! All those times I listened to you talk about her, all that childhood stuff, the stupid fucking firefly story! She's got you whipped!"

I shoved him right out the front door. He fell on his ass, but stayed there on the concrete screaming up at me, his long bangs now disheveled around his face despite the oil.

"Unfuckingbelievable! I thought you were better than that, bro," he said.

"Your shit will be on the sidewalk by tonight," I said, glaring down at him. "Don't ever fucking come in here again. You understand? After you get your shit, that's it. Don't come back here or I'll beat the fuck out of you."

"Whatever, man," he said and pushed himself to his feet. "At least give me my car keys."

I looked over my shoulder at Bray and she went into the living room, coming back seconds later with his keys in her hand. Mitchell reached out for them, but I took them from her instead and pushed her carefully behind me.

"Don't go near her ever again. Not for anything."

I dropped the keys in his hand.

"Yeah, fuck you," he said casually and turned and walked toward his car.

"I'm so sorry," Bray said after I shut the front door.

She stepped up to me, clasping her fingers gently around my hands at my sides.

"I did not expect it to go down like that," I said, looking toward the wall, thinking about Mitchell.

"He'll come around," she said. "He's just not right in the head."

"I know."

Bray helped me pack up all of Mitchell's things, which wasn't much, just boxes of his clothes and movies and CDs. Thankfully, the only furniture in the apartment that was his was a small TV stand and a bar stool from Dickey's Bar and Grill that he bought at an auction after Dickey's closed down. We carried everything out-side and set it near the front door instead of on the sidewalk. I didn't want anything to get stolen or rained on.

But two days came and went, and Mitchell never came back to get it.

# SEVEN

## Bray

$\mathcal{E}$lias took the falling-out with Mitchell really hard the first few days. It was only to be expected, since they had known each other even longer than *we* had known each other. Despite everything, Elias knew that it wasn't his fault, and he wasn't going to sit around and blame himself. Mitchell had brought this all on himself. Eventually, Elias went from feeling bad about what happened to indifferent.

He still had me, after all.

By Friday night, we were debating whether to go to the river or not, because Mitchell would almost definitely be there.

"I say we go, Elias. Don't let him ruin our good time."

Elias kissed me on the forehead and squeezed me around the waist as I sat straddled on his lap.

"OK. We'll go. Just stay away from him, all right?"

I draped my arms around his neck and then kissed his lips. "I'll be too busy with you to worry about him," I said suggestively.

Elias smiled and squeezed my butt in his hands. "How did we get like this?" he asked, studying my face and my lips.

"It was inevitable," I said in a quiet voice. My fingers touched the contours of his cheekbones and probed him as if he were a beautiful, delicate statue. He hadn't shaved in a while, but I found the growing stubble sexy on him.

"Do you remember our first kiss?" he asked, smiling at me.

"Of course I do," I said. "The first night we met."

He shook his head and his hands slid up my back.

"No, I mean the first *real* kiss."

I swallowed hard. On the inside I was screaming as another memory infected my thoughts in that moment, but on the outside, I looked as blissful as he did.

"Yes. I remember," I said distantly.

Elias's blue eyes softened, not sensing the turmoil going on inside of me. I was thankful for that.

"I've always wondered about that day," he said. "When you asked me to kiss you, did you really just want to practice? Be honest."

I swallowed again and my hands began to shake. I steadied them, interlacing my fingers around the back of his neck. The memory of our first kiss was one of my most cherished. I would never forget it. But the other, more solemn memory that always came with it nowadays was what I couldn't bear.

"I did want to practice," I answered, hiding the pain in my heart. "But it was just an excuse. I really just wanted you to kiss me."

Elias's smile widened. And then he touched his lips to mine, slowly brushing the tip of his tongue between them. I wilted in his arms.

He made love to me that morning before we packed the car and headed to the river. And I noticed—very hard not to—something about Elias that I never expected, but that drove me absolutely mad for him. Every time we would have sex, he was different, he would *feel* different. Sometimes aggressive, sometimes explorative, though it seemed like he was holding something back. I had been with several guys, but none of them had anything on Elias. Sex with him was never the same. He was focused, determined, meticulous, and experienced. And each time I went in, I found myself wondering what he was going to do to me this time. Just anticipating it was thrilling. And sometimes scary. In a good way.

For the first time in my life I didn't feel wrong about the way I was inside. I didn't feel ashamed. But instead, I felt like I could *almost* be myself completely with Elias. But only almost. I wasn't ready yet to lay something like that on him. I was afraid of making him look at me differently, or lose respect for me.

Because the truth was, I was addicted to sex.

I wanted it all the time. In every way. On the outside I was a seemingly innocent girl by today's standards. Before Elias, whenever I would have sex with guys, I always felt ashamed afterward. I didn't want any of them, sexually or otherwise. I wanted Elias in every way imaginable.

Now that I had him and was picking up these familiar sexual vibes from him, my mind began to spin with the possibilities.

Were Elias and I more alike than we ever knew? Was that even *possible*? Was Elias just as addicted to sex as I was?

By this time, even without knowing the answers to those questions yet, I thought that life really couldn't get any better. We were in complete and absolute love, finally living the dream with one another that we had always dreamed about. There was so much to do, so many things about ourselves and about life to explore together, and we had our whole lives ahead of us in which to do it.

But on the night of April 20, everything we knew would

change, and that life together we had waited so long to have would come crashing down around us like some cruel fucking joke.

———

We made it to the secluded party spot on the river just after dark. It was getting slightly cooler as the night approached, but that never stopped anyone we knew from swimming. Summer in Georgia wasn't officially here, but it might as well have been.

There were a lot of people at the river, some I knew, most I didn't. Tents had been pitched throughout the woods, spaced far enough apart for privacy. Two separate campfires burned, and people sat around each of them talking and drinking. The smell of pot filled the air. Not even two minutes in, as Elias and I carried in our camping gear, a group of people offered us a joint. We stopped and took a hit before heading into the woods to stake our claim on a spot for the weekend.

"I haven't seen him yet," I said about Mitchell as I set our ice chest down beside a tree.

Elias unzipped the tent bag and started setting up. "Well, maybe we'll get lucky and he won't show."

"Hopefully," I said.

After we were satisfied with our setup, we walked through the trees the short distance back to the main camp, where everyone was sitting. Music was playing from a portable radio, but the river was so close that it nearly drowned out the music coming from the tiny speakers.

We sat down next to a couple and immediately the guy passed a joint to Elias. Elias took a long hit and shotgunned it to me, exhaling it into my mouth. My eyes watered and burned a little, but at that point I didn't care.

"I'm tellin' ya, man," another guy to our left said in a half-joking manner, "once you get married, it all goes to shit. Should jus' keep things like they are." The guy took a hit and let the smoke trickle out of his lips and funnel back through his nostrils.

"He would know," the blonde-haired girl sitting next to him said. She took the joint from him and put it to her lips, pressed between the tips of her thumb and index finger. "My dear idiot brother here has been married twice." Her voice strained and cracked as she held the smoke deep in her lungs. "Was with his ex for six years. Perfect together. Got married and—" she snapped her fingers "—*poof*! Instant destruction of a perfectly good relationship."

Laughter ripped through the air.

Elias pulled me from beside him and over between his legs, wrapping his arms around me from behind. I could tell he wasn't paying any attention to the conversations going on around us. Not the one about that guy's bad luck with marriages, or the one on the other side of us about some girl's recent endometriosis diagnosis. He was enjoying his high, and I was enjoying mine with him.

We zoned out for a while, me sitting between his legs, leaning against his chest. We listened mostly to the mix of the radio and the nearby river, which somehow blended harmoniously. Being high has many strange and unexpected perks. After a couple of hours, most of our company either went swimming, or drank too much then hit their tents to pass out.

Elias nuzzled his mouth at the back of my neck. My body folded forward, attacked by a tickling sensation that raced down my spine.

"Want to go for a swim?" he asked, then whispered hotly into my ear, "Or, you can go to the tent with me."

I giggled and tilted my head to one side, exposing my neck to his mouth. He dragged his teeth across the skin, raising chill bumps all over my body.

"Why don't we do both?" I suggested and licked his tongue playfully with the tip of mine.

He smiled and drew his head back. "You want to swim in the tent?"

I teasingly elbowed him in the ribs. "No," I said and turned around on my knees to face him. I leaned inward toward his ear, bit his earlobe, and said, "You can fuck me in the water."

And that was just what we were doing when Jana and Mitchell finally made their grand appearance.

Mitchell jumped off a rock several feet high into the water not far from us. It scared the crap out of me, but Elias was so close to getting off that he wasn't about to let something like that stop him. It was always harder to get off when under water, so the thirty minutes we spent with my legs wrapped around his waist and him slowly thrusting in and out of me wasn't going to be for nothing.

Elias grabbed me closer, one arm around my back, the other positioned partway in between my butt cheeks, and held me still when I startled.

"Ignore him," he said, staring deeply into my eyes, his face just mere inches from mine, as he tried to stay focused.

He never took his eyes off mine. It made me insanely crazy for him. I pushed my bikini-covered breasts firmly against his rock-hard chest and kissed him. He devoured my mouth, pushing in and out of me beneath the water the whole time. Water dripped from his lips and his cheeks and I licked it off of him. The gesture made him thrust deeper, his fingers digging painfully into my back.

"Oh look," I heard Mitchell say, "It's my best friend. Who kicked me out for a girl."

Elias's concentration was unshaken. I, on the other hand, was getting pissed. And a little worried someone—mainly Mitchell— would notice what we were doing. He certainly didn't need any more fuel for the fire he started.

Jana jumped into the water next, thankfully slightly farther away from us than Mitchell had.

"Come on, Mitchell," I heard her say. I never looked away from Elias's eyes. "Don't do that shit here. You'll ruin everyone's night, not just theirs."

The two of them swam away in the opposite direction and left us alone.

But apparently Mitchell's presence and misplaced grudge against Elias, instead of the apology Elias had been hoping he'd get if he saw Mitchell tonight, was too much of a distraction. He pulled out of me without getting off and then hugged me.

"I'm sorry," he said, kissing the top of my head.

"What are you apologizing to me for?" I kissed his lips. "He's a fucking asshole. Enough to kill anyone's buzz or orgasm." I brought my hand out of the water and flicked droplets at his face. "You can finish with me later. However you want it."

For a second, it seemed Elias was just going to smile and join in with my impish gestures, but I saw something shift in his eyes when I said that last part. He looked at me with a deep curiosity.

"However I want it?" he asked, searching for further explanation.

I rested three of my fingers on his nose and then dragged them down his face and onto his lips, where he kissed each one individually.

"Yeah," I responded coyly. "You know you can do anything you want to me, right?"

He still looked incredibly curious, that sidelong look in his darkening gaze, but I could sense that he was as afraid to come out and say what he was thinking as much as I was. We were still feeling each other out. Testing those boundaries. Hoping that there *were* no boundaries. But we were each afraid of scaring the other one off. We should've known that nothing could ever do that. It would've saved us a lot of pent-up sexual frustration a lot earlier on.

A giant gush of water covered us like an angry ocean wave. Elias and I broke apart from each other's grasp. I couldn't see; the water burned my eyes as well as my nostrils and the back of my throat.

"What the fuck, man?!" I heard Elias shout.

I pushed the heavy, wet hair back away from my face and finally got my eyes open. I saw Elias first, and he had a murderous look on his face. I swam back over to him and draped my arms over the back of his shoulders, wrapping my legs around him from behind.

Mitchell was grinning enormously, proud that he'd splashed us.

"Let's just go to our tent," I said.

He ignored me. "You're twenty-seven years old, man," he snapped at Mitchell. "A little old to be acting like that, don't you think?"

"Seriously, baby, let's just go."

Mitchell laughed and laid on his back, floating on top of the surface. He spit water into the air. Jana, floating upright next to him, dodged it and made a face. Mitchell didn't say anything else, but there was no shortage of spiteful looks exchanged as Elias and I left the water and got as far away from him as we could.

"We can go home if you want," Elias said to me. He pushed back a low-hanging tree branch to clear the path for me, and his other hand rested on my lower back.

"No," I said. "I want to stay. Screw him. I can't believe he's even acting like that. I feel like we're back in junior high school."

"Well, it's like you said, it's the drugs. He's definitely not himself."

We made our way up the rocky path leading back to our tent, hand in hand. But before we got there, my left flip-flop broke.

"Shit." I bent over to fool with the strip between my toes, trying to make it hold long enough so I could walk the rest of the way through the woods.

Elias lifted me up, swung me around on his back, and carried me the rest of the way. My arms were hooked around his neck and his were hooked around my thighs. We hung out at the tent for a long time, but neither of us could sleep. We had uncomfortable sex inside the tent, and then we talked for a while until we decided to explore the bluffs. I "borrowed" a passed-out girl's flip-flops from another tent nearby, and Elias and I headed deeper into the woods.

# EIGHT

## Bray

*W*hat if we get lost?" I asked, gripping Elias's hand. "We didn't exactly bring any survival gear."

"We're not going far," he said. "I saw a ridge when we were swimming. People were hanging out on top of it." He pointed. "It's just up ahead. Jared and a few of the other guys went this way to get to it."

I had seen it, too, and wondered how everybody got over there.

After several more minutes of pushing our way between trees and bushes and stepping over dead branches and stray rocks, we emerged from the woods into a clearing at the top of the ridge that overlooked the river many feet below. A campfire had burned here recently; I could smell the leftover heat and smoke still rising from the charcoaled sticks on the small pile. A few empty beer bottles were strewn about the ground.

We walked to the edge of the ridge and looked out at the river; the moonlight was reflected off the water like hundreds of little diamonds. Some of our friends were still in the river below, floating on small plastic rafts, but it was fairly quiet everywhere, as the party had begun to die down for the night.

I sat down near the edge of the ridge and drew my knees toward my chest, wrapping my arms around my legs. The breeze blew through my hair, and I closed my eyes and raised my chin to the sky, taking in the tranquility of the night.

Elias sat down next to me, propping his wrists on his bent knees. "I almost went to South Carolina after you," he said.

I glanced over. He was looking out at the water. "Why didn't you?" I asked.

"Mitchell told me you were engaged."

I started to turn to him, shocked by what I'd heard, but I realized it didn't surprise me much. "Well, he lied," I said in a calm voice instead. After a pause, I added, "I wish you would've come after me anyway."

Elias looked right at me, the emotion in his eyes pulling me in. The breeze brushed through the messy dark hair that framed his beautiful, stubbly face. "I know," he said and looked away. "And you should've called me instead of Mitchell." There was no blame or resentment in his voice.

"I know," I said.

"I guess there are a lot of things we could've and should've done differently," he said. "But you came back regardless. And we're together now, despite all of that. And that has to count for something."

Silence fell between us for a moment, giving us both time to reflect.

"Did you love her?" I asked about Aline, and I knew there was no need to clarify who I was talking about. I knew enough about her from Mitchell.

"Yeah," he said and I felt an uncomfortable twinge in my stomach. "But she wasn't you. I can love a lot of people. Aline. My parents.

Hell, even Mitch's dumb ass. But I could never love anyone the way I love you."

The twinge softened and became something warm.

"Did you love *him*?" Elias asked.

"No," I answered honestly. "I, uh..." I sighed and looked out ahead of me again. "I think I used him," I admitted to Elias *and* to myself. And while I felt like a horrible person for it, suddenly I felt the need to spill the truth because I had been holding this inside for so long.

I went on:

"Even before I left, before we got together on your twenty-second birthday, every guy I was with, I think deep down was a substitute for you. It's why none of them lasted, why I couldn't date anyone for more than two months. I told you before, Elias, I was always scared of being with you. Of ruining what we had."

"I know," he said, but it was all that he said. I got the sense he wanted me to continue.

And so I did. I took another deep breath and began to tap my fingers against my knees out of nervousness.

"Lissa introduced me to Garrett," I said. "He was a friend of her brother's. I don't know what the hell was wrong with me, or how I managed to stay with him for a year, but I did. I didn't love him, but I guess I needed him. He wasn't you, but he was there."

*And I needed sex*, I wanted to say, but couldn't. *I didn't want to sleep around with a bunch of different guys, so I found one and stuck with him. I used him for sex. I used him to pretend that he was you. I used* him. *I'm awful.*

I couldn't say these things out loud. I wanted to. I wanted to so bad that every word was on my tongue, pushing against the back of my teeth. I needed to get the truth out—about Garrett, about all of the other guys after him—to feel the impending relief. But I was still scared. I knew that I could trust Elias more than anyone in this world, that Elias would stand behind me no matter my flaws. But it was a double-edged knife, because I was terrified of losing that one person. And I had seen people lose others over much less.

"There's something you're not telling me," he said, surprising me.

My gut twisted in knots.

"You know you can always tell me anything," he went on, but I couldn't look at him. "There is absolutely nothing you could ever say or do that would make me leave you."

He knew I was hiding things from him, and he was desperate to know my secrets. And I was desperate to tell him. But he didn't want to push me. He wanted me to tell him when I was ready, but he was letting me know that it would be OK.

And I believed him. I looked over, into his eyes, and he smiled warmly back at me.

I was going to tell him right then. Suddenly, it felt right. That small window a person is given in which to say or do something they've always been afraid to had opened up for me in that moment. I felt elated and alive and longed to not feel suffocated anymore by the weight I carried on my chest.

But the window closed too quickly, and I shut down.

It was as if he could sense it right away, too, because I saw the hope and determination in his eyes fade seconds after the window closed. But he wasn't mad. Disappointed, yes, but never mad at me. That only made me love him more.

He reached out his hand and cupped the back of my neck, pulling my head toward him. He pressed his lips to my forehead.

"Y'know, I think I'd rather sleep up here than in that stuffy tent," I said after a minute of quiet.

Elias pursed his lips and thought about it, then his head bobbed in agreement. "Not a bad idea," he said and stood up. "Let's go back and get the blankets." He reached out his hand to me.

"I can wait here," I said. "Unless you want me to go with you."

"No, I can go," he said. "It's not that far. I'll be right back."

He leaned over and kissed me on the lips, then walked across the opening and disappeared among the trees.

It was so peaceful sitting on the top of the ridge all alone, looking out at the dark landscape and how the river snaked a path through the trees below. I gazed up at the sky and closed my eyes again to savor the wind on my face. It had been a long time since I felt this free, not since I was a kid. I hated that with growing up came the knowledge that life won't always be like it was when we were children. I wished we could just grow backward.

I heard footsteps behind me coming from the trees, and I thought initially that Elias was back sooner than expected. Two figures emerged from the woods far away from where Elias had gone back in.

As the two moved closer into the moonlight, I saw that the skinny blonde-haired one was Jana. The other was a girl with supershort black hair whom I had never seen before.

I stood up as Jana stumbled toward me, the black-haired girl following close behind.

"What the fuck are you looking at?" I thought I heard Jana say, but I wasn't completely sure, as her words were slurred and choppy.

She was clearly drunk. And maybe high on something, too. Her more so than her friend, who didn't have any trouble standing up straight.

"Are you all right?" I asked, peering at Jana.

Her black bikini top sat sloppily over her breasts, barely containing them. The straps were left untied from around her neck and hung freely. She had on a pair of men's shorts, and she wore no shoes. I noticed one of her big toes was bleeding.

"I'm fanfuckingtastic," she said with a big drunken smile. "Hey, aren't you Elias's girlfriend?" Her finger unfolded from her hand and pointed at me shakily.

Then she looked over at her friend and said, "This was the girl I was telling you about."

Jana stumbled again and almost fell. I grabbed her instinctively and held her up by the elbow, but she shoved my hand away. "I got this," she snapped. "Don't...I'm great, I told you."

I didn't really want to help her anyway, so I was happy to let go.

"Yes, I'm Elias's girlfriend," I finally answered.

She attempted a grin, but it was quickly overrun by the lazy fluttering of her eyelids as though she was struggling to keep her eyes open.

"He's a good lay," she said to me and then smiled at the black-haired girl, who looked bored, or just ready to get back to the party rather than stand up here with the two of us.

I gritted my teeth at Jana's comment but held my composure.

Jana laughed and almost fell over again. This time I didn't try to stop her. I *wanted* her to fall.

"They both fucked me at the same time," she added, that grin finally winning its battle with the inevitable unconsciousness. But she didn't seem to be gloating about it, just reminiscing a little too openly. "Him and Mitchell. God damn." Then she looked right at me and pointed again. "Have you done them both? Surely you have, since you lived with them and all." She said it so casually, as if she and I were talking about what to have for breakfast. Clearly she wouldn't be saying these things if she wasn't so messed up. No, I take that back—she definitely would.

"Ummm, no, I haven't," I answered, trying to stay calm when really what I wanted to do was hit her in the fucking mouth.

"Let's go back to the fire," the black-haired girl said.

"Well, you should," Jana said to me, ignoring the girl's suggestion. Her upper body swayed backward slightly like a tower hit by a gust of wind.

Then she stuck her finger in my face. "Hey. Oh my God!" Her breath was rancid. "We could totally have a foursome. You game? Or shit, a fivesome!" She pointed at the girl and the girl's face soured. "Wait"—she had a dumb moment look on her face all of a sudden—"that's an orgy, right?"

I swallowed hard and took a step back away from her. "No," I said. "I think I'll fucking pass."

"Uh, yeah, me too," the black-haired girl said. "Jana, I think you need to find your tent and sleep it off. Seriously."

"Fine. Whatever," Jana said, but she wasn't responding to the girl. She was still talking to me. Her eyelids started getting heavy again. "Probably better, anyway. I think I fucked up when I screwed them. I mean it wasn't that long ago, but I think I might be pregnant with your boyfriend's baby."

The breeze burned my eyes as they widened and I sucked in a sharp breath. "What the hell did you say?"

The black-haired girl shook her head and took a step back. "I'll see you later. No bitch drama for me tonight." And then she walked off toward the path that Elias took and left Jana and me standing alone.

Jana's head swiveled on her shoulders and she tried to stifle a laugh, pressing the side of her index finger against her lips.

*Now* she was gloating.

"Yeah, I'm like five days late," she said twirling a hand in the air, pleased to be filling my head with this information. "And I'm *never* late. So yeah, I'm pretty sure I'm knocked up."

I punched her right between the eyes and her head snapped backward. I don't know how she managed to stay on her feet that time. It was an uncontrollable reaction to hit her, in retaliation to her taunting me about it. I regretted it a second after I pulled my fist back. My knuckles stung painfully.

With her hand cupping her nose, she just laughed.

"For your sake," I said with anger rising in my voice, "you better hope that's not true."

I started to walk away, back through the clearing and toward the trees. She followed.

"Or what?" she mocked me. "You won't do *shit* except babysit our kid on the weekends. Fuck you." She laughed.

I kept walking toward the trees, but I was blinded by anger and hatred and so many other emotions that I didn't realize I was walking in the wrong direction, more toward the area Jana had come from rather than to where Elias had gone.

She kept following me, and I kept walking. All the while, she yelled curses at me and taunted me. Tears streamed down my face. My fingernails dug into the palms of my hands, almost breaking the skin. I couldn't get the images out of my head: her pregnant with Elias's baby, him divided between the two of us, him leaving me to be with her, thinking he was only doing the right thing. I even saw him marrying her. Their life together flashed before my eyes, and before I knew it I was standing at the edge of a ravine. I had taken a wrong turn at some point, and the only way back was past Jana, who was closing in on me from behind with her hateful, spiteful words and that laughter in her voice that made me want to kill her. Figuratively, of course.

"Move!" I said, turning to face her. I went to push my way past her, but she grabbed me by the arm.

"Fucking *move*!" I roared.

A white-hot pain seared through the side of my head. I spun on one heel and fell backward, tripping over a rock. Before I could get to my feet, I reached up and touched the side of my face where she had hit me, letting the realization of what she did sink in. Then I sprung to my feet and was mere seconds from beating the shit out of her. I was in her face, our noses practically touching, my hands clenched into fists at my sides.

But I couldn't bring myself to hit her again. If she was pregnant, I couldn't hit her because I felt like I'd be hitting that baby, too. I hated her. I fucking *hated* that bitch for coming into my life and ruining what Elias and I had gone through so much together to have. But I couldn't hit her back. I started to walk away, but she grabbed me from behind, both of her hands winding tightly in the back of my hair. She became violent, like an animal, so quickly it made my head spin. She screamed something I didn't understand, and all I could do was try to pry her hands off me.

Finally, I managed to whirl around at her, flinging her hands away and into the air above her.

"GET! OFF!" I wailed and pushed her in a last desperate attempt to be free of her.

She stumbled backward.

I froze and watched in absolute horror as she missed the tree, tripped over her own feet, and fell right off the side of the ravine.

Through the seemingly infinite silence that suddenly consumed me, I heard her body hit the rocks below with a stomach-turning crunch.

I stopped breathing in that moment. No, *everything* stopped in that moment. The wind. The sky. The river. The world. Everything....

# NINE

## Elias

*W*hen I made my way back to the top, I found Bray wasn't sitting near the edge of the ridge where I had left her. I moved farther out into the clearing with our blankets draped over one shoulder.

"Bray?" I said, looking around.

I brushed it off for a second, thinking she was probably just taking a piss behind a tree somewhere, and I set our blankets on the ground.

But then I got a sinking feeling in the pit of my stomach.

I walked quickly toward the edge and looked over. My heart started to bang against my rib cage. I peered down as far as my sight could penetrate the darkness, but took a step back upon realizing that if she had fallen there was no way I'd be able to see from way up here.

She had to be somewhere around close by. She *had* to be.

"Bray?" I called out again. "Where the hell did you go?"

Still no answer.

Panic set in quickly. I stood there as still and as quiet as I could for several long seconds in case she was coming through the woods, but I heard nothing. I arranged both hands around my mouth and shouted, "BRAY!" and my voice echoed through the wide-open space. But still nothing. I felt sick to my stomach. She wouldn't have left like that way out here. And if she did, I would've seen her on the path coming down as I was making my way back up.

I ran toward the tree line, searching for any sign of her, for another path she might have taken. I refused to believe that she had fallen off the edge.

Just as I noticed another path through the woods that seemed to head south and I started to go toward it, I heard footfalls in the leaves. I didn't wait to see if it was her, I ran blindly straight into the woods. A skinny branch slapped me across the forehead on my way, but I didn't stop.

Bray and I nearly crashed into each other.

"Shit, baby! Where the hell did you *go*? Scared the *hell* out of me!" I started to pull her into a hug, but something about her was off and I stopped. She didn't respond or even raise her head to look at me.

"Are you all right?"

I took her hands into mine. Hers were shaking. Her whole body was shaking.

I cupped her face in my palms and raised her head so that she'd look at me. She was crying, and something in her eyes . . . I couldn't place it, but it haunted me. I wondered if she even knew I was standing right in front of her. Her hair was messy, with pieces of leaves stuck within a mass of strands. Dirt was smeared across her left cheek. She looked like she'd been in a fight.

I touched her split lip, where a thin line of blood glistened near the corner. "Bray, you're scaring me. What happened to you?" I shook her gently and then more aggressively when she still didn't respond. "What happened? Talk to me!"

Her lips trembled and more tears seeped from the corners of her eyes. And then as if a floodgate had been opened, she started screaming through her tears, "It was my fault! Elias! Oh my God!"

"*What happened?*" I roared, scared for her and for myself, my heart about to burst through my chest.

"Jana!" her voice trembled and she began to stutter. "Sh-she fell. Jana f-fell. Right off the cliff!"

"What?" I said, suddenly almost completely calm. I don't think what she had just said registered in my mind yet.

Then suddenly, it *did* register and my heart stopped.

I crouched down in front of her, squeezed her trembling hands within mine, and I looked up into her reddened, tear-soaked eyes as she stood before me.

"Bray, look at me. *Look* at me." She did. "Are you *sure?*"

She nodded in an unsteady, jerking motion. The tears never stopped flowing. Her pretty face distorted with every kind of pain and anguish and guilt that a person could possibly feel at once.

"Show me," I said with intent, trying to contain the dread and panic. "Take me to where it happened."

She shook her head at first but then nodded. "OK."

I followed close beside her as she led me through the woods toward the edge of a ravine not even two minutes from the clearing. I held her hand tight as I stepped to the edge and looked over. The drop was no more than fifty or sixty feet, where I could clearly see Jana's body splayed out on the rocks.

"Holy shit...."

Bray ruptured into heartrending sobs, and she buried her face in her hands. I seized her and pulled her harshly against my chest, squeezing my arms tight around her shaking body, my hands holding fast to her head.

"Shhh, baby please, stop crying. Listen to me. We have to go down there. We have to make sure. Can you do that? Bray, can you help me?" I tried my best to calm her down. I held her gaze until she seemed fully coherent and cooperative. I wiped the tears from her cheeks.

She nodded slowly.

"We'll figure this out, OK? Now let's go."

It took us what felt like a very long time, thirty minutes at least, to find the easiest way partway down the ravine and to Jana's body. And once we got there, I knew before we even got close enough to see if she was breathing, that she was dead.

Jana was dead. Jana was dead.

The words kept running through my mind, over and over again like a broken record. I think for two minutes straight I had an out-of-body experience, because nothing around me felt real. I couldn't tear my eyes away from the body. The rock beneath her head was painted with glistening red that appeared black in the darkness. Jana's eyes were open, staring up at the sky, lifeless and empty, though still full of *something* ... they were full of the truth of what happened. I finally looked at Bray standing next to me, on the verge of full-blown traumatization. At any moment she was going to crack. She was going to slip into oblivion, and I didn't know if I'd be able to pull her out of it.

I pulled her against me again, even tighter this time, and felt her ribs moving against mine. "Stay with me," I said. "We're going to figure this out. Do you understand?"

And I held her there. We stood together next to the body.

I thought of my mother and the things she always said to me when I was growing up: *Always do what you know in your heart is right. No matter what, Elias.*

And I wept going over those words in my mind. I cried and shook and lost myself as much as Bray had done for a moment, crushing her against me, never wanting to let her go. But finally, I pulled Bray away from my chest and clasped my hands around her upper arms. "Baby, look at me and tell me...*swear* to me...that this was an accident."

She fell to her knees on the cool rock and I went down with her.

"Please, Bray, tell me the truth."

"It was an accident! I swear! I pushed her off of me, but she stumbled back too far and tripped and went over the edge! I didn't think I'd pushed her hard enough! I didn't *want* to push her off!" She screamed every word at me but it felt more like she was trying to convince herself, to make herself understand what just happened. Her face was stricken by pain. So much pain. Her fists were clenched against her thighs.

I tried to grab her head, but she jostled herself to the side and started puking on the damp bank next to the rock we stood on. I pulled her hair back and away from her shoulders and held her loosely around the waist while she threw up. She cried so much that her voice was strained when she tried to speak between vomiting intervals. "I didn't mean—" and she'd vomit before she could get the rest of the words out. "I wasn't try—"

Finally, she fell against my body when she couldn't puke anymore, and I enveloped her in my arms and rocked her gently, brushing her hair away from her forehead.

"I-I don't want to go to prison," she said. "They'll send me to prison, Elias. I can't prove it was an accident. Elias, they'll charge me with murder." Her voice started to rise again and her body became stiff in my arms. "Please don't let them take me to prison!"

She was crying heavily again.

"Shhh...that's not going to happen. You can tell them the truth. Just tell the truth and this will work out. I have to believe that."

I didn't believe that...

"No, Elias," she cried. "They won't believe me. People know you slept with her. Mitchell knows. I'm the new girlfriend. People will assume. And..." She stopped cold.

"And what?"

Her hands were trembling harder.

"Bray, what is it?"

"She...she told me she thought she might've been pregnant." She hesitated again. She didn't want to finish. "With your baby."

I froze.

"That's ridiculous," I said. "I-I mean, it's not impossible, but I used protection. It wasn't even that long ago." My head was spinning now with the possibilities, my heart a heavy, uneven series of beats. I was almost as traumatized as Bray was at this point. "How would she even know something like that so early? I used a condom. It didn't break. If she was pregnant, I doubt it was mine. Possible, but unlikely." I was rambling now. Nervous as hell that something like that could've been true.

"She was just fucking with you," I added, completely believing that, because it was the only thing that made sense.

"It doesn't matter, Elias. She's dead and I was the last one to be seen with her! There was a girl here with her just before it happened! And I, more than anyone out here, had motive. They won't believe it was an accident! They'll *crucify* me!" She buried her face in my chest, her fingers digging into the back of my neck.

I decided to do the right thing, just like my mother always said. In that moment, it was the right thing to do...

"Let's go," I said, pulling her to her feet. "We have to get out of here."

Bray looked at me with confusion in her eyes, but it took all of two seconds for her to understand and follow me. We found our way back to the ridge in the clearing. We didn't speak, overwhelmed by what had happened and exhausted by the uphill climb. I held her hand tight the whole way, afraid to let her go for even a second.

I was afraid to let her go...

I grabbed our blankets from the ground and tossed them over my shoulder.

Finally, I spoke. "Now listen to me, OK?"

She nodded.

"When we go back to the main camp we have to act normal. Hopefully no one will notice us, but if they do we *have* to act normal."

"Are we leaving...now?" she asked nervously.

"Yes," I said. "If they find her while we're still here..." I stopped. I sighed. But I had to be truthful with her. "Bray, I'm not confident enough to believe that you won't break down in front of everyone. We can't stay here for that. Do you understand?"

She nodded again. "But it won't be normal for us to leave in the middle of the night," she pointed out.

I hadn't thought of that. A heavy breath rattled through my chest. I looked out toward the ridge for a moment.

In the end, I could think of nothing. Nothing was going to make this better. I knew deep in my gut that unless she turned herself in, that if I didn't talk her into doing the right thing, that from this point on everything would just get worse.

I pushed myself away from her and threw the blankets on the

ground in a rage. "AHHH!" I shouted, balling my fists beside me, my arms bent upward. I went to the edge of the ridge. "God damn it!" My hands gripped the back of my head and I just stood there like that, staring into the dark sky.

Bray came up behind me. I felt her hands slip around my waist from behind, the softness of her cheek pressed against my bare back.

"I won't turn myself in," she said softly, as if she knew what I was thinking. "Elias, I know in my heart that this will be the end of us. I'm scared. I'm scared of losing you, of being taken away from you and put away. Haven't we been apart long enough?"

Those last words wrenched my heart. My fingers dug in between hers against my stomach. I choked back the tears.

"If you don't want to leave with me," she continued, "I'll understand. It's probably better that you don't. Because this wasn't your fault. You don't need to ruin your life because of me. But I want you to know—"

"I'm not going to leave you," I stopped her, turning around to face her. "I'm not going to lose you. It's you and me, it always has been. It always *will* be."

I smashed my lips against her forehead.

We made it out of the camp that night without a scene. Only one person stopped us to ask why we were leaving, and Bray pretended to be sick. It wasn't hard for her to pull off especially since she looked like she had been to hell and back. And she smelled faintly of vomit.

It was daylight when we arrived back at my apartment. Everything was different. The way the early morning sun hung over the trees and how it always made the wind chimes hanging outside my neighbor's front door glisten and sparkle. The sunrise seemed darker; the reflected light on the shiny metal trinkets, lifeless. I didn't hear any birds. I had always heard birds chirping in the early morning, but not this morning. Maybe they were there, carrying on like they always did, but I didn't hear them. Even the paint on the apartment walls appeared dull and faded. The comfort I always felt when I'd walk through my front door after work was replaced with something ominous. Nothing was the same and it never would be again.

Bray and I knew that skipping town would look suspicious, and put us on the police's radar. But we also knew that it didn't matter much at this point, because what we had already done was enough to make us the number one suspects. The motives that Bray pointed out. Mitchell having it in for me and knowing everything about those motives. Us leaving the camp before the first night was over. It didn't matter what we did from that moment on. We just knew that we had to get away. We hoped that maybe Jana's body wouldn't be discovered. It was our only way out.

Of course, the bodies are almost always found, sooner or later. And since we didn't try to hide it and left it out in the open, I knew too that "sooner" would trump "later."

# TEN

## Elias

We drove southeast toward the ocean and wound up in Savannah. Things quieted down while we were on the road. We sat mostly in silence for the four-hour drive, but every now and then one of us would bring up the what-ifs and the maybes, which always rendered us silent again, left us to think heavily about this ever-expanding web of disorder we were creating for ourselves. One question would produce three more, but never any answers. By the time we found a small shithole of a motel to stay in, we had exhausted the topic. For a short while, anyway.

I chose this motel, likely the first choice of hookers and drug dealers, because it was one of the few that accepted cash and didn't care if I'd "lost" my driver's license.

The only thing that worried me as I stood at the front desk waiting to get my room key was that I was already in fugitive mode. It was like something was triggered in my brain that told me that we had to be careful in everything we did. Use fake names. Pay only with cash. Don't call home. Don't answer the phone when home calls us. And we hadn't even officially been targeted as suspects yet. Hell, we didn't know if Jana's body had even been found.

"I'm starving," Bray said, sitting down on the end of the bed.

"I'll get us something," I said. "There's a few fast-food restaurants farther down the road."

She reached out to me, and I took her hand and crouched on the floor in front of her. She brushed her fingers across my unshaven face. I kissed them.

"I love you," she said with a weak smile. She was exhausted. Physically and mentally. We both were.

I raised up on my toes enough to reach her lips. "I love you, too," I said after I pulled my lips away from hers. Then I stood up and grabbed my keys from the nightstand. "I'll be back soon," I said and left her in the room.

Instead of stopping at a restaurant I drove right past them all and went straight to my father's house about ten minutes away.

He welcomed me at the door with open arms. "Elias! It's good to see you, son. Come on in."

If there was any person in the world whom I could trust and count on even more than Bray, it was my father. Unlike my mom, who was always the voice of reason, the do-gooder, my dad was the one who wasn't beyond doing the wrong thing if, in his heart, it happened to be right. His was another kind of voice. Like father, like son. In more ways than one. I favored my father. I inherited his dark hair and blue eyes.

"You didn't mention you were coming to Savannah las' time we talked," he said.

He brought two bottles of beer from the kitchen and handed me one as I sat on his old beige sofa.

"It was an unexpected trip," I said.

"Well, I'm always glad to have ya here," he said with a proud smile. He pushed his glasses up to the top of his nose.

We took a sip of beer at the same time and silence ensued.

"Dad, I'm in trouble." I got right to the point. Not only was I not afraid to tell him, but I didn't want to leave Bray alone in the motel for longer than I had to.

My dad cocked an eyebrow and his beer hung inches from his lips in pause. Slowly he lowered it. "What kind of trouble?"

"The worst trouble I've ever been in."

He set the beer on the coffee table. All traces of him being happy to see me dimmed on his face. He looked intent and worried and, as I had expected of him, very fatherly and ready to do whatever he had to in order to help me.

"Talk to me, son."

"You remember Brayelle, don't you?"

He nodded and smiled again briefly. "Of course I remember her. Cute little girl. Beautiful like your mother later on when she grew up. Had a mouth like a biker chick." He laughed and then said, "She was the one your mom whipped you over because you snuck out that summer I went to Michigan. Brayelle always was the Bonnie to your Clyde."

His words stunned me. He had no idea how relevant the seemingly innocent comparison was.

He smiled again and winked at me. "Yeah, I knew all about her." He grinned.

"Then you knew how I felt about her," I said.

"Umm-hmm." He took another swallow. "You were in love with that girl from the moment you saw her. I may not've been around much, but some things are easy to figure out in just a few visits. You two were always together." He rested his back against the chair. "I used to look at your mom like that."

"Well, something happened last night," I began. "I'm not going to tell you the details—don't want to drag you into it any more than I am just by being here. But I want you to know that it was an accident."

He narrowed his gaze on me subtly. "Was it her accident, or yours?"

"It was Bray's."

"And you're *sure* it was an accident?" He looked at me in a short, sidelong manner.

"Yes, she said it was an accident, and I believe her."

"Do you?" He raised his back from the recliner and slumped over forward, resting his arms across his pant legs. "Think about it, Elias. Think about it long and hard, because the answer really is the difference between you doing what the law says is right and you doing what your heart says is right. You have to be sure. One hundred percent, son."

I thought about it, just like he said to do, but I didn't have to think long. I already knew.

"I *know* it was an accident," I said. "She wouldn't lie to me. And I could tell she was telling the truth. Bray may be brazen and a little over the top sometimes, but she'd never intentionally do something like that."

My dad nodded once, accepting my explanation, trusting in me and what I believed. "Y'know, Elias, as your father, first and foremost I have to tell you that I don't want to see you ruin your life to protect someone else's." He set his beer down again and got up from the chair. His camouflaged T-shirt hung sloppily over the top of his jeans. "But I'd be a fool and a hypocrite to expect you not to follow your heart." He turned and looked down at me. "What do you need?"

I stood up with him, leaving my beer on the coffee table, and I hugged him long and hard. I wondered if it would be the last time I ever saw him, at least without a thick wall of security glass separating us.

I left my father that day with some extra cash to get us by for a little while at least, but more important, with his advice, which I always took to heart. He told me that I should try everything in my power to talk Bray into turning herself in before it was too late.

"Are you sure that's what's stopping you?" he had said. "Because you think it's too late?"

"Yes," I had lied. "We're already in this too deeply to turn back now."

But my father was a smart man. He could see right through me and I knew that he could. Bray and I still could've turned back and done the "right" thing, but I couldn't lose her again, and Bray didn't want to lose me. We had already established that before we left the ridge that night. And that was the way it was going to stay.

I went back to our motel room with burgers and fries.

We ate in silence. Silence seemed to be the norm for a while. And we watched television, both afraid we'd turn the news on at ten o'clock and see our faces staring back at us from the screen next to a reporter. But for the first several days, from Savannah to Fernandina Beach to Daytona Beach, we were still in the clear. Bray's cell phone hardly ever rang. Just once when her sister, Rian, called to see how she was doing. Bray let it go to voice mail.

My mom, on the other hand, called me constantly. Not wanting to worry her any more than she already was, I ignored my own rule about phone calls and answered after the third concerned voice mail. I told her that I was on vacation and not to worry. I don't think she believed me deep down, but she accepted it. My boss at Rixey Construction called only twice. After that, I was pretty sure that was the end of my job. But my mom was the only reason I didn't get rid of my and Bray's cell phones earlier. In the back of my mind I worried they'd eventually be what led the police right to us, but I couldn't listen to reason. The thought of my mom worried sick to death over me kicked my reason in the ass. Until this day. I finally decided that it was time we ditched our phones, and so I stuffed them in a Burger King bag with our leftover fries and tossed everything in the garbage. Bray looked at me like I was crazy, but she understood.

By the end of the month, we were in West Palm Beach soaking up the sun and enjoying the somewhat warmer weather that a little farther south had to offer.

And we were already beginning to get settled into a false safe zone.

"We can't afford too many more motels," I said as I came out of the shower. "I have some money in the bank, but if I withdraw it or write a check, everybody will know where we are."

It was the only reason I borrowed cash from my father in the first place. We left Athens so fast I didn't think to stop at an ATM and withdraw the money before we left.

"How much do we have?" Bray said, coming up to me. She fit her fingers between the towel and my waist and pulled my body toward her.

"A few hundred bucks, but that's it. We'll need that for gas, unless we find a place to park it for a while."

She kissed me lightly on the lips. "I say we find a place to park it then," she said, but she wasn't thinking much about the conversation. She was horny.

That was one thing that never changed about the two of us. Despite all that was going on, nothing ever ruined the many intimate moments we had on a daily and nightly basis. She seemed as addicted to sex as I was. But I'd never say that to *her*. And I definitely wasn't going to complain.

"I don't like all this driving around anyway," she added, tugging on my bottom lip with her teeth.

I slipped my fingers down the front of her panties.

"I don't either," I said and found her wetness.

She gasped when I slid my middle finger between her lips and touched her clit.

"Then what do you think we should do?" she asked breathily.

"I dunno, we'll figure it out later." My mouth closed around hers and I sucked on her tongue, then I pushed her backward onto the bed, where I fucked her for a long time.

# ELEVEN

## Bray

*I*t would seem that it was too early for Elias and me to stop being afraid and on edge about what happened. I admit it. But really what we were doing was looking for any way out of that mind-set, because if we didn't, it would've killed us. We just wanted to live life. And, well, it's easy to forget about the significant things when you find other things to cover it up. Partying quickly became our means of salvation, the way out that we longed for. We learned fast how to replace misery and fear with happiness and enjoyment, and with drugs and alcohol. We couldn't afford much ourselves, and the last thing we wanted to do was waste what little money we did have on shit like that, but we got by with freebies usually. A joint passed around a room. A group of partygoers already lit on alcohol, offering to buy the table the next round. And occasionally guys would buy me drinks when they thought I was alone.

Our first night hitting the bars and nightclubs in Florida was the first domino to fall in a swirling maze of hundreds of dominoes.

And every fucking one of them would later prove to be a bigger mistake than the last.

"Hey, that's our song!" I said over the music bumping through the speakers inside the club.

I grabbed Elias by the wrist and tugged. He slid down from the bar stool and hit the dance floor with me. He had always been a hot dancer, and it helped that he had the body for it. But usually, it took a few drinks for him to loosen up enough to dance in public. He wasn't afraid of it; he just never cared for it much.

Even that started to change with our new lifestyle.

"Since when did this become *our* song?" he shouted over the music.

I danced my way around, putting my back to him, raising my arms up and around both sides of his neck.

He ground his hips against me from behind, his fingers splayed against my thighs.

"Since that time at Matt's party, remember?"

The beat picked up, and his grinding hips moved with it flawlessly. I about fucking died. The boy could dance.

I danced back around, facing him again, moving my upper body in a lithe, swaying motion against his.

"Oh yeah, I remember that night," he said, leaning toward my ear. "But if I recall, after we danced to it in front of everyone, you left with Dane Weatherby."

"Dane was just a friend," I countered. And he *was* just a friend. "I was his shoulder to cry on that night. Nothing more. But you and me, we had the whole room. We owned it!"

Elias grinned and fit my hips in the palms of his hands, his long fingers spread like claws as he grinded against me some more.

He was *so* getting laid tonight.

"I guess we did, huh?" he said with a grin.

Suddenly Elias snatched me forward, his arm around my waist, and pulled me out of the path of a tipsy couple barreling through the crowd.

"Oh, sorry about that, man!" the guy said.

He was as tall as a tree and had short brown hair buzzed around the back. He grabbed hold of a strawberry-blonde woman's elbow to keep her from falling over. She laughed and fell into his arms on purpose. Her huge boobs bulged into view from the force of his arm, which he held across her chest.

"I think I've had too much," she said, raising her wine cooler out in front of her and then happily taking another drink.

The guy apologized again. And again. I wondered if he was just too drunk to remember he had already gotten that much out of the way.

"It's all right," Elias said, still holding me around the waist. "No harm done."

We started to walk away from the dance floor and back toward the bar, but we only got halfway before the couple came up behind us.

"I've never seen you in here before," the guy said.

"You must come here a lot, then," I said, still being pulled along by my fingers. "To remember every face in a place this populated."

A small part of me was worried he'd seen my face on a Most Wanted poster somewhere. But it was just the paranoia kicking in.

"We're here every weekend," the girl said.

She never stopped smiling. Neither of them did. They wore permanent, drunken smiles.

We finally made it back to the bar. Elias put his hands on my hips and lifted me onto the stool. He then sat on the empty stool next to me.

"I'm Anthony," the guy introduced himself. "And this is Cristina." He smelled of musk cologne.

I started to show them the same courtesy, but Elias jumped in a second before. "I'm John and this is my fiancée, Julia."

Fiancée? That certainly got my attention. So much so that I had already forgotten the fake name he gave me.

"You live around here?" Anthony probed. He leaned against the bar next to an empty bar stool rather than sit. Cristina, who I assumed was his girlfriend, continued to use him as her makeshift crutch.

"No, we're from—"

"—Indiana," Elias jumped in.

I narrowed my eyes at him secretly from the side.

He softened his baby-blues, as if to say, *Sorry, babe.*

Instant forgiveness. He was in the right, though, because I had been about to say Georgia, just as I had been a second away from telling them our real names.

I didn't know if I'd ever get used to this covert lifestyle of lies and highways and shitty motel rooms. But Elias was with me, and that made it all OK.

"How long will you be in town for?" Anthony asked.

"A day or two," Elias said. "Then we'll be heading back home."

As Anthony helped Cristina onto the bar stool, his hands pushed underneath the fabric of her short flowered skirt. I noticed he wore hemp bracelets like mine, five or six thick ones wrapped around his left wrist. I wore them on both. Probably for different reasons.

Cristina called for the bartender, and he came over.

"Are you staying close by?" Anthony asked. He put up his hand and added, "If you don't mind me asking."

"Why are you asking anyway?" Elias was wary of this guy, but just like me, it was only the paranoia.

Anthony smiled and paid for Cristina's drink. "I own a beach house not far from here. We're always trolling the clubs lookin' to find people to invite. You're welcome to come."

Cristina almost fell off the bar stool and her drink thumped over onto its side. She fumbled the bottle back into an upright position. Clearly she didn't need any more to drink.

"I think you've had enough," Anthony said, reading my mind.

She whined when he took the bottle from her.

"Not in the mood to clean up after her tonight," Anthony said, still with a big smile plastered on his face.

"Hey!" Cristina shot back, feigning offense and reaching out for the bottle. "Don't be an ass!" She laughed.

Anthony ignored her and turned back to us. "So, are you up for it?"

"I don't think so," Elias said. "But thanks."

"All right, but if you change your mind, I'll be around here for another hour or so."

"Thanks, man," Elias said with a nod.

Anthony helped Cristina down from the bar stool and walked her on her wobbly legs through a small crowd, and they disappeared amid the throng of people.

"Maybe we should've gone," I said over the music. "The guy owns a beach house. We could probably crash there for a few nights. He seems pretty cool."

Elias held up two fingers and the bartender came over. He ordered a beer and one for me. "I don't know, maybe," he said.

I could tell he thought it wasn't such a bad idea, considering we had begun thinking about staying put somewhere for a while to save money.

We drank a couple more beers and danced some more before we decided to head back to our motel. The more buzzed Elias got, the more he wanted to take me somewhere and strip off my clothes. But he stopped before he got so buzzed that he wouldn't be able to drive us back.

We gave up the idea of joining Anthony and Cristina and never went looking for them. But we found them anyway, by accident, lingering outside the nightclub in the parking lot.

"Hello again! John and Julia, right?" Anthony said, walking toward us.

Oh, *that* was the fake name I couldn't remember.

We met him halfway. Cristina was sitting down on the blacktop with her back and head pressed against the side of a car tire. I could see straight up her skirt; she was too drunk to notice she was on display to anyone who happened to walk by. Both of her knees were drawn up against her chest.

"Hey, man," Elias said with a half smile. "We thought you had already left."

"Yeah, well, that was our intention," Anthony said. "But I lost my damn car keys."

"No shit?" Elias said.

"Maybe someone turned them in inside," I said, looking back at the club briefly.

"Already checked. I had a guy out here about ten minutes ago with a wire hanger, but we couldn't get it unlocked. Looks like I'll be calling either a locksmith or a cab."

Elias looked over at me. I knew what he was thinking, because I was thinking the same thing.

"Well, we could give you a ride back to your place," Elias offered.

I smiled at them both, glad to see that things with this whole beach house idea were starting to go my way.

"Help me up," Cristina whined, reaching out her hand.

I went over and helped her up instead, regretting it a little once I realized how heavy she actually was as she leaned against my shoulder.

"Nah, man, thanks but I don't want to put you out," Anthony said.

"We don't mind," Elias countered. "We're staying in a motel nearby and we're not in too much of a hurry to go back there."

"Well, you two can crash at my place tonight if you want," Anthony offered.

Elias thought about it for a moment and glanced over at me again, wondering how I felt about all of this.

"Sounds like a plan," I said and gripped Cristina around her waist.

I wished Anthony would take over. I didn't sign up for this. Or maybe I did, in a way . . .

"Then I guess it's settled," Anthony said as if he were making an announcement, both arms raised out at his sides. "Where's your car?"

"End of this row," Elias said.

Anthony finally noticed the struggle on my face and relieved me of drunken-Cristina duty. They followed us to Elias's car, parked at the very end of the lot.

"I just thought of something," Elias said after opening his door and pressing the master lock on the inside. "We're only paid up in our room until tomorrow. Somehow I doubt we'll be awake before checkout."

"Just swing by and get your stuff then," Anthony suggested. "As long as you don't need a U-Haul to move it, you can keep it at my place."

Elias laughed. "That won't be necessary," he said. "It'll all fit in my trunk."

We left the club parking lot and rode back to the motel first, which was on the way to Anthony's beach house. Since our new guests were going to be riding in the backseat, we stuffed our bags with everything we owned in the trunk. I made it a point to stash my purse back there, too, just in case either of them were the type to help themselves to my belongings.

Cristina was seconds away from passing out next to Anthony. He guided Elias back onto the main highway and we rode for quite a while, longer than I had expected since Anthony had mentioned before that the beach house wasn't far from the club. And he didn't talk as much after about ten minutes. The highway became darker and less traveled as it got later.

I started getting nervous, though I wasn't sure why.

Gut feelings are a bitch.

# TWELVE

## Elias

Anthony leaned forward between my and Bray's seats. He reached out and touched the bracelets on Bray's left wrist. I didn't like that much.

"Did you make those?" he asked. He peered in closer and tried to finger the bracelets individually, but she snapped her hand away.

"Ummm, no I bought them," she answered.

I could sense the nervousness in her voice. He had made her uncomfortable. Not. Fucking. Cool.

With my hands still on the wheel, I turned my head slightly to look over at him. I thought I was going to have to tell him to back off, but he saw the look in my eyes and fell back against the seat before I could say anything.

"Hey, sorry," he said, smiling. "I didn't mean anything by it."

Whatever. By now, I wasn't feelin' it anymore, hanging out at his place. It wasn't just that he touched her bracelets, it was something else, a vibe, the way Anthony seemed to go from helpful, smiling party guy to creepy backseat hitchhiker in such a short time.

"How much farther is it?" I asked, glancing at him in the rear-view mirror.

"Just a few more minutes," he said.

A few minutes came and went. I thought we would probably be getting off at the next exit, but when he didn't say anything about it ahead of time, I flipped on my blinker anyway and planned to take it, if not for any reason other than to drop them off at the nearest convenience store.

"Where are you going?" Anthony asked. "We don't get off here."

"Well we're getting off here anyway," I said and proceeded to veer onto the exit ramp.

The sound of a gun cocking at the back of Bray's head and the shiny black glint of the barrel in the corner of my eye caused my heart to jump into my throat.

"Don't take that fucking exit," Anthony demanded with a threatening edge in his voice. "Stay on the freeway."

At the last second, I remained in the same lane and watched helplessly as the exit ramp flew past my car.

"*Elias?*" Bray said from the passenger's seat, her voice filled with fear.

"Elias, huh?" Anthony probed. I saw him push the gun against her head harder. She closed her eyes momentarily. I was white-knuckling the steering wheel. "Thought your name was John."

"What does it matter?" I asked. "What the hell *is* this?"

"What the fuck do you *think* it is?" Anthony said, laughing.

Cristina was still passed out against her door.

"Look, man, I know how this goes," I said, but I could hardly look at him. I was far too preoccupied with the gun against Bray's head. "I've got cash on me. Whatever you want. Just please don't hurt her."

Bray's lips were trembling, the only part of her stiff body that was moving. I wanted to pummel this motherfucker to death.

"Pull over up there," Anthony demanded with a nod of his head, indicating the side of the road.

"All right. All right." I tried to keep calm. It took everything in me, but I had to keep my head clear. Hopefully he planned to rob us and run off into the woods. But if I even for a moment got the feeling that he was going to shoot us down, I would make a last, desperate attempt. I wasn't about to let this fucking lowlife shoot Bray without at least *trying* to stop him.

The car came to a stop and I put it into Park. And I waited.

I was hopeful when I saw headlights blazing toward us from behind, but the lone semi drove right past us, pushing wind against the car.

"Empty your pockets. Wallet. Anything you have on you. Put it on the dashboard."

"I take it you don't have a beach house?" I said sarcastically as I did what he told me to do.

"Fuck no," he said and laughed. "And that car in the parking lot wasn't mine, either." He barely looked away from me long enough to say to Bray, "You too. Whatever you have put it on the dashboard."

I thought about using that split second he looked away from me to grab for the gun, but I couldn't risk it. It likely would've gone off and killed her right there next to me.

There was no saliva left in my mouth. My whole body was stiff and sweating. Aside from getting that gun away from Bray's head, all I could think about was beating the fuck out of this guy. All I could see was red. I wanted so badly for him to slip up and give me the opportunity to take him down and cave his face in with my fists.

"Now get out," he demanded, looking right at me.

My heart dropped into my feet then. Was he going to take off in the car with her in it?

"Take the fucking car," I said, raising my hands up in front of me. "Just let her out."

*"Get. The. Fuck. Out."* He moved the gun to the back of my head now.

I only felt slightly better about that. At least it wasn't on Bray anymore.

I placed my hand on the door handle carefully, popped it open and stepped out, keeping my hands raised up, my fingers level with the top of my head.

From my peripheral vision, I noticed another set of bright headlights coming toward us off in the distance. My eyes darted to and from it, then to Bray, still sitting in the front seat. Cars sped by on the other side of the freeway, but it was too dark for anyone in them to see what was going on.

"Let her out," I said as I stepped around to the grass on the side of the road. "Please just fucking let her out."

Cristina's red-blonde head raised up from being pressed against the window. She rubbed her eyes and dragged the palms of her hands over her face and head like she was trying to wake herself up.

Then she noticed Anthony getting out of the backseat with the gun in his hand, pointed right at me.

"What—Anthony? What the hell are you *doing?*" Her voice began to rise with alarm as realization set in. "What the fuck! Anthony, no!"

"Shut up!" he yelled at her from outside the car, his eyes still on me as well as the gun. "Now get your girlfriend out. I don't need more than one bitch flapping her fucking jaws at me the whole ride."

Without a thought, I swung Bray's car door open and grabbed her by the arm, pulling her out faster than she could get out herself. The car coming toward us was so close. I pulled Bray against me and then pushed her around behind me. I looked up as the car neared.

"Don't even think about it," Anthony said, pointing the gun at me through the side window.

And just like with the last exit ramp, I watched as our last hope for help sped by at seventy miles per hour. Bray was shaking behind me, her fingers digging into my ribs.

"Thanks for the ride, man!" Anthony said just before he jumped behind the wheel and sped away with Cristina screaming curses at him from the backseat.

I watched until what were once my brake lights became tiny red dots in the distance and then blinked out.

"Son of a fucking *bitch*!" I punched at the air in front of me, wishing it was more than air. Then I turned to Bray. *"Oh shit!"*

She stood there trembling with her face buried in her hands.

I dropped the anger and became the comfort she needed. "Baby, come here." I tried to pull her toward me.

"Leave me the fuck alone!" she roared, her hands falling straight down at her sides. She took several steps back farther into the grass. I followed. Tears shot from her eyes. "Just . . . just leave me alone."

I knew she wasn't mad at me. She just needed a moment. She'd just had a goddamn gun pointed at the back of her head.

She sat down on the grass, her hands shaking as if she were freezing. I crouched in front of her and rested my hands on the tops of her knees.

"What the fuck are we doing, Elias?" She looked up into my eyes, tears glistened on her cheeks in the bluish dark. "What the fuck are we doing here?"

I sat down fully and held her hands. "We can go home if that's what you want, Bray, all you have to do is say the word."

She shook her head no. She wasn't sure of anything, just as I wasn't. She asked me what we were doing here, but it was only a moment of realization. She knew that things were so much worse than getting robbed and left on the side of a freeway hundreds of miles away from home. I knew Anthony had little to do with what was going through her mind at that moment. He was just the messenger, a small and insignificant piece of a much larger picture that we were lucky enough to have forgotten all about for just a little while. This situation only brought back to reality the gravity of the bigger situation surrounding it.

"I don't want to go back," she said, raising her eyes. "I want to keep going. I just want to keep going."

"Then that's what we're going to do," I said.

I pulled her over into the throne of my lap and covered her with my arms.

"We have no car. No money. No phones. Fuck, we don't even have any clothes!" She clutched my fingers, tangling them with hers. "We can't call the cops. What are we going to do?"

"The beach isn't far from here," I said. "The exit we passed is probably about a ten-minute walk. We'll go back the way we came and stop in at one of the gas stations there and I'll call my father. I have money in the bank. I'll have to risk that much at least. We can't do this without money."

She turned around halfway at the waist. "No," she said. "We can't get our families involved, you know that. They might already know by now why we ran. We can't risk *anything*. I'm not going back."

That look in her eyes told me she was terrified. Bray had been about as scared as one can be when I was with her back on that ridge. But this was a different kind of paralyzing fear. It was as if she had already made up her mind to believe that she was going to go to prison for Jana's death, no matter what we did or how long we did it. I knew in this moment that I would never be able to talk her into turning back. She was going to run until things got worse, *much* worse, and until the day she died.

And like I vowed to her and to myself in the beginning, I was going to run with her. Because I fucking loved her. And love makes a person do crazy fucking things.

"I have an idea," I said.

"What?" Her voice shuddered.

I got to my feet and took her hand, bringing her up with me.

"Come on," I said and pulled her gently alongside me down the shoulder of the freeway.

We were exhausted by the time we got to the ocean nearly an hour later on foot. Neither one of us ever expected to be hiding out on a beach in Florida to get some sleep, hoping the cops didn't shine their flashlights in our faces and run us off or haul us to jail.

"I don't know if I like this," Bray said, looking all around as we came upon the back of a beachfront hotel. "What if we get caught?"

"We won't as long as we act like we belong here."

The beach was empty at this hour, and the hotel was pretty much quiet except for a few of its guests sitting out on their balconies. Bray questioned me when we walked into the hotel and took the elevator up to the third floor and then came back down. I told her we needed a room number and she shrugged it off, not really understanding what for but accepting it. We passed by the pool and an outside shower, and we made our way down a wooden walkway and onto the beach. We lay down on the sand out in the wide open, and Bray curled up next to me.

Not ten minutes later a security officer found us and we got the damn flashlight in our eyes after all. "What are you doing out here?"

I raised myself up from the sand, partially shielding my eyes from the light.

"Just enjoying the ocean," I said and then pointed at the hotel behind me. "We're staying in room three forty. Vacationing from Missouri."

He shone the light around the sand beside us.

"Where's your room key?" he asked and I panicked a little inside.

I stood up and patted my cargo shorts back and front pretending to be searching for it and realizing it wasn't there. Bray got up, too.

"Oh crap," she said. "I probably dropped it by the pool. I'll go look for it. Be right back."

"Hurry up," I called out to her, as she ran barefooted through the thick sand and back toward the hotel.

I had no idea how we were going to get out of this one. The only thing we could really do, I thought at that point, was run like hell. He was just a security guard, after all, and unlike a cop he probably wouldn't care to chase us far. But I wanted to avoid a chase, even a short one, at all costs. We didn't need any attention drawn to us. What we needed was a quiet night to ourselves so that we could think about what we were going to do next, because we had literally run out of options. We had nothing. No money. No car. Just the clothes on our backs and each other, and I was worried now more than ever about us being able to go any farther. Even if we got through this minor issue with the security guard, I still didn't know how we were going to press on. I couldn't tell Bray yet that I felt like we needed to go home. She was hell-bent on moving forward.

She wouldn't have accepted it. But I began to realize that something more was going on with Bray. Something that I couldn't quite put my finger on, but it left me with a sense of deeper responsibility, as if she was incapable of being fully responsible for herself. I didn't want to believe that. Bray was a smart and confident girl, but I started to feel like her reckless decisions no longer mirrored my own. They weren't based on fear and natural worry, constantly licked by the voice of reason, like mine had been. Her reckless decisions began to seem fueled by something far more dangerous, something devoid of rationality.

I started to think that I was hurting her more than I was helping her, but I wasn't yet sure what else to do.

I carried on with the security guard, trying to play off my tourist act as smoothly as possible while I waited on Bray. Though waiting on her for what, I didn't know.

"Where are you from in Missouri?" he asked me.

"Springfield," I said. "We come here every year."

He nodded and shone the flashlight around on the sand again, probably looking for evidence of alcohol or drug paraphernalia. He wasn't a heavyset man, but he was a bit out of shape, with a small beer gut that hung somewhat over his pants. I noticed when he moved the flashlight around, the skin under his bicep jiggled.

"How long are you here for this time?" he asked.

"We're heading out tomorrow," I said. "Been here since Wednesday." I looked thoughtfully at him and added, "I didn't see you around here last night. We laid out here for a while around this time."

"I had two days off this week," he said, and I was a little surprised at how well my improvising had played out. "But you should be careful out here at night. And you can't be sleeping on the beach."

"No sir," I said. "That's what we have the bed for." I glanced back at the hotel.

Just then, I saw a figure shrouded by the shadows of the hotel's massive pool deck, moving toward us. It was Bray and she was carrying something over one shoulder. As she got closer, kicking up sand behind her as she trudged through it, I saw that it was a see-thru mesh beach bag with what looked like a beach towel and other random items inside.

*Where the hell did she get that?*

I smiled—probably squeamishly—back at the security guard and then shoved my hands into my pockets.

"I'm surprised it didn't get stolen," she said.

She stopped next to me, somewhat winded, and reached inside the bag. "Here it is," she said, holding up a card key to the security guard with the hotel's name printed on it. "I'm glad you asked about it because I might've lost my whole bag over by the pool."

The security guard shone his flashlight on the card key and then looked us over again.

My confidence in pulling this off shot up a few notches. We stood there in a long, stressful silence waiting on what the security guard would say next.

"Just be careful," he finally said. "And remember what I said about sleeping out here."

I smiled back at him. "Definitely."

Bray and I let out our breath once he was out of earshot. We watched him until his dark figure disappeared around the side of the hotel building. We thought we were in the clear, at least for the time being. We sat down again, side-by-side in the sand, and looked out at the black ocean.

"So where did you get the bag?"

"Found it by the pool." She laughed. "A serious stroke of luck. And we sure needed it, after everything that has gone wrong."

Just as she said that, we heard voices approaching us from behind.

"That's her!" a girl said.

Bray and I both knew the group of three were talking about us and coming right toward us. Even if we hadn't been the only other two on the beach, we still would've known. I looked down at the bag and then our eyes met. We stood up together just as two girls and the tall tattooed guy walked up.

"There it is," the blonde-haired girl said, pointing at the bag beside Bray's feet. "That's my bag."

And that was how we met Tate Roth, part savior, part...something else.

# THIRTEEN

## Bray

*I* grabbed the bag from the sand and held it out to the girl. "Sorry about that," I said. "I was just borrowing it." Her hair was so damn long, tumbling like a blonde wave down her back and nearly past her waistline.

She snatched it from my hand and began digging inside to see if I'd stolen anything. The brown-haired girl standing next to her looked at me once unemotionally, but she never said anything. "Borrowing it?" the girl said with harshly narrowed eyes. "No, bitch, it's called *stealing*."

I stepped toward her in a challenging fashion and Elias put his arm between us.

"I didn't steal it," I said through my teeth. "We just...needed it." She was completely in the right, but I couldn't help but snap back after what she called me.

"Look, we apologize," Elias said, surrendering. "Bray found it by the pool. The security guard was on our asses about being out here."

The tattooed guy listened to all of us quietly, a faint smile resting in his hazel eyes. A part of me got the feeling he thought the whole thing was amusing.

"Don't ever touch my shit—"

The guy hushed her by gently pushing her back a few steps with his muscular arm.

"It's obvious what's going on here," he said in a pretend authoritative tone. "These two are trying to slum it on the beach." He grinned and looked me over once before turning to Elias. "The question is why. Homeless or stranded with no other place to go. Or just looking to fuck in the sand. It is, after all, one of the things on the universal bucket list."

"Tate, let's just go before I beat this bitch's ass," the blonde-haired girl said.

I pushed my way past Elias's arm and went toward her. "You can fuckin' *try*," I said mere inches from her face.

We were both dragged away from each other. Elias had his hands around my upper arms.

"Calm down, Jen," the guy said, setting the blonde back on her feet. He laughed under his breath and added with his mouth on her ear, "Damn, baby, save it for *me* later."

I yanked my arms out of Elias's hands angrily, but I stood there rather than going after Jen again. Then Elias grabbed my hand and started walking with me away from them. I bent over at the last second to snatch my flip-flops from the sand.

"Hey, man, wait!" the guy said, and we stopped. "No harm done. Look, tell me what's going on. Maybe we can help you out."

"Thanks, but no thanks," Elias said and started walking off again. "We've already been 'helped' by someone who relieved us of our car just over an hour ago."

"No shit?" the tattooed guy said, coming around in front of us. We stopped. "Are you fuckin' for real—someone *stole* your car?"

"Yeah," Elias said. "So we're fresh out of trust. But thanks anyway."

"*Help* them?" Jen shouted from behind. "Tate, you've got to be fucking kidding me! They steal my stuff and now you want to *help* them?" She slung the bag over her shoulder, grabbed the quiet girl by the elbow and started tramping through the sand back toward the hotel. "Asshole!" She said and gave the guy the finger.

The guy just smiled and waved her off.

"Don't worry about her," he said, turning back to us. "She'll forgive me later. Where are the two of you from?" Then he pointed at me. "Bray, was it?"

Neither Elias nor I had realized until now that Elias had called me by my real name. It was too late to try being John and Julia, so we went with the flow.

"Yeah, this is Bray, and I'm Elias."

"Tate Roth," he said, and shook Elias's hand.

"And we're from Indiana," Elias added.

Good idea to keep with Indiana, at least.

"Indiana, huh? What brought you to Florida? Vacationing before the summer crowds?" Tate asked.

We didn't answer.

Tate was tall, with short, blondish-brown hair that was somewhat longer on top, tousled and spiky, and it looked like he never really brushed it. But the look worked for him somehow. There was a full-sleeve tattoo down his right arm and tattoos on both of his calves. And he was built a lot like Elias, not too overly muscular where his shoulders dwarfed his head, but rather just right. He seemed harmless. Charming, even. The kind of person you can't help but instantly like despite that cocky sort of grin he wore and his hot-tempered company.

"Why don't you come up and hang out with us in our room?" Tate said. "No shady shit here. Just a friendly offer."

"We'll pass," Elias said and interlocked our fingers.

"From the looks of it," Tate said, "it's either up there with us or out here with the sand fleas and the security guard who makes rounds every hour."

Tate's offer was enticing, despite our unfortunate run-in with Anthony and Cristina. But I could tell that Elias wasn't up for finding out if Florida had a lot of Anthonys.

"Can you give us a second?" I asked Tate, putting up my finger.

"Sure thing," he said with a nod and a confident smile. Then he lit up a cigarette.

I pulled Elias by the hand and we stepped several feet away from Tate.

"I think we should," I whispered.

"Well, I don't," Elias came back. "That guy almost fucking shot you tonight and I couldn't do anything about it. We'll figure this out on our own, Bray. I'm not going to risk something happening to you again."

"What other choice do we have?" I asked, my whisper becoming harsher. "And you're right, you couldn't do anything when Anthony had that gun on me, but that wasn't your fault."

"I let them in the car with us," he said. "It wasn't any different from picking them up off the side of the road somewhere."

"We *both* let them in the car," I corrected him. "Neither of us could've known he was going to pull a gun. He seemed perfectly harmless."

"Like *this* guy?" Elias noted, pointing toward Tate with his thumb.

"Seriously, what are the chances that we'd get robbed twice in the same night? We don't have anything left to steal."

"Something worse could happen," Elias said. While that was

true, I had to believe that it wouldn't, and Elias was just being overly protective.

"Like what?" I asked, shaking my head but still trying to be understanding. "There's two girls and one guy. And the girls... I could take either one of them."

"Uh, actually," Tate said from his far-off spot, holding up his middle and index fingers with the cigarette wedged between them, "there are five of us. My brother and his current lay are upstairs in our suite. But you're right, you could probably take Jen or Grace. Though Jen is a spitfire. She won't go down easily."

"Come on, Elias." I took his hands. "We have nowhere else to go."

Elias sighed and shut his eyes briefly.

Minutes later we were walking into a fifth-floor suite set up like a small one-bedroom apartment. Coming in behind Tate, we were greeted by the casual glances of two more people we hadn't seen before. The first was another blonde, this one with much shorter hair than Jen's, a vacant look in her eyes, and freckles splashed across her cheeks and the bridge of her nose. Something bothered me about her, and she hadn't even spoken yet. And there was another guy, who looked younger than Tate but very much like him, with the same light-brown hair and soft hazel eyes. Those two lost interest in us quickly. But Jen, who had been out on the beach with us, held her glare on us all the way through the room.

Grace, on the other hand, smiled at me. Of the three girls, Grace was the one I felt the biggest connection with. She had a kind and caring air about her, and I liked her instantly.

Jen snarled and then gave Tate one helluva pissed-off look. He bent over and kissed her on the side of her temple. I blinked, stunned, when her hand shot out and slapped him across the side of his neck. "Get the hell away from me," she snapped.

Tate was surprisingly unfazed by the blow. I halfway expected the smile to drop from his face and for him to snatch her up from the couch and at least yell at her for slapping him. But his smile remained, and he just kissed her again. Ultimately I shrugged it off, realizing quickly that we weren't the only people in the room with a complicated love life.

Jen went back to her quiet conversation with Grace sitting beside her.

"This is my baby brother, Caleb," Tate announced. Caleb nodded from his spot on the floor. And then Tate pointed at the blonde sitting behind him in the chair with her knees at each of his shoulders. "That's Johanna. And you've met Jen and Grace." He turned to Jen, who refused to give him her attention, let alone look at us. "Say hello to our guests, Jen. No need to be rude."

I got the feeling Tate was taunting her in his own quiet way, but I also got the feeling that Jen was used to it and probably liked it more than she was letting on. Still so pissed off at him that she would probably slap him again if he stuck his head near her too closely, but she liked it just the same.

"Pick a seat," Tate said, waving his hand about the room. "We're only here for tonight. Headin' out in the morning back to Miami. Home sweet home."

I sat down on Elias's lap at the table by the window overlooking the beach. Tate opened the mini fridge in the kitchenette and reached inside. He had three bottles of Heineken wedged between his fingers when he straightened up, and he held two of them out to us. Elias took them and opened mine before handing it to me.

Tate plopped down on the couch beside Jen, slouching down far into it with his long, tanned, and muscular legs splayed into the floor. Jen made a hateful face as his shoulder pressed against her back, but she continued to give Grace all of her attention and didn't exactly push Tate away. She and Grace were looking into a cell phone screen, Jen's finger moving across the glass.

"So if your car was stolen," Tate said, "how are you getting back to Indiana?"

These were the kinds of questions that Elias and I didn't want to answer. Me, worried about screwing up whatever story Elias had in mind to tell them, I just kept quiet and let Elias do all the talking.

"We're not going back anytime soon," Elias said. He drank from the bottle and set it on the table, then rested his elbow next to it. "We're just traveling."

"By foot now?" Tate pointed out and took a sip.

"I guess so."

When Elias didn't offer any more information and the room got quiet, Tate took the hint.

"Hey, it's all right," he said. "I understand. TMI too soon." He looked at Caleb and said, "Why don't you roll one up?"

Caleb leaned back and away from Johanna's chair and reached inside his back pocket. A rolled-up plastic sandwich bag appeared in his hand. He settled between Johanna's bare legs again and started rolling a joint. I watched him for a moment, still struck by how much he and Tate looked alike. Same hair color and build, except Tate appeared taller and Caleb only had one tattoo that I could see, an Asian girl on his left arm surrounded by swirling wind or water, I couldn't tell at this angle. He and Johanna seemed the quiet type, or maybe they were just really into that movie playing on the television in front of them. Caleb kept looking up at it while rolling the joint.

Here I was thinking Johanna was Caleb's girlfriend, not remembering Tate had called her Caleb's "current lay" when we were out on the beach. But then Grace left Jen on the couch and walked over to Caleb, too. She sat down in between his legs when the joint was fully rolled, and he wrapped his arms around her from behind. Johanna leaned forward and rested her hands on his shoulders.

All kinds of sexual images began flitting around inside my head. And then, Caleb caught my eyes. I looked away quickly and turned sideways on Elias's lap, laying my head down on his shoulder.

I heard the grinding snap of a lighter, and then the sweet aroma of what Tate called "grade-A shit" filled the air.

"Someone turn on that bathroom fan," Tate said. "Fucking smoke alarm will go off."

Everyone seemed to be either really comfortable or too far away from the restroom, so I got up from Elias's lap and did the honors. Then just before I left the restroom doorway, I snatched a wash-cloth off the rack next to the mirror. I went over to where the smoke alarm was mounted on the ceiling, stepped up onto the side of the bed so I could reach it, and covered the round plastic nuisance with the cloth.

"Good thinking, baby doll," Tate said, holding out the joint for Jen now.

Without giving Tate the luxury of a look, Jen reached around her shoulder and took the joint from his fingers.

"You said you all live in Miami?" Elias asked from the chair as I went back over and sat on his lap.

Tate let out a long, deep breath and stretched one arm above his head across the back of the couch. "Yeah, Caleb, me, and Jen live in Miami. Those two—" he motioned toward Johanna and Grace "—they wouldn't survive in Miami."

Grace's head fell to one side and she propped her hands on top of Caleb's bent knees.

"What's that supposed to mean?" she said. It was the first time I'd actually heard her talk, and I thought her voice was sweet and soothing, much unlike her fire-breathing companion, Jen.

Jen still sat peering into her cell phone.

"You're too damn white, girl," Tate said and laughed.

"White? Like Caucasian?" Johanna said with an air of curiosity. Immediately, I got the dumb-girl vibe from that one.

"No," Tate said and rolled his eyes. "White like a vampire. Don't get me wrong, Grace, that milky-white skin will give any guy a hard-on in a second, but you know what I mean."

Jen whirled around at him and punched him in the chest, hard. Tate's body reacted by jerking forward, his feet raising from the carpet a few inches. He laughed and held one hand over the spot.

"Tha fuck you say that for?" Jen said. "I'm sitting *right here.*"

Tate was trying not to laugh, but the smile on his face pretty much gave it away.

"Damn, baby, chill the fuck out." He reached out for her arm, but she snatched it away. "You keep that shit up and I'm going to *fuck* you up."

*Whoa* . . . I wonder what he meant by that. He definitely didn't seem the abusive type—Jen wore the championship belt in that category from what I'd seen—but his threat made me wonder.

Tate, with his smile still intact, turned back to us. "No, we just got back from a long drive to Norfolk to pick up my brother." He motioned at Caleb. "It was just me and Jen on the way up. Didn't know we'd have a car full on the way back." Then he pointed at Grace and Johanna again. "These two bobbleheads are friends of Caleb's. They wanted to get out of Virginia for a while. We had room in my Jeep. You can paint the rest of the picture."

"Why didn't you just fly?" I asked.

Tate and Caleb looked at each other and then Tate looked back at me.

But Elias was the one who answered, "Because they couldn't carry their drugs on the plane."

A smirk tugged the corners of Tate's mouth.

# FOURTEEN

## Elias

*T*ate stopped midsmile and pointed at me from across the room, beer dangling from his hand, and said, "You're not a cop, are you?" I think he knew I was as much a cop as he was.

"Hell no," I said, shaking my head.

His smile returned and his arm dropped beside him again.

Grace, the brown-haired girl sitting between Caleb's legs, pushed herself forward on her knees, raising her ass in front of Caleb, and she stretched out her arm toward us. Bray leaned forward on my lap and took the joint from her fingers and then put it to her lips.

Caleb saw an opportunity and smacked Grace before she sat back down. Grace looked back at him with an awry smile. I was having a hard time figuring the two out. I didn't sense any real emotional attachments between them, but a sexual attachment was unmistakable.

We were all fairly high after the joint made its third pass around the room. Bray and I were warming up to our new friends quicker than either of us expected. Maybe it was the weed, but even Jen began to ease up on Bray some. Every now and then she'd make a nonsarcastic comment to something Bray said, and things were beginning to look up between the two. Though Jen wasn't about to ease up even a little on Tate, who finally gave up trying to talk to her and zoned out on the couch.

I had no clue as to how much time had passed when I noticed how much Grace and Bray were hitting it off. Bray and I had moved from the chair to the floor at some point, sitting with our backs against the wall. Grace sat beside Bray, and they talked nonstop for a long time while I zoned out like Tate and stared across the room at the television. I wasn't completely fried, but my mind wandered so much I couldn't say what I was watching. I saw their lips moving on the screen, but I couldn't hear a word.

Caleb snapped my mind back into reality when he called for Grace and looked at me with a familiar predatory gaze. Taken aback by it, I paid more attention to what was going on around me. Did I miss something? I had no fucking clue why Caleb looked at me like that, but when Grace got up and went over to sit with him, I got the feeling he was threatened by me when it came to Grace. It was odd. I had barely said two words to her. Bray was the one doing all the talking. I just shut my eyes and leaned the back of my head against the wall and ignored him. I stayed like that, Bray now lying on the floor with her head in my lap, until Jen and Tate arguing woke me up again.

"I'm going to bed," Jen spat. She pushed Tate away when he tried to slip his arm around her waist. "You can sleep in here."

Tate laughed and followed her toward the separate bedroom.

"Take your clothes off when you get in there," Tate said. "I'll be in there in a minute."

Jen whirled around and slapped him across the face so hard that I felt the sting. I drew my head back, my eyes widening in a mild display of shock. Bray lifted her head from my lap.

Tate was still smiling, but I noticed his teeth grinding behind the handprint that started to appear on his cheek. He grabbed Jen's wrists.

"Leave. Me. Alone," she growled.

Tate let go.

For a second, it looked like a standoff as the two of them stood face-to-face, unblinking, each waiting for the other to make a move. Finally Jen turned around and walked into the bedroom, slamming the door behind her.

Among the seven of us, only Bray and I seemed to find their display concerning.

Tate stretched his arms high above his head and yawned, stretching his whole face. Then he dropped his arms back at his sides and looked at us.

"Crash wherever you want," he offered. "I'm going to hit the sack."

"Sure thing," I said somewhat distantly.

Tate disappeared inside the room with Jen, and before he even got the door closed all the way, Jen's shouting at him to "Get the fuck out!" among other things, was what I heard.

"I said take off your fucking clothes," I heard Tate say through the wall.

"Go fuck yourself," she told him.

Then I heard a loud *thwap* and felt my eyes widen in my head.

"You fucking want to hit me?!" Tate roared. "Fucking hit me again! Do it!" I could picture him turning the other cheek.

I glanced over at Caleb who sat just as he had been all night between Johanna's legs and Grace between his. He ran his fingers through Grace's hair and his other hand brushed against Johanna's knee.

*Thwap!*

Jen screamed, and then I felt the floor shake and what sounded like a scuffle. I stood up. It was instinct. Jen may have needed to shut her mouth a long time ago, but I couldn't stand to know she was being hit on the other side of that door.

"Don't worry about it," Caleb said stoically.

I glanced down at him, but then just looked back toward the door. There was definitely some kind of physical fight going on in there. Bray was standing next to me. I was so focused I didn't even know when she got up from the floor.

"Why the hell not?" I asked Caleb. I kept looking back and forth between him and the door.

Caleb remained impassive, or maybe he just didn't feel I was worth wasting any more of his breath on. He shook his head and lay back against the cushion between Johanna's legs.

"It's not what you're probably thinking," Grace spoke up instead.

"Well it sure as hell sounds like it," I said.

Bray grabbed my hand. "Baby, don't get involved. Please." She was scared, because we were outnumbered.

Grace added, "Tate would never hit Jen." Her face softened and she tilted her head to one side, leaning her back against Caleb's chest. He slipped his hands up her shirt. But she kept her eyes on me. "The only one in there you have to worry about is Tate," she added with a small chuckle.

Caleb dragged his fingertips across the skin on her neck.

Squeezing Bray's hand, I looked away from them and focused all of my attention on the sounds coming from the other side of that door. Soon, I began to understand. Before long, the argument and the scuffle turned into moans and whimpers and the sound of the bed hitting the wall.

The thought of their fiery relationship made me hard. And, I admit it, so did Caleb's relationship with Grace and Johanna.

Before the night was over and after the lights and television had been shut off, bathing the room in partial darkness, Caleb was fucking Grace and Johanna on the couch, which had been folded out into a bed. They didn't care that Bray and I were still wide awake in the same room. And it wasn't exactly something new to me, by any means.

But I realized for the first time, by how easily Bray accepted it, that it wasn't exactly anything new to her, either.

She crawled on top of my lap as I lay on my back against the floor. She leaned over and pinched my bottom lip between her teeth, pushing herself against my hardness through our clothes. She wanted me as much as I wanted her. And I was about to fucking burst. Maybe she was as turned on by everything going on around us as I was. I couldn't fault her for that. But I never expected her to want to fuck me out in the open. With a threesome happening just across the room. Hell, I wasn't about to ask questions. I just wanted her on top of me. Naked.

"Ride me," I whispered hotly onto her mouth.

She grinded her hips against mine even harder then. I grabbed the sides of her face in my hands and kissed her with predatory intent before letting her have her way with me.

We fell asleep wrapped in each other's arms.

———

It was a tight squeeze by the time we made it to Miami. Tate and Jen occupied the front seats while Bray and I shared the back with Caleb, Grace, and Johanna. And it became clear to me that Bray did, in fact, have bones in her ass somewhere, despite me always assuring her that she didn't have a bony ass.

Tate and Jen were an enigma, needless to say. After that so-called fight they had in the hotel, the very next morning it was as though it had never happened. They were like an entirely different couple. Jen was all smiles and flirtatious with Tate, and they couldn't keep their hands—or mouths—off of each other.

Liam, Tate's roommate, was a hardcore-personality type with a Mohawk who reminded me of Mohawk Guy. Except Liam wasn't your average systems engineer who made the ladies "swoon," as they call it. No, Liam Foster was another kind of animal who enjoyed making the ladies come. Worse than Caleb Roth ever thought to be, Liam was the reigning king of womanizing.

He was screwing some chick on the couch when the seven of us walked into their apartment in Miami.

The light-haired girl looked up at us in horror and tried to worm her way out from underneath him, but Liam wasn't having it and pushed her back down.

"Fucking be still, girl," he said, thrusting in and out of her.

"Liam, there's people in the fucking room!" she said through her teeth.

"So what?" he said. "They'll get over it. I'm almost done."

"Fuck, Liam!" she shouted.

"That's what I'm trying to *do*!" he said in return.

"Ugh! You know what I mean!"

Liam stopped midthrust. He looked over at us.

"Is this bothering any of you?" he asked.

"Fucking yes it bothers me!" Jen spat. She pushed her way through us and went into the kitchen.

The rest of us pretty much shook our heads and averted our

eyes. Tate waved it off and headed into the kitchen after Jen. Bray and I started to follow, while Caleb sat down in the recliner and brought Grace down in his lap. Johanna just stood there.

Liam looked down into the girl's aghast face. "Are you satisfied?"

"Hardly," she said with a sexually sarcastic undertone.

"Well, you will be soon, but you've got to let me finish."

As if that was enough reason for her, she said "Fine" and dug her fingernails into Liam's back.

We entered the kitchen before he returned to business.

"Sorry, I know it's really not my place to ask, but doesn't he have a room?" Bray spoke up.

"Dammit, Tate," Jen snapped, "that's fucking nasty. Why do you let him do that shit?"

Tate opened the fridge and leaned over inside. "I'm sorry, babe. I'll talk to him." He looked at me then. "Yeah, he does have a room. But Liam is...well, he's hard to explain." He came out with a bottle of mustard and a package of sandwich meat and set it on the counter.

"Liam's a sick man-whore. Simple to explain, really," Jen retorted, got a bottle of water from the fridge, and left the kitchen.

"He's moving back to Phoenix in a few months," Tate said. He reached inside the bread bag that had been pushed up against the toaster and pulled out two slices. "I love Liam and all, but I look forward to having this place to myself."

"Does Jen live here?" Bray asked, probably trying to imagine how that would work with Liam's broadcasted activities.

"Want a sandwich?" Tate cut in real quick.

Bray shook her head and I did, too, when he glanced at me.

"No, Jen has her own apartment not far from here. We can't

live together. Tried it once. Didn't work out. She can't stand my shit bein' all over the place, and my biggest fear is getting so used to each other that she thinks it's OK to take a shit with me in the bathroom. Not. Fucking. Sexy." He pointed the mustard bottle at us to emphasize each word.

"So, we're going to a party tonight," he added. "A great underground band is playing. Liam's brother is the bass player. You up for it?"

Another party. I had a feeling we'd be doing a lot of that from here on out.

"Yeah, definitely," I said and Bray agreed.

Miami ended up being more a drop-off place. After watching Liam's brother's band play we spent only one night there, most of us laid out on beanbags and furniture in a tiny two-bedroom apartment. The next day, Tate drove Caleb to some guy's house, and the rest of us sat outside in the Jeep while Caleb went inside and did business with the drugs he brought back with him from Norfolk.

I liked our new friends, but something about Caleb kept me on edge. Part of it was the drug dealing, but there was something else, too. I couldn't put my finger on it, but I got really bad vibes from him. He never talked much. Mostly he gave his attention to Johanna or Grace, or both at the same time, and at times he spoke to Tate. But he wasn't the kind of guy to warm up so easily to someone new. Maybe never. But he left us alone, and that was good enough for me.

It seemed that my and Bray's problems—the small ones, anyway—had been solved now that we were with Tate. Jen and Grace both shared clothes with Bray. And Tate, realizing that I was just as needy in the clean clothing department, offered me some of his extra stuff. We had a ride and always a place to go, whether we were crashing at some random beach house with friends of Tate's, or in a hotel room somewhere on Tate's dime, or just on the beach in places Tate knew we wouldn't get caught. Bray and I were finally able to breathe since Jana's death. Life became more relaxed. Our safe zone had started to cocoon us. And we had only been with them for a little over a week.

Things were going smoothly—so smoothly, in fact, that the changes I started seeing in Bray didn't concern me as much as they would have if I had been in a more alert frame of mind.

It took one night in a waterfront beach house to know that I didn't know my girlfriend, the love of my life, as much as I thought I did.

And it broke my fucking heart.

# FIFTEEN

## Elias

*T*he beach house was one of the most immaculate I had seen, overlooking the ocean. It had a massive boat dock just steps away from the backyard, which itself looked like something you'd see in a landscaping magazine. Every room in the house was like walk-in luxury, with expensive ceramic tile floors and intricate paintings and designer furniture that I was afraid to touch and leave fingerprints on. I thought that a place like this, so rich and clean, couldn't possibly belong to any of Tate's friends. The last few houses we had visited looked more like my apartment did back in Georgia: a bachelor pad.

Turned out, this was Jen's parents' house, and they were in the Bahamas on vacation. So, naturally, we turned it into a party spot.

The music bumped through the speakers in the living room ceiling. Bray and I were sitting together, kicked back on the couch with a mixed drink in our hands while Tate and Jen and a few others danced to "Pony" by Ginuwine in the center of the room. There were people sitting on every piece of furniture, and as I got up and went into the kitchen to trade my mixed drink for a beer, I saw that even the countertops were occupied.

Caleb was one of the occupants. He sat near the sink with a half pint of Jack Daniels between his legs. Johanna was on his left, leaning her head against his shoulder. She had a dazed look in her eyes, but with her that wasn't unusual—she always appeared dazed even when she was sober.

"I have a question for you," Caleb said.

I was surprised by his voice. He had never made much of an effort to have a conversation with me before. Now that he had, I was leery of it.

I shut the fridge and leaned against the counter beside it, twisting the top off my beer.

"Yeah, what's that?" I asked before taking a swig.

Caleb moved the whiskey from between his legs to one side. He took his time. "Why didn't you call the cops when your car was stolen?"

"What makes you think I didn't?"

"I heard you talking about it with your girlfriend the other night."

So Caleb was the quiet, observant type. I didn't give him enough credit. Up until this point I didn't take him for the type to give any kind of shit about what other people had to say.

"It wouldn't have done any good," I answered, and I knew my excuse was lacking but I couldn't tell him the truth. I really just needed to avoid this conversation altogether.

Caleb smiled slimly. I didn't think I'd ever actually seen that guy smile before. He was onto me.

"The only reasons someone wouldn't call the cops if their ride got stolen would be either you stole the car first, you're in some kind of trouble and *can't* call the cops, or you're lying about it." He smirked subtly.

I wanted to punch him, but I couldn't punch him for being intelligent.

"Hey man, no judgments here." He put up his hands briefly. "I can't talk. I'm not exactly Kirk Fucking Cameron. Whatever you two did, it's none of my business. I just don't want you getting us mixed up in your shit, all right? I've got enough of my own to last me the rest of my life."

*It takes a criminal to recognize the actions of a criminal*, I thought.

I couldn't really agree to his request in good conscience. As long as we were with them there was a chance they'd get mixed up with what we did. But to be fair, Caleb was right: he couldn't talk. From what I knew about him, he was an asshole and a drug dealer. And from where I was standing, drug dealer trumped accidental death by a long shot.

"Nothing to worry about," I said and pushed away from the counter.

"For your sake," he said, "I hope you're right."

I left the kitchen without any further conversation.

Caleb would always be the mood killer for me as long as we were around them.

But Caleb did something more than kill the mood, he got me to thinking. Were the police looking for Bray and me yet? Had they found Jana's body? Suddenly, I had to know. I left the kitchen and weaved my way through people standing in the hallway until I found Jen. I asked her if there was a computer in the house I could use, and she directed me to her father's office.

I closed myself inside the office. Alone. Just me and the Internet. I sat down at the desk in the leather office chair with wheels and cupped my hand over the cordless mouse, bringing the flat-screen monitor to life in front of me. The light from the screen illuminated the dark room. I opened a web page and started to type in our names and "Georgia" and a few other random keywords, until I realized it wasn't such a good idea to do it that way on someone else's computer. I backspaced and typed in one of Georgia's news station names instead.

And then I just stared at the list of results, my finger wanting to click the mouse button. But I couldn't. As much as I needed to know, I was too afraid. Bray and I were having such a great time together, able to forget about the looming future that I knew would eventually come, but I wasn't ready to bring it on sooner. I wasn't ready to see that smile on Bray's face I woke up to every morning disappear and become only a memory.

I wasn't ready.

I erased my search from the browser's history and then closed the page out, leaving the room the same way I found it. Dark and empty and with all of the answers.

I went back into the living room, and as my gaze fell on the couch where Bray had been sitting, I saw that she wasn't there. I looked around for her, casually making my way from room to room and between Tate and Jen practically fucking each other while still dancing to "Pony," which seemed to have been put on repeat. As I glided past the sliding glass door in the sunroom, I saw Bray sitting outside in a patio chair talking to Grace.

Feeling playful and deprived of screwing with Bray's head the past four years, I quietly crept my way out the door and approached the two of them from behind. It was much quieter out here; I heard the sound of the breeze coming off the ocean and the calm waves brushing against the dock nearby. The bumping music inside the house was muffled by the walls.

I snuck up quietly, intent on scaring Bray enough to make her pee herself. But as I drew nearer and caught snippets of their conversation, my steps began to slow and my ears began to burn.

"God, I just can't imagine...," I heard Grace say with a gasp.

I saw the top of her head from over the back of the patio chair, and she leaned over as if to look down at something.

"Grace, just... please don't say anything else about it," Bray said, and I noticed her move her hand from between their chairs. "I don't want Elias to know."

Grace nodded slowly. "Yeah. Sure. Not a problem." And then she added, "Is that why you wear so many?"

I stepped up as close as I could to better see, but not enough to be seen. Grace was looking down again. I cocked my head at an angle to get a better view between their chairs, and I saw Grace's fingers probing the hemp bracelets around Bray's right wrist.

And then Bray noticed me standing there.

She jerked her hand back from Grace again and scrambled to finger the bracelets back in place. I walked the rest of the short way over to them.

"Hi baby," she said to me, looking over the back of the chair with a forced smile.

I leaned down and pecked her on the lips.

I glanced at Grace and then back at Bray, hoping Grace would get the hint and leave. But she didn't. I looked down at Bray's hands, my eyes scanning the bracelets.

Suddenly, I felt betrayed by them. Not by Bray, but by the bracelets.

I gave Bray a moment, a chance to just fess up, because she must've known that I'd heard parts of their conversation that she never wanted me to hear. But no one said anything. It was an awkward moment; Grace being there was what made it the most awkward.

"What did you not want me to know?" I came out with it.

Bray looked away.

I glanced over at Grace again, but now that she felt trapped, she wanted out of there. She looked back up at me squeamishly, stood up and said, "I need to find Caleb," and then scurried across the brick walkway, which was laid out in a mosaic pattern.

A new song filtered into the night air for a moment until it was shut off by Grace closing the sliding glass door.

I pulled the empty chair around in front of Bray and sat down. Her knees were drawn up, and to the side, her bare feet on the seat. She wouldn't, or *couldn't*, look at me.

I reached out for her hands. "Are you going to tell me?" I turned her hands in mine, my thumbs caressing the delicate skin of her palms.

"No, Elias. I can't."

I pressed down on her hands with all of my fingers and she tried to pull them away. "No," I said and held them tighter, forcing her gaze. "I want you to tell me." I searched her face for emotion, her eyes for information, but found only pain. I already had an idea about what I was going to find, but I didn't want to believe it.

She tried once more to pull her hands away, but I held them firm in mine and gently pushed my thumbs underneath the bracelets. My heart fell. I stopped cold. I couldn't move or say anything to her. And she still couldn't look at me for longer than two seconds at a time.

I took a deep breath into my lungs and then rubbed the pads of my thumbs over the scars on her wrists. I closed my eyes to compose myself, but my moment of calm was shattered when Bray snatched her hands away when I was at my weakest, leaped from the chair and ran past me.

"Bray!" I ran after her. "Stop! Please!"

She kept running, over the mosaic bricks and then through the landscaped grass and past the dock, heading toward the rocky beach.

"Stop! God damn it, stop!"

I grabbed her by the elbow and she swung around to face me, her long, dark hair whipping about her face. She tried desperately to push my hand away, but I refused to let go. The more she struggled, the firmer my grip became.

"*Please, Elias! Just leave!*" she roared. Tears streamed down her face.

I pulled her toward me, but she still fought, and with her free hand she tried to shove me backward.

"*Talk to me*, Bray!" I screamed. "Tell me why you did it!"

Having no other option, she let her weight drop and she fell against the sand. I let go before I went down with her. She wailed into the night and buried her face between her knees, rocking back and forth. I sat down in the sand with her. I tried to comfort her. I tried to touch her. Talk to her. Understand her. But she was inconsolable. I was lost. This wasn't the Bray that I knew, the girl that I grew up with. This wasn't the fun and crazy and life-loving beautiful girl I shared my entire life with. She was still the girl I loved, no matter her flaws or her weaknesses. That would never change. But this girl sitting in the sand in front of me with suicide scars across her wrists and such pain in her heart that it shook *me* to my core... this was another side to that girl I loved. A side that I never saw, never even knew existed.

"Please," I said softly, in a last desperate attempt.

She raised her eyes and gazed out at the dark ocean. Tears clung to her long, dark eyelashes. But she wouldn't speak.

I could only wonder what she was remembering...

# Bray

*The memory...*

Blood dripped from my fingertips like little crimson beads, pooling on the floor beneath the chair. Each drop actually sounded more thunderous than the last, as if in death the body's senses heighten. That little voice in my head, the one telling me I was tickling the threshold between sanity and despair, had finally won.

Elias was gone. I felt alone. So alone. I had grown so apart from my parents that we talked only on special occasions. They gave up on me a long time ago, and so I gave them the space they seemed to want from me. My only friend, Lissa, wouldn't understand me if I sat her down and tried to make her understand. Although she had a big heart, she was much more comfortable watching another's problems from the sidelines rather than wanting to be a part of the solution. I had no one. But worst of all, I didn't have Elias. I had left him, moved away from my life with him in Georgia, because I knew I didn't deserve him. I was too messed up; I had far too much baggage that I was too afraid and ashamed to set at his feet. I just wanted him to be happy.

Dark clouds littered the evening sky, but nothing would come from them. Choking incense burned heavily on the side table, and in intervals the coils of smoke were broken apart by the wind creeping through the opened window. Buried beneath the fragrance, a layer of metallic blood lingered. I could smell it like vinegar pressed against my nostrils, taste it in my mouth and in the back of my dehydrated throat.

But nothing was more potent than the memories. In my final hour, they had come back to haunt me, and all I had the strength to do was try to force them away. I gazed beyond the choking smoke, my eyes heavier with every troubled breath. The sound of Lissa's voice out in the hall suddenly paralyzed me. The fear of her stumbling upon my gory predicament caused my heart to quicken. Soon though her footsteps faded as she shuffled down the hallway.

I closed my eyes. The painful memories still pressed against my skull, tearing holes through the backs of my eyes. The pictures were so clear, so lifelike and so cruel.

And I was powerless to stop them from tormenting me.

*I could feel the early morning spring rain against my skin, the coolness of each drop on my cheeks and my girlish bare shoulders. I ran with thirteen-year-old Elias through the pasture near Mr. Parson's pond—two gullible, free, young barely-teenagers with little worry in the world except getting caught and grounded, or forced to eat ramen noodles for dinner. We headed out in a mad dash and jumped into the water with a great splash. Elias fell beneath the surface and swam toward my legs, grabbing me at the knees. Just like he had always done when we came here. I kicked my legs wildly, trying to get away, laughing so hard that brief tears formed in the corners of my eyes.*

*Elias emerged from the water, pushing back the soaking mop of dark brown hair on his head.*

*"I wish we could stay here forever," I said.*

*He splashed at me gently. "I do too," he said. "Who says we can't?"*

*I chuckled, covering my mouth with my hand.*

*"School. Our parents. They might have a problem with it."*

*Elias lay back, floating atop the water with his arms stretched out beside him.*

*"You know that boy in Mrs. Rowe's class, Brayden Harris?" I began. "I think he likes me."*

*Elias lifted, eyeing me suspiciously.*

*"I want to learn how to kiss," I added. "Like a real kiss with tongue, y'know? I don't want to look stupid when I do it for the first time."*

*"You don't need to even have a boyfriend, much less be kissing." There was a strange edge to his voice that I couldn't place.*

*"Oh come on, teach me how, please," I begged. "I'll be embarrassed!"*

*"No."*

*"Why not?" I splashed at him. "I know you kissed Mitchell's sister before. Mitchell told me all about it."*

*"I did not kiss her."*

*"No?" I narrowed my gaze at him. "So then you've never French-kissed? Ever?"*

*"Yeah," he said, looking somewhat unconfident. "Sure I have. Just not Mitchell's sister." He visibly shuddered and made an awful face.*

*"Then who?" I tried crossing my arms, but it made me bob precariously in the water.*

*"That's none of your business," he said, crinkling one side of his nose. "Don't you know you're not supposed to kiss and tell?"*

*I rolled my eyes and splashed him again.*

*"You suck," I said.*

*He looked faintly stunned, and the whites of his eyes became more noticeable. I laughed because I thought it was funny how he was so offended by such a generic put-down. But I always did like to push his buttons, so I added, "You suck big, hairy, disgusting—"*

*A tsunami took the breath right out of my lungs and replaced it with dirty pond water. I choked and coughed and tried to rub the burning water from my eyes, only making it worse since my hands were wet.*

*"Damn it, Elias! I hate you for that!"*

*"No, you don't," he said matter-of-factly.*

*I twisted my bottom lip between my teeth and snarled. "OK, so maybe I could never hate you"—I rolled my eyes for added effect—"but if you don't help me practice and I get made fun of when I do it wrong the first time, it's on your ass." I rounded my chin arrogantly.*

*"You're hopeless, Bray. You know that, right?"*

*I could tell by the surrendering tone of his voice that I was going to get my way.*

*"Please?" I whined.*

*"All right, I'll try to show you," Elias agreed with hesitant words that he almost swallowed. "I mean, it'll be weird kissing you like that, being my best friend and all."*

*My face lit up. "I don't care! Just be glad I'm asking you and not Mitchell or Lissa!"*

*We exploded into laughter.*

*"Yeah, that would be pretty disgusting," he said.*

*Elias drew near, placing his hands upon my wet cheeks. For a moment, my lips formed a pucker and I closed my eyes so tight that I felt lines crinkling around my nose.*

*"No, not like that," Elias said. "Relax your face and don't do that smoochy-thing with your lips."*

*I followed his direction and when it felt natural, his lips gently covered mine. He slipped his tongue into my mouth, and my whole body tingled in a way I had never felt before.*

*My belly swam like warm mush and fluttered and made me feel weird between my legs. I didn't understand it, but I liked it, almost how I liked it whenever Elias would scratch my back or play with my hair. It was heavenly and warm.*

*The kiss broke and we looked into each other's eyes. But before things got awkward, we started splashing each other relentlessly.*

*I screamed at the top of my lungs as Elias swam around and jumped on my back, pressing both hands on the top of my head and trying to dunk me. I went under twice and swallowed more pond water before I could get away.*

*"You jerk!" I shrieked.*

*His dark hair bobbed in the water as he began to swim back toward the dock.*

*"You still suck, Elias Kline!" I called out to him, my voice carrying across the water. "And that's why you won't admit to kissing Mitchell's sister! Because you sucked at it and don't want anybody to know!"*

*With his back to me, his arms came up and he fixed his hands against the edge of the dock. His body shot up out of the water and he sat down against the wooden planks.*

*"You're wrong, Bray!" he shouted back.*

*"Is that so?" I sneered.*

*"Yeah," he said. "I never French-kissed her because you were my first."*

I shook the memory out of my head and screamed at the top of my lungs, pounding my fists against the bloody arms of the chair. Tears shot from my eyes.

I looked over at the razor blade on the side table, forcing the memory of Elias out of my mind entirely. I struggled to lift my head, but it felt like it weighed fifty pounds.

The room began to spin. Long, flowing curtains blended with the beige paint on the walls. The sounds from the house were now more audible than ever before. The ticking of two clocks sounded more like six. The shuffling of Lissa's feet seemed still right outside the room. The clock ticking on the wall in the hallway clacked so loudly in my ears I wanted to press my hands over them to stifle the sound, but my arms were too heavy and limp to lift.

My mind was receding fast into blackness. I had always thought this was a slow way to die and that maybe the mind goes before the body.

But I never got the chance to find out.

Lissa burst into the room, saw me in the chair, my wrists covered in blood, and she started screaming.

"Brant! Brant!" I felt her hands cover my wrists. *"Call nine-one-one!* Brant! Fucking call nine-one-one!" I thought her voice should be unbearably loud in my ears like everything else had been just seconds ago, but this time all the sound around me had become dampened by death slowly stripping away my conscious mind.

# SIXTEEN

## Elias

*B*rayelle?" I spoke up when I could no longer stand the silence.

I didn't expect her to answer and was prepared to leave her alone on the beach if that was really what she wanted, but she surprised me when she said, "I did it wrong." She kept her gaze on the dark ocean out ahead of us.

"You...you did *what* wrong?"

"The way I slit my wrists."

A knot formed in my throat. Hearing those words come from her lips did something to me, something really fucked up. It hurt. It hurt like hell hearing her admit it, even more so than seeing her scars.

I couldn't speak. And I couldn't look at her. Pain and even resentment for what she had done assailed me.

She sniffled and said, "Lissa found me. I did everything wrong. The way I cut them, the house I chose to do it in. The hour. I—"

"*Why* did you do it, Bray? Why?" I looked right at her. "I want you to tell me the truth. If I had anything to do with why you did it, I want to know."

I didn't want to know. I needed to.

I swallowed hard and stared at her from the side, my forearms perched on the tops of my bent knees.

She still wouldn't look at me and as the silence grew between us, I knew without her having to admit it that I was part of the reason, after all. I just hoped like hell I wasn't *the* reason.

"Elias...I lied to you when I said I was afraid of having more with you than we already had because things would change and we'd grow apart. That was all just an excuse. A watered-down version of the truth."

I couldn't believe what I was hearing. Instantly, my mind began scrambling to find what could be the truth before she told me, but I came up short.

She steadied her breath. I sat quiet and motionless and confused.

"I've been pretty messed up all my life," she said. "You've known that. Better than anyone."

*No. I haven't.*

"Crazy, fucked-up mood swings. Highs and lows that gave me whiplash. That gave everyone around me whiplash. I clung to you from the day I met you. I couldn't have known that there was something wrong with me when I was a little girl. I was just *me*. I didn't know I was any different from anybody else. Who knows stuff like that when they're kids?" She shook her head shamefully, as if she had been trying to convince herself of this for years, that it wasn't her fault.

"But I clung to you because you were the only person who wanted to be around me, who went out of his way to be around me." She laughed lightly and it caught me off guard. "Did you know that Lissa was scared of me?" She glanced over at me briefly, but looked back out at the ocean. "I had no idea. Not until I turned fifteen. I got that ceramic music box from my grandma for my birthday, the one with my name engraved on the side. Lissa dropped and broke it right in front of me. It was an accident, but I'll never forget the look on her face. She thought I was going to beat the shit out of her." She laughed lightly again. "That was crazy, of course, but she told me that day that she had always been afraid of me. The other girls at school when we were growing up, they *all* thought I was a nutcase."

Then the soft look of nostalgia darkened on her face.

"No one really wanted to be around me," she said, and I could hear the pain in her voice. "I never knew it. No one ever told me. Not until Lissa told me that day." She sighed and shut her eyes softly and repeated, "No one ever told me, they just all talked shit about me behind my back. Lissa admitted to it, but she was the only person who remained my friend. But she never really wanted any part of my problems. And who could blame her?"

I scooted over closer to her, touching my shoulder to hers. But that was all I did. I didn't want to interrupt. It felt like the things she was saying to me were things she had wanted to say to me, to *anyone*, for so long.

"My mom caught me curled up in a ball on my bedroom floor clawing at my wrists with my fingernails. I was sixteen. I wasn't trying to kill myself. I didn't even draw blood. I...well, it's so hard to explain." She clenched her right hand into a fist and gritted her teeth. "I just had so much *anger* inside of me. Chaos. It's the only way I can describe it. I had to get it out. I felt like I was going to explode and I just needed a release. It was itching on the inside. I had to get it out. I can't explain it."

She glanced at me again only briefly. Silence ensued as she jumped from one memory to another.

"All those trips I was taking with my mom to gymnastics..."

Elias, I've never taken a gymnastics class in my life. I was seeing a shrink. A fucking *shrink*. She didn't want anyone to know. *I* didn't want anyone to know."

Finally, Bray turned her head and looked straight at me, giving me all of her attention, her eyes filled with intensity and with intent.

"You were the only person in the world who I felt deep down accepted me for the way I was, even though you had no idea there was something wrong with me. Who didn't run the other way or talk about me to other people. Even my parents...Elias, they loved me, I know, but they were so exhausted by me. They didn't want to deal with it anymore. I was always getting into trouble. Sneaking out. Getting picked up by the cops. Sent to Juvenile. They didn't want to deal with me anymore."

She looked away and a tear escaped her eye. She tried to hide it, but I reached up and wiped it away with the pad of my thumb.

"Tell me," I urged her. "Tell me everything." I had known growing up with her that she spent so much time with me because she had problems at home. I had seen it, the way her parents regarded her, how her father favored her sister and looked down on Bray, but until now I never knew why. I never knew, just like Bray had said, that there was something wrong with her, that she had lived all her life with this eternal struggle.

She gathered her composure, forcing down the other tears that threatened to turn her into a blubbering mess.

"I overheard my dad telling my mom once that he didn't care anymore, that I was just a spoiled brat that hated authority and that I deserved whatever I got. They gave up on me. My mom and dad just *gave up*. They didn't care where I went or what I did. I got worse after that. My highs and lows went from being a bad teenager to a very sick one. Some days I was the happiest person on Earth, while other days I wouldn't get out of bed. I wanted to lay there forever. I would stare up at the ceiling and wish that the world would just crumble to bits around me."

She caught my eyes.

"You *were* part of the reason, Elias," she said, finally answering my question about the suicide attempt. That knot just got bigger in my throat. "Lissa, trying to be a good friend I guess, talked me in to seeing another shrink when I moved to South Carolina with her. I thought she was really trying to get involved and be proactive by helping me. No one who knew about my problems had ever really done that for me before. Sure, my parents sent me to a shrink, but I always felt like they did it for themselves and not for me. Or like it was their duty. So, when Lissa sat me down that day and she looked me in the eyes—she even held my hands, Elias. She came at me with all of the right things—I felt like, *Wow, she really cares about me and wants to help.* So, wanting to show her how much I appreciated the gesture, I agreed to go."

Bray stopped and looked back out at the ocean again. The wind blew softly through her hair, pushing a few dark strands across her lips. I moved around to sit in front of her and then reached up and pulled the hair away, tucking it back behind her ear. But she never stopped looking at the ocean even with me in front of her. Her mind was lost in her darkest memories. I waited patiently for her to go on. She needed this moment to reflect, I knew.

"I never wanted to take medication. I was afraid that if I took it that would make it real, that I would *believe* I was crazy. I would prove my parents right. So I never did. The medication I was prescribed when I was sixteen, I only pretended to take. But in South Carolina, I was so caught up in Lissa wanting to help me that I took the medication the shrink she talked me into seeing prescribed."

She paused and said, "It was the worst thing I could've done."

"Why?"

"Because it was ultimately what made me want to kill myself."

Confused, I just stared at her, longing for the answers.

"That shrink was a quack," she said. "Had to be. After Lissa found me sitting in a chair with blood pooling on the floor beneath me, I woke up in the hospital to my parents and two women with tablets in their hands and judgment on their faces. They committed me. My parents left me in the care of the State and they went back to Georgia. Lissa, she visited me once but that was it. That was when I knew she was just like my parents. She cared about me, but she was exhausted by me and wanted to hand me over to someone else to deal with."

I rested my hands on her knees.

"I was under the State's thumb for two weeks before they released me. Before they felt I was no longer a danger to myself. I convinced them that I had never tried or really wanted to commit suicide before I started taking those pills. And it was the truth. I mean, yeah, I did have suicidal thoughts. I had them a lot, I won't say I didn't. But I never attempted it until after the medication. Idiots prescribed me something else, slapped me on the wrist and said, *We hope we never see you in here again, Miss Bates*," she said, mimicking a man's voice. "And they sent me on my way. After three more months living with Lissa—who by then avoided me as much as possible—I was done with her and with South Carolina." She raised her eyes to me again. I felt a hot chill run through my back. "I was done hiding from the only person in the world who I knew loved me. And so I came home. To you."

I just stared at her.

Ocean water continuously pushed against the shore. The clatter of voices and music steadily funneled from the beach house

many feet away, though faint and not at all distracting. The wind
was mild, moving between the two of us quietly, as if it had a mind
of its own and wanted to give us this time together without inter-
ruption. Bray sat Indian style with her hands in her lap. Tears still
clung to her lashes, but she couldn't cry anymore. I could sense that
she wanted to look me in the eyes, but now that she had told me all
of this, she was ashamed.

I reached out and took both of her hands into mine and I
turned her wrists up. She didn't protest, but she watched me curiously. I wedged my thumb and index finger between the bracelets
on her left wrist and when my finger found the scar, I caressed it.
Then I lifted that wrist to my lips and I kissed it. I did the same to
the other one and then placed both of her hands back into her lap,
and I held them there.

"Before I have to say what I intend to say to you," I began, "you
have to tell me how I was partly to blame for this."

Confusion flickered in her eyes. She shook her head no, her eyebrows drawn inward creating tiny wrinkles in her forehead.

"No, Elias," she said. "No part of you was to *blame* for this."

I didn't speak. I didn't want to. I only wanted to listen.

"Two days before I did it," she said in a soft, distant voice, "I
started thinking about the last phone call I had with Mitchell. He
had told me that you were in love with Aline, and I knew that I
had lost you forever. You were all I had. The thought of never having you in my life just made my mind-set worse. It made *everything*
worse. I thought of you when I put that blade to my skin. I thought
of when we first met. Our first kiss. Our first everything. Yes, I
thought of you, but it wasn't your fault."

"And it wasn't yours," I said. "You know that, right?" I held her
hands more firmly.

She nodded. "I know." It seemed like she wanted to say more than that, but she looked back down into her lap instead.

"I'm really pissed off," I said, and her head shot back up before I could finish. I wrenched her hands. "Why didn't you ever tell me? You told Lissa. You confided in her. You sit here and basically tell me that I was the only person who loved you enough to understand, that I was all that you had." I stared harshly into her shrinking face. I *wanted* this to sound as angry and as resentful as it did. It needed to be said that way, to be taken that way. "Yet I was the one person you didn't tell, the one person you didn't confide in, the one person you didn't go to for help."

Tears stung the backs of my eyes. I took a deep breath to contain them.

"I was the one person you knew loved you more than anyone ever could, yet you didn't trust in me enough to let me be there for you."

I had hurt her. Tremendously. Her bottom lip began to quiver and her hands began to shake beneath my own. But I refused to let go of her. She was going to face this truth if it was the last thing I ever said to her.

"Why didn't you come to me? Why did you constantly push me away?"

"I told you why!" she roared.

I remained calm. "No, you didn't. You told me that everything you said was a lie, a watered-down version of the truth."

"Yes! It was watered down! It was…it—" Her jaw snapped shut.

Finally, she sighed and said, "I *was* afraid. I was afraid that I would only push you away like I did everybody else. Especially if you knew the truth. You looked at me like I was beautiful. Perfect.

And that's what I wanted to be for you. I never wanted to shatter your image of me by telling you the truth. I was embarrassed and ashamed."

"*Of what?*" I said with disbelief.

Her eyes began to fall away from mine. I pulled on her hands to shake her attention back to me.

"Seventeen years I've known you, Bray. *Seventeen years.* I have loved everything about you. Your foul mouth. Your crazy-ass, brazen antics. Your fearless attitude. Your highs, your lows, whatever they were, I only saw a girl with a vivid personality. A girl who sometimes *did* give me whiplash, I won't lie, but I liked that about you. You kept me on my toes. You challenged me. Don't you understand? I went out of my way to be around you *because* of the way you were. And if you were ever going to scare me away or make me think badly of you, would I have made you the center of my world for *seventeen* years?"

I caught a tiny smile hidden in her eyes.

I let go of her hands and stood up from the sand.

"Out in the open. Everything. Right now. No more secrets or lies between us."

I began to pace, but then stopped and looked down at her and said, "When I was fifteen, and we crashed at Lissa's house that night of her birthday party, I touched your boob when you were sleeping."

Her mouth fell open with a spat of air. I was smiling from ear to ear.

"Pervert!"

I nodded. "Yeah, I was. A total fucking pervert. Hell, I *still* am. I always *will* be. But yeah, I touched your boob without your permission or you knowing about it. And I don't regret it."

She just shook her head, smiling the more I spoke.

I rested my chin in my hand for a moment, pondering. Then my index finger shot up. "OK, you want another one?" I slapped my hands together. "Senior year. You were supposed to go to the prom with that jack-off—what was his name?—anyway, he called you and cancelled because *I* threatened him."

"What?"

I nodded again. "I did. I knew he was a fucking douchebag. The thought of him trying to get in your pants made me fucking mental. I tried to talk you out of going with him, but you were hell-bent. So Mitchell watched the restroom door while I cornered him inside right after he had taken a piss. I told him that if he didn't back off, I'd fucking kill him."

"I can't believe you did that," she said and she wasn't smiling anymore.

"Well I did, and I'd do it again. Are you going to leave me now? Have I run you off?" I knew I hadn't. I was trying to prove a point.

She shook her head.

"You want something worse about me?" I asked and at this point, even I was a little afraid to go on. But this was our moment of truth. If I was going to make her understand anything, I had to show her a side of me that I knew she wouldn't like.

I reached out and took her hands, pulling her to her feet.

"I did coke for a year after you left," I said. "And twice, when I couldn't find any—because I was becoming addicted fast—I actually smoked crack. Right off a soda can. That's about as fucked up as it gets."

She looked like I had just slapped her across the face.

I put my thumb and index finger a centimeter apart in front of us and said with a squinted eye, "I was this close to becoming a full-blown addict. This close to being strung out twenty-four-seven, sleeping in fucking Dumpsters, giving blowjobs for blow. It was why I think I was so hell-bent on helping Mitchell get off that meth. I saw what it was doing to him. The same thing my shit almost did to me."

Bray let out a long, concentrated breath and dug both of her bare feet deeper into the sand.

Then she looked back up into my eyes. "Did you?"

"Did I what?"

"Ever do any of those things?"

I shook my head. "No. In fact, what sobered me up quicker than anything was when I went to a drug house with this guy— I didn't even know his name—and I was offered a line of coke. Primo shit. The other guy there, the one selling the stuff, was going to blow *me*. He would've given me a line and all I had to do was let him suck my dick. I almost did. I thought, hey, at least it's not the other way around. But then the guy who I went there with, he stepped up before I could answer and said he would let the guy do it if I wouldn't. And then two minutes later, there I was, watching this drug dealer suck this guy off who I rode there with. I thought, that could be me, getting violated for drugs. Willingly." I took a breath, softened my face and said, "And then I thought of you."

Bray took my hands into hers, consolation and understanding and even a little bit of horror lay resting in her face.

"I thought of you and of when we were kids swimming in that pond. Just seeing your face looking back at me in my head made me want to stop that shit. It didn't matter to me that I thought you were engaged—" I pointed at her. "I was pissed about that, just so you know. I thought that should've been *me*. Anyway, it didn't matter to me that you were in love and that I thought I'd lost you forever,

I wanted to be a better person for myself and because I knew you would hate to see me like that. I never touched coke or crack again and I never will. None of that life-killing shit. No fucking way. And smoking weed became a rare recreational thing for me."

Without giving her a chance to respond, I added quickly, "Would you have left me if I said yes? If I admitted I took part in something like that?"

This time, even though my heart told me that no, she wouldn't have left me, another part of me felt ashamed enough about everything I had told her that I thought maybe she might. It was when I truly understood what *she* went through with me all those years. I didn't agree with how she handled things, but I understood it at least.

"No," she said softly. "There's nothing you could do or say to make me leave you." And even though we had both said this very same thing to each other a few times in the past two weeks, it felt new and more real every time it was said.

She leaned in and kissed my lips. "Now it's my turn," she said.

I honestly didn't expect it. I knew I had told her that I wanted us to get everything out in the open. Right there. Right then. But I think a part of me assumed she had no other secrets. Hell, the ones she had been keeping were pretty bad in and of themselves. What else could she have possibly been hiding from me?

# SEVENTEEN

## Bray

*M*y hands fell away from his and rested at my sides. I took a step back, swallowed, and announced, "I like sex. A lot."

He raised a brow. "And that's a problem why, exactly?"

I wanted to laugh at that, because it was funny to me admitting to a guy that his girlfriend loved sex and he was supposed to frown upon it. But I couldn't laugh because it was the next part I was the most afraid to admit.

"Well," I said, "it's a problem because I...I've been with quite a few guys."

*He's going to be so disgusted with me and just walk away, I know it...*

"The same can be said about me with girls," he responded casually. "Did you use protection with them?"

I was dumbfounded by his response. Not his admittance, but his lackluster reaction to mine.

"Yeah," I said. "I-I mean, once or twice it didn't go down that way. Heat of the moment, I guess. Stupid as hell, I know, but I always did after that second time. And I'm clean. They tested me for everything when I was in the hospital."

He looked up in thought for a moment and then nodded. "Well, so am I," he said casually.

It didn't matter that he seemed OK with the truth. I was still worried and felt the need to explain further. Just in case.

"It started out I was only trying to fill a void," I said. "I think I was just looking for affection. But then it turned into something else." I ran my hands over my face and then the top of my head and sighed.

"What's wrong?" he asked.

I swallowed and looked at him nervously. "I had a threesome with this guy and his girlfriend. And I liked it." I couldn't look at him anymore. I felt so ashamed. I felt like the biggest slut on the planet. I didn't deserve him. "I think that's what changed me. I'm sorry, Elias. I really am."

"Why?" Just like before, there wasn't a trace of disappointment or disgust in his voice. "Bray," he said, and I looked up, "I had a threesome with Mitchell and Jana. And it wasn't my first."

"I know," I said. "Jana told me that night on the ridge." I thought about Jana for a moment. I saw her dead eyes looking up at the night sky. The blood on the rock underneath her body.

I forced it away.

"So then what's the problem?"

"Doesn't it bother you that your girlfriend has been with so many guys, or that I've done really kinky stuff?"

He shook his head and looked at me as if I were being ridiculous. "So it's OK that I do it and not you?" he asked. And before I could say anything, he added, "Baby, this isn't 1950. You have as much right to as much sex as you want, however you want, as I do. You didn't cheat on anyone or screw someone's husband." He narrowed his gaze and said, "Did you?"

"No."

"Then you have nothing to be ashamed of. Definitely not with me. As long as your love for sex doesn't land you in some other guy's bed now that we're together, we're good. I'm not an asshole. I'm not going to throw your past up in your face."

I should've known all along that Elias, of all people, would not judge me. Not on my sexual history. Not on anything. The only thing I regretted was the seventeen years I wasted not realizing it sooner.

Elias took a hold of my hands again and wedged his thumbs underneath my bracelets to find my scars. "I love you, Bray," he said, and the moment changed in an instant. "But you're gonna have to promise me something. You have to promise that you'll never do anything like this again. It scares the hell out of me to even *think*"—he put pressure on my wrists with the emphasis of that word—"of you killing yourself. You can't leave me in this world without you. Do you understand? Look in my eyes and tell me that you'll never try anything like that again."

"I won't," I said. "Like I told you, I only did it once because of the side effects of that medication."

"But you did it once," he pointed out. "You had it in you all along. You even admitted to having suicidal thoughts before that, Bray. That means you had it in you. And that is terrifying to me. Just knowing that it's there."

"I won't," I said again, hardening my gaze. "I'm past that now. I'm stronger than that."

He thought about it for a long moment. I hoped he believed me.

Then he leaned in and kissed me long and soft. The feel of his lips against mine and the emotion in that kiss melted me. I felt weak in the knees, and I draped my hands around his neck, interlocking my fingers. He lifted me up around his waist and held my butt in his hands.

"Elias," I said softly onto his lips when the kiss broke.

"Yeah?"

"You said that it should've been you."

He drew his head back slightly to better see my whole face. "Huh?"

I kissed the tip of his nose.

"Earlier," I went on, "when you said that about my ex. You said you were pissed when you thought I was engaged, that it should've been you."

His eyes smiled and shortly after, his lips followed. "I did say that, didn't I?"

"So then why don't we?" I blushed. "You know...get engaged."

His smile turned into a grin. "Are you asking me to marry you?"

My whole face flushed as hot as a Georgia summer. I wiggled my way out of his arms and stood upright in front of him again, shuffling my toes in the sand. "I-I don't know...I guess so," I said meekly.

"Might as well," he said. "I think it's safe to say after seventeen years we're pretty much stuck with each other. So sure, why not? We've been doing all kinds of crazy shit as of late. Might as well add it to the list."

I just stood there, blinking rapidly, with my lips parted. Then I pursed them, crossed my arms, and popped my hip to one side.

"That was the most romantic fucking proposal I've ever heard in my life," I said with heavy sarcasm.

Elias smiled hugely, baring his prefect set of white teeth. "Wasn't it, though?" he joked.

My arms unfolded and I slammed the palms of my hands into his chest, knocking him on his ass in the sand. He just looked up at me and laughed.

I started to walk off, fuming pissed, but I loved it just as much, and he knew it.

"Baby, where the hell are you going?!" He couldn't stop laughing.

I raised my middle finger in the air high above me and just kept walking. I could hear his laughter carrying on behind me over the growing music as I approached the beach house.

"I'm going to get drunk and stand in the center of the room and tell everyone that your cock is two inches long! And then afterwards, I'm going to—"

He grabbed me from behind and pulled me down on the grass and sand.

"My cock is *not* two inches long," he laughed, sitting on top of me.

No, it definitely wasn't, that was for sure...

I smirked up at him.

He grabbed my hands with both of his and pinned them above my head. The prickly sensation of grass tickled the backs of my arms. Then he leaned in and kissed me. When he pulled away his eyes searched my face. "Will you marry me and my two-inch cock?"

I smiled. It wasn't exactly romantic, but for some reason it felt right. "Sure, why not?" I replied.

He took me in for another kiss and we stayed like that, him sitting on top of me on the sand until Grace interrupted us—which was probably a good thing, because we were heading right in the sex-in-public direction.

"Ho-ly shit! You've got to see this!" she said waving her hands out in front of her frantically, a crazed smile lighting up her face.

We followed Grace back inside the beach house. A crowd had gathered in a circle inside the large living room. Elias tugged on my fingers; I followed in close behind him, and we pushed our way to the front of the crowd to see Tate and Caleb exchanging blows.

I heard a crunch as Tate's fist made contact with Caleb's face. Caleb stumbled backward into a guy on the other side of the circle, but he bounced back just as quickly and returned the blow. Tate dodged it and came around behind Caleb, grabbing him around the waist with his thick muscled arms, and he squeezed Caleb so hard I thought he was going to bust a vein in Caleb's head.

Caleb managed to raise his arms above him and grapple Tate's head. Tate lost his grip, and Caleb whirled around and grabbed the back of Tate's neck, forcing his body over forward. Caleb's knee came up, and I heard another stomach-twisting crunch. I yelped. The music and the sound of bystanders chanting was loud, but apparently not loud enough that it covered the sound of Tate's face being pummeled into Caleb's knee.

Elias pulled me back when Tate and Caleb started getting closer to us. They were moving around in a circle, both of them bent forward in battle-ready stances with their clenched fists out at their sides, each waiting for an opportunity.

I didn't notice until I managed to tear my eyes away from the fight for a split second, but Tate's girlfriend, Jen, was standing at my right side. I looked over at her questioningly.

"They do this all the time!" she shouted over the noise, then turned back to the fight. "Come on, baby! You got this!"

I was so confused. But I think Elias was enjoying it. Any moment now I half-expected him to whip out some cash and pass it to the nearest sideline bookie.

Tate buried one hard right jab into Caleb's ribs, then a left, then one dead center in Caleb's gut. Caleb doubled over, and a second later Tate hooked him underneath the jaw with an uppercut.

Caleb fell backward on his ass and tried to shake off the blow, but it was clear he had lost.

Tate raised both arms in the air as if he were in a boxing ring, and the room erupted in cheers. Jen stepped out and kissed him. Molested him. With those two, there never seemed to be boundaries.

Then Tate reached down and gave Caleb his hand, helping him to his feet. They hugged and joked around, and then it was all over. Everyone went back to partying. Caleb moved past us without even looking at us and looped his arms through Grace's and Johanna's. They disappeared into the kitchen. Tate, with Jen at his side, walked toward us.

I looked at Tate like he was crazy.

"Hey, it was Caleb's idea," he said.

"Is he *drunk*?" I asked.

Tate laughed. "Probably. But he'd challenge me sober."

He patted Elias on the back while Jen handed Tate the extra beer bottle she had been holding.

"We're heading to a secret spot on the beach next," he said, looking at us. He took a swig before he finished and made a subtle face, as if it tasted sour. "Headin' out in the morning. We'll probably stay there for a few days. Are you two still good to go with us?"

Elias and I exchanged a glance.

"Yeah, we are," I said.

"I'm game," Elias added.

Tate grinned and pointed at us both, the beer bottle hanging from the same hand. "You two are gonna have to tell me what's up with you sometime." His grin got bigger.

I glanced at Jen, and she smiled at me. Did she know something I didn't? Instant paranoia. But I was relieved when she said, "Yeah, seriously. Tate and Caleb have a bet going on. A few more days and they'll both be trying to pry it out of you just to see who won." She pushed up on her toes and kissed Tate on the side of the mouth.

"A bet?" I asked.

Tate laughed. But it was Jen who elaborated. She pointed at Tate and said, "Yeah, *he* thinks you two robbed a bank or something. Caleb thinks you killed someone."

I felt myself gasp sharply, but I don't think anyone heard. Elias's hand slid down and linked with mine. He tried to play it off, or was trying to divert their attention away from me with my deer-in-the-headlights face. He laughed out loud and shook his head in disbelief just to distract them.

Tate laughed along with Elias and patted him on the back one more time. Then he and Jen left us and went to mingle.

Before we crashed, with Jen's go-ahead, Elias and I made use of an upstairs bathroom, where we soaked for a long time in a hot bath. The music had died down an hour ago and everybody had either found a place to sleep or left. The low humming of the central air-conditioning unit could be faintly heard from the bottom floor as we sat together in the tub next to the window overlooking the beach. I lay with my back and head lying against his naked chest. One of his arms rested along the side of the cast-iron claw-foot tub. Elias had dimmed the lights in the bathroom earlier, which left the room in a low copper-colored glow that spilled onto the white marble floor near the elongated sink. The moonlight cast a grayish-blue hue on the tub through the window.

Elias continued to massage my scalp with his fingertips long after he had rinsed the shampoo from my hair. I nearly fell asleep against his chest, lulled by his touch, but when I shut my eyes, I saw Jana's face staring back at me.

"Elias," I said in a low, distant voice as I stared toward the window. "Even if nothing ever happens to me, even if I get off with a slap on the wrist, I don't think I can ever forgive myself for what happened to her."

Water trickled from Elias's arm into the tub as he reached underneath the water for my arm and pulled it against my breasts. He laid his head against the side of mine and I could feel the warmth of his breath from his nose as he exhaled softly against my cheek.

"I know, baby," he said quietly. "I can't tell you not to let it get to you and I can't say that you shouldn't feel guilty because it was an accident, even though that's what I feel, but I'll be here for you. Always."

"I know you will..."

He traced the bone along my forearm with the tip of his finger, up to my shoulder and then along my collarbone. I closed my eyes and let the shiver running along my spine subside.

"Can I ask you something?"

"You know you can," he said softly with his cheek pressed against my wet hair.

I reached up and touched his face, trailing my fingers along the well-defined curvature of his jawline, the tiny stubbles of his unshaven face gently prickling my sensitive skin. I continued to look out at the ocean, lost in the memory of Jana on the ridge with me that night, before she died.

"If she had been pregnant with your baby," I began, "what would you have done?"

I felt his chest rise and fall heavily against my back.

"Well, I would've been there for the kid," he said. "I would've helped her raise it, but you would always be in my life. With me. Just like you are now."

His hand covered mine over my chest and he slid his fingers in between mine, locking them together.

I didn't say anything in response. He knew it was what I had needed to hear.

I breathed in softly, and Jana's face finally vanished from my mind. I saw only what was really in front of me then: the dark sky peppered by hundreds of tiny white dots and the waning moon hanging high above the horizon. Although I loved the night sky in any season and in any place, it never felt quite the same as when I saw it at home, above Mr. Parson's pasture.

"If you could go back in time, any time, and stay there, would you?" I asked.

"Well, I don't know," he said with reluctance, as if he needed more time to think about it. "I mean, if I could go back and *change* anything in my life, I guess I would. But as far as staying somewhere, I'm not sure."

"What would you change?"

"The night on the ridge, of course," he said and laid his left arm over my belly underneath the water.

"But let's just say you *had* to choose a time in your life to go back to and live, stay there forever, what time would you choose?"

He was quiet for a long moment and then he said, "I'd choose our childhood. The day we first met up until—"

"—until we lost our innocence?" I interrupted.

I felt his chin move against the side of my face as he nodded once. "Yeah," he said. "I'd choose our childhood."

"Me, too," I said.

"But I like being with you now, too," he added. "Despite the circumstances, I think that if I had to choose between our childhood and our adult lives together, I'd probably choose the way we are now."

I swallowed uneasily and then brought his hand from underneath the water and pressed my lips to his wet knuckles.

"What would *you* choose?" he asked, though I wished he hadn't.

"I..."

He squeezed his arms around my body and said, "I know what you would choose. Don't feel bad about it. But baby, when this is all over, when we're free to live our lives and enjoy our time together, you won't feel the same way."

"Maybe not," I said, but I wasn't so sure.

# EIGHTEEN

## Bray

One night of partying went by at Tate's secret spot on the beach, but we didn't sleep there that night. Elias got so shitfaced after drinking way too much whiskey that I thought he had alcohol poisoning. Since I was the most sober one among our group of seven, Tate tossed me the keys to his Jeep, and I drove us to a hotel in St. Petersburg. But not until after I got us lost and drove farther out of our way than I had to. It wasn't easy navigating a giant Jeep Sahara through a state I had never driven through before, with a load of drunks and one very sick fiancé puking his guts up on Tate's floorboard. Tate was too drunk to care. I held my breath the whole way, hoping like hell we didn't get pulled over by the cops.

I felt so awful for Elias. I pulled over twice to let him get some air. And by the time I got him into the bathtub and ran down the hallway with a dripping ice bucket in one hand, he had finally calmed down on the vomiting. I cleaned him up and helped him into the bed.

I had taken it upon myself to get a room separate from everyone else. Tate said he didn't care when I asked him as we stood at the hotel's front desk. I put the rooms on his credit card. The front desk clerk almost didn't rent us the rooms because we looked like a bunch of beach hoodlums and we stank like whiskey. But I think she took pity on Elias.

It seemed like all of us slept for twelve hours straight. Except when check-out time came around—Tate woke up long enough to find me in the room next door, get his credit card back, and go downstairs to pay for another day.

By early evening, we were all awake and out on the beach, soaking up what was left of the sun. Elias was feeling much better. He said he doubted it was the alcohol that made him sick; it was probably the burritos we'd eaten an hour before he started drinking.

"I'm telling you," Elias said, "that felt like food poisoning. It wasn't the alcohol. I've drunk way more than I drank last night, and I've never puked like that before."

I grinned at him. "Are you just saying that to make yourself feel better about drinking tonight?"

"No," he said. "But if I do drink tonight, I think I'll lay off the hard stuff."

"Good idea," I said, and laid my head on his arm as we walked alongside each other down the beach.

Jen had a suitcase full of clothes with her in the Jeep, and she lent me a bikini. Elias didn't care to swim, but Tate offered him his extra pair of trunks if he changed his mind. This was beginning to bother Elias. A lot. Tate paying for everything, paying for us, for me. I tried to tell him that it wasn't something he could control. He couldn't access his bank account. What money we did have was probably snorted up Anthony's and Cristina's noses by now. One last time Elias was going to call his father and give his dad access to his account somehow, so his dad could wire us some money, but I stopped him. It was too much of a risk.

But either Tate was loaded or he just didn't care about maxing out his credit cards. I couldn't know. But he didn't have any qualms about paying for everyone most of the time. Caleb paid for beer and food, but usually it was Tate footing the bill, except when we stayed at friends' houses and such. That was pretty much a freebie all around.

Before the night started to fall, Tate talked everyone into heading back to that secret spot on the beach, which was well over an hour from the hotel.

We had already checked out of our room, and I had to pee, so before we got on the road I found a public restroom in a nearby restaurant. The stalls were full when I made it inside. I waited next to a sink, trying to avoid having to hold myself or do the pee-pee dance, until finally one toilet flushed and out of the stall stepped a girl with a blonde braid draped over her shoulder.

I smiled, and she smiled in return. Really, I just wanted her to walk away from the stall faster so I could jump in there and pee before it was too late.

Afterward, we hung around the beach for a while longer. I saw that same girl from the restroom sitting several feet away from us next to a tall, brown-haired shirtless guy with a huge tattoo down his side. When the girl stood up once, I saw that she had one, too. I was instantly intrigued. I had always liked tattoos, the way they looked on other people, but I never got around to getting one of my own. The tats these two had looked like masterpieces even from this far away.

"Damn," I heard Johanna say. "Do you see that guy over there?" I was more curious about Johanna saying anything at all, much less openly gawking at some random guy on the beach while Caleb was standing just feet away from us talking to Tate.

I shrugged it off, accepting that Caleb, Johanna, and Grace's relationship was weird enough to me as it was. I didn't care to delve deeper into it. If Johanna wasn't worried about what Caleb might think, then I wasn't worried *for* her.

"Which guy?" I asked, pretending not to have noticed.

I didn't want Elias to think I had zoned in on him like Johanna had. I mean sure, the guy was smokin' hot, but he had nothing on my man. No one did.

Tate and Caleb walked back up then.

"Hey," Tate said from behind, "we're going to head out soon."

"Why don't we invite some more people this time?" Johanna suggested. She stood up and dusted sand from her bikini.

Tate looked at Caleb, who shrugged. "Yeah, sure, that's a good idea, actually," Tate agreed.

Elias and I stood up. All of us started scanning the beach and since it still technically wasn't summer, there weren't many people to choose from. A middle-aged couple sat to our right, the woman wearing a purple one-piece with large flowers printed all over it and a huge floppy hat on her head. An old man jogged past, very tanned and in better physical shape than most forty-year-olds I had seen, and glistening with sweat and suntan lotion. A young married couple with two children sat close to the water in beach chairs. It was safe to say that the cute blonde in the red bikini and her tattooed boyfriend were the only candidates.

"I saw that girl in the restroom down at the restaurant earlier," I said, nodding in her direction. "Why don't we invite them?"

I noticed Tate eyeing her a little too obviously. Jen slapped him on the arm, and he pretended to be wounded. Thankfully, Jen forgave him quickly, because I really wasn't in the mood to hear them arguing, and I doubted anyone who came along with us to party would be, either.

We went over to the couple.

"From around here?" Tate asked.

I sat down on the sand next to the girl and brought Elias down with me. I hoped they wouldn't take offense to us invading their space like that.

They didn't seem to mind. "No, we're from Galveston," the guy answered.

"And Raleigh," the girl added.

"We're from Indiana," I said, smiling at her.

Tate wrapped Jen in his arms from behind, probably his way of making her feel better about his straying eyes from before. "I'm Tate, this is Jen," he said, then introduced everyone else. "Johanna. Grace. And that's my brother, Caleb."

"I'm Bray," I said. "This is my fiancé, Elias."

We had long ago given up using false names.

The girl sat up and brushed the sand away from her hands. "Cool to meet you," she said. "I'm Camryn and this is *my* fiancé, Andrew." She had a pretty smile and an air of kindness to her. Andrew had bright green eyes and two distinct dimples that set evenly in his cheeks when he smiled.

Elias reached out to shake their hands.

Tate said, "We're heading to a private spot on a beach about thirty minutes from here." I knew that was a serious bit of misinformation, but if he told them it was a longer drive than that they probably wouldn't have come. "It's a great secluded party spot. You're both welcome to come along."

Camryn turned to Andrew. They seemed to be having some kind of inner conversation.

Andrew then said to Tate, "Sure. We can follow you out."

"Kick ass," Tate said.

The two of them grabbed their belongings and followed us off the beach and to the parking lot.

"They seem pretty cool," Elias said. I was sitting on his lap in the backseat, my head hitting the roof every time the Jeep would drive over even the slightest bump. "Did you see those tats they had?"

"Yeah, that was some sick ink," Tate said from the driver's seat. He glanced over at Jen in the passenger's seat. "Makes me want to get another one."

Jen rolled her eyes and went back to painting her toenails, her feet propped on the dashboard. I wondered how she could paint in the moving Jeep without getting turquoise nail polish all over her feet.

It was dark by the time we got there.

"You probably shouldn't have told them it was only a thirty-minute drive," Grace said beside me. She was sitting halfway on Caleb's lap and her hip kept bumping into mine, making the ride that much more uncomfortable.

"Yeah, you're probably right," Tate said.

We turned onto a partially paved road and the last couple of minutes of the drive were the worst as the Jeep shook and jolted over the broken road littered with potholes and debris. My head felt like a battering ram. The headlights bounced through the darkness until finally the road opened up into a wide space of sand and rocks.

Camryn and Andrew pulled up next to us in their black vintage car and shut off the engine.

"Hopefully they won't be too pissed," Tate added and hopped out of the Jeep.

Without hesitation, the rest of us got out quickly. I stretched my legs and rubbed my calves and the lower part of my back with my fingertips. Elias came around behind me and massaged the back of my neck. I let out a soft moan. "I don't know how much more piling up in that Jeep I can handle." In response, he kissed my bare shoulder.

Tate lifted the ice chest from the back of the Jeep and dropped it in the sand.

"We've got plenty of beer," he said, raising the lid and reaching inside. He tossed a bottle of Corona to Andrew.

Elias and I stepped up beside Camryn. Tate popped the cap on another bottle of Corona and offered it to her.

"Thanks," she said and took it.

"If you've got any blankets, might want to bring one," Tate said. Jen joined him then, prancing over in her skimpy white bikini. I think she may have felt a little threatened by Camryn, but not so much that she treated her badly. "And I've got a kick-ass system in this baby," Tate added, patting the back of the Jeep. "So I've also got the music covered."

Andrew popped the trunk on his car and grabbed a blanket.

"Where are my shorts?" Camryn asked, rummaging around in their backseat.

"Right here," Andrew said. He tossed them over the car toward her, and she caught them.

"I don't plan on swimming in that abyss at night," I heard her say as she slipped the shorts on over her red bikini bottoms.

"I'm glad I'm not the only one!" I said. I was always afraid of swimming in the ocean at night.

She smiled at me over the roof of their car and then shut the door. "Have you been out here before?"

Tate and everyone else were walking toward the beach carrying all of our stuff. As usual, Tate left the doors open on the Jeep.

The speakers blasted rock music; Tate and Caleb's mutual playlist, which consisted mostly of some singer named Dax and several different bands he had been in. Last night it was Pantera. The night before, old-school Snoop Dogg. All of our musical tastes had no boundaries, really.

"We were out here last night," I answered, "but Elias got drunk way too early and started puking up his insides, so I drove us back to our hotel."

Elias shook his head at me, disappointed. I think I embarrassed him.

Camryn and Andrew followed us down to the beach, where Tate was already setting up camp. Tate tossed a match onto a pile of tree branches and ignited the lighter fluid he had squirted all over the pile. Fire curled up and over the top of the branches and illuminated the darkness. Elias and I sat down with two beach towels next to Camryn and Andrew. Tate and the others were on a giant blanket.

I noticed Johanna was seriously checking Andrew out. I was put off by it, but I never said anything. It was rude the way she kept eyeing Andrew with his fiancée sitting right there. I had never really had much reason to dislike her until I witnessed this. She sat next to Caleb, the guy she had been screwing for no telling how long, making sure her pose was natural but at the same time sensual, as if she hoped Andrew would notice her barely tanned skin underneath her hot pink bikini, which barely held her boobs in place. At one point, I saw her twist her long, blonde hair and drape it over her shoulder on one side, as if to mimic the way that Camryn wore hers. I thought *I* had issues. No, Johanna had me beat in the issues department. And I may have been promiscuous, but I had standards. Johanna didn't know the concept.

"Those are some wicked fuckin' tattoos," Tate pointed out.

Camryn pulled away from Andrew's chest to give us all a better look. She raised her arm above her head and exposed her side, as well.

"Yeah, no doubt," I said, totally fascinated by the ink and wanting some of my own more and more. I crawled across the sand toward them to get a better look. "I've been curious about yours."

"Turn around here, babe, and show them how it fits," Andrew said and lifted Camryn around on his lap. He lay down on the sand and brought her body down on top of his.

They lined up their tattoos to form a seamless picture, and my eyes grew wide with fascination and envy. I didn't even know the story behind it yet, but my heart ached just seeing the two of them lying together like that, like two pieces forming one whole person right in front of my eyes. Momentarily, I thought of me and Elias. I pictured the two of us in their place. Andrew's half of the tattoo was of a woman wearing a long, graceful see-through white gown that was pressed against the sensual curves of her body by the wind. Tendrils of flowing fabric blew behind her as she reached out her arms to the male figure inked on Camryn's ribs. I gaped down at the detail, mesmerized by the beautiful complexity of every perfect line. The tattoos were enormous, stretching from the tops of their ribs down almost to their hips.

I glanced back at Elias with an idea rampant on my face. He looked nervous. And he should've been, because he knew what I was thinking: that I was ready to drag him to the closest tattoo shop.

"That. Is. Awesome," I said, looking back at Camryn and Andrew. "Who are they?"

"Orpheus and Eurydice," Andrew answered. "From the Greek legend."

"A tragic tale of true love," Camryn added.

Andrew squeezed his arms around her.

"Well, nothing seems tragic about the two of you," Tate said and lit up a cigarette.

I finally managed to pry myself away. "I think it's beautiful," I said as I made my way back to sit between Elias's legs. "And I guess it better be, because I know that had to hurt like hell."

"Yeah, it definitely hurt," Camryn said. "But it was worth every hour of pain."

We all sat around the blazing bonfire and talked mostly about benign things for a long time, but it didn't take long for Camryn and me to hit it off. Even before she started getting buzzed and overly talkative, we talked more than anyone. Normally it would be me and Grace, but she was too wrapped up in Caleb this time to be my sidekick. At one point, I was so into my conversation with Camryn, and I felt so comfortable with her, that I almost slipped up and mentioned we lived in Georgia. Elias noticed how close I was getting to saying things I shouldn't, and that was when he entered the conversation and started talking about concerts we had all been to.

"Maroon 5 are great live," I said.

"I know!" Camryn said with excitement in her eyes. "I saw them in concert with my best friend, Nat, and they were amazing! Not too many bands who sound almost just like they do on their album."

"Yeah, that's the truth," I said and took the last drink of my beer. "Did you say you're from North Carolina?"

Camryn sat Indian style on the sand.

"Yeah, but Andrew and I don't really live there now."

"Where do you live?" Tate asked. He took a long pull from his cigarette and held the smoke in his lungs. "Texas?"

"No, we sort of…travel," Camryn said. She had pretty bright blue eyes; I'd noticed them when the light from the fire hit her face at just the right angle. And a cute, oval-shaped face.

"Travel?" I asked. "What, like driving around in an RV?"

"Not exactly," Camryn said. "We just have the car."

"Why do you travel?" Johanna asked.

I saw the way Andrew looked at her upon hearing her voice, and he wasn't pleased, to say the least. It was pretty obvious he had noticed the way she had been eyeballing him all night. He ignored her and looked back over at us. "We play music together."

"What, you're like in a band?" Johanna asked with a valley-girl accent.

I rolled my eyes. Her desperation was getting ridiculous.

Andrew looked right at her this time, which kind of surprised me. "Sort of," he said, but that's all the answer he gave her. I realized it was intentional.

"What kind of music do you play?" Caleb asked. He sat, as usual, between Grace and Johanna, not caring in the slightest what anyone thought of him being with two girls.

Andrew took a drink of his beer and answered, "Classic rock, blues and folk rock, stuff like that."

"You'll have to play for us!" I said excitedly. I was buzzed myself by this time.

Camryn turned around to look at Andrew, and she was animated by the idea. "You could. You've got the acoustic in the backseat."

"Nah, I'm not up to it right now," Andrew said.

"Oh come on, baby, why not?"

"Yeah, man, if you've got a guitar with you and know how to play, that'd be awesome," Tate jumped in.

Caving to the peer pressure, and probably more so to not wanting to say no to his fiancée, Andrew got up and walked to his car.
He came back carrying a guitar.

"You're going to sing with me," he said to Camryn as he sat
back down beside her.

"Nooo! I'm too buzzed!" She kissed him on the mouth and sat
next to me and Elias, probably to get out of it.

"All right, what do you want me to sing?" Andrew asked.

"Hey, whatever you feel like, man," Tate said.

Andrew sat there in thought for a moment as though shuffling through a hundred different songs in his mind and decided on
"Ain't No Sunshine" by Bill Withers. My mom used to listen to that
song all the time, so I was no stranger to it. And damn, Andrew
could sing. As if he wasn't already tattooed and gorgeous and could
play the guitar like a pro, his voice was something to be reckoned
with. I sat up between Elias's legs, my body swaying side to side
with the music, letting it run through me.

All of us were getting into it, even Elias, who wasn't at all
threatened by Andrew, because he knew he had no reason to be. I'd
made sure of that early on.

Andrew belted out the last chorus and the song ended.

"That was great!" I said excitedly.

"Man, you weren't fuckin' playin' around," Tate said and lit up
a joint.

"Play another one," I said, laying back against Elias. He
wrapped me in his arms, and I felt his chin press softly against the
top of my head.

Tate passed the joint to Camryn first but she just looked at it
for a moment. She shook her head at Tate and said, "No thanks—I
think I'll just stick to liquor tonight."

Andrew played a few more songs by the bonfire and Camryn finally did sing one with him. They were both very talented. I thought they should be playing shows somewhere.

Tate came back from the Jeep carrying a stack of Solo cups, a bottle of Seagram's 7, and a bottle of Sprite. Jen went to work mixing drinks and passing them around.

"Have at it, man," Tate urged Andrew. "Don't worry about driving anywhere tonight. Cops don't even know about this place."

"Yeah, sure, I'll have a cup," Andrew said.

When it came Camryn's turn, the two of them went back and forth about whether or not it was a good idea, but ultimately she decided that it was. She had already turned down the joint.

Maybe it was the weed and the alcohol, but before too long I was talking to Camryn about, of all things, tampon brands and eventually the best kind of shampoo. She asked me about my bracelets, to which I made sure not to let her get as close as Grace had the other night at the beach house, worried it would be a similar scene all over again. I could open up to Elias about what I did, but no one else out here had any business knowing. The music continuously funneled from the Jeep.

"Andrew, I need to pee," Camryn said.

He took her cup from her hand and set it on the sand. "I need to take a piss too," he said.

Tate pointed behind them with another cigarette between his fingers and said, "Go around that way. There's no glass and shit to step on over there."

Andrew set his cup next to Camryn's and helped her up. Once they slipped into the darkness, Elias thought it was a good idea, too, and stood up. "I'll be back in a few," he said. He looked down at me. "You need to use the bathroom?"

"Nah, I'm good," I said.

He smiled and walked in the opposite direction of Andrew and Camryn, past the vehicles, to relieve himself.

Grace left Caleb's lap and came over to me, laying her head on my shoulder.

"Have you been watching Johanna?" she whispered.

I looked over at Johanna trailing her fingers down Caleb's bicep muscle, a vacant look on her face. She always appeared high or just not all there in general. I wondered what went on inside her head, other than thoughts of Caleb, and now this new guy, Andrew. Eventually, I had to believe that nothing else went on inside there.

"You mean her drooling over Andrew? Yeah, kind of hard not to notice. Doesn't Caleb care?"

Grace chuckled and raised her head from my shoulder. "Not really," she said. "He pulled me behind the Jeep earlier and told me he wanted her gone."

"That doesn't surprise me."

She shook her head, glanced over at Johanna and Caleb again, and then added, "There's something seriously wrong with that girl."

"That's an understatement. How long have you known her?"

"Just a few months. She moved into my apartment building."

Caleb got up and started digging around in his pockets. It may have been just to get away from Johanna for a moment.

"Why doesn't he just tell her that he's not into her anymore?"

"Because she lives in Virginia," Grace said quietly. "He may be an ass sometimes, but he won't leave her stranded so far away from home. I told him when we were at the Jeep he should just get her a bus ticket back to Norfolk."

"What did he say to that?"

Grace brushed her long, dark hair away from her shoulders. She drew her knees up, leaned back, and propped herself up on her elbows.

"He said that's probably what he'll do."

"Hey," I said, "why are you with him, anyway? I mean, he doesn't exactly seem like boyfriend material."

Grace smiled and let her bare knees sway side to side. "I'm not lookin' for a boyfriend," she said. "I just want to have fun. Got out of a bad relationship not long ago, and I ain't in any hurry to jump into another one."

I could understand where she was coming from. Not that I felt the same way, though.

"So, what did Elias say about your wrists?" Grace asked, lowering her voice.

I crossed my legs and hid my hands in between them, my fingers moving over the bracelets absently. I didn't want to talk about this, but I really liked Grace and I wanted her to know that.

"He was upset, naturally," I said. "But we're OK. Elias understands me."

Grace smiled slimly, glanced at my wrists, and then let her body slouch farther in between her shoulders.

"I never told anyone this before," she said, looking out ahead of her, "but I had an older brother. Jacob. He was in the military. Two years in Iraq." She glanced at me once and said, "He put a bullet in his head six weeks after he got home," and then she looked away. Her gaze was fixated on the darkness, but I knew she was seeing her brother's face.

My heart fell. I twisted around on the sand to face her. "That's...so fucked up, Grace. I'm so sorry."

She nodded and smiled a little. "Yeah, that's the best way to describe it. Fucked up. He was in a bad place for a really long time. No one knew." She gestured one hand in a backtracking fashion. "Well, we *knew* something was wrong. He was different when he came home. Isolated. And he had real bad anger issues. But we didn't know he was capable of suicide." Then her face fell, shadowed by the memory and her own guilt, which I knew she'd probably carry around forever. "We didn't know until it was too late. The second chancers are lucky." She pointed at me then, and her smile grew. "You're lucky. Don't ever forget it."

I didn't really know what to say to that. I wanted to agree with her, but knowing that her brother wasn't so lucky, I felt awful and thought it best to say nothing at all.

Grace changed the mood quickly as she raised up and dusted the sand from the palms of her hands. Then she reached around and pulled her bikini bottoms from her butt crack.

"Damn, I have too much ass to be wearing Jen's bathing suits," she grumbled as the bikini elastic snapped around her butt cheek.

"I think I do, too," I said and laughed with her.

Tate and Jen were making out over on the blanket, Jen's small body looking like a permanent fixture on top of his. Johanna looked bored sitting over there by herself, twirling her hair around her index finger. Caleb walked from cup to cup, dropping something into each one as he passed by.

"What's that?" I asked when he made it over to us.

One side of Caleb's mouth lifted into a grin. He dropped whatever it was into my cup. And then one in Elias's.

"Just a little something to shake this party up," he said. "Completely harmless, I swear."

I wasn't used to seeing Caleb so mischievous. He hardly ever smiled.

Grace raised her cup that had been sitting beside her in the sand. "Don't forget about me," she said.

"Hell no, baby," he said and dropped something into hers last.

I wasn't sold at first, and Caleb noticed.

"I swear!" he repeated with a breathy laugh.

Grace leaned in toward me then and said, "If anything, this stuff will make you and Elias want to do sexual shit you've never tried before." She grinned, reaching out her hand to Caleb, and he helped her to her feet.

I was so sidetracked by her comment and my already intense high that without really thinking about it, I took a heavy drink from my cup.

Elias emerged from the darkness after his bathroom break just before Camryn and Andrew did.

I never said anything about what Caleb had done. It wasn't that I was intentionally hiding it. I just didn't think about it anymore. At the time, I was already on my way to being drunk. I had shared three joints over the course of the night and was pretty fried. My judgment was severely impaired. I didn't think of what Caleb did as being wrong, because the high side of me believed him when he said it was perfectly harmless. After all, he and Grace were doing it. He had even put some in his own brother's cup. I know what I did was wrong and stupid and thoughtless and reckless and a thousand other things. I know. But everybody makes mistakes. This just happened to be one of my most regrettable.

# NINETEEN

## Elias

*I* remembered taking a piss. I vaguely remembered cutting the end of my pinky toe on the way back to the bonfire on a jagged rock that had been hidden underneath the sand. I remembered sitting down next to Bray, drinking my gin and Sprite, laughing and carrying on with her and everyone else.

But sometime during that—I can't recall when because time itself seemed to shift abruptly—everything changed. Bray was lying on the sand next to me, looking up at the stars, laughing and pointing and talking about how colorful they were and then—

I was standing by the ocean. I didn't know how I had gotten there. I looked behind me. The bonfire had been reduced to a dim orange glow, barely holding on to the oxygen it needed to keep from burning completely out. And then—

I was sitting on a rock. The ocean water was pushing against it two inches away from my feet. It gurgled and spit and told me to move. I looked down. The water was black. I looked over, back toward the bonfire again. It had completely faded, and only a thin coil of smoke rose above the branches. I stared at my hands in front of my face and I could see every line like on a map. I ran the tip of my finger over each one: every road, every river, every shortcut. I could hear my heart beating in my ears like a bass drum, constant and unrelenting. I could taste grains of sand between my teeth and trapped in my gums and in the creases of my lips. I thought it was glass and I panicked. But then I was calm when the glass dissolved in my mouth.

I was alone. Bray was gone. Everyone was gone. It was just me sitting there on the rock. I heard music. "Night is the Notion" by Dax Riggs blasted through the speakers. I heard someone else singing along with it, but I couldn't see anyone. I was completely alone.

Time seemed to skip backward, then—

"Holy fuck, Tate," I heard Jen's voice say, but I couldn't see her anywhere. "This is some good shit. Ho-ly fuck. I'm seeing rainbows and shit. It's the Reading Fucking Rainbow...." She began to sing the *Reading Rainbow* song.

And then I woke up. It was the next morning.

I sat there on the sand for a long time, trying to pull my head together. I don't remember doing anything last night except gin and weed. But I was definitely on something.

And I was *pissed*.

My attention was diverted when I saw Bray walk quickly across the sand and kneel down next to the blonde, Camryn, trying to comfort her as she vomited violently.

"Get off of him!" Jen screamed at the top of her lungs

Andrew was fighting Tate, walloping on him with his fists.

"Andrew!" Camryn tried to scream, but it came out raspy and painful. She was clearly in a bad physical state. She couldn't even stand on her own.

"What the fuck is wrong with you, man?!" Tate roared.

He was trying to back away from Andrew, but Andrew just

kept swinging. He punched him over and over, eventually knocking Tate in the sand.

Caleb tackled Andrew from the side and they both rolled across the sand away from Tate. Andrew grabbed Caleb by the throat and lifted him over his body, throwing him hard against the sand and was on top of him in seconds. He punched Caleb three times before Tate was behind him, pulling him off.

"Chill the fuck out, man!" Tate shouted, trying to defuse the situation. But Andrew rounded on Tate and caught him in the chin with an uppercut. Tate staggered backward, holding his hand over his jaw.

I knew Tate wasn't going to take much more. Rage had begun to churn in his eyes.

"You drugged us! I'll fucking *kill* you!" Andrew roared.

From the corner of my eye I saw Camryn stumble to her feet and start running toward the fight, and before I could do anything, Caleb barreled straight toward Andrew again and knocked Camryn down as she came between them.

I ran out after them.

Andrew couldn't hold his own against both Tate and Caleb at the same time for long. I remembered hearing Jen say the night before that Tate had the drugs, and so I did the only thing I knew to be right. I jumped into the fight to help Andrew, despite Tate being our so-called friend.

"Move!" I growled as I pushed Camryn out of the way, both to keep her from getting hurt further and so that I could get in there. Tate had it coming. He shouldn't have drugged us.

"Stay back here with me," I heard Bray say as she dragged Camryn the rest of the way to the side.

I punched Caleb first.

The four of us fought hard, exchanging blows so fast I almost couldn't tell who was hitting who. But I ended up fighting Caleb more. Andrew focused on Tate. By the time the fight was over, all of us were bleeding from the mouth or the nose. My jaw felt like it had been beaten on with a hammer.

"Just back off of him!" Tate said to Caleb, grabbing him from behind by both arms and securing him there. Caleb was going to come after me again. Tate was just ready to end this.

I did the right thing, I thought, but I had also sided with the people who weren't helping Bray and me get around. I knew that after this, she and I were screwed. Unless Andrew and Camryn decided to become our new ride, Bray and I were going to be right back in the situation we were in before we met Tate and everyone at that hotel.

But something deep down told me that Andrew and Camryn weren't going to be as accommodating.

Andrew had murder in his eyes. Even when he looked at me. I couldn't blame him. If I were in his shoes—I *was* in his shoes. I walked behind him over to Bray, who was helping Camryn as she lay next to a stinking puddle of vomit being soaked up into the sand.

"Shit," Andrew said, looking at Bray. "Will you run to my car and get a bottle of water out of the ice chest in the back?"

Bray nodded quickly, stood up, and ran off to do it.

Andrew rolled Camryn over onto his legs and he brushed her hair away from her face.

"They fucking drugged us, baby," he said.

"I'm going to kill that bitch. I swear to God, Andrew," Camryn said.

They started talking about something entirely different than the drugs or the fight, I assumed. Something about one of the girls.

I had no idea, but it wasn't about Bray, and that was all that mattered to me.

I stepped up closer and crouched down next to Andrew. "I'm sorry, man, we didn't know. I swear," I said.

"I believe you," Andrew said.

Bray scurried back with the water, and Andrew reached out for the bottle. He twisted off the cap and poured some in his hand first, wiping Camryn's forehead and mouth.

"Look man, I'm sorry," Tate said, coming up behind us. "Didn't think you'd mind. We just dropped some in everybody's drinks. We didn't bring you out here with any fucked-up intentions."

Andrew released Camryn carefully, whirled around, and punched Tate again.

"Please, Andrew!" Camryn shouted.

I grabbed Andrew and Caleb grabbed Tate and we held them off of each other.

Finally, Andrew relented and shook me off. He helped Camryn to her feet. "Let's go," he said.

They grabbed their guitar and blanket and headed straight for their car.

"Come on, Bray," I said, taking her hand. "If we have to, we'll walk."

She locked her fingers with mine and we set out in the same direction. I grabbed my shirt from the sand, and Bray grabbed her flip-flops as we walked toward them. Andrew was putting their stuff in the trunk as we approached. He went over to his side of the car, laid his arms across the roof and then dropped his head in between them.

"God damn it!" he shouted and hit the roof with his fist.

Camryn, probably wanting him to cool off before she said anything, got inside the car and shut the door.

"I'll give you two a ride back if you want," Andrew said just before we walked past.

Bray and I discussed it with our eyes and got inside the car.

"Thanks," I said from the backseat, but I don't think either of them heard me.

Bray sat with her head on my shoulder the rest of the way back, but I got the feeling maybe she was mad at me. She didn't say a word.

Andrew dropped us off at the hotel, and that was the last time we ever saw them.

We were alone again. No car, no money, no nothing.

Bray sat down on a bright yellow concrete parking space barrier, resting her elbows on her knees and her head in her hands. I sat down beside her.

"What Tate did was wrong, Bray. I had to jump in."

"Tate didn't do it!" she shouted, lifting her head from her hands.

"What do you mean?"

She took a deep breath and laced her fingers together, dangling between her knees. She gazed out at the half-empty parking lot.

"Tate had nothing to do with it," she said. "Caleb did it. Tate was too busy with Jen to even notice what Caleb had done."

"Wait—how do you know this?" What I really wanted to ask was, *You* knew *about this?* But I was too busy trying to make myself believe that couldn't possibly be the truth.

Bray wouldn't look at me. "I saw Caleb do it," she said, even though I could tell she didn't want to. "He walked around dropping something in everyone's drinks."

I stood up. It took me a long moment, but I finally said, "How could you know this and not tell anyone?" I was extremely pissed off, I felt so betrayed, but I was doing whatever I could to hold it all inside. As much as I loved her, I wanted to walk away from her right then. I began to pace.

"I know I fucked up, Elias. I know and I'm sorry. I wasn't thinking straight—"

"Yah *think*?!" My head reared back and my hands dropped at my sides. "Bray, you should've *told* me! Jesus Christ!" I threw my hands up above me. "I went to jail once because of this very same thing! Or did you forget about that?"

She started crying, burying her face in her hands. I wasn't about to console her, not this time. This was almost unforgivable.

"I can't take back what I did," she said, her voice strained by tears. "And I can't make you believe me when I tell you I didn't say anything because it didn't seem like a big deal. I was fried. I'd drunk a lot. I. Fucked. Up." She stood up from the concrete barrier and threw her hands up in the air. "I made a bad decision! It definitely wasn't my first, and you know it won't be my last!"

"You're right," I interrupted. "It wasn't your first. Two weeks ago you accidently caused a girl's death. And you didn't want to report it. That was one of the biggest mistakes you ever made in your life."

She stood with her mouth agape.

"It was *your* idea!" she shrieked. "You had just as much to do with me running as I did! Don't you *dare* put this all on *my* shoulders!"

She shoved the palms of her hands against my chest, but not with enough strength to knock me over. "God damn it, Elias!"

I grabbed her by the elbows. "Stop screaming!" I screamed back at her. I shook her and then my voice calmed and I said with more composure, "Just calm down. You're right. I'm as much to blame. I shouldn't have said that to you."

She let out a long, unsteady breath and then she dropped her head between her shoulders.

"What are we going to do now?" she said, her voice strained with worry.

I pulled her body against mine and wrapped her in my arms. "There's nothing else we can do except go home."

"But I'm scared," she said, the side of her face pressed against my chest muscles. "I'm *so* scared…"

"I know," I whispered and squeezed her gently. "But we can't keep doing this, especially with nothing but the clothes on our backs. We can go back now. Maybe it's not too late."

On the outside, it appeared I was only thinking of our current situation. But on the inside, where Bray couldn't hear, I was thinking a lot about getting her some help. Every day the decisions she chose to make were becoming more irrational. I knew that I couldn't help her on my own, that as much as I wanted to be able to, that even as deeply as I loved her, it would never be enough to save her from herself. Something dark began to grow inside of me, a frightening feeling that I couldn't quite read but I knew was very tragic.

Just then, Tate's black Jeep came humming through the parking lot toward us. Bray pulled away from me and stood at my side, her hand clenched tight within mine. I wasn't up for any more fighting, and I was prepared to surrender and let Tate and Caleb know that.

Tate put the Jeep in Park and hopped out, leaving the motor running.

"Look, Tate," I said, putting up one hand, "I'm not going to fight you anymore. I did what I had to do back there and I'm not apologizing for it, either, but I'm done fighting."

Tate shook his head and laughed gently. "I'm not here to fight you, man," he said. "I came to pick the two of you up. Though I gotta admit, I thought you'd be long gone with the tattoo twins by now."

Bray and I glanced at one another. I was confused.

"No hard feelings," Tate said. "You were in the right, and I admit it. We shouldn't have done that without you knowing about it. If it was me, shit, man, I would've went off on you too."

"But it *wasn't* you," I pointed out and then looked toward Caleb sitting in the backseat. "Why didn't you say anything?"

Tate pretended to not understand. His smile transformed into something a bit more apprehensive. He forced a laugh. "What are you talking about?"

I put my back to the Jeep and lowered my voice. "Why did you take the blame for what Caleb did?"

Tate gave up trying to cover for him, sighed, and glanced back at Caleb once. Then he looked back at me.

"Because he's my brother," he said. "Caleb has some issues. He's on parole for some shit that went down back in Miami with a girl. If he gets into any more trouble, he'll go to jail for a long time. I'm just looking out for my little brother."

He reached out and patted my shoulder and then lit up a cigarette. "I'll talk to him," he added. He put the cigarette between his lips and took a long pull. "It's about time he and I had a brotherly heart-to-heart anyway. He's starting to fuck up a lot again."

I shook my head, resolved to take Bray and go back to Georgia now that I finally got her to somewhat entertain the idea. I looked at her. She looked at me. And then I said to Tate, "Look, I appreciate it, you coming back for us like that, but I think it's better that we go home." Bray's hand tightened around mine and at first I took it as her way of quietly agreeing with me, standing beside my decision, but that wasn't it at all. She caught my eye and I saw in hers nothing but pleading and refusal.

I tried to ignore it.

"Besides," I said to Tate, "your brother is unstable. I don't feel like I can trust him anymore."

I never trusted him really to begin with, but after what he did last night, what little trust I did have was gone. I now realized that in this particular situation, Bray was almost no better than Caleb. She knew what he had done and didn't tell anyone, just like Caleb. But I made up excuses for her: She wasn't on parole. She wasn't the one who dropped the drugs into everyone's drinks. She—who was I kidding? Bray was just as much at fault. The only difference was that I loved her.

"Caleb won't be a problem," Tate said, trying to change my mind. "Like I said, I'll talk to him. Shit, I've already had it out with him on the way here about what went down. He may be 'unstable' and a prick at times, but he always listens to me. And he knows I'll kick his ass if I have to."

"Elias?" Bray said softly. "Let's just go with them. Please."

I knew it had nothing to do with any of them but everything to do with being afraid to go back home and face what happened. I was going to refuse. I had it settled in my mind that Bray and I were going back to Georgia. Nothing that Tate could say or promise was going to change that.

But then I saw something flicker across Bray's features just as she let go of my hand and took a half step back. She wasn't going to go back with me. I knew by that look on her face, that pleading, solemn darkness that had consumed her—if I chose to go back, she would stay with them. I wouldn't be able to force her. I knew she wouldn't have *wanted* to leave me and that it would take everything in her to do it, but there was *no way* she was going back.

All I wanted to do was protect her.

I had already made up my mind by then to stay, but I wanted to know some things about Tate first, before I openly agreed.

"Why do you care where we go, anyway?" I asked.

Tate smiled and blew out a stream of smoke. "We just like having you around." He started gesturing with his cigarette hand. "I have to go back to work in a week. I had almost a full month of vacation time racked up at my job. If I didn't use it I was gonna lose it. So that's what I'm doing. And hell, it's been great. I'm getting paid to hop around Florida and party."

I never took him for the hard-working type, much less being *such* a hard worker that he had that much vacation time he had never used. This actually kind of blew my mind. And I felt very small all of a sudden. Here I was, jobless, homeless, standing in a parking lot with nowhere to go and no way to get there. I had worked all my life, from the age of sixteen. I helped my mom out with bills and groceries just about every month. Now, I felt as much a lowlife as that piece of shit who stole my car.

Tate went on, "Damn, man, I thought it was just going to be me, Jen, and my brother. Now, with Ditzy Dope-for-Brains and Grace the Powerpuff Girl back there, sometimes I feel like I'm going to lose my shit. As if Jen beating the shit out of me at least once a week and Caleb fuckin' up wasn't enough. You two are a breath of fresh air."

"She beats the shit out of you?" Bray asked with an air of serious disbelief.

Tate threw his head back and laughed. Then he flicked what was left of the cigarette across the parking lot. "Well, I let her, of course. I like it, she likes it but pretends she doesn't. It all works out." He shrugged and added, "So what do you say? Go back home or stay with us for just one more week and help keep me sane before I have to crawl back into that nut-suffocating suit?" He cocked his head to one side thoughtfully.

"You work in a suit?" Bray asked, her eyebrows drawing inward.

I admit, I was just as astonished by the possibility as she appeared to be.

Tate smiled with teeth. "Yeah. Unfortunately."

Jen slid the window down on the Jeep and yelled, "Baby, come on! Your gas light just dinged!"

Tate looked back at us with what I thought he meant as being puppy-dog eyes, but he looked more confident and impish than innocent.

I thought about it for a moment. Bray looked like she was holding her breath the whole time.

"All right," I said, and both of their faces lit up. "But seriously, man, talk to Caleb. I know you're his brother and all, but if he fucks up like that again, and Bray or I are involved, I won't come to you for permission to beat the fuck out of him."

Tate nodded. "It's a deal."

We shook on it and were on our way to Panama City.

# TWENTY

## Elias

*P*anama City was the turning point. I didn't think that things could get any worse, but lately rock bottom was just never the bottom anymore. We had stayed there for four days, and the week Tate had left of his vacation time was suspiciously extended.

It began on Sunday night when Tate got a phone call. We had been staying at the house of one of Caleb's friends, Adam. He was someone Caleb apparently had gone to college with. Like Tate and his job, I never took Caleb for the college type. Come to find out he had to drop out when he was sent to prison after that thing with the girl in Miami that Tate had mentioned to me previously.

Adam's house was several miles from the beach. I was glad for that, because I was getting sick of looking at the ocean and dusting sand out of my shoes.

I missed home. As much as I wanted to be with Bray, I missed the summer river parties and the southern lakes. I missed my mom's fried chicken on Friday nights. I missed hanging out in a friend's backyard with a beer and listening to the crickets and frogs with their strangely calming melodious racket during long summer nights. And the fireflies. Always the fireflies. But what I missed the most was my quiet life, the one where I went to work every day and came home to my own apartment and could kick back and watch television. I didn't have to worry about anything except maybe Mitchell. But he was fixable. This situation, I knew, wasn't.

As I sat on the back porch of Adam's house in Panama City, listening to Tate get upset while on that phone call, I pictured being home. I wondered—every single day, in fact—what life would've been like if that night at the river had never happened. I thought of Bray and how she came back into my life, and how everything was so perfect, the way I had always imagined it. A part of me couldn't help but blame her for how everything ended up…destroyed. I felt guilty for thinking that way, not only because it was half my fault, but because I didn't want to feel that way about her at all. I loved her so much. But I had begun to feel a lot of anger and resentment toward her, too. I…OK, I started to realize that Bray, despite all that I loved about her, was ruining her life and selfishly taking me down with her. And my tolerance for forgiveness was beginning to fade.

It was my fault as much as it was hers, but I had tried on several occasions to talk some sense into her. I tried to get her to go back. I knew I never should've let her leave in the first place. But I was weak in that moment, standing next to Jana's body with Bray next to me shattered and lost and afraid and in so much pain. It was a fucking mistake to run with her. I know. I fucking *know* it more than anyone. But I couldn't take back what I had done. All I could do was try to fix it along the way. But Bray fought me at every turn and for that I began to feel resentment.

"Listen, man," Tate said into his cell phone pressed to his ear. "I'll get it, all right? No—No, just hear me out. I'll bring it myself.

I can leave first thing in the morning after the bank opens and I can be in Corpus Christi by tomorrow night. Yeah. This is my cell phone number. Don't call Caleb about anything. No, just let me deal with it." He began to nod heavily as if wanting the call to be over with already. "I know, man. Do me a favor and don't deal with him anymore." A few more nods and broken sentences and he hung up. I saw his teeth grinding as the cell phone disappeared in his fist. I thought he was going to smash it on the concrete beam holding up the porch roof, but he calmed himself at the last second.

"I know it's none of my business, Tate, but why are you still covering for him? Sounds like some serious shit."

He sat down heavily in the empty wrought-iron chair. The cell phone clanked against the matching table as he tossed it carelessly on top. He ran both hands over the top of his head and let out a long, aggravated breath.

"And why are you covering for *her?*"

His question shocked me motionless. I don't think anything moved other than my eyes for a long while. It wasn't the manner in which he said it—there wasn't any bitterness to his tone—but that he said it at all. Because he knew more about me and Bray than I assumed he did.

"Maybe I'm out of line," Tate went on, "or I have no idea what I'm talking about, but in my opinion"—he pointed at me—"I think you'd do anything for that girl."

"I guess I would," I admitted.

"The question is, how far would you go?"

I looked away and thought about it. Then I turned back and said, "Probably as far as you'd go for your brother."

Tate nodded, slouched down a little in the chair with his long legs splayed out in front of him, his fingers locked over his stomach.

"Then you just answered your own question. Why are you two running, anyway?"

"Who said we're running from anything?"

Tate smiled faintly and shook his head. "It's kind of obvious. Even though your car and your shit was stolen—which, by the way, you never got the police involved in—I haven't seen either one of you try to call anyone back in Indiana. No *Hey Mom, we're doin' great*, or *Yeah, bro, we've been partying with this masochist pothead and his asshole brother, but we're still alive*." He laughed and then shook his finger at me. "You're not homeless—you're both too groomed and healthy for that. What did you do, Elias? Or rather, what did *she* do?"

I looked away from his eyes and began staring at a porch light on the other side of the street.

Tate raised his back from the chair and leaned over, letting his hands dangle between his knees. "No disrespect, but your girlfriend, fiancée, whatever, she's a loose cannon. Don't get me wrong, I think she's a great girl from what I know about her. But she seems unstable."

I wanted to punch him, but my conscience wouldn't let me. I knew what he was saying wasn't far off the mark. So I sucked it up and left it alone.

He leaned back in the chair again and locked his hands behind his head. "I guess sometimes good people do bad things, almost always in the name of love." He laughed lightly. "But after all is said and done, is what we do really 'bad' or just necessary?"

Tate surprised me the more I got to know him. I wondered how he got where he was when he had such a strong hold on his own life despite all the partying he did, but then I realized that he and I weren't really so different.

"It's all right if you two don't want to go to Texas," he said. "It's probably better that you don't, anyway. Maybe Adam will let you stay here until I get back."

Then suddenly he added as if an afterthought, "Well, whatever you're covering up for her, by now you're probably in as much trouble as she is."

*What just happened?* I thought as I stared right through Tate. Just minutes ago I was full of resentment and had started to envision my next conversation with Bray. I was going to lay down the law and tell her that I was going home and she was going with me if I had to drag her back kicking and screaming. But out of nowhere, the resentment was gone. I now realized Tate was in a similar situation with Caleb, and I wasn't so alone in my plight. I wasn't the only guy running around doing stupid things for a person that he happened to love. Maybe I took Tate's words and subconsciously twisted them into advice, because deep down I was struggling to find justification for what I had done and what I continued to do.

I never asked Tate exactly what Caleb did to warrant a trip to Corpus Christi. I didn't think it was right, since I wouldn't tell him any more than I had about us, so it was only fair. But I left Tate at the table that night with a new outlook of moving forward with Bray. I still knew that what we were doing was wrong, but I wanted desperately to find another way out of it. I couldn't let Bray go to prison. Like Tate had said about Caleb, she wouldn't make it in there.

So from that point on, I made it my mission to use the time we were away with Tate to figure out how to get her out of this. It wasn't just about running anymore. What I was doing now had purpose.

Later that night, after Tate and Caleb argued behind closed doors in the guest bedroom, the only agreement the two of them came to was that Johanna and Grace had to go back to Norfolk. Everyone in the house heard the conversation:

"Dammit, Caleb! Why do I keep having to bail you out of shit? You owe this guy *eight thousand* dollars. What'd you do with the money, Caleb? You know what, I don't even wanna know."

A loud *bang* vibrated down the hallway. I could imagine it being Tate's fist against the wall inside the room.

"I hope he doesn't tear my place up," Adam said from the couch. He was a tall, skinny guy with sandy-brown hair and stylish black-rimmed glasses that made him look like a stereotypical intellect sipping a latte.

"We're leaving in the morning," I heard Tate say with a demanding edge in his voice. "I'm going to pay this guy off and then I'm done. I'm fucking done, little brother. Eight thousand dollars is about all I have left in savings."

"Nobody asked you to bail me out."

"If I don't, who *will*, Caleb? Dad? You've already milked him dry of his savings. Kyle? Shit, bro, if he finds out I'm helping you he's going to kick *my* ass. Everly? Baby sister is siding with Kyle, bro. I'm all you've got *left*."

Then he said, "Why don't you just call Mom? Talk to her and see how she's doing? You haven't called her in a year. You know she'll let you move back in. You can get away from all that bullshit. Get a decent job and start putting your life back together. Maybe Cera will take you—"

"Don't even go there," Caleb snapped. "Just don't—"

A long, dark silence lingered.

"I think it's time you sent Johanna and Grace home," Tate said. "It's not a good idea to take them to Corpus Christi."

"Yeah, and what about your new freeloader friends out there?"

"I don't know yet," Tate said. "But you need to worry about you and this shit you've gotten us into. Send the girls home."

"I'll take them to the bus station tonight," Caleb said.

Grace and Bray locked eyes from across the room upon hearing that. They both looked dejected. But I could tell right away that Bray was forcibly trying to hide the fact that she was utterly heartbroken. I hated to see it. I hated to know that the one person Bray was closest to besides me was about to walk out of her life and that there wasn't anything I could do about it.

Thirty minutes later after the arguing and Tate scouring the house and outside in the yard for his keys, Bray and Grace were saying their good-byes.

"Here's my number," Grace said as she slipped a torn-off piece of a magazine page into Bray's hand. "Call me when you get back to Indiana. Maybe we can visit sometime." They fell into a tight embrace.

"As soon as I get another cell phone, I'll call you with my number," Bray said.

I could tell that Bray was on the verge of tears. They hadn't known each other long, but they'd bonded, and Bray always had a hard time bonding with people. Besides me, Lissa had been her closest friend growing up, and it turned out that Lissa wasn't as close to Bray as she thought she was. As I stood there watching the two of them say good-bye, I thought to myself how I wished it could've been different, that they could've met under better circumstances. Because I knew that once Grace walked out that door, they'd never see each other again.

# TWENTY-ONE

# Elias

Caleb drove Grace and Johanna to the bus station.

Adam came strolling out of the shower wearing a pair of black running shorts and a towel draped around the back of his neck.

"Since Caleb will be chickless tonight, he can have the couch," Adam said, drying the back of his hair. Then he pointed at Bray and me. "You're welcome to crash in the office. The couch bed in there is really comfortable." He stopped just before he made his way down the hall. "Though if I were you I'd change the sheets."

This was good news. I didn't think I could sleep another night crammed onto the couch in the den with Bray like we had the past few nights at Adam's.

Adam disappeared inside his bedroom like he did at the same time every night. Tate was outside on the back porch again. All of us thought it best to just stay out of his way while he was seething over this thing with Caleb. Except for Jen, of course, who was outside trying to talk to him and calm him down. Even she knew better than to act her usual self around him while he was like this.

Secretly, I envied the two of them, the chaotic yet strong relationship they had.

I wanted to be alone with Bray for a while. I got up and took her hand. "Want to go for a walk?"

She smiled up at me. It was such an innocent and sweet smile that I felt even guiltier for the resentment I was feeling.

"Lead the way," she said and placed her hand into mine.

We left the house and walked down the street for a long time, then we cut through a parking lot toward a baseball field. There were two light poles near the chain-link fence at the end of the field that cast a dull gray glow over the dirt and white painted lines. We slipped through an unlocked gate near a dugout and walked out past the pitcher's mound and sat down on the grass.

"I hate it that Grace had to go," I told her.

She laid down beside me on the grass and looked up toward the sky. Thick clouds completely covered the stars. I sat upright next to her with my legs angled upward. I picked at a few blades of grass and rolled them in my fingertips.

"Yeah," Bray said with a trace of sadness in her voice. "But I still have *you*."

I smiled down at her. Tiny pieces of torn grass fell from my fingers and were carried off by the wind.

"Tate's really pissed about whatever Caleb did," I said.

"Yeah. He really is."

Silence fell between us again. I reached down and pulled a couple more blades of grass from beside my shoe.

"Elias?"

"Yeah?"

"What did you really bring me out here for?"

I had been trying to figure out how to tell her and also trying to figure out if this was what I needed to do.

Her hand touched my arm. I looked down at her and smiled faintly.

"Elias?" she asked again, being very patient.

"I'm going to be your witness," I said.

She rose up from the ground, a blank look in her eyes.

"What the hell do you mean?" She knew exactly what I meant.

"I can say that I was there when it happened." Already she was beginning to shake her head no. "No one can prove otherwise. I'll tell the police, a jury, whoever I need to, that I was there and I saw what happened and that it was an accident."

"No," she said with complete resolution in her eyes. "I won't let you do that."

"You don't have to *let* me," I said. "I'm going to be your witness."

She stood up and crossed her arms with her back to me.

"Bray?"

She snapped around. "No! I said no!" Her arms fell at her sides and her face was wild with anger and concern. "What if they ask you to take a lie detector test? Or, they get us in separate rooms—because they will—and one of us slips up and tells them something different?" Her voice began to rise. "Jesus, Elias! One tiny detail, one seemingly insignificant detail and they have us. They'll have *you*. They're trained to spot things like that! They're trained to trip us up!"

I stood up in front of her. "We have some time while we're still with Tate to get the story straight. Make it simple and straightforward. Don't include a bunch of small details. Just give them the basic picture and stick to it."

"No. No fucking way."

She turned her back to me again.

"We have to do *something*," I said. "We can't run for the rest of our lives, Bray. They'll catch us sooner than later. The longer we run, the worse we make it for ourselves."

She wouldn't respond or look at me. I watched her from behind as her head fell over forward between her rigid shoulders, her arms crossed again tightly over her stomach.

"Then I'll say it was me," I added.

Even with her back to me I could tell her face had locked up along with the rest of her body, as her head rose solidly from between her shoulders, she slowly turned around. I had never seen her look so stunned before.

Both of her hands came out in a flash and she shoved me hard, but I didn't fall. Then she grabbed my shoulders and shook me. "Don't *ever* say that again. You fucking hear me, Elias? Don't you *ever* say that!"

I just stared into her wild eyes, seemingly unfazed by her outburst. I needed to keep my cool, because one of us needed to be calm and it clearly wasn't going to be her.

I reached up and tried to cup her face in my hands but she shoved them away.

"I can't believe you said that!" she snapped.

"You can't believe I said it, or that I'd actually do it?"

"It doesn't matter. I won't let you go down for me."

She began to pace.

"I can't go down for you, but you'll let me go down *with* you?"

She froze. I knew my words would hurt her, but they needed to be said. Because it was exactly how I felt.

"There's not that much of a difference, Brayelle."

"Is that what this is about? You're just trying to prove a point?" Resentment laced her voice.

"What point would that be?"

She shook her head with dismay. She couldn't respond. Maybe she didn't understand her own question, I didn't know, but I admit even I was somewhat confused by my own. *Did I just openly blame her?* I thought to myself.

Not wanting her to feel that way even if it were true, I took her into my arms and kissed the top of her head.

"You're not going to lie for me and say you were there and you're not going to go down for me, either."

"Then what am I doing here with you?" I asked calmly, surrendering, knowing that her resolve was unshakable.

"Maybe you shouldn't be," she shot back, but I knew it wasn't something she wanted to say.

She stayed in my arms and didn't try to pull away. I wouldn't have let her if she did.

"Is that what you want, Elias? To leave?" She sighed and nuzzled her cheek against my chest muscle. "If you want to leave I'll understand." The pain was soft in her voice, but pain nonetheless. It wasn't to make me feel guilty at all, but it did anyway.

"Well, I'm not leaving you," I said. "But we need to figure out what we're going to do. Partying every night and running around with Tate isn't going to make this go away. A few more days. That's it, Bray. We need to figure this out in a few more days, or we're going back together and I'm going to be your witness."

"You can't do that."

"If it's the only option we have then I *will* do it."

I placed my hands on her arms and took one step back, looking down into her tightened face. "Just promise me that," I said. "If we don't think of anything else, you'll at least let me be your witness."

"What if I'm lying? Would you still be my witness?"

That caught me off guard. "I know you're not lying."

"How do you know?"

"Because I trust you. And because I know you."

Her gaze strayed, but it wasn't because she was hiding anything.

"Just promise me that you'll go along with it."

She didn't answer at first. I knew she didn't want to. Finally, she nodded.

"Good," I said and hugged her close to me again.

We stood there quietly for a moment. I had a feeling that even though she agreed, when the time came, if it ever did, there was a chance she might change her mind.

"Elias, what's going on with Caleb and Tate?" she changed the subject. "What if this is our last stop with them? I doubt Adam will want us here after Caleb leaves. And besides, I'd feel weird about staying anyway."

*Yeah, so would I*, I thought.

"I'll talk to Tate," I said. "Ask him to keep us around for a few more days at the most. Long enough for us to figure out our next move."

Bray didn't look convinced. "Yeah, but you heard him talking to Caleb. They sent Grace and Johanna back for a reason."

"I know," I said, but I knew she was right so it was all I said.

Thunder rumbled in the sky and the thick, dark clouds lit up in the distance, revealing what the tops of the trees looked like painted against the black backdrop that had shrouded them. The crawling branches that reached upward along the infinite dark looked ominous as the flash of light faded.

I felt a drop of rain. And then another.

"So much for a quiet walk together," Bray said.

And just then, the sky opened up and it began to pour. Bray shrieked and tried to cover herself unsuccessfully with her arms and then the screaming turned into laughter. We were both drenched in under five seconds. The rain pounded down so fast and so hard that we had to shout over the noise to hear each other; each drop like a million nails being thrust into the dirt on the baseball field.

"It's a long walk back!" I said.

Bray started spinning like a ballerina in the middle of the field. She laughed and raised her arms above her and turned her face upward toward the sky and just let the rain wash over her. She opened her mouth and spun around and around. I watched her for a moment, mesmerized by her innocence. I saw that little girl I met so long ago, running with me through that pasture without a worry in the world. Just seeing her like that, it made me smile, but deep down it also crushed me. I knew that she would never be that innocent again, that our life together would never be as carefree as it was when we were children.

"Dance with me!" she shouted.

"What?"

"Dance with me!"

I had heard her right the first time. I just didn't understand why here, why now.

"There's no music!" I said over the rain.

She grabbed my hand. "You don't hear that?!" she said, motioning to the patter of rain and thunder around us.

She started spinning around me and I stood in the same spot following her until she grabbed both of my hands and pulled on them. Next thing I knew, we were spinning together, holding each other's hands tightly and distributing equal weight on our arms. At first, I felt like an idiot and hoped Tate wasn't spying, or worse, Caleb. But I was quickly lost in Bray's laughter and her smile and her beautiful blue eyes. The thunder got louder, the lightning more intense. I was beginning to worry about us being out in the open like this, in the center of a baseball field just asking to be struck down by the finger of God. But soon, I didn't care. We were those two innocent children again, living free and loving life. And not even lightning could ruin this moment. It wouldn't dare.

We stopped spinning, and I twirled her around by her hands as I stood in place, and then I dipped her. Leaning over her body, I pressed my wet lips between her breasts as her white shirt was weighted down by the endless rain. I planted kisses up the center of her throat until I found her plump lips, dotted by droplets of rain. Rain washed in heavy rivulets over our faces, into our parted mouths. I searched her eyes staring back into mine, and I longed to taste her. In every way. Every square inch of her body. But right now, just her lips.

I raised her body back up and gazed into her eyes, my hands secure at her back and still holding up her weight. She smiled at me, that same bright and beautiful smile that never failed to instigate my own. I watched adoringly as the rain clung to her eyelashes and streamed down her cheeks and glistened on her lips. I would've given up anything to stay with her forever in this moment, blocking out the world around us and forgetting what awaited us out there.

I lifted her from the ground with my arms wrapped around her lower back and I kissed her deeply, savoring the taste of her warm tongue against mine.

Perfect. Beautiful. She could never shatter my image of her, no matter what she did.

We finally tore our lips apart, gasping for breath. Before we even caught our breath, we ran straight to the house and dove into the office where we would be sleeping that night. I immediately started to strip off her clothes, peeling her wet shirt from her skin. I just couldn't get her undressed fast enough. I hardly ever moved my lips from hers when I tried to undress myself.

I urged her onto her hands and knees onto the couch bed, and I immediately positioned myself behind her. I leaned over her, laying my chest across her back, and I searched for her lips with my own.

We were still out of breath from running and the effort it took us to get out of our wet clothes, so we were breathless when we spoke.

"Do you remember what you said?" I whispered hotly onto her mouth from the side. I pressed my hard cock against her from behind and trailed my tongue down the back of her neck as I lay on top of her.

"What did I say?" she said breathily, her mouth constantly searching for mine.

I pressed myself against her again, and I felt her skin prickle with shivers underneath my naked body.

I bit her bottom lip. "That I could do anything to you I wanted."

Just picturing it made my cock throb painfully.

"Y-Yes." She shuddered.

Her hand came up and she wound her fingers through my hair. "Did you mean it?"

"Yes, I meant it." She gasped when I pressed against her this time. She knew what I wanted to do to her, that I wanted to explore her in ways I'd never explored her before.

"Elias...," she said softly, cautiously.

I kissed her collarbone. "Yeah, baby?" I replied just as softly.

She paused for a moment. "I...well, I've never done this before."

It wouldn't have mattered to me if she had. The moment with her would still have been special. But knowing that I was going to be her first excited and elated me.

"I'll be gentle," I said with a caring smile in my voice. "I promise."

She nodded. "OK." Her voice was sweet and willing.

I lifted my chest from her back and reached up around her head, pulling the pillow out from under her cheek. It was soaked with rain-water from her hair. I couldn't stop looking at her ass, the smooth, round shape of her cheeks that I wanted to dig my fingers into and slap a few times just to make them sting. But I focused on her needs first and helped her position the pillow underneath her belly.

I took my time with her, loosening her up and keeping her wet so it would hurt less. She whimpered when I slipped the second fin-ger inside and she tightened around them. I kissed her back upward and along her spine, creating a path to her ear.

"Stop me if you change your mind," I whispered and took her earlobe between my teeth, my fingers still moving carefully in and out of her ass. "I don't want to hurt you."

An unsteady breath shuddered through her lips and when she didn't say no, I withdrew my fingers and gently placed the head of my cock at her entrance. She gasped sharply, and both of her hands began to clench the sheets. I slid myself inside her a little farther, and her whole body became stiff underneath me.

"Ow, ow, ow...," she whined softly and I stopped.

Her legs were shaking, her hands grasping even more of the sheet into her fists. Her cheek lay pressed against the mattress, her lips parted and her breath getting heavier.

"I can stop, baby," I said gently, wanting her to know that it was OK, that I wouldn't be disappointed.

"No, no, don't stop," she whimpered.

"But if I'm hurting you...," I said, worry lacing my voice.

She pushed her ass toward me, taking my cock a little more. She moaned and her thighs hardened in an instant. Then I saw her hand slip in between her legs.

"No," I whispered and moved her hand away. "Let me do it." I began to move my two middle fingers in a firm, circular motion on her clit, and then I felt her open up even more to me, almost every part of her body surrendering to mine. And when she still didn't tell me to stop, I pushed my cock deeper inside her ass. God, she was so tight, constricting around me so hard that I felt my spine quiver. I threw my head back, a loud moan escaping my lips.

It didn't take long and I succumbed to an intense climax. A deeper moan reverberated through my chest, and I pulled out and came on her backside. Bray collapsed onto her belly, and I went down beside her. I kissed along her spine, her shoulders, and her cheek as it lay pressed against the pillow. I combed her wet hair away from her neck with my fingers and kissed her there. And then I gently rolled her over onto her back and planted kisses along her collarbone and her throat and her breasts.

With her head tilted to the side, Bray smiled over at me.

"What is it?" I asked, hiding my impatience. I just wanted to know why she was smiling like that.

She reached her right hand over her body and touched my face. She traced her index finger lightly down the bridge of my nose and brushed the backs of her fingers down my cheek. "I'm just happy," she said. "No matter what's going on out there. Or what's waiting for us. I'm happy right now."

I smiled back at her and took her hand into mine and laid it on my chest.

"But *that* will take some getting used to," she said with a smile in her voice.

"Did it hurt?" I asked, worried now that maybe she'd endured the pain just so that I could get off. "I mean, I know it had to hurt some, but—"

She shook her head. "It hurt a little, but I liked it, too."

I breathed a small sigh of relief and then looked up at the ceiling.

"Though...," she started to say in a "nevertheless" manner, and my head fell back over to one side to face her, "...I doubt I'll ever be able to get off like that."

A blushing smile cracked in my face and I let out a small laugh. Then I rolled over onto my side, pulling her naked body against mine. I kissed her shoulder before I nuzzled my head next to hers.

"Say no more," I said, as my free hand slid down her belly and toward her inner thigh. I pulled her legs apart and took my time getting her off with my fingers.

———

Sunlight poured in through the crack in the curtain from the office window the next morning. I remembered that Tate planned to leave first thing after the bank opened, so when I glanced up at the clock on the wall and saw that it was already noon I woke up quickly the rest of the way.

I shook Bray's shoulder gently. "Bray, baby, get up."

It worried me that Tate might've already left; I didn't hear any voices in the house except from the television.

I crawled off the couch bed and got dressed pretty quickly. Bray followed, though she wasn't nearly as awake as I was. Her eyes were still heavy, and she seemed out of it as she clasped her bra behind her and pulled her shirt over her head.

"I hope he didn't leave already," I said.

Bray followed me out of the room and into the den. Tate and Jen were still there. And so was Caleb. Adam was still there, too, and they were all staring at the television.

Bray and I stopped cold in our tracks behind the couch when we saw our faces on the television screen. I clutched Bray's hand. She was shaking.

# TWENTY-TWO

## Elias

*E*lias Kline's car was found abandoned on Luther Road near the Charlotte County fire station last evening. He and Brayelle Bates are wanted for questioning in the death of Jana McIntyre, whose body was found near the Ocoee River in Georgia last month. Authorities believe…"

I let the rest of what the reporter was saying fade into the back of my mind somewhere.

Everyone simultaneously turned and looked at Bray and me, wide-eyed and as speechless as we were. I felt Bray's fingernails digging into my hand, and I could feel her heartbeat pounding through my palm. Or maybe it was mine.

"It was an accident," Bray blurted out.

"Holy shit, you're wanted for *murder?*" Jen said. She was turned around fully on the couch facing us, her knees pressed into the cushions. I couldn't tell whether or not she was disturbed by it or fascinated.

"Questioning, not murder," Tate corrected her.

"I knew it," Caleb said, smirking. "I mean I didn't *really* think that was it. It was a joke. Damn. But a deal's a deal." He held out his hand to Tate sitting next to him. "Pay up, bro."

"Subtract it from what you're going to owe me after we get to Corpus Christi." Tate never took his eyes off us. "What happened?" he asked, looking straight at me.

"Just what Bray said. It was an accident."

"If it was an accident, why'd you run?" Caleb asked.

Bray burst into tears. I pulled her into my arms.

"We ran because we didn't think anyone would believe us," I said, holding Bray's head in my hand, pressed against my chest. "It was self-defense. But the girl stumbled back too far, tripped, and fell over the edge."

"The edge of *what*?" Adam asked. He looked far more nervous than anyone, his mouth partially agape, the whites of his eyes beginning to show.

"A cliff. Overlooking the river. It was an accident."

Tate got off the couch and came toward me. Bray continued to sob into my shirt.

"What the hell are you gonna do, man?" He looked truly concerned and not at all accusing or put off, as I expected them all to be. Maybe he understood more than I knew, having to deal with his own issues with Caleb. "Seriously. I'm not going to judge you, but shit, man, you know they'll catch you." I saw him glance over at Bray. He knew this was all about her. He looked back at me. Sympathetically. I wondered what he was really thinking, but then thought it better that I didn't know. Because I had a pretty good idea and I didn't like it.

"We don't know yet," I answered.

Bray couldn't take anymore. She broke away from me and ran back into the office and closed herself inside. I started to go after her, but I needed to deal with Tate and everyone else first.

I looked at Tate.

"Better cut them loose," Caleb warned from behind. "We've got enough shit to deal with."

Tate looked back. "Yeah, you're right," he said reproachfully. "We've got enough to deal with because of the shit *you* got us into. I love you, little brother, but you're the last person in this room to be talkin'."

I really appreciated Tate for that.

"I hate to say this," Tate went on, looking at me again, "but Caleb's not too far off the mark."

"I know," I said. "And I don't expect you to keep us around anymore. If it was me, I know *I* wouldn't."

"So then what are you going to do?" Jen asked.

"Well, they definitely can't stay here," Adam said, looking more nervous every time my eyes passed over him. "And I'm sorry, but the sooner you two leave the better. I'm not trying to be a dick, but—"

I put up my hand. "No, Adam, you're right. No hard feelings."

I looked around at everyone else. "But I just hope you all believe that it was an accident. We could never do anything like that on purpose, not even out of anger."

"You keep saying 'we,'" Jen said. She got off the couch and stood next to Tate.

I nodded. "Yeah, uhh—"

"They were both there," Tate stepped in. I saw a warning look hidden in his eyes. He was covering for me, and I was surprised by this. "It was Bray's accident, but Elias saw it happen, so he's calling it 'their' accident. I'd do the same thing." He shrugged.

I thanked him with a private look.

"You knew about this?" Jen asked.

"No," Tate said. "It was just a wild guess." Then he said looking back at me, "Am I right?"

I nodded.

"Look," Tate went on. "I would help you get back, but all of my extra cash flow is going to the Caleb Fuck-Up Fund—"

I shook my head at him, waving a hand in front of me in refusal. "No, I wouldn't take your money anyway. You've done enough already by letting us hang around the past couple of weeks. I have money in the bank and I intend to pay you back every dime. I've just been afraid to access my account." I inhaled a deep breath and glanced at the floor in thought for a moment. "Bray and I were going to figure out what to do within the next three days and then, whether we came up with anything or not, we were going to go back to Georgia."

"What could you possibly do other than just turn yourself in?" Jen asked.

It was a fair question.

"I don't know," I said. "I really don't. Maybe I'll call my father and see about getting a good lawyer. I just…don't know." And it was the truest thing I had said in days. Sure, I could go back to Georgia and say I witnessed the accident, but any other ideas continued to elude me, and it seemed as if they always would. But the part of me that wanted to do everything in my power to help Bray wouldn't let me believe that. So I stuck to my three-day rule. I thought that maybe by some miraculous chance a better idea would fall into my lap and blindside me out of nowhere. Not likely, but possible.

Tate reached into Jen's purse on the side table nearby and took out a pack of cigarettes. He tapped the end of the pack with his finger, and a cigarette shot out the open end. He had it between his lips and lit seconds later. He smoked too much.

"Shit, Tate," Adam argued from the side. "Not in the house."

"Oh, sorry, man," Tate said and started to head to the back door just a few feet away that led out onto the porch. He drew his head back, indicating for me to follow, then he said to Jen, "Baby, get your stuff ready. I don't want you to miss your plane."

I left the den and went outside with Tate. "Where's Jen going?" I asked.

"I got her a plane ticket back to Miami," he said, and took a long pull from his cigarette. He sat against the concrete porch railing. "She starts a new job in two days. But she didn't want to go with me to Texas, anyway. And I wouldn't have let her."

I figured that must have been why he didn't leave early this morning like he had planned: he wanted to wait until after she got on her plane.

"Why don't you just tell Caleb to leave what drugs he has left on him here so you two can fly to Texas? Corpus Christi is a long drive."

Tate flicked his ashes over the porch. He was slow to answer, which made me think there was more to it.

"I guess since you're not exactly a threat to Caleb anymore, you being in more shit than even he's in, then it's OK I tell you that he's still on parole and isn't supposed to leave Florida. He could go right back to prison if they ever found out he was in Virginia. It's the main reason why we've been driving everywhere."

"Geez, what did he do?"

"Sentenced to five years for rape. Only served two, and he's on a five-year parole."

I blinked. "He *raped* a girl?" I couldn't believe it. Caleb was a dick, sure, but I never would've taken him for the type.

Tate shook his head. "My brother didn't rape that girl. And

before you think I'm just backing him because he's my brother, I know he isn't like that, and I know for a *fact* he didn't do it. That bitch fessed up to someone my sister, Everly, knows. She admitted that she'd lied just to get back at Caleb." He shook his head and ground his teeth together behind his tightly clamped jaw. "Caleb told me everything. He was going through a bad breakup with his girlfriend, Cera. He got shitfaced one night, met this girl at a party, one thing led to another, and he fucked her. Well, Caleb felt like shit the next day for sleeping with her. He loved Cera. So, when he told this girl it was just a one-time thing, apparently she didn't like that much. My brother was loyal to Cera." He pointed at me as if to underline what he'd just said. "That might not seem like him, loyal, but he loved her. He was going to marry her. Anyway, that bitch got pissed off because he wouldn't acknowledge they were 'together'"—he quoted with his fingers—"so she cried rape. Claimed she regretted it after the alcohol wore off, but by then she was too afraid to tell the truth because then charges could be pressed against *her*." He hopped up on top of the concrete railing and let his legs dangle over the side.

"Did you report what you overheard?"

"Fuck yeah I did, right after I confronted her myself—it was the one time I really wanted to punch a girl," Tate said as smoke streamed out of his nostrils. "I told Caleb's lawyer and the police, and I tried to get that now *ex*-friend of my sister's to stand up in court and tell everyone what she was told, but she denied it." Tate shook his head, smiling disappointedly, as if to this day he still couldn't believe it. "Long story short, Caleb was sentenced and served some of his time. His girlfriend of five years left him, and that was the end of Caleb's life. Wearing a bright fucking rape badge on your chest is pretty much a life ender, even if you didn't really do it. After that, Caleb wasn't the same anymore. He got out of prison and he was changed. I didn't even know him anymore. I still don't. When I look in his eyes I don't see my little brother anymore, and I don't think I ever will."

I thought about Bray then, about the possibility of her going to prison. "You think the time in prison made him that way?" I asked.

"Nah," Tate said, wrinkling his nose. "He wasn't in prison that long. I think it was a combination of everything. Losing Cera. Being convicted of a crime he didn't commit. Facing a bunch of asshats when he got out. Some people did everything short of stoning him to death in the street. He lost his job and a lot of his friends because they all believed he was a rapist. Shit like that can really mess with a person's head."

I leaned my back against the concrete beam and crossed my arms. All I could picture was Bray, dressed in an orange suit. And after hearing about what Caleb went through, I became even more hell-bent on keeping her out of prison when I thought I couldn't possibly be any more determined than I already was. Suddenly, I was terrified for her. The system failed Caleb Roth. I knew, with every fiber of my being, that it was just as likely to fail Bray.

She was right all along. She was right to be afraid. She was wrong to run, but her fears were absolutely justified.

"Go ahead and come with us to Texas," Tate said. "Use the ride there and back to figure out what you two are gonna do." He pointed at me briefly. "But my advice, if you want it, you need to talk that girl into turning herself in."

I was confused, and I know I must've looked that way. After what Caleb went through unnecessarily, I thought Tate would know Bray would probably go through the same thing.

"She thinks it's too late for that," I said. "And I can't say I disagree with her."

"Maybe so," he said, "but that's some serious shit right there. You kill somebody, accidental or not, it's not something that'll ever get swept under the rug. The longer you run, the harder they'll hunt you down, and the more you make yourself look guilty as hell."

"Yeah, I know. Trust me, I know. I've thought about nothing but that since we left Georgia."

Jen pushed the back door open, her eyes, wide with worry, framed by her long, cascading blonde hair. "Elias, I think you need to get in there with your girlfriend. She locked herself in the bathroom."

Fearing the worst, and knowing what Bray was capable of, I rushed past Jen and ran back into the house.

# TWENTY-THREE

## Elias

*I* rapped harshly on the bathroom door. "Bray?"

I could hear her sobbing, but she wouldn't answer, so I knocked and called out her name again. Jen and Tate came up behind me, but I was too busy trying to get the door open to pay attention. I twisted the knob both ways, knowing it was locked but hoping by some chance it might still pop open. "Bray, open the door, baby, please." My heart was thrumming in my throat.

"I heard her crying when I walked by," Jen said from behind. "I stopped and asked if she was OK, but she didn't answer. I dunno why, but it just kinda freaked me out."

"Bray! Open the damn door!" I pounded on it harder with my fist.

"Move out of the way," I heard Adam say in a calm manner, as if he had it under control.

I stepped to the side and Adam went up to the door and stuck a thin L-shaped piece of metal in the doorknob. The door clicked and popped right open. Adam stepped away and I wasted no time rushing in there. Bray was sitting on the bathroom floor next to the pedestal sink with her back against the wall, her knees drawn up and her head atop them. She rocked back and forth on her backside, her body a trembling mess, her arms pressed together against her chest. I checked her over from afar, at first afraid to approach her.

No blood. There was no blood, and a great sense of relief washed through me like a crashing wave. As relieved as I was, I felt guilty for thinking she would ever do something like that after she promised me that she wouldn't. I wasn't giving her enough credit.

I sat down beside her on the floor and glanced back at everyone standing in the doorway.

"Let's give them a moment," Tate said and reached out for the doorknob. Just before the door closed he added, "I hate to rush you, especially right now, but we have to head out in fifteen minutes so Jen can make her flight."

I nodded and he closed the door the rest of the way.

Immediately, I turned back to Bray. Placing my hands on the sides of her face, I tried to lift her head. She fought me at first, but I managed to get her to raise her eyes to me. Her face was streaked with the black mascara she had borrowed from Jen. I tried to take her hands, wedging mine between her thighs and her chest to reach them, but she refused, jerking them away. Her dark hair fell over her shoulder and further concealed them.

"Why are you hiding them?"

That feeling in the pit of my stomach began to twist deeper.

"Elias..." Her voice was soft and pleading.

She didn't want me to look.

I clenched my jaw so hard that pain shot through my teeth and I reached in and grabbed her by one wrist, feeling the coarse hemp rope material her bracelets were made from scratching against my fingers. I expected them to be moist with blood, but they were dry. She screamed at me and thrust her body backward, accidently hitting her head on the wall, but I wasn't about to let go. Her eyes were feral and imploring.

"Stop, Elias, *please*!"

"No! What are you hiding?!" I wrenched her wrists into view and forced my fingers behind the bracelets, pulling them apart so I could see her skin. Still no blood. No cuts. I looked at the other one. It was the same, but as I moved a little to the left and the light in the ceiling filled in the shadow my body had been casting on her, I saw that her wrists were red and inflamed. Red streaks stretched from just below the balls of her thumbs downward to the center of her forearm.

Scratch marks.

I froze, my hands clamped down on her forearms so hard that she couldn't move them. "What the hell is this?"

She shook her head. Tears streamed down her face, dripping off the end of her chin.

I shook her so hard that the back of her head hit the wall again. "What the hell *is* this, Bray?!" I roared in her face.

"It's not *that*!" she screamed back in my face. "It's not what you're thinking!" Her face was contorted by pain.

"Then tell me what it is!" I remembered her telling me about this before, when her mom found her clawing at her wrists and sent her to a shrink afterward. But I needed to know more. I needed to know everything and she was going to tell me or we'd sit here like this forever.

She started to twist her body in a way that if I didn't let go her arms would break, so I released her.

"Just go. Go home, Elias. Please just go home." Her voice was strangely soft and distant, it felt like every part of her had given up.

She buried her head on her knees again, wrapping her arms around her legs.

"No, I'm not leaving this room until you tell me what that is."

Her head shot back up. "If I tell you, will you go home?"

"No."

"Then forget it. I'm leaving here, Elias. Not with Tate or with anyone else. I'm leaving here on my own." Her voice was firm, resolute.

"What are you talking about?"

She was scaring me. Her wrists. This burst of despair and pain that came out of nowhere and blindsided me. This crazy shit she was saying about leaving without me. She shook her head back and forth over and over again, looking at anything but me. And it was infuriating. I rose from the floor and into a crouched position, pushing up with my knuckles pressing against the linoleum. She still wouldn't look at me and I had given up expecting her to. Was she serious? Did she really want me to leave? What was she planning to do?

My heart sank. I knew I couldn't leave her. I wouldn't have, anyway, but I knew that even if I had wanted to I couldn't.

"I wasn't trying to kill myself," she said in a soft voice. "I was… I just do that sometimes."

"Do what?" I couldn't for the life of me understand what the hell she was saying to me.

"I've done it since I was a teenager," she said. "It's no big deal. It's just a release. I wasn't trying to kill myself. I told you I'm stronger than that." She finally looked up at me and her face was full of darkness and finality. She was tired of who she was, tired of hiding, from me, from herself, tired of pretending to be someone she wasn't, because she knew she wasn't what society deemed normal. I felt it as I looked down into her eyes.

She was *tired*.

"I'd say that clawing at your wrists with your fingernails is a pretty big fucking deal, Bray."

"To you, I guess it would be." She was eerily calm and her tears had already begun to dry up. She sniffled back the few remaining.

"What's that supposed to mean?" I asked.

She hesitated and looked at the pedestal sink next to her. "You would never understand."

"Try me."

"They always say that."

"I'm not 'they,'" I said. "I'm the one person in this world you know loves you more than anything. Never throw me in the closet with them. I don't belong there. I never will."

Her throat moved as though she were swallowing more tears that were trying to rise to the surface.

Finally she said, "Sometimes the darkness feels like it's right there beneath the skin. It's *right there*. I hate it when I can feel it, because it's like it's taunting me. It knows I can't get to it. I scratch and claw"—her voice began to shake, her eyes were brimming with tears again, tears of anger—"and I try to get it out but I *can't*. I can't because I know I'd hurt myself if I went that far! But I try *so* hard!"

I sat down in front of her again and took her gently by her forearms, my thumbs pressing in the center of the soft underskin. "Tell me. I want to know everything. How it feels. What makes it go away. How often it comes back. I *need* to know, baby."

She choked the tears back and sniffled. "It doesn't happen very often anymore, not like when I was a teenager," she said. "And it eventually goes away after I've cried it out." She laughed drily. "Well, I always *try* clawing it out, but it never works. It always comes back. And whenever it comes back, I always go for the wrists first."

She looked me in the eyes. "Elias, I wasn't trying to hurt myself. I just wanted it out."

I believed her. I couldn't understand exactly how she felt, but in a way I could. I couldn't imagine living like that. I tried to picture myself in her place, going through the motions all her life, and it only made me squirm inside my skin. I thought she was much stronger than I could ever be for dealing with something so dark, so strange, practically all her life. I knew I could never have done it.

"Elias, I want you to go home." Her tone was calm, but abandon lay evident in her eyes.

I was an idiot to think she had forgotten about that part. I shook my head. "You know I won't do that."

"Look, this isn't some cry for attention," she said as she speared all ten fingers through the top of her hair, pulling the hair away from her tear-streaked face. "This isn't me telling you to go home because I need to hear you say that you won't. I really mean it, Elias. You need to go home. This isn't your problem and I'm tired of *making* it yours."

"It *is* my problem," I said. "Whatever you go through I go through with you. I always will."

The palms of her hands slapped against the floor on each side of her. "Dammit, Elias! Stop *doing* this! You deserve better than what I could ever give you, and I'm never going to be able to change. Ever. Stop being my safety net and just go. I *want* you to."

"I don't care if that's what you want," I said. "I'm not leaving you. I'm with you to the end, whether you want me there or not."

She gritted her teeth and inhaled a deep, infuriated breath. She was telling the truth about really wanting me to leave. It was exactly as she had said, that this wasn't about needing to hear me say that

I wouldn't. She was determined to make me leave her behind and angry that I refused. But I didn't care.

"Three more days," I said. "You agreed to give me that much. I expect you to hold to it."

"So you're just going to walk around going absolutely nowhere with me? Everybody here knows about us now. It's only a matter of a very short time before one of them calls the cops and we're hauled off to jail." Her steely gaze shot through me when she said, "And I'm *not* going to jail. Do you understand? I won't go to jail."

The way she said it, the way her eyes held every ounce of resolve that I knew could never be shaken, tore a hole in my soul. Bray had revealed to me the darkness that lived within her, the darkness that made all the reckless decisions and that always controlled her when she was at her weakest, that which I feared would later send her right into the throes of death. My Bray was no longer the one sitting on that bathroom floor. That brave, strong, fearless girl who loved to laugh and play in the rain. The darkness that lived underneath her skin, that she fought so hard to be free of, was in control of her now, triggered by how close we were getting to the end of all this, triggered by the events that she knew would inevitably be set into motion. *I won't go to jail.* Her words ran through my mind over and over again, and I knew that she'd die before she let that happen.

Bray would *die* before she let that happen.

"You promised me three days."

She looked right at me. Her tears had completely dried up.

"Then three days it is," she said, nodding. "We have three days left together. I want to make the most of them."

Her words rendered me speechless. My heart, which only beat

for her anymore, took my voice and my mind when it fell into the pit of my stomach.

We had only three days left together, and I knew that they would end either in separation or in death.

And I could never prepare myself for either.

## TWENTY-FOUR

## Elias

*T*ate and Jen said their good-byes at the airport. By this time, she was so worried about Tate's safety that she only glared at me and Bray with accusing eyes. She was adamant about Tate calling her every chance he got to let her know that he was OK. But her fears didn't lie only with us. She was equally worried about what could happen to Tate when he got to Corpus Christi. In her eyes, Caleb was no better.

Jen was a great girl. She and Tate were perfect for one another, I believed. And the more difficult my and Bray's relationship became, the more I envied the two of them. I wanted nothing more than for Bray and me to be like they were. Free. If Bray wanted to beat the shit out of me, I would've welcomed it. I would've welcomed anything over what we had and what we were now going through.

We hit the road just after one o'clock in the afternoon and were in Baton Rouge, Louisiana, by seven o'clock. We pulled into a small motel when one of Tate's tires blew out. It was so loud it sounded like a gunshot.

"You change the tire," Tate told Caleb, "and I'll call Rocky."

"Why are you calling him?" Caleb asked.

"Because obviously we're not going to make it there when I told him we would."

Caleb went around to the back of the Jeep and took the spare tire down from the mount.

Tate rented two rooms first and handed me a key when he came out of the front office.

"I'll put it on your tab," he said with a smirk.

"How long is that tab, anyway?" I asked in jest. "At least eight hundred bucks, I'm sure."

"Shit, man, I'm charging you interest," he said, grinning. "We'll get it all squared away when this is over with."

"Sounds good to me," I said, and he disappeared inside the door two rooms down from where the Jeep was parked.

All of the rooms opened to the outside rather than inside onto a maze of hallways. I looked at our room key, which was an actual key—that's how old the motel was—instead of a card. Our room was right next to Tate and Caleb's. Bray finally got out of the Jeep after Caleb asked her to so he could jack it up.

"I'm going to get a shower," I called out to Bray. "Want to come?"

A faint smile appeared around her eyes, and she crossed her arms as if there was a chill in the air, even though it was a sticky, humid night.

"I'll take one after you," she said.

I knew what she was doing. She was trying to distance herself from me. To prepare me. And while I didn't exactly think that was the way to go about making the most of the three days we had left together, I couldn't bring myself to argue with her about it.

I slipped inside the room and left her outside with Caleb while he changed the tire.

# Bray

I hadn't told Elias yet about me overhearing his conversation with Tate on the back porch at Adam's house. The conversation about Caleb and his rape sentence. The office room Elias and I had stayed in was right next to the back porch. I'd listened to them from the window. I had also heard their conversation about me, Tate telling Elias that he should talk me into turning myself in. Tate was right in all of the advice he gave Elias, but I felt beyond redemption. There was no hope left for me. I hated it that I was dragging the one person in the world I loved more than any other through the mud with me. But he wasn't going to leave me alone. No matter what I did or said to him, Elias would never leave me to my fate. I both loved and resented him for it. I resented him only because it hurt that much more, knowing that I was ruining him.

I sat down on the faded yellow concrete parking chock in the empty spot next to the Jeep. Caleb was pumping the metal lever on the tire jack, raising the Jeep off the asphalt.

"Mind if I ask you something?"

Caleb glanced over at me briefly.

"If I said no, would you still ask?"

"Probably," I said.

I caught his eyes rolling as he looked back at the jack.

"What is jail like?"

Caleb stopped pumping the jack for a second, but he didn't look at me. When he went back to work he answered, "Jail or prison? Jail is pretty manageable. Prison is a whole 'nother nightmare. Why do you ask?" He glanced back at me with a gleam in his eye. "Worried about what they're going to do to you in there?"

My heart skipped a beat. He enjoyed asking me that. I didn't let it get to me.

"Yes," I answered honestly. I still had no plans on going to jail or prison, but I wanted to know what it was like just the same.

Caleb pumped the jack lever one final time and stood upright, wiping light sweat from his forehead with the top of his forearm.

"No idea what it's like in women's prison," he said. "But I imagine it's not too much different. The short time I spent locked up, it really wasn't that different from what you see on TV. Not as harsh where I was. No one raped me in the ass or made me their bitch, but if I had shown even a fraction of fear they might've tried. Guess I have Tate and Kyle to thank for that." He laughed lightly. "They beat the shit out of me growing up. I had a lot of practice. But yeah, I did get into fights, and I did get my ass beat once, but I had friends on the inside. They looked after me while I was in there, and I look after them while I'm out here."

My expression shifted from interest to confusion, but he wouldn't elaborate. I knew whatever he'd been doing for his "friends" on the inside must've been illegal.

"Did you kill that girl?" He looked right into my eyes.

"Not on purpose," I said.

He nodded and then reached in the back of the Jeep and pulled out a tire iron. Bending over in front of the blown tire he attached one end to a lug nut. "Then you should've just went to the police," he said, spinning the tire iron once. "You really fucked up by running."

"I know," I sighed. "But there's nothing I can do about that now."

I gazed contemplatively out at the falling darkness, the way the grayish-blue light fell over the parking lot. The horizon was pink and orange as the last of the sun fell behind the clouds. I thought about how blunt Caleb had been just now, how right he was.

"Did Cera ever see you while you were in prison?"

Caleb stood upright, still clasping the tire iron in his dirty, blackened hand. I knew I would strike a nerve bringing up her name, but I didn't care much.

"You're overstepping your bounds," he warned.

"Did she?" I pressed.

He glared at me.

"It's obvious you still love that girl," I said, further angering him. "And I don't think you're a bad guy. An asshole at times, and a womanizing pig, but you're clearly not a bad guy. You just happened to end up with the shit end of the stick. I just want to know if she loved you as much as you loved her."

A deep sigh escaped Caleb's lungs. His head dropped for a moment as if he were quietly arguing with himself for giving in to me at all.

Then he sat down beside me on the yellow chock. The tire iron clattered softly against the asphalt as he put it down next to his low black Nike shoes. He rested his arms atop his bent knees. Absently, I studied the tattoo of the Asian girl on his left arm. We looked out at the colorful, darkening horizon.

"No," he said. "Cera never came to visit me. Not even once. I was convicted of raping someone, and she believed everyone else over me. But I didn't blame her. I still don't."

I looked at him, but he didn't look back. "I guess it would be hard to put your faith in someone who was accused of rape," I said. "But... I think if she truly loved you then she would've known that you were innocent. She would've been able to feel it."

"Cera did love me," he said with a hint of acid in his voice. "You don't spend five years of your life with someone, happy every morning when you wake up next to him, a smile in your voice every time you talk to him on the phone, if you didn't love him."

I nodded. I couldn't argue with that.

Then he said, "Elias loves you. A little pussy-whipped, I think, but it's still love."

I was surprised by the sincerity in his face.

He grabbed the tire iron and stood back up. "Yes, I think Elias will visit you when you go to prison," he said, and it sobered me in the darkest of ways. "That is what you want to know, isn't it?"

I didn't answer, but I didn't really have to.

He started loosening another lug nut.

"And if he doesn't," he went on, "it doesn't mean that he doesn't love you, just like Cera. It just means he's confused and a little scared. That's all it is."

Caleb was lying to himself, and he knew it. He turned the tire iron harder, the muscles in his arms hardening with each push. I saw the side of his temple where a vein was beginning to bulge, and the way his jaw clenched tightly as he ground his teeth. He knew deep down that Cera may not have loved him as much as he thought she did, but he struggled with not allowing himself to believe it every single day of his life.

"Don't you have something better to do?" he asked as he dismounted the bad tire and dropped it on its side. "Go shower with your fiancé. Watch TV, hell, I don't care much, just anything but hanging around out here with me." He looked at me from a bent-over position in front of where the tire used to be and then grinned. "Unless you want to be Grace's replacement? I have no fucking problem putting your little ass up on that hood and licking your pussy until the sun comes up."

My eyes popped wide open. I swallowed hard. I stood up and dusted off the back of my shorts.

Normally, I would be offended by that, but Caleb was harmless, and I knew that sex and his extreme personality was his way of coping with the way his life turned out. I mean, sure, it wasn't that Caleb wouldn't do something like that even with Elias just feet away, but he was still harmless. I just shook my head and rolled my eyes at him.

He smiled and nodded toward the room where Elias was and said, "Get outta here."

I smiled back and walked away.

Elias was still in the shower when I walked into the room, glad he thought to leave the outside door cracked so it wouldn't lock me out.

I sat down on the bed and looked at the cigarette-stained phone on the nightstand.

I picked it up, placed the receiver to my ear and punched in my parents' number.

"Hello?"

"Hi, Mom."

"Where the hell *are* you, Brayelle?" she said harshly into my ear. "I've been calling you! Where's your phone? The police are everywhere looking for you! You need to come home. Now. Where are you? We'll come get you. Tell me where you are." I wondered if she'd stop talking long enough to catch her breath.

"It doesn't matter where I am."

My mom pulled her mouth away from the phone and said to my dad, "It's Brayelle. No, no, I'm talking to her. Just wait." And then her voice was loud again. "What do you mean it doesn't matter? What have you done? Did you or that guy have a hand in that girl's death? Tell me the truth. You killed her, didn't you? It's just like that girl and that boy, Mitchell, said. You were fighting with her that night. You shoved her off that cliff because of Elias Kline. Didn't you?" She was all but screaming into the phone.

"You believe that, don't you?" I asked calmly, but my heart was slowly breaking every second that went by that my mother was treating me like a criminal, having no faith in me whatsoever.

My dad grabbed the phone from her. I heard her voice fade quickly and then her arguing with him.

"Brayelle, it's Dad. Tell me where you are and I'll come get you."

"Why?"

"Because you need to come home and you need to face what you did."

"Face what I did?" I mocked and bit my bottom lip. "I-I guess I should've known that both of you would accuse me."

"We're not accusing you," my dad said sternly. "We just—"

"—not accusing me?" I snapped cutting him off. "That's exactly what you're doing. Neither one of you has asked how I am. Neither of you has asked me if it was an accident."

"Well, if it was an accident, then why did you run?" my dad asked.

"Because I was stupid and I was scared."

"Brayelle, only the guilty run."

My heart broke completely when he said that. I felt like I wanted to cry, but I had already cried so much that I had no tears left. I sucked in a sharp breath, rounded my chin, and said, "Dad, I just want you and Mom to know that I love you very much. And I love Rian and please tell her that for me. I know I wasn't the best kid growing up, and I gave you both a lot of hell and for that I am so sorry. I am *so* sorry. I'm sorry I couldn't be more like Rian."

"Honey, why are you saying these things?" My dad's tone began to change, and maybe he really was starting to worry about where this was heading, but I wasn't going to fall for it.

"Just tell Mom and Rian that I love them."

"Brayelle?" He sounded genuinely worried. But it was too late for that.

I hung up.

# Elias

I stepped the rest of the way out of the bathroom.

"What are you doing?" I asked, as Bray set the phone back down.

"Nothing," she said.

"Who were you talking to?"

"No one," she said. "Well, I was talking to myself. Rehearsing. I was going to call my mom and dad, a-and maybe my sister, but I changed my mind."

I nodded and draped the towel over the back of my neck. I had heard everything she said to her parents on the phone, but she didn't want me to know, and I thought it was better that I just pretended not to know.

Her conversation put a knot in my chest. The things she had said to them sounded like good-bye, the kind of good-bye that always ends badly. I thought about that painting that had been our life together, the black-and-white one that continuously filled with colors as each event unfolded and made us who we were. But that painting had become something so dark that Bosch couldn't touch it.

"Caleb said he would eat me out on the hood of Tate's Jeep," she said.

I didn't know whether to go outside and beat the shit out of him or just continue to stand there, dumbfounded by her swift change of mood.

Ultimately, I opted for beating the shit out of Caleb.

I turned on my heel and went for the door, still only dressed in my boxers, but Bray was behind me in a flash and she grabbed me around the waist.

"No," she whispered onto the shell of my ear as one hand came down and grabbed a handful of me. "Caleb was just being Caleb. He didn't really mean it."

I didn't give a shit. I opened the door anyway, but Bray slammed it shut with the palm of her other hand and I whirled around just as she pushed my back against the door. She stripped off her shirt and took me into a deep kiss, pinning me against the door with her hand still grabbing my cock, rock hard beneath her palm.

She pulled the wet towel from around my neck. I grabbed both sides of her head and pulled her hair, forcing her neck back and pushing the tip of my tongue down the center of her throat.

"What do you want to do to me?" she asked, squeezing and pulling my cock in her hand as her fingers tightened around it.

A low growl reverberated through my chest. My teeth clamped down on her chin, and then I slid my tongue into her warm mouth.

"I want what you want," I said breathily and kissed her even harder, wrapping my arms around her body and crushing hers against mine.

Her hand came out of my boxers and she dug all ten of her fingernails into my back. "I want everything," she said, and it sent a tremor through my cock.

I turned her around, stripped her shorts and panties off, and forced her onto her knees in the center of the bed.

## Bray

When you know you're going to die soon, all bets are off. You feel like the person you always wanted to be, the fearless, uninhibited member of society who doesn't give a flying fuck what anyone else thinks. You want to do and say all of the things that you were always afraid to do and say. You want to drink and do drugs until you can't see straight, punch a random stranger in the face just for looking like an asshole, fuck until you can't feel your legs anymore.

Elias raised my ass in the air and shoved my face against the mattress before spreading my legs apart with both hands, exposing me to the cool air. He slid a finger between my nether lips and played with my clit, rubbing and teasing and exploring until I couldn't help but bite down on my bottom lip out of frustration.

"Fuck me," I moaned. "Please, just fuck me."

"Not yet," he said, and I felt the heat from his breath closing around my pussy. A loud moan moved through my throat as I felt the sensation of my clit being sucked hard between his lips and then tugged on with his teeth.

I tried to reach between my legs to touch his face, to feel the movement of his jaw as he licked me, but he caught my fingers in his mouth and sucked on them before grabbing both of my wrists and pinning them behind my back.

"Be fucking still," he said.

He spread my legs apart even further and slipped his tongue inside my wetness. I gasped and moaned and whimpered. I wanted to see it, I wanted to watch him lick me, but with my cheek pressed against the mattress, all I could see was my ass raised in the air and Elias's legs, bent at the knees, behind me. He licked me fast and hard, and I pushed my ass toward him. Then he sucked on my clit again, so hard I tried to pull away, because it was too intense.

"God, please don't stop," I begged him.

He flicked the tip of his tongue against my little bead, spreading my lips with the fingers of his free hand. When he let go of my wrists, I found the sheets above my head and grasped them tight. Two fingers slid into my pussy, and he moved them in and out of me while he licked my clit as I began to crawl upward across the bed.

"Oh goddamn!" I closed my eyes and held fast onto the pillow, as he curled his fingers into a hook inside of me, forbidding me to move any farther. He held me there, licking and sucking and fucking me with his fingers until my body became stiff as I felt my orgasm coming on.

"I'm going to come," I said through uneven breaths. "God, please don't fucking stop."

He stopped.

"No, please, Elias, don't stop!" I wanted to cry. No, I *was* crying. Every part of my body was opened up to him, wanting him, yearning to feel him inside of me. But I needed that orgasm. I fucking *needed* it.

He shoved his cock deep inside of me where I ached for him, hitting the spot. I gasped and grabbed fistfuls of the sheets again. The surprise and the intensity of it took the breath right out of my lungs. Tears streamed down my face. Tears of emotional pain. Of anger. Of guilt. I wanted it out of me. All of it. And instead of clawing at my wrists for a release, I wanted Elias to fuck it out of me. The bed banged against the wall as he slammed against me from behind. His strong fingers dug partway into my thighs and my ass cheeks as he made sure to keep me spread wide open for him to see.

I still wanted to watch. I wanted to see what he could see, his hard cock moving in and out of me, glistening with my wetness. I felt the orgasm brewing again so quickly. I wanted to call out to him, tell him I was about to come again, but I was afraid he would stop again.

I got very still. Very quiet. But I think he knew I was going to come, *because* I was so quiet and still.

"Say it," he told me, still thrusting in and out of me. "Say it, baby."

"I'm going to come," I whispered.

He thrust hard and held his cock deep inside of me for a moment. Then he did it again and held it there for another moment.

I felt my eyes rolling into the back of my head.

"Oh goddamn, Elias...if you fucking stop I'll kill you. I'll fucking *kill* you!"

He slammed into me harder and held himself there, so deep I could've sworn I felt it in my soul.

I gasped and shuddered as an explosion went off deep inside my belly, my legs trembled and shook and felt like jelly the more I tried to hold myself up on them. I felt myself constricting around his cock as I came, and tears of relief and pleasure streamed down my face.

Elias let out a moan and pulled his cock from inside of me just before he came on my backside.

Everything was quiet except our heavy breathing.

He collapsed on top of me, the sweat of his naked chest mixed with the sweat on my back. He kissed me there with his arms wrapped around my stomach. I felt the tip of his tongue moving up my spine and between my shoulder blades. He rose up and made his way back down and kissed me between the legs softly. Chills attacked my body all over. He kissed my thighs, giving each one the same amount of attention.

I rolled over onto my back, and Elias crawled up my body, his hands pressed into the bed on either side of me, and he kissed me all the way up. My belly button. My stomach. My breastbone. And with the same grace and attention that he gave my thighs, he kissed each breast.

I cupped his face in my hands and guided him toward my lips. His warm naked body fell between my legs and he kissed me with so much passion that I never wanted to open my eyes again. I wanted to die in this bed, just like this, with him on top of me. If I'd known he would've given me that kind of death, I would've asked it of him. But I didn't want to ruin the moment. Because I knew in my heart that it would be the last moment like this I would ever share with him.

Three days. I promised him, and I had every intention of staying true to my word.

Three days.

## Elias

"I love you, Bray," I whispered as I lay with my face nuzzled against her breasts. I wanted to hear her heart beating. "I love you more than you will ever know."

She wound her fingers gently through the top of my hair. "How is that?" she asked in a quiet voice.

"Because I would do *anything* for you," I said. "You just don't realize yet what 'anything' truly means."

"Maybe I will someday," she whispered, and I shut my eyes softly, holding in the tears. "I love you, too, Elias. More than you could possibly ever know."

"How is that?" I asked.

I felt her lips against my hair. "Because I'd never ask you to prove your 'anything.'"

We fell fast asleep, our bodies tangled, the sound of her heartbeat so soothing in my ear.

# TWENTY-FIVE

## Elias

$\mathcal{C}$aleb saw my fist coming, but he didn't have time to react. I heard the crunch and felt the pain sear through the bones in my hand as he fell against the side of the Jeep.

"You ever fucking hit on Bray again," I said, pointing my finger at him, "I'll beat you unconscious."

"Elias!" Bray came running out of the motel with wet hair. "Baby, please! I told you he wasn't serious!"

I felt both of her hands pulling on my arm, but I didn't move from in front of Caleb. And he wasn't fighting back. He massaged his jaw with one hand and just looked at me with no emotion.

Tate came out of his room, wondering what was going on. "Something tells me you deserved that, little brother," he said, looking between Caleb and me.

"I guess I did," Caleb said, and a small smile crept up in his eyes. I almost hit him again on principle, but I stepped away from him and let Bray feel as though she was pulling me back.

Tate gave me a nod of approval and said, "All right, we need to hit the road. Rocky is expecting us by four o'clock. I want to get this over with." He looked at Caleb. "Get your shit together," he said, and he wasn't talking about personal belongings.

———

Two hours passed and we were getting closer to the Texas state line.

Tate glanced at me over his shoulder from the driver's seat. "When we get there I'll drop you and Bray off at a store or restaurant somewhere. It's not a good idea if you come with us." He looked at Caleb in the front passenger's seat and then put his eyes back on the road. "It's probably not a good idea that you come, either."

"No way, Tate," Caleb argued. "I'm fucking going with you."

"Look, I can just go in, meet with Rocky, hand him the money, and go about my day. If you're there it probably won't go as smoothly."

"I'm not letting you go in there by yourself," Caleb snapped.

"But you'll let me use my savings to bail your ass out," Tate retorted.

Caleb stared right through Tate from the side.

"Hey, Tate's right," I spoke up from the backseat. "I may not know what this is all about, but I have a pretty good idea. Caleb, you're likely to just create tension."

"Nobody asked you," Caleb snapped, turning his head to look back at me. "Why don't you deal with your own damn problems? Remember? You got cops looking for your ass. Deal with the dead-girl issue and stay out of mine."

I hated to admit it, but Caleb had a point.

Bray and I spent the rest of last night talking about what other options we had. Of course, there were none, so the conversation was very short. Then mostly we just stared up at the ceiling, wrapped in each other's arms. I never wanted to let her go. I felt the same from her. Eventually, our minds drifted from the matter at hand and we started reminiscing again. We talked about our childhood and about all of the things we missed and enjoyed and loved. But time passed all too quickly, and the present snuck up on us again. We thought about what else we could do, but still came up short. Stared at the ceiling some more. Fell asleep. And that was that.

But Bray was different. She hadn't been herself since we saw the newscast back in Panama City. Since I found her on the bathroom floor. I got the feeling that she wasn't really worried anymore about finding other solutions. She seemed more laid-back than concerned or on edge. It scared the hell out of me, and I didn't know why.

We stopped at a gas station to fill up.

"I've got to pee," Bray said and hopped out of the Jeep.

Tate tossed me a folded-up twenty-dollar bill. "Mind getting me a bottle of water and a Reese's? Oh, and see if they have a hot bar. Grab me a hot dog or somethin'."

"Sure thing," I said. I took Bray's hand and walked with her through the lot and into the store.

Inside, I pointed over Bray's head toward the far back corner. "Restrooms are over there." She weaved her way through a few people in the aisles toward it. I found everything Tate asked for and stood in line. Bray was out before it was my turn, so she stood next to me until finally I checked out.

Bray had wanted to check the newspapers sitting in the metal display near the register. Thankfully, she didn't find anything about us inside.

We got back on the road.

"I'm going to pay you back, bro," Caleb told Tate.

They had been arguing about money and all of the times that Tate had used his to bail Caleb out of something since he got out of prison. They went from money to their parents to their sister and then back to money again. Bray and I kept to ourselves in the backseat, and eventually I didn't hear much anymore. I held Bray close to me on the seat, my arm wrapped around her from the side.

"I know you called your parents," I said softly with my cheek resting against the top of her hair.

"I had a feeling," she said.

"You know, maybe if you sat down with them and just tried to talk," I began. "Tell them what I know about what's been going on with you. Make them understand."

"They don't want to understand."

"What makes you think that?" I squeezed her arm gently in my hand.

"Elias, they gave up on me the day I turned eighteen. Well, technically, they gave up on me before that, but until I turned eighteen they at least had to pretend they were doing everything they could for me. I could see it in their faces. Well, when they'd look at me anyway. But mostly, I was just a ghost..." She tilted her head back so she could see me. "Other than just wanting to be around you, why do you think I spent so much time with you?"

I pressed my lips to her forehead, and she laid her head back down.

Memories of when we were teenagers moved slowly through my mind. I swallowed and took a deep breath and squeezed her arm again when a particular memory came into view:

*"I only got one C," Bray said, coming up to me at school in the hallway, her eyes lit with excitement. She shoved her report card into my hand. "Math, of course. But it's better than the D I had last nine weeks."*

"That's awesome," I said. "I can help you study. Told you I'd help."

She snatched the report card away from me and smirked. "I can do it myself," she said and kissed me on the cheek. "Besides, if my parents found out you helped me, they'll think I can't do it on my own." She wore a bright yellow T-shirt with an anime character with pink hair imprinted on the front, hip-hugger jeans, and a pair of black flip-flops. Her long, dark hair was pulled behind her into a ponytail.

"Are you still coming over tonight?" she asked me.

I dialed in the last number of my locker combination, pulled the door open, and shoved my books inside.

"Definitely," I said, smiling. "I'm bringing the marshmallows."

"And the beer," Bray whispered and pressed her hip against mine.

My eyes grew wide as I looked around and over the top of her head to see if anyone was listening.

"Not so loud," I said in a harsh, low voice. "Besides, I said I'd try to get a few beers. My mom hasn't touched the ones my Aunt Janice left over at our house last month, but it makes me nervous that she might notice them missing." I retrieved my book for my next class and shut my locker door.

"I know, I know," Bray whispered. "But just get two then. Make Mitchell and Lissa find their own. Mitchell's dad always has beer."

"I dunno, Bray, if my mom finds out, she'll kill me."

She laid her head on my shoulder. "Just try. If you can't, then it's OK. We always have marshmallows." Then she grinned with a crafty glint in her eye. "But if we play Spin the Bottle, you might have to kiss Lissa, and I'm sure you don't want to be sober for that."

I inwardly cringed. "Spin the Bottle is lame," I said. "Who does that anymore?"

"Who cares? It's still going to be fun."

I met up with Bray after school, and we walked home together down the dirt road toward Mr. Parson's land, like we did every day. Bray was excited about her good grades. Last year she had gotten mostly Cs and Ds, and she was depressed for a long time about how disappointed her parents were. Bray was a smart girl, intelligent even, but when it came to school she couldn't focus. She got bored easily, and it was hard for her to get along with most of her teachers, so she got into trouble a lot.

"They're going to be so proud," she said later, as we made it to the end of the driveway at her house. She let go of my hand and said, "Want to come in with me this time?"

I shook my head. "Uhh, nah, your dad doesn't like me much. I'll just see you in a couple hours for the marshmallow roast."

She grabbed my hand again and started pulling me along. "My dad always looks like he doesn't like people," she said.

I let her pull me, but I really didn't want to go inside. I never liked to, because her parents always eyed me with suspicious looks, as though I was something evil that needed to be exorcised. I crawled inside her bedroom window a lot over the years, after her parents had gone to sleep, and I never got caught, but I was always pretty terrified.

"Bray, really, let me just catch up with you later."

*We made it to her front porch. A little swarm of bugs buzzed around the porch light just above the door. An old wooden swing hung from the porch roof on one side; two lawn chairs were pushed against the side of the house on the other side, with a table situated between them. Cigarette smoke lingered faintly in the air, as though someone had sat out here and smoked in the past hour.*

*The screen door opened with a creaking sound as she pulled it back. She was smiling so brightly. I knew she wanted me to be there when she showed her parents her grades. And I wanted to be there for her.*

*We entered the living room together, the smell of pot roast and potatoes and garlic filled the air and made my stomach rumble. It was always a little too much on the warm side in Bray's house. I didn't know if her parents just didn't like to turn on the air conditioner or if it was because her mom cooked a lot and it kept the house heated. Every time I went there it seemed like I smelled freshly cooked food of some kind.*

*Bray dropped her backpack on the floor and looked back at me, her smile getting bigger as she walked around the back of the couch to where her parents were watching TV. I stayed where I was, at the entrance to the living room, where it felt safer.*

*"Mom, Dad, you're not going to believe this," Bray said and started unfolding her report card.*

*"That you didn't clean your room last night when I told you to?" Bray's mom snapped as she looked away from the TV.*

*Bray's smile almost faded, but she was too excited to show them her grades, so she didn't let the comment about her room not being clean get to her. "I promise I'll clean it right after I show you this.*" *She unfolded the report card the rest of the way and held it out to her dad first.*

"*Why don't you clean your room now, Brayelle?*" *he said sternly, not even looking at the paper in her hand.* "*It's always about later with you. You'll do it later. You'll get to it later. Do what your mother said and clean your room now. Elias can go home. You won't be roasting any marshmallows tonight. You're grounded.*"

*Her face fell. I saw it. But she gathered herself quickly and tried once more to get them to look.*

"*Daddy please just look at my grades.*" *She pushed the paper further into his view.* "*I only got one C. The rest are Bs, and I have an A in Art.*"

*Her dad snatched the report card from her fingers, looked down into it, then back up at her.*

"*Better than the last one,*" *he said still with the same uncaring emotion as I always expected of him.* "*But bringing up your grades doesn't excuse you from having to do your chores, or keep your room clean. Rian has good grades, does her chores every day, and her room is spotless. If she can juggle them all, why can't you?*" *He dropped the report card on the table and turned back to the television.*

"*Honey, please go clean your room,*" *her mom said, probably with a bit of guilt for the way her dad was treating her. But the woman never stood up for Bray, and I just never understood it.*

"*But—*"

"*Now!*" *Her dad shot up from the chair, and the remote control hit the hardwood floor.*

*Bray stepped backward away from him. Her parents were never abusive to her, but from what I had seen over the years, the way they talked to her at times was almost as bad.*

*Her mom looked at me and said in a calm manner, "Elias, it's best if you head home."*

*Bray's blue eyes were brimmed with tears. She looked at me once, grabbed her report card off the table and tore it to shreds in front of them. She screamed something inaudible, clenching her fists down at her sides and threw the ripped pieces of what was once something very dear to her at her dad and then ran off to her room. The door slammed shut so hard behind her that it rattled the pictures hanging on the walls in the living room.*

*Bray's older sister, Rian, walked through the front door just as I was going to leave.*

*"Hi, Elias," she said, but I pushed my way past her without a word. "Is Brayelle home?" she called out to me.*

*I turned to face her as I stood at the door with my hand on the knob. "Yeah," I said icily. "But some home this is."*

*I slammed their door almost as hard as Bray had and ran down the dirt driveway and away from that house.*

I looked down at Bray curled up next to me in the Jeep, and I combed my fingers through her soft hair, choking back the memory. I guess Bray was right. They didn't want to understand her.

# TWENTY-SIX

## Elias

$\mathcal{C}$aleb raised his back from the seat and pointed up ahead. "Pull in there," he said. "I need to piss."

Tate took a left at the stop sign and pulled into the parking lot of an old run-down liquor store on the corner. Various beer and whiskey advertisements completely covered the windows. An ice cooler sat beside the front door with a faded polar bear plastered on the side. There was only one car parked outside, on the edge of the building underneath a metal carport. It was probably the owner's car.

"Hurry up!" Tate shouted out the Jeep window as Caleb walked quickly inside. I heard the faint ringing of a bell when he swung open the door.

The three of us sat in silence for a moment. Bray had almost fallen asleep before we stopped.

"Are you two hungry?" Tate asked.

"No, man, I'm good," I said and then looked down at Bray as she sat against me with her head on my shoulder.

"I'm not hungry," she said.

"You sure? I can run in and get you a stick of jerky or something," Tate offered. He was turned around in the driver's seat and facing us, with his right hand wedged behind the headrest of the passenger's seat.

"No thanks," Bray said.

Tate nodded and turned back around. He tapped his thumbs against the steering wheel and turned the song up on the radio. Awolnation's "Sail" streamed from the speakers. We were all getting into it, bobbing our heads and singing along to the words.

"I might as well take a piss, too," Tate said after a minute.

He opened the door and started to take the key out of the ignition, but I stopped him. "Leave 'em," I said. "This is a great song."

"All right." He shut the door and jogged toward the front of the liquor store.

I leaned between the two front seats and reached out for the volume button, turning it up.

Bray and I became lost in the music. I leaned my head back against the seat and shut my eyes. She laid her head on my lap and shut her eyes. We let the music roll through us like medicine, and for a moment it was all we cared about. For that brief moment, we took advantage of shutting off the outside world.

A gunshot rang out, and our eyes popped open. Bray rose upright from my lap. "What was that?"

"Sounded like a shot."

I looked out the window beside me to see Caleb and Tate running toward us, Caleb with a gun in his right hand.

"Oh shit!" I cried.

We both froze and looked at each other as if to ask, *What just happened?* But neither of us could move.

Tate swung his door open and jumped inside. "Get the fuck in!" he yelled at Caleb.

A second later, Caleb was in the passenger's seat, and we were speeding away from the liquor store with dirt kicking up behind the Jeep's tires.

"*What the fuck?*" Tate roared at Caleb, white-knuckling the steering wheel as we got back onto the desolate highway.

"*I didn't mean to shoot him!*" Caleb leaned over and rammed his own head into the dashboard several times.

"What happened? Oh my God, what the fuck *happened?*" Bray said frantically. She rose up behind him, trying to look over his shoulder.

"You *shot* someone?" I grabbed Bray by her waist and pulled her away from Caleb and next to me.

"*Back off!*" Caleb screamed at us.

He looked at Tate, his eyes full of fear and anger and regret. "I-I fucking swear it, Tate. I-I didn't mean to hit him. I was only trying to scare him."

"You robbed the store?" Bray asked. "I can't believe he robbed the fucking store!" She was looking at me again.

I put my hand over her mouth gently. "Bray, please, just be quiet," I whispered.

She was shaking. *I* was shaking.

Tate slammed his fists down on the steering wheel. I counted six times before he almost lost control of the Jeep and had to grab the wheel to steady the vehicle. We fishtailed in a quick jolting motion until the Jeep straightened up. I could smell the burnt rubber from the tires.

"What are we going to do?" Caleb said nervously.

Tate swerved to the side of the road and came to a sudden stop. I caught Bray just before her mouth hit the back of Caleb's seat.

Tate fumbled for his cell phone somewhere in the front seat and called nine-one-one.

"A man was just shot," he said into the phone and then proceeded to give the operator the location of the liquor store.

Caleb got out of the Jeep and started walking down the center of the road. Tate followed. We watched them argue in the street for a moment.

"I did it to get money to pay Rocky!" Caleb yelled. "So you wouldn't have to use all of your savings!"

"And robbing a liquor store makes it better?!" Tate roared. He hit Caleb in the face.

Caleb stumbled backward and almost fell, but he didn't hit back. "I was only trying to scare him! I shot but I aimed at the wall! I didn't mean to *hit* him!"

"What are we going to do, Elias?" Bray asked, her whole body trembling.

"I don't know, but we can't stay with them."

Just then Tate jumped back inside and Caleb followed. Before we could even protest, the Jeep lurched into forward motion. We fell heavily against the seat and then forward again.

"Let us the fuck out!" I tried to shout over the radio and Tate and Caleb screaming at each other in the front. But I don't think Tate even heard me, he was so blinded by rage.

"I'm not doing this anymore with you, Caleb!" Tate said. "This is it! I'll always love you. You're my brother. But I never want to see you again!" Then his voice began to rise. "What the fuck, man! I just pulled the same stunt they did!" He pointed at us. "I fucking ran to protect your ass! What the fuck was I *thinking*?! I'm not going down for you! Not anymore! *Not like this!*"

We sped by a maroon-colored minivan.

"Slow down, man," I said nervously from the backseat. "You're going to get us all killed."

Minutes later we pulled into another convenience store parking lot. Bray and I jumped out quickly before Tate even put the Jeep into Park. I grabbed her hand and pulled her next to me.

Tate and Caleb started fighting in the front seat. Tate was on top of him, pummeling Caleb with his fists. But this time it was far from being a harmless brotherly squabble. Tate was a merciless animal, raining down blow after blow after heavy, bloody blow onto Caleb's face. I was afraid he was going to beat him to death.

I let go of Bray's hand and she screamed at me as I ran around to the passenger's side of the car and opened the door. Caleb fell out halfway and I grabbed him by the arms and helped him out the rest of the way. Tate was outside of the Jeep and standing over Caleb on the asphalt before I even had a chance to pull my arms from underneath his.

"Back off, Tate! You're going to make a bad situation worse!" I put up my hand, hoping to get him to back down. His balled fists hung bloodied at his sides. His face was twisted with rage. His tats almost looked alive as the muscles in his arms hardened and became more pronounced against the white backdrop of his shirt, also stained by Caleb's blood.

"Please, man, just back off," I pleaded one last time with him.

Tate's conscience took control of him again and he took two steps back. His chest rose and fell with heavy, deep breaths that he could hardly steady. I finally let go of Caleb and stood back as he picked himself up from the ground. Blood streamed from both of his nostrils. His left eye was already swollen. He reached up and wiped a trickle of blood from the corner of his mouth with the side of his hand.

I looked over to see Bray running into the convenience store.

I ran after her, and I could only wonder what the hell she was doing. I followed her to the ladies' restroom facilities and without a thought, I barged right in. I didn't give a damn if there were other people inside. I was worried about Bray. I was worried about what she was capable of.

The stall door shut with a vociferous *bang!* and seconds later I heard her throwing up. I wondered why she didn't just throw up outside, but it was such an insignificant curiosity that I didn't bother to ask.

"Baby, are you all right?"

"Yeah, I'm fine. I'll be OK." She threw up a few more times and I went over to the sink to wet some paper towels for her.

Bray came out of the stall and I started wiping her face and mouth.

"What are we going to do?" The floodgates opened and she broke down in tears, pressing her arms against my chest. I wrapped one arm around her back and the other behind her head.

"I think three days is too long," I said. "I think it's time we went home."

She looked up at me, and I kissed her forehead.

"I'm not going home," she said softly. "I never planned to."

I shook my head. "W-What are you saying? Bray, we have to go home. There are no other options."

"I love you, Elias, but I'm not going home with you. I'm not going to jail."

We were interrupted by a few screams inside the store and then I heard, *"Everybody get on the floor!"*

It was Caleb's voice.

And that was how we ended up here. In this moment. Holed up in the back of a convenience store with cops surrounding the building.

# TWENTY-SEVEN

*Present Day*

## Elias

*C*aleb has been holding me, Bray, and five other people inside the store for the past two hours. The store clerk and two customers have been sitting in the candy bar aisle just feet from us. I can smell urine. I think the woman with the brown hair and wearing a long, flowered dress pissed on herself at some point. Bray and I haven't moved from the wall in the hallway next to the restrooms.

My mind is overloaded with . . . with a little bit of everything. A part of me wants to feel absolutely numb to all of this, but it's only a small part. The rest of me is fearful but focused. I have to stay focused to get Bray out of here unharmed. I don't think Caleb will hurt us. I really don't. But I'm still afraid of what he might do, how far he will go.

Tate never made it into the store when the cops swarmed the parking lot and jumped out of their cars, drawing their guns. Caleb told us that he had pushed Tate away when Tate tried to follow him inside. He didn't want Tate to go down with him like this. What-ever that meant.

I still have a bad feeling sitting sour in my stomach. As if what's already happened isn't enough, I still feel like the worst is yet to come.

"Bray?" I try again to get her attention.

She doesn't answer. She appears stoic. Vacant.

I try another approach, with Caleb at least. I feel like Caleb is the one I need to fix first. To keep Bray safe, I have to talk Caleb down. An hour ago, I tried to talk him into giving himself up, but it was useless, as I had a feeling it would be.

I push myself to my feet. The gun in Caleb's hand is pointed right at me the second he notices.

I raise my hands out at my sides. "It's just me." He starts to lower the gun. "I just want to talk."

"*Five more minutes!*" an officer's voice on a loudspeaker calls out. "*We're sending him back in!*"

He's referring to the man—a cop of some sort—Caleb agreed to let in thirty minutes ago. He wanted to hear Caleb's demands and I'm sure to assess the situation inside for the officers outside. Bray and I stayed by the restrooms, out of sight.

"Talk about what?" Caleb says acidly.

His eye has turned blue and purple over the past two hours, and it's so swollen the skin is raised nearly an inch over what is normal.

"You say you're not going to hurt anyone," I begin, "so just let everyone go. Show them you mean it. You keep these people in here like this, they're hostages."

"So fucking what?" he says. The woman in the dress looks up at him but is afraid to meet his eyes. "They're already gonna charge me with having hostages. Doesn't matter now."

"Then let them go. You didn't intend to have hostages, so let them go. I'll stay here with you. But let Bray go, too."

"I'm not going anywhere," Bray finally speaks from behind me.

I turn around to see her looking up at me from her sitting position on the floor. I leave Caleb carefully, backing my way away from him so that I'm not making any sudden movements, and I go straight over and kneel beside Bray.

"You need to get out of here," I say.

"No. I don't," she says simply. "If I go out that door, I go straight to jail. I told you, I'm not going to jail. And I meant it."

My heart is racing. Time is running out, and all I can think about is what's going to happen when it does. Every possible scenario has run through my mind like a wide-awake nightmare, each of them ending with Bray facedown in a pool of her own blood.

Five minutes later, the guy in the casual clothes who somehow still reeks of cop reenters the store with his hands raised above his head. And just like before, Caleb keeps the gun trained on him.

"Where is my brother?" Caleb asks.

"He's still outside waiting for you," the man says in a calm voice. "He's worried about you, Caleb. He just wants you to come out of here safely so that you can go home."

Caleb laughs. "*Home?* Are you fucking *kidding* me? You think I'm fucking stupid? I won't see home for a long time."

"No, you won't," the man says, still with both hands where Caleb can see them at all times. "But you will someday, and the longer you stay in here like this, the worse you make it for yourself, the farther away the prospect of seeing home becomes. What about these people?" He points at the male clerk and the two women sitting in the aisle. "*They* want to go home. They haven't done anything to deserve this."

I wonder why the man didn't include Bray and me, why he's acting as though we aren't sitting here several feet away and as much a part of this as they are.

Just as I think that, the man looks at us, his dark eyes peer at us underneath dark, bushy eyebrows.

"And what about Brayelle Bates and Elias Kline?" he says and my heart stops.

*How did they find out so soon?* I think to myself, but then it becomes obvious. We've been on the news. It wasn't hard to figure out. But still, his saying our names like that took me by surprise.

Bray has the same reaction. Her eyes grow wide. She looks at me for a split second before giving the man her full attention.

"They still have a chance to go home," the man goes on, though he's looking right at us, making sure that we get the message he was sent in here to give. "Everybody knows that they're scared. But no one is accusing them of murder. Innocent until proven guilty. They want to go home to tell everyone what happened that night on the river, tell their side of the story, to have a chance at life." He looks at Caleb again. "But you have to let them go home so they can do that."

"I'm not keeping them here," he says. "And *she* doesn't *want* to go."

The man looks at Bray. "Is that true?"

"You're not in here for me," Bray says. "I'm the least of anyone's worries. Leave me out of it."

"I'm afraid that's not something I can do," the man says.

"He's the one with the gun, you asshole," she snaps. "Just leave me alone!"

The man turns to me. "And what about you?" he asks. "Are you a part of this?"

"Wait a damn minute!" Caleb shouts. "What the fuck is *that* supposed to mean? You accusing them of being a part of this?" He points the gun forward at the man. "See, fuck the system! Fuck 'innocent until proven guilty'! They already think you're guilty, that you are as much a part of this as I am, even though I'm the one holding the gun to his fucking head. See how the system works? They send innocent people to jail every fucking day while murderers, child molesters, and *real* rapists are set free because of some stupid goddamn technicality. *Fuck* you and your system, you piece of shit!"

The man takes two steps back and raises his hands a little higher. He's getting worried that Caleb might get trigger-happy. So am I.

"No, I'm not accusing them of anything," the man says in surrender. "But it looks bad on them if they stay in here when they have a chance to be set free. It makes them look even guiltier of Jana McIntyre's death than they already do." Then he adds, "And I know about your rape sentence, Caleb. I've seen men get sent to jail for rape, men just like you who don't fit the profile. It happens all the time. You're not the only one." He looks at us once more. "And accidents happen all the time, too. Sometimes people run when they're scared. It's the worst thing you can do, but it happens. All the time. None of you are alone."

"Are you saying you believe us?" Caleb asks. "Or is this your way of gaining trust?" He doesn't give the man a chance to answer. Caleb already has it set in his mind what he believes and nothing this man can say will ever change that. He laughs. "That's exactly what it is. You come in here wearing your stupid fucking running pants and your stupid fucking running shoes, trying to look like a civilian, when really we all know you're just another cop trying to fit in with the little people. Gain our trust. Make us believe your bullshit lies."

"Your brother is outside right now, Caleb," the man cuts in. "He's worried. He told me to tell you that he will visit you every single day while you're locked up. He said that he didn't mean what he said before, that he never wanted to see you again. He wants you to know that no matter what, he'll put you first and visit you every day until the day you get out. Because he loves you and nothing can keep him away from his little brother."

I hear Bray rupture with sobs and I look down at her. It's as though what the man just said struck a nerve.

Caleb's eyes are now brimming with tears, too. His mouth is twitching at the corners, his nose wrinkling under the deep setting of his eyebrows as he tries to hold the tears back. But he can't hold them in and they begin to run down his cheeks in rivulets.

"Is my brother in trouble?" Caleb asks, the gun, still shaking, pointed at the man. "Is he going to face charges for running with me? It wasn't his fault! He wasn't even thinking straight when he ran out of that liquor store with me! He had nothing to do with it! He only ran because *I* was running! *He wasn't thinking straight!*"

"Calm down," the man says, motioning forward. "No, listen to me, Caleb, I'm sure I can get him out of it. He did run, yes, and he shouldn't have, but he called nine-one-one, and the man you shot is going to live. Your brother is going to be fine."

"He's going to live?" Caleb asks, his voice desperate and nearly breathless.

I see the relief wash through him beneath all of that anger and rage and fear.

"Yes," the man says. "He's in stable condition. It was a shoulder wound."

"And my brother? You fucking swear on your life he's not going to be charged?"

"Caleb, I'm not going to swear it," the man says, "because I want to be completely honest with you. But his chances are very good. The only thing he did wrong was run, but he didn't go far. He did everything else right. I believe he'll be fine. And I'll do everything I can to make sure that he is. I know he's innocent. He's got a good heart. I've been doing this for a long time and I know a good man when I see one." He pauses, looks at me and then back at Caleb. "I'm looking at two good men right now. And one good woman. People who were in the wrong place at the wrong time. People who have screwed up and who will have to face charges no matter what, but people who still have a chance to prove that they're good people."

The woman in the flowered dress breaks into sobs of her own. The clerk holds her next to him.

"Let them go, Caleb," the cop says.

"I will," he says. "You go back outside and I'll send them out after you."

"What about you?" the man asks suspiciously. "Are you going to give yourself up?"

"I want to think about it," Caleb says. "But I'll let them go."

The man nods, accepting what Caleb gives him. He leaves the store.

Caleb paces back and forth in front of the drink coolers, staying out of sight of the front windows. Then he stops and points at the three hostages.

"Go," he says motioning his free hand toward the front doors. "I'm sorry that I put you through this. I'm so sorry."

The woman in the flowered dress raises her eyes to him and then immediately bolts out of the store sobbing hysterically.

"Bray," Caleb says turning to her, "I'm sorry for being such a dick." He looks at me. "I really am."

"I know," I say.

Bray just sits there quietly with her back pressed against the wall. Her tears have dried up, her face devoid of any emotion.

Caleb goes to the door and opens it enough that he can yell out, *"I'm going to come out! I'm going to surrender!"*

Bray gets up, and her movement surprises me. She walks past me and goes toward the end of the candy bar aisle.

I follow behind her.

*"Put the gun on the floor and come out with your hands up!"*

Caleb sets the gun on the floor right in front of the door, raises his hands high above his head, turns around, and pushes the glass door open with his back.

The second the door closes, I see Bray's dark hair whip behind her as she runs toward the door. I panic inside when she falls to the floor and grabs Caleb's gun and then backs herself against the bread display.

"What are you doing?" I approach her carefully. My heart is hammering against my rib cage. "Baby . . . please . . . please don't—"

She shoves the gun underneath her chin, pushing her head back against a loaf of bread, and her finger rests on the trigger.

I fall to my knees, tears streaming down my face. I feel like I'm going to throw up my heart is beating so fast.

"God, please, Bray . . . *please* . . . if you do this, if you take your life in front of me it will kill me. I love you *so fucking much*. I always have. I always will." I'm choking on my tears, and the back of my throat burns. "You remember that pact we made when we were kids? Best friends always. Do you remember?" I inch closer on my hands and knees. My hands are shaking so badly I can hardly hold my body up. Bray's face holds no emotion. None. She just looks at me through glass eyes, but the more I talk to her, the more I remind her how much I love her, the more I see the faintest of emotion flicker inside the glass. I see the Bray I've known and loved since I was nine years old, the one stronger than the darkness that lives inside of her. "I know you remember. But you're more to me than my best friend. You always have been. My heart beats for you. If you die, every part of what makes me human will die."

Her hand begins to shake. It makes me nervous. Her finger on the trigger...I don't want her to shake.

"God damn it, Bray...*I love you! Don't put me through this!*"

"I can't be locked up!" she screams. "I can't live like that! Away from you! You're all I have in this world! All I've ever had!"

"I'll be there!" I scream back at her with every ounce of emotion my body can produce. "I would never leave you alone! Do you understand me?! *Never!* I don't care how long it takes, Bray, I will wait for you!"

And then the significance of the moment hits me.

"*I will die for you, Bray! I will die WITH you!*"

Her lips quiver uncontrollably. She stares deeply into my eyes for what feels like forever. And then she shakes her head no, the barrel of the gun moving with the movement of her head.

"*Don't say that!*" she roars.

"I *will*!" I scream, and then I try to calm myself enough to make her understand. I inch closer. "Brayelle, this, this moment right here is the 'anything' I vowed to you last night. You didn't ask me to prove it, but I'm going to prove it anyway—don't look away from my eyes," I say, and she looks back up. "Stay with me. Right here." I point at my eyes with my index and middle finger. "If this is what you really want, then I go down with you. I don't want to live without you, either. We're in this together. We always have been. I won't abandon you now. I'll die with you if you think death is the only way."

She shakes her head, over and over, and tries fruitlessly to produce words.

"I don't want you to die because of me," she finally says, her voice raspy from crying so much and so hard.

"I want to live, Bray," I say breathily, and with desperation. "I want to live a life with *you*. I want to marry *you*. I want to grow old and have babies with *you*. I want to *live*. But I'm prepared to die. Do you understand?"

"Why are you *doing* this?!" Her features are tortured, her body trembling.

*"Because we belong together! In life and in death! Because without you I'm dead anyway!"*

She throws her head back against the bread shelf and screams, dropping the gun on the floor. I grab her and scoop her up in my arms and crush her so hard against me that it takes the breath out of my lungs. We cry into each other, her fingers grasping my shirt, mine digging into her back.

"Baby, I fucking love you so much. I'll never let you go," I murmur into her neck.

The police burst through the door, but I can only faintly hear them. They're ghosts, like Bray had always been to her parents. I only see and hear and feel Bray when they're pulling us apart. I only hear her yelling out my name as everything else around us is mute. My heart breaks as she is reaching out for me and I know I can't reach back. Everything seems to happen in slow motion.

"I won't abandon you," I say almost in a whisper, as she's being dragged away with her hands behind her back. "I won't abandon you."

And then she's gone.

# TWENTY-EIGHT

*One year and two weeks later...*

## Elias

*I* have written her every day. I've visited her every week during visiting hours. I've spent every waking moment not only proving to Bray that I would never abandon her, but fulfilling my own need to be with her.

Bray was sentenced to three years for involuntary manslaughter and for leaving the scene of a crime, but her attorney expected her to actually serve less than half of her sentence. Having no prior criminal record except a harmless stint in juvenile and offering to take a polygraph test really helped her case. Bray passed the polygraph, but it almost wasn't admissible in court because Jana McIntyre's family initially didn't agree. But in the end, they relented.

Turned out that Jana McIntyre had more of a record than Bray had. Jana spent most of her teenage life in and out of juvenile detention and juvenile court for behavioral crimes, most of them related to violence. But the one key thing that Bray's attorney made sure to bring to light in court was Jana's three-month stay in juvenile for attacking a girl in the school gym and beating her unconscious.

This helped back Bray's story about Jana attacking her on the ridge and Bray shoving Jana only to get her off. Bray might've been given a lesser sentence if she hadn't admitted to pushing her out of anger rather than self-defense. But at least she told the truth. It *was* self-defense, and the judge believed this, given the details of the situation, but it wasn't life or death for Bray, and she had acted more out of anger than fear.

Also, since Jana's death was considered suspicious, an autopsy had been ordered. Along with enough alcohol to put her three times over the legal limit, a host of drugs were also found in her system.

And there was nothing noted about Jana being pregnant at the time of her death.

As for me, I got off much easier than Bray.

Two years of probation was all I got for my involvement. I didn't have to spend any time in prison. But being without Bray and knowing that she was locked up and lonely all that time was my own personal version of prison.

And she made me swear that I wouldn't try to be her witness. I was going to do it. I had planned everything out in my head, even though we never really got the chance to plan the story together, but she told me if I did it she'd never speak to me again. She told me that she would only tell them the truth: that I wasn't there when it happened, and that I was only trying to help her by claiming that I was.

I knew then that if I tried to go through with it, I would only make a bad situation worse.

Bray hasn't been doing well. Every time I see her I notice that she has slipped deeper into the darkness that lives inside of her. I haven't slept much since she's been away, worried that every time my phone rings it will be Rian, Bray's sister, telling me that Bray attempted suicide. Or achieved it. I like to think that she'll never try because she's strong and refuses to let the darkness consume her again, but a part of me believes deep down that it's only because nothing is available to her. Because of Bray's previous suicide attempt in South Carolina and her bipolar II disorder diagnosis, Bray was put under suicide watch. It's hard visiting her. As I sit with her across the tiny white plastic table every week I feel like she is slipping completely away from me.

"What's on your mind?" I asked on my last visit. I reached across the table and held her hands. I smiled, trying to comfort her.

She smiled back, but I could sense that it was forced. "Just getting out of here," she said. Her gaze drifted.

"Did you get my letter?" I had asked.

She nodded and raised her eyes to me again. The faint smile I saw resting at the corners of them wasn't forced this time. "Every day but Sunday."

I often wondered how much those letters helped keep her afloat. Well, I call them letters, but technically not all of them were. I wrote notes to her on everything. Anything that happened to be available wherever I was when I thought of something I needed to say.

On the back of a takeout menu from a nearby diner:

*I was thinking about that day in tenth grade, the day the storm knocked the lights out in the school. You and Lissa snuck out to smoke cigarettes in the bathroom. Your hair smelled like an ashtray for a week after that. I was just wondering, did you actually wash your hair that week? I missed the smell of that strawberry shampoo you always used. I'd stand next to you at your locker just before lunch and I'd smell your hair. Creepy, I know. Deal with it. But that was a bad week for me. I think it threw me off my game. Anyway, I love and miss you.*

*Elias*

On the back of a grocery store receipt:

*I was sitting at a stoplight (the one that never changes down the road from your parents), and I just wanted to tell you that when you get home I'm going to do naughty things to you. Maybe even at this stoplight.*

*Elias*

On a napkin at a Denny's restaurant:

*Bray,*

*I got a speeding ticket today. Fifty in a thirty-five. I was late for work. I guess I should tell you, I got a new job. Roofing. Hot as a bitch in the summertime, but it pays good money. I'm going to buy you something nice with my first check. Oh, and pay the speeding ticket.*

*Love you,*
*Elias*

On one of those blank pages they always add to printed books—ripped it out of an old book at the dentist's office:

*I'm getting a root canal today. You know how much I love going to the dentist. Remember in fourth grade? I know you do. I cried like a girl for an hour because my mom was taking me for a checkup. I don't think I ever thanked you for not telling Mitchell about that. Thank you. Because I'd still hear about it today if you had. Which brings me to some news. Mitchell and I are talking again. He's clean and doing much better. He's his old self again for the most part. He wanted me to tell you that he's sorry for what he did, and he can't wait to see you when you come home. I know you're pissed at him, but I thought I'd relay the message. But don't worry, he's definitely not living with me. I only have room for one other person, and I'm just waiting for her to come back.*

*I love you.*
*Elias*

I'd tuck each one in an envelope, slap a stamp on it, and mail it the same day. I wanted to make sure she got something every single day she was there, at least on days that the mail ran.

She writes to me, too, though not every day, and while I'm OK with that, it has started to worry me. Her letters often feel distant, emotionless. Sometimes I'll get a letter out of the blue riddled with the Bray I fell in love with, cracking jokes and being a pervert. She'll talk about the things she wants to do with me when she gets out, the life she wants us to have. I'll smile as I read it, feeling like she's starting to come around and that things are looking up for her. But as I read on, the pessimist eventually comes out of her before I get to the end of each letter. I keep telling myself, *The next one won't be like this, Elias. It won't end like this.* But so far, every one of them has.

I know she's getting help where she is, but that hasn't stopped me from looking for the right psychiatrist for when she gets out. I've scoured the Internet and the phone book searching for the one.

I want Bray to have the best, and I'll do everything in my power to make sure that she does.

Three hundred and seventy-nine days Bray has spent behind bars, and in two weeks she will be released. I'm going to visit her today, and while this is supposed to be something for both of us to look forward to, I'm nervous. I'm nervous because of the last letter I got from her just five days ago. It wasn't anything that she said in the letter, it was what she didn't say.

*Dear Elias,*

*I know you've never missed a visiting day, but I wanted to make sure you didn't miss the next one. It's very important that you be here.*

*Love,*
*Bray*

I get out of my car and go through the front doors of the building and check in with the officer at the counter. Like I do every week, I count the lockers in the small room adjacent to the check-in area just after I secure my wallet, cell phone, and keys inside one. I don't know why I count them. I just do. Maybe it's out of nervousness, like how as I'm allowed past the heavy security door I always read the signs posted on the walls about firearms and visiting hours, and reminders about how it's against the law to bring contraband in to the prisoners. I always read the signs. Sometimes more than once. And I always stop at that word *prisoners* and it hurts me, like someone is reaching inside my chest and folding a fist around my heart.

The long hallway is stark white, the tile floors and the white walls blending in with one another to appear seamless in my peripheral vision. The fluorescent lights shine overhead so brightly that I can almost see my reflection in the floor. I take my time, passing a few doors that lead to other strange rooms, and I have no interest in knowing what's behind them. A fatherless family walks by: a woman with two small children, their hands clutched in hers. I wonder if they were here visiting their father. Bray doesn't belong here. She's no criminal. She didn't murder anyone in cold blood or kill someone because she was under the influence of anything that impaired her judgment. She's not a drug dealer or a thief or an abusive spouse. She doesn't fucking belong here. I guess prison really doesn't discriminate.

I turn the corner at the end of the long hall and enter a room. A guard points me to a table where I sit. And wait. There's a clock high on the wall and to my left. Plain. Black and white and boring. There are several round, plastic, white tables positioned about the room. Eight families are already inside waiting at other tables. I realize as I glance around that I'm the only one here alone. I look down at the bright white table and trace my finger along an indentation that looks like it had been carved with something sharp, maybe a paperclip. It smells like bleach and Pine-Sol in here. The back of my nostrils begin to itch, and I take a deep breath, hoping to force back the brewing sneeze.

I look up at the clock. She should be coming in here any second now. I place my hand against my chest to feel my heart beating, because it's beating too fast. Why was it so important that I make this visit? What is she going to tell me?

Just as I feel like my mind is going to come undone with the possibilities, bright orange moves against the stark white walls, and I look up to see Bray coming toward me wearing her usual orange jumpsuit, white socks, and thick plastic sandals that squeak against the floor.

I stand up. I smile at her as she approaches and she smiles back, but I don't feel like it's real, and my heart twists in knots.

"Hi baby," I say and hug her gently. Physical contact is limited here.

Her hug is tight and doesn't at all reflect the smile she gave me, but that only makes me feel a fraction better. Her hair is pulled into a tight ponytail at the back of her head. She's wearing no makeup, of course, and although she looks tired, physically and mentally, she's still the most beautiful thing I've ever seen.

We sit down.

"Two weeks," I say, smiling even brighter, trying to lighten the mood. "You'll be back with me in no time."

"Elias?" she says and my heart stops. I don't know why, but I have a bad feeling. I swallow a knot in my throat, but another emerges behind it.

"What's wrong?" I ask.

She inhales a deep breath into her lungs and then reaches up and wipes underneath her left eye with the edge of her finger.

Then suddenly, she smiles. I feel the corners of my eyes hardening in confusion and I cock my head to one side curiously. A smile of my own teases the corners of my lips.

"What is it?" I ask, suddenly beaming.

Bray shakes her head. "It's nothing," she says and reaches her hands across the table, enclosing them over mine. Her fingers are cold and frail. She leans over and kisses the tops of my warm, calloused ones. And while I'm worried the guard might say something to her about that, I don't care much, either.

"Then what was with your letter?" I ask.

She slides her hands away. "I just wanted to see you," she says.

"But you knew I'd come," I say. "I-It just...sounded urgent. Is there something you're not telling me?"

She sighs. "Yeah, but it's not really that big of a deal."

"Well, what is it?"

She hesitates and says, "My release date has been moved to the ninth."

"But why?" I ask. "I mean it's only four days more, but—"

"It's just some kind of technicality," she answers.

Wanting her to stay positive, I make sure to do the same. I let my smile reappear and I say, "Well, that's fine. I mean, sure, four days sucks, but it's just four days. You'll be OK, right?"

She nods. "Yes."

Something doesn't feel right. I feel like she's lying to me. But why would she do that? Why would she lie about something like that?

I'm just being paranoid. That's ridiculous. No way I'm going to accuse her of not being truthful. Not now. She doesn't need that from me.

"Good," I say and reach out to hold her hands like she did mine.

"So, tell me about Mitchell," Bray says.

"Well...he's not on meth anymore," I say. "And he's working at that tire and lube place over by our old school. He really does feel like shit for what he did. To both of us. Not just me."

Bray's smile is soft and forgiving. "Well, you tell Mitchell that it's OK," she says. "I'm not mad at him. He couldn't help what he did. How's your mom doing? And your dad?"

"They're great," I say, nodding. "Mom got engaged to James. I just found out last Thursday. They're getting married in March. My dad is the same as he was before. A hardworking loner. He wanted me to tell you he wants us to visit him in Savannah when you come home. He really likes you. Always has."

Bray's eyes light up with her smile and then she looks down at the table.

My smile fades and I'm reluctant to ask, but I have to. "Are… your parents, or Rian, still contacting you much?"

She shakes her head. "My mom has visited several times. I think she feels guilty. My dad…well, he's visited me, but it feels like it always has, like he's only here out of obligation. But I forgive him. I don't want to feel angry or hurt by anyone anymore. I just want to be free. To *feel* free. In my heart, y'know?" She tilts her head to one side and her eyebrows draw inward thoughtfully.

Maybe I do know what she means, but then again, I feel like there's something much more to it than that. Something about what she said fills me with an uncomfortable feeling. I can't place it, but it worries me.

Having nothing more to go on, I simply nod and say, "Yeah, I know. I understand that need." And then I ask, "What about Rian?"

Bray's smile brightens a little again.

"She's visited several times, usually in the first half of the day." I was glad for that, because I wanted my time with Bray to be mine and not to have to share it with someone else. Like right now, I always visit in the late afternoon hours, after I get off work. "But she's been writing me a lot."

"How do you feel about that?"

She shrugs. "I'm not sure. I mean, I'm glad she's making an effort, but I just have a hard time trusting her motives."

I completely understand that.

Bray, as usual, is distant. I want to reach across the small table and pull her into my arms. It depresses me that I can't, that I can't hold her, kiss her, be myself with her and make her smile. I feel completely fucking helpless.

Bray's eyes keep straying. To the wall behind me, toward the door she was walked through minutes ago, toward the guard sitting at the long, rectangular-shaped particleboard table next to the white wall. Everything but me.

I look over my shoulder to see that the guard is reading a newspaper, so I scoot my chair over a little closer to her. Finally, her eyes fall on mine again. I smile at her, revealing my teeth. It feels kind of goofy, and apparently it is judging by that weird, amused look she's giving me in return. Then I grin impishly and get the blushing reaction out of Bray that I was shooting for.

I enclose her left hand underneath both of mine.

"When you get out of here," I say in a low voice, "we're gonna have a lot of sex to make up for lost time."

She lowers her eyes again, but this time it's only because of the hot blush overshadowing her features. I stroke the very center of the palm of her hand softly with the tip of my pinky finger, gazing into her eyes with a mischievous quality. And then I whisper, "I'd say, at least a full week straight of nothing but sex. Everywhere. In every way. In every part of you." I faintly lick the dryness from my lips, taking my time about letting my tongue hide away back inside my mouth, all the while still stroking the center of her palm with my finger.

Her eyes flutter.

While it was my intention only to make her feel better, give her a sense of normalcy, just talking about it, thinking about it, and touching her hand in such a suggestive way, it's made me so hard that I have no doubt about what I'll be doing first thing when I get home.

Bray's blushing face turns softer and she says, "I really do miss you."

I smile softly back at her and kiss her knuckles once before letting go of her hand. "I miss you, too. But it won't be long and you'll be home, where you belong, with me. There's so much that I want to say to you and show you. I feel like even though we've known each other all our lives and that we've been through so much, once you get out of here it'll be a new beginning. A do-over. This time we'll get it all right."

Bray's face warms with a smile, softening her eyes, making her appear loving and ... strangely sympathetic.

Thirty minutes is over before we know it, and she's standing up.

"Bray, I love you," I say, as she starts to walk away. "More than anything."

She turns at the last second, the last one in a line of orange jumpsuits, and smiles back at me with a look of pure devotion.

"I love you too, Elias," she says sincerely, yet the tone of her voice is lifeless.

She follows the line out the door, and I can't help but feel that it's the last time I'll ever see her.

# TWENTY-NINE

## Elias

*R*ian called me an hour ago and invited me over to discuss something "important." Before I agreed, I made her promise me that nothing had happened to Bray. Like I said, it's always my worst fear when I get a call from Bray's sister. Since we're not married, if something were to happen to her while in jail, they would likely call her blood relatives before they'd call me, even though Bray put me at the top of her emergency contact list.

Rian said that it was not about anything like that. Thank God.

"I want my sister to come home with me when she's released," Rian says as she sits across from me at the kitchen table. Her long, dark hair, much like Bray's, is draped over both shoulders; her almond-shaped green eyes, not at all like Bray's, are scrutinizing me. She and Bray look very much alike, but Rian has always appeared more stern and intimidating. Just like their father. I think it's one reason I never liked her much: she is too much like Mr. Bates, whom I pretty much despise. A mug of hot coffee covers the bottom half of her face as she takes a slow sip. Then she sets the mug down in front of her, her manicured fingernails tapping the ceramic.

"Why would you want her to come here?" I ask. "She should be with me."

"And she will be," Rian says. "But she went through a lot with you—"

I slap the palm of my hand down on the table, and stare her down. "All the more reason for her to come home with me where she belongs."

"No, Elias, you don't understand." Her head falls gently to one side and dark bangs fall around her eyes. "I want my sister to know that you're not the only person in this world who cares about her."

I laugh drily. "Really? And I'm assuming you're talking about yourself and your parents?"

"Look," she says, staring at me with an unwavering gaze, "I know you think I don't care about her because our parents were hard on her growing up, but I love my sister. I tried to have a relationship with her, but she always pushed me away. I didn't understand her destructive personality, so I gave her the space she seemed to want. But I always loved her."

I sigh and shake my head. She's fucking unbelievable.

"You *let* her push you away, Rian. Instead of standing by her and *trying* to understand her, you opted for the easy way out. And don't even get me started on your parents." I throw my hands up in front of me and then lean back in the chair. There are many more things I want to say to her, but I hold back.

"I agree with you about our parents," Rian says. "Even I could see that they were just tired of dealing with Brayelle. But I'm only three years older than my sister. You treat me as if I'm just like they are, that I am just as guilty as they are—but you have to understand, I didn't know any better for most of our lives. I mean...I knew what my sister was going through, but I didn't know how to help her. I was young."

I can't look at her. Not because I don't agree with what she said, but because I don't want her to be right. I want to blame her because Bray's parents aren't sitting in front of me to blame.

"What will bringing her here do?" I ask icily.

"I just want some time alone with her. I want to make things up to her and make her understand that aside from you, she also has me and that I'll never shut her out again."

"Have you asked Bray if that's what *she* wants?" I want to smirk because I already know the answer. I know there's no way Bray wouldn't want to come straight home to me when she's released. But I keep my cool and wait for her answer, ready to be an adult about it and not gloat like a kid.

"Yes," Rian says. "I talked to Brayelle about it the last time I went to visit her. She said she would come home with me."

My mouth figuratively falls on the floor. "What?"

*Don't smirk or smile at me or I'll lose my shit on you, Rian.* Coming here, I completely expected something like this from her, for her father's genes to shine through and make her intolerant about Bray's well-being. Although Rian rarely interfered in Bray's life and her illness, the few times she did, she always made it worse.

But she doesn't smirk or smile. In fact, she appears soft and sympathetic toward my feelings, which only makes me feel like an asshole.

"She said that? Why would she say that?" My heart is hurting.

Rian pushes the ceramic mug to the side and folds her ring-decorated hands on top of the table. She looks across at me with nothing but sincerity in her eyes.

"Elias," she says gently, "my sister loves you very much—*too* much, in my opinion—"

"*Too* much?" I narrow both eyes at her. "What the hell is that supposed to mean?" I push myself to my feet, causing the chair to skid across the linoleum behind me a few inches. I've never been this way before, so difficult and offensive. I realize it as I stand here glaring down at Bray's sister with so much animosity. But I just can't bring myself to accept that Bray would do this without me knowing, would agree to come home with a sister who was never there for her, her whole life. I can't accept that Bray wouldn't tell me. I can't accept that she wouldn't want to come home with me first thing.

It doesn't make any sense!

I'm starting to see what my last letter from Bray and the last visit with her was all about.

I try to compose myself, sucking in a deep, concentrated breath. I shut my eyes and let what little calm I harbor settle over me.

"It's too much when a person's life revolves around another person," Rian says. "I know that Brayelle feels like she's nothing without you, that she can't *live* without you, Elias. No one should ever live that way. It's unhealthy. You have to know that."

"You don't know what you're talking about," I snap. "What makes you say that?"

"Because that's what she told me."

I throw my head back and laugh. I lean forward, pressing the palms of my hands against the wood grain table, peering down at Rian with a look of disbelief and disappointment twisting my features.

"You really have no idea what's going on with your sister," I accuse. "It's unbelievable to me that after all that's happened, after everything Bray has gone through, the suicide attempt in South Carolina, the shit she went through with you and your parents, constantly shoved to the side by your father while your mother looked the other way." I feel lines deepen around my nose as I glare angrily down into Rian's calm and unemotional face. "I was the only person who ever gave a shit about her. *Of course* she's going to say she can't live without me. She's going to even believe that at times, but you want to know the truth? Let me enlighten you, Rian." I stand upright again, letting my hands slide away from the table. "You're not seeing the bigger picture here. All you see is what you *want* to see. You sit there and listen to the things your sister says, and instead of trying to understand what's really going on with her, why she is the way she is, you blame *me* and ignore the fact that underneath it all, you and your parents are more to blame than I am."

I slash the air in front of me with my hand. "Bray is sick, Rian. She's *sick*. When it comes down to it, it's not my fault, it's not your fault, it's not even your parents' fault. We're only to blame for her not getting the help she needed a long time ago. Even I'm guilty of that. I never should've left with her after what happened last year. I contributed to her illness by what we did." I lean over again, bracing one hand on the table and pointing my finger at her with the other. "But you know what? At least I can say that I didn't know she needed help until after we ran. I had no idea that she was seeing a shrink when she was a teenager. I had no fucking idea that she tried to commit suicide when she was in South Carolina. I had absolutely no idea that her problems ran deeper than I could imagine. And you want to know *why* I didn't know?"

I slap the table again. Rian blinks and leans further back in the chair. "Because I loved her for the way she was. I never pushed her away. I accepted her and everything about her, and the only way I saw her differently from anyone else was that I *loved* her, unlike anyone else. But you and your family and her so-called fucking friends shoved her in the corner because she wasn't like you, because you couldn't spare the extra effort to really know and understand her." I point at myself. "She wasn't sick around me because I was all the therapy she needed, at least until her illness reached its worst." I pause and take a deep breath and calm myself. "I want to get her the help she needs. If it's all that I ever do, to help her get through this, I'm fine with that. But she trusts me. She loves me."

Rian swallows and loses eye contact with me for a long moment. I want to think that what I said will make some kind of sense to her, that it might wake her up enough to understand that she has seriously misjudged the situation. That she's wrong. I meant every word I said to Bray when I sat in front of her on the floor of the convenience store that day, when she held that gun underneath her chin. I would die for her or with her. That day in the store, tomorrow, a year from now. I will still die for her or with her if it ever comes down to it. Two people can love each other so much that not even death can separate them, but I will never believe that two people can love each other *too* much. Bray may feel like she can't live without me, and I feel the same way, but when it comes down to it, when a person commits suicide seemingly over another person, it's never only about that person, about losing them. There's always a plethora of underlying issues that would cause someone to take their own life. And a single person is never to blame.

I find it sad that I'm the only one in Bray's life who understands that.

Yes, I will die for her. Yes, I will die *with* her. Still to this day, and every day after it. But it's different when it's brought on by love and devotion than when it's caused by depression and mental illness.

I turn my back to Rian and cross my arms.

"She said she'd come home with me," Rian says.

I hold back my need to lash out at her. I hate her right now. I hate her for not listening. I feel like all she cares about is what she thinks is best while disregarding anything else.

"If Brayelle says she doesn't want to, then I'll bring her to your place myself. All I'm asking is for you to keep your distance and not interfere. This is what she wants, and you should respect that." I hear her sip her coffee and then place the mug back upon the table.

Finally I turn around to look at her. I start to speak, but the words stick in the back of my throat, and I swallow them down.

The screen door shuts hard behind me as I storm out of the house and down the concrete steps.

————

"Damn, man, that's fucked up," Mitchell says several days later. We're sitting in the living room of his apartment. I stopped by to visit him after work this evening and told him only the basics, nothing too personal. "I remember when we were all in eighth grade, Rian picked Bray up one afternoon from school." I nodded, and he went on. "They were fighting about something and I heard Rian tell Bray that she wished she'd just kill herself and get it over with."

My brows draw inward.

"Never really thought anything of it," he goes on. "Brothers and sisters say shit like that all the time."

I nod, agreeing, but it makes me sick to know Rian had ever said something like that to Bray, even if she had no idea what kind of impact saying that might've had on her.

"So what are you going to do?" Mitchell asks, pushing his bangs away from his face.

I shake my head and then rest it against the back of the love seat cushion. I look upward at the ceiling fan as it spins around and the little pull string on the light taps against the glass globe. "I'm going to give Bray what she wants. As much as I hate it, I don't want to come between her and her sister, especially if Rian's trying to make an effort to be there for her. A lot late, but better late than never, I guess.

"Besides, it's not like Rian would be able to keep Bray away from me if Bray wanted to see me. She can kick Rian's ass, so I'm not worried about Rian holding her prisoner in the house or anything."

Mitchell laughs. "Yeah, I have to say that about Bray; she always was mean."

I laugh lightly, thinking about it. "Yeah, I guess she was."

"Well, you want my advice?" Mitchell asks.

I don't really want the advice of a former meth-head-slash-asshole, but he is a good friend on the mend, so I accept it anyway.

"Tell that warped sister of hers to go fuck herself and you drag Bray's ass home with you. That's my opinion." He nods sharply and takes a big gulp of soda.

*Yeah, thanks for the advice, Mitch, but as much as I'd love to take it, I think I'll go the adult route.* I don't respond to him out loud.

"So, when did you say she's getting out?" Mitchell asks.

"Two more days," I answer. "They pushed the date back four days, or she'd already be out."

Mitchell purses his lips contemplatively. "That's weird they'd do that."

"Not really," I say, but I don't know my reasoning for believing that.

"Well, sure," Mitchell says, "they might extend someone's sentence for fuckin' up in there or something, but usually it's longer than four days for something like that. It just seems odd to me."

I think about what he said, and, I admit, I agree with him for the most part. But over the years I've learned not to put too much stock in what Mitchell says.

I leave Mitchell's house and head home just before dark, and all I can think about is Bray. I park my car in the front of my apartment and turn off the engine. It's a hot July night, so I turn the key and slide the windows down. The lights in the dashboard fade after I pull the key out and drop it on my lap. The back of my head falls against the headrest, and I close my eyes and let the warm breeze filter through the opened windows and brush against my face. The crickets and frogs start to come alive as the night falls, their song all around me is clamorous yet relaxing. Nothing can beat a Southern summer. Bray and I grew up in them together, loving the heat and humidity, the noisy nature at night and the birds that always woke up before the sun in the morning. We loved fishing and wading in the creeks catching crawdads and chasing the fireflies in the pasture.

Always the fireflies.

Two more days and Bray will be free. She'll be free to live her life, to start over with me and to find the happiness she's always sought, always fought for. The happiness she deserves. I picture her face, that bright smile that I've always seen in everything good. And for a long time, sitting with my back pressed against the seat in my car, my shirt beginning to soak with sweat, I get lost in the memory of her face, that bright smile she always charmed me with. The way the wind always blew her hair across the softness of her cheeks, the glistening of her blue eyes, the innocence of them. Every moment of our life together drifts through my mind like an old film with little imperfections and tiny blips and discolorations on the screen. I hear the constant clicking of the reel, but no voices. Bray runs ahead of me through the pasture, her dark hair whipping up behind her in the wind. She looks back with her bright smiling face and laughs and shrieks as I close in on her from behind.

I catch up to her and grab her around the waist. We fall to the ground amid the tall, prickling yellowed grass. I'm on top of her, staring down into her big beautiful blue eyes. Her chest rises and falls beneath mine as she tries to catch her breath.

And we just stare at each other, not saying a word. I want to kiss her and deep down I know she wants me to. We were fourteen and fifteen when this happened. Maybe if I had kissed her that day, the time when I knew more than anything that I wanted her for myself and the day when I was going to tell her that. But we were both dating other people. Maybe if I had given in, everything would've turned out differently. If I had just given in...

So I do. This time I do it. I wash everything else out of my mind. I push out the song of the crickets and the frogs, the feel of the wind on my face, and I *make* this moment real.

"Why are you looking at me like that?" Bray asks, staring up at me with her long hair spread behind her against the grass.

I study the shape of her lips, the softness of them, and I imagine what they must taste like. Because it's been so long since I tasted them, when we shared our very first French kiss ever. I feel her fingers curling gently around the fabric of my shirt as her arms are bent upward, tucked between our bodies.

"Because I love you," I say and she blushes.

"You love me?"

I nod.

"I love you and I want us to be together forever," I say and study her lips again, forcing myself not to kiss her yet.

Her fingers move from my shirt and come up to my cheeks. She traces a finger along my cheekbone and then over my eyebrows and down the bridge of my nose.

"I love you too, Elias," she whispers and her thumb rests on my bottom lip. "And I want to be with you forever."

My mouth closes around hers and I kiss her deeply. I feel her heart beating against mine.

And then I wake up from the daydream and look out the windshield of my car. Rian is standing on the sidewalk looking in at me, a piece of paper clutched in her right hand. Immediately, I know something's wrong, and my heart sinks like a hot stone straight down into the balls of my feet.

# THIRTY

## Elias

*I* get out of the car. "What's wrong?" I'm terrified of the answer.

She's been crying. She reaches up and wipes her nose with the back of her free hand. I hear her sniffle lightly.

"Rian, w-what is it?" I keep glancing at the paper dangling from her fingertips, knowing it's the bearer of tragic news, and I want to burn it.

The uneasiness in Rian's voice scares me further. "Brayelle's been home for two days," she says.

Maybe I didn't hear her right. I feel my head move from side to side, as if to shake her words out of my mind and start anew. I put up my hand. "What did you say?"

Rian swallows hard and clutches the paper in her hand more firmly. I'm getting so impatient I feel like grabbing her by the arms and shaking the words out of her.

"She didn't want me to tell you, but she got out on schedule and came home with me."

My voice rises almost to a full shout. "Rian! Just say what you came here to say!" I step up closer when really what I want to do is leave her. I don't want to look at her, but she's the only way I'm going to get any of the answers that I'm desperately seeking right now.

"I don't know where she is!" Tears begin to stream down her cheeks. "She's been acting really strange since she came home. Talking to me with this sincere look in her eyes. I-I felt like she was forgiving me for everything. She wasn't mad. Sh-She didn't even want to talk about the past." Her tears begin to choke her. "She hugged me. She's hasn't hugged me since we were in sixth grade."

My heart is beating so fast I feel it in my fingers and in my toes. My head is on fire, hot from the fear and anger and adrenaline racing through my veins.

Bray has been back for two days. She didn't want me to know.

No.

Oh God no...

She planned this all along. She made me believe she was getting out late so I couldn't stop her.

Finally, I grab Rian's upper arms tightly in my hands and I shake her. "Where *is* she?!"

"I told you! I don't know! The last time I saw her was a couple of hours ago!" Tears barrel from her eyes. "She left this on her bed."

Rian places the crumpled piece of paper into my hand.

I look down at it and I'm terrified to read it, everything in my heart and soul telling me that it'll kill me if I look into its secrets, like opening Pandora's box. The light weight of the paper in my hand somehow burns my fingers, right down into the bones.

I open the paper and read the text scribbled in Bray's handwriting:

*I miss the Georgia night sky and the warm summer breeze on my face. I miss running across the prickly grass with my bare feet. I miss the stars and the laughter and the heat. I miss our innocence. I miss the fireflies. I want things to end where they began, the two of us floating around in a jar together, lighting the way for each other through a confined space that could only feel infinite. Because nothing else mattered then. Nothing on the outside could ever touch us, hurt us, or threaten us. Because innocence is bliss. And I want mine back. I just want it back....*

The last thing I see are Rian's teary eyes staring back at me. I let the paper fall from my fingers and I take off running toward Mr. Parson's land. I leap over the chain-link fence behind Donna Sanders's house and land on my feet. And I just keep running, past the neighborhood and the church and the old factory at the end of the street. I run faster than I've ever run in my life. By car it would take two minutes longer to reach the pasture than running straight through the woods. I can hardly breathe I press on so hard. My heart pounds against my rib cage, trying to burst through it. My calves are as hard as stone, my shoes hitting the ground so fast and so hard that I feel every shock sensation rush into the tips of my toes and up the back of my calf muscles.

I don't stop running.

Leaping over a small wooden fence, I run past an old shed, and the darkness of the deep woods swallows me whole. I keep on the path, jumping over the same rocks I've jumped over since I was a kid. Small low-lying limbs snap me in the face as I run past, not stopping long enough to push them out of my way. The song of the crickets and the frogs and the cicadas rises louder in my ears as if they're singing to me, urging me on, telling me to hurry.

Tears burn the backs of my eyes and down into my throat. I part my lips and breathe in sharply, forcing the tears back and letting anger and fear and determination push me forward. Because I know that the tears will only slow me down; they'll rock me to my core and bring me to my knees.

I trip and fall over debris in the forest bed, feeling my ankle twist painfully beneath me. But I pick myself up and keep running. I can feel the solitude of the pasture out ahead. I can faintly smell the stagnant water that always lingers around the bank of the pond. I'm so close. So close. I push myself even harder, veering left and off the path toward the edge of the field. I can see it through a break in the trees. I can see the light of the moon spilling out over the clearing until finally I burst through the last bit of trees and find myself on the outskirts. The water in the pond glistens in the distance. I keep on running toward it, my heart tearing to shreds the closer I get. And then when I finally get there, I stop dead in my tracks as if inches from running into a brick wall.

I feel like I can't move any part of my body anymore, yet somehow my feet move around in a circle. I see behind me and beside me and the stars above me as if I'm spinning, but I don't know how I'm moving at all.

My heart has stopped beating. Only my brain is keeping me alive, my mind, frantic with fear and confusion, is frozen in time.

"No…," I say aloud, yet I don't recall ever moving my lips.

I step forward. "No…"

My gaze falls downward and for a moment all I can see is the dried grass around my running shoes. But then my head jerks back up and I look at the pond again, at the figure floating on the top of it.

*WHY CAN'T I MOVE?! WHY CAN'T I FUCKING MOVE?!*

I scream something unintelligible even to me into the night and finally break free from my frozen imprisonment, willing my legs to push forward. My feet hit the water with tremendous force, and my shoes taking on the weight of it nearly knocks me down. Tears pour from my eyes. My hands and legs shake and tremble uncontrollably. My stomach swims in a sickening, churning lake of bile. My mind still frantically searches for my heartbeat but never finds it.

I force my body through the water, pushing myself through foot by foot, feeling all the while as if dozens of hands are grabbing at me from below, trying to pull me under.

*"Bray! Brayelle! No! NO!"* I cry out.

I've never felt so much pain. My body has never endured so much torment. I know this is what Hell must be like.

I nearly collapse.

When I finally make it to her, I grab her, pulling her limp body into my arms. "Bray, no! Please wake up! Please wake up!" I slap her cheeks, squeeze them in my fingers. I close my mouth over hers and exhale deeply several times, but I don't know CPR. I can't see through my tears. I can't breathe, my lungs feel like cement blocks.

Her arms float atop the water out beside her. Her long, soaked hair, seemingly black, moves atop the surface like seaweed. Her face is white and lifeless and hollow. Her eyes are closed, as though she's only sleeping. I cry out her name again, over and over, erupting with painful, burning sobs, pulling her body closer to mine and crushing her against me.

*"God damn it, no!"* I wail.

I hear voices shouting somewhere behind me in the pasture, but they're muffled behind this glass wall my mind has put up around us. I see flashes of bright light bouncing through the darkness and coming toward me, but I can't look at anything other than Bray lying limp and lifeless in my arms.

I don't know how I managed and I don't remember doing it, but I find myself sitting on my knees on the bank of the pond with Bray still clutched against me, her legs splayed out, still floating in the water. I cry into her heavy, wet hair and I squeeze her so tight that I imagine it'll hurt her and she'll wake up and tell me to stop.

"*Why?* Why did you do this? Why did you do this?" I cry out, rocking her back and forth within my arms.

The bouncing dots of light moving toward me become brighter; the shouting voices, louder.

I don't want to let her go. The voices are telling me to let her go. But I can't. I just want to die with her.

But then amid the shouts and the chaos and the light I hear someone say, "She has a heartbeat."

*She has a heartbeat.*

I fall against the soaked earth and look up into the night sky. Slowly my heart begins to beat again and breath finds its way back into my lungs. But I'm paralyzed. All this time I'm thinking Bray is still wrapped in my arms; that we're looking up at the stars together. But then I realize I'm lying on my side and I am alone. How long have I been here like this? Seconds? Minutes? Hours? Days? I don't know the difference. I look out into the pasture with my cheek pressed against the wet ground. A single blade of grass stands upright near the corner of my eye and somehow I reach out and move it away. The dark horizon is black on blue, meeting with the earth in the far-off distance. I see tiny green-yellow blinking lights flash off and on lazily in the night. One gets closer. Off. On. Never in the same spot. Off. On.

"Elias?" I hear a man's voice say with a country accent. "Elias Kline?"

The little firefly floats away.

I turn over onto my back to see Mr. Parson kneeling beside me in his brown boots and plaid short-sleeved shirt tucked into his old-man Levi's.

"Elias? We have to go now. Can you come with me?" His voice is calm and gruff. The smell of Old Spice fills the space around us.

"We got to go to the hospital," he says.

I feel trapped within myself. I hear him speaking, but at first I can't respond. I can't move from this spot. All I want to do is lie here and die.

"Lemme help you up," I hear him say, and then I feel his arms fitting underneath mine.

I don't protest. I don't have the strength to.

Minutes later I'm in the front seat of Mr. Parson's old Chevy truck, my head pressed against the glass of the passenger's-side window. It smells of old, worn-out leather and oil and metal in here.

"Y'know," I hear him say, but I'm still too weak to raise my head, "I always knew 'bout you and Brayelle Bates sneakin' into my pond when you were growin' up. 'Course, I never minded much. Only when I had'ta go out there sometimes an' pick up after yas."

I watch the dirt road change to gravel and then to asphalt. All I can think about is Bray. The only face I can see is hers staring back at me. And when I see her lifeless face, her eyes closed, pond water streaming over her eyelids and lips, I *force* myself to look at her, punishing myself for not being there sooner.

"An' there was one night," he goes on, "I was walkin' in the pasture lookin' for m'dog and stumbled on you two sleepin' in the grass. You was curled up like two pups. I just left you alone. Harmless really." He laughs lightly and I can sense him looking over at me. "Though that wife o'mine was afraid you two were doin' more on our land than jus' swimmin'. She wanted to tell your folks. But I said she better leave it alone or I'd make her get out there on that damn bush hog and clear the pasture herself." His laughter rises.

My mind begins to drift farther and I can't see or hear anything else anymore. Only Bray. I think of every good thing between us and I picture every smiling moment that we shared. Everything. All the way to the hospital. And when the truck pulls up to the doors of the emergency room, I'm too dazed to understand where I am.

Finally, I lift my head from the window. The bright lights outside shine on my face and I look up at the automatic glass doors to peer inside the hospital. But I'm too afraid to go in. I'm too afraid to get out of the truck.

The hospital doors break apart, and Rian steps through them with my mother beside her.

"Oh, Elias," my mother cries and reaches for me. I don't even know how the truck door was opened. "I'm so sorry, honey. This is awful! I'm so sorry." She squeezes her frail arms around me. I don't even know how I got out of the truck.

I'm afraid to ask her why she's sorry. I don't want to know.

Rian's cheeks shimmer with tears. A tissue is crushed in her hand. She reaches out to hug me, and although I want her and my mother and everyone to leave me alone, I still don't have the strength to act upon any of my thoughts or intentions.

I'm sitting on a chair in the ER waiting room. I don't know how I got here, either. All I see is the cream-colored tile floor, wet and dirty from what my drenched running shoes have tracked in. I'm leaning forward with my elbows resting on the tops of my legs, my hands folded together, draped between my knees. Rian and my mother are sitting on either side of me, but I don't know which. I hate the smell of this place, so sterile and plastic and offensive. The sound of strange beeping machines in the triage room just feet away frays my nerves even further. I hear the squeaking of leather shoes moving across the floor, the intercom popping in the ceiling, and I see the flash of red lights bouncing against the tall glass window from an ambulance that just pulled in.

I feel a hand on my knee, and I recognize it as my mother's when I place it with her voice.

"You did everything you could do, baby." The pain in her voice sears right through me. Is she trying to prepare me, or is she hoping to keep me calm?

I keep my eyes trained on the floor.

Time passes, but I can't tell how much, and a nurse steps into the waiting room and calls Rian's name.

I'm scared to look up. I know this is the moment, it's the moment in my life when I will either die from happiness or from pain.

"Are you Ms. Bates's sister?" the nurse asks Rian.

I still can't raise my head. My fingers are digging into the back of my scalp, trying their best to penetrate my skull. My right leg shakes uncontrollably, the heel of my foot bounces up and down against the floor in rapid succession. My mother's hand touches my back.

"Yes...," Rian answers and I feel her stand up beside me.

There is no air in the room. It's all being held inside my lungs.

"She's in stable condition. You can come back and see her now."

The air bursts from my lungs all at once and I fall from the chair to the floor on my knees. Sobs rack my entire body. I feel even more hands on my back, but I can't raise my head to see whose they are. I cry so hard into my hands that I almost puke. "She's alive," I say out loud to myself. "She's alive…" My nostrils burn from the stinging tears.

Finally I raise my head to see Rian and my mother standing over me.

"No, I, uh…," Rian starts to say. I notice her glance at me and then look back at the nurse. "Please let Elias go back first."

# THIRTY-ONE

## Elias

$\mathcal{T}$he room is brighter than I imagined. The walls, floor, and ceiling, stark white bathed by fluorescent lights running along the ceiling panels. The nurse pulls a long curtain closed after I'm fully inside the room. The stench of rubbing alcohol and something chemical rises up into my nostrils.

For a moment, I just stare across the short distance of the tiny room and look at Bray, lying upon the elevated bed with white sheets covering her motionless body. Her hair is still drenched, lying against the pillow. Her arms are visible, extending down at her sides. Hospital bracelets have replaced her hemp bracelets on one wrist, and an IV tube is taped to the other. I look at her sleeping face, so soft and calm, as if her body hadn't just gone through something so horrific. She looks...peaceful.

The nurse makes a few marks on a paper attached to a clipboard and says, "She's going to be fine. But you should get with her family and discuss what options there are for admitting her. From what I understand, this is Ms. Bates's second suicide attempt."

Everything else she says I just hear bits and pieces. Drug overdose. Nearly drowned. If she hadn't been found sooner...

The nurse leaves me alone in the room with Bray, and I turn off the light shining over her bed. Quietly, I pull a chair around to the side of her bed and I sit. I take her hand into both of mine and tears roll out of me as I lean over, planting my lips on her knuckles. I stay like this for a long time. Just me and Bray, closed off in the solitude of the room. Every now and then I hear faint voices and footsteps moving back and forth outside the room beyond the tall curtain and the glass doors behind it. Bray never stirs. Not once. Her chest rises and falls as she breathes on her own. I wonder what she's dreaming, if she's dreaming at all. She looks so peaceful and soft lying there, even though her hair is dirty and wet and her skin is sickly pale. I fall asleep sitting upright in the chair.

Later in the night, they move her to a room and out of the ER. Rian and my mother join me there, all of us sitting around her bed. No one says much, just a few words here and there to any number of nurses that come in to check on Bray through the overnight hours.

My mother decides to leave when Bray's parents finally show up.

"You call me soon," my mom says, holding my hands. "Keep me updated and I want you to come home and stay with me for a couple of days."

I nod. I don't intend to do that, but this isn't the time or place to argue with her about it.

She kisses me on the forehead and I hug her tight before she walks past Mr. and Mrs. Bates in the doorway, dressed like they just left church.

I step aside when Mrs. Bates walks quickly over to the side of Bray's bed and sits down in the chair I had been sitting in for the past couple of hours. She takes Bray's right hand into hers and kisses her knuckles just like I had done.

"I'm so sorry I wasn't there for you, Brayelle," she says with tears in her voice.

Mr. Bates looks at me coldly. "You can go now," he says.

I go into territorial mode in two seconds flat. My teeth clamp together behind my tightly closed lips. It takes everything in me to keep from knocking him on his ass.

"I'm not going anywhere," I lash out as quietly as I can.

Mrs. Bates sobs into Bray's hand. Rian stands off to my left, quiet and attentive.

Lines deepen around Mr. Bates's nose and he rounds his square-shaped jaw, trying to retain his composure. His hands are clasped together down in front of him.

"We're her family," he says through his teeth.

"No, *I* am her family," I say sharply, cutting off whatever else he had been prepared to say. "And I'm *not* leaving this room."

"Please, Dad, just stop," Rian says, stepping up. "Don't *do* this. If anyone belongs here with Brayelle, it's Elias. And I know you know that deep down."

"I don't—"

"*Robert!*" Mrs. Bates snaps at her husband. Then she lowers her voice and points her bony finger at him. "That's enough. Elias saved her life." She glances at me and adds, "From what I understand, more than once. So just *back off*!"

Mr. Bates looks between the both of us, and thankfully he decides to leave it alone for now. He doesn't approve; he just doesn't want to make a scene.

The three of them stay for nearly an hour, and Bray remains asleep. I don't know if it's from the drugs that were in her system, or from something the hospital gave her, or just pure exhaustion, but whatever it is, I'm starting to wonder if she'll ever wake up.

They go to leave after talking privately with a nurse outside in the hall. But Mrs. Bates comes back inside the room and kisses Bray's cheek before turning to me.

"Thank you for being there for her," she says with a trembling bottom lip.

"I wouldn't be anywhere else," I say in response, and she smiles slimly and walks past, barely touching my shoulder with her delicate fingers.

It pisses me off that they're leaving before Bray even wakes up. A part of me wants to run out into the hall and tell them everything I've always wanted to tell them, that they're poisonous people who should have done more to help Bray throughout her life. Why are they leaving? I feel like hitting something.

But then Rian comes back into the room and she's smiling at me softly. "I talked my parents into letting you be alone with her," she says.

I stand up from beside Bray's bed and turn to look at her very changed sister. Her dark hair is pulled into a sloppy bun with black hair clamps pinned to the top of her head. She's wearing the same clothes as before, when she found me outside my apartment. Her gym shorts are stained with hot pink paint. Her white T-shirt is stretched out and dirty.

"Why?" I ask.

She sighs and glances briefly at the floor.

"Because you were right all along," she says. "I just didn't want to believe it. And I meant what I said before, Elias, about you belonging here. More than my parents. More than me. You really are Brayelle's family, and I know you always have been." She wipes her finger underneath her left eye before the tear escapes. "Thank you for taking care of my sister. For being there for her when she didn't have anyone else."

Rian starts to step back out into the brightly lit hall, but I stop her.

"Rian." She looks back at me, wiping more tears from her eyes. "Bray forgives you. You know that, right?"

She smiles a little underneath her pain and then nods. "I hope so," she says. "But I still want that chance to prove to her that I love her."

Then she turns and walks away, letting the tall wooden door close softly behind her, shutting off the light the room had been borrowing from the hall.

I take my seat next to Bray again, and I reach up and run my fingers through her tangled hair. I brush her long bangs back to keep them away from her face. I kiss her lips and I watch her sleep until my eyes get heavy again. The early morning sunrise begins to peek over the horizon, sending thin, dust-filled beams of light through the sliver in the thick curtains on the window.

And when I fall asleep, I sleep soundly with the knowledge that Bray, the love of my life, is going to be OK. She's going to live and she's going to grow and she's going to get better.

Because I'm going to make sure of that.

# THIRTY-TWO

*Three months later...*

## Elias

*T*hey're here," I call out to Bray from the living room of our new rental house just outside of Savannah. I let the curtain fall back over the window.

Bray hurries in from our bedroom wearing a sexy brown knit dress that stops just above her knees and a pair of black calf-high leather boots. Her hair is pulled into a ponytail with a few loose strands left to hang freely about her face.

I walk over and fit my hands on her hourglass waist and lean in to kiss her lips. She smells like freshly washed hair and coconut body wash.

"Damn, baby. I should bend you over the chair." I kiss her again and grab two handfuls of her butt.

Bray's face flushes, and she retaliates by hitting me playfully on the chest. "Stop it," she teases. "We've got company." Then she reaches up and squeezes my cheeks in her hand. Her tongue sneaks out and licks my pooched-out lips.

There's a knock at the door.

"I'm so nervous," she says.

I laugh lightly. "Why?"

She shrugs, and I take her hand as we approach the front door. "I don't know," she says. "It's just been so long since we've seen them."

"Yeah, but they're not snooty distance relatives or anything like that." I twist the doorknob.

"*Heeey!* Long time, man!" Tate says when I open the door.

He shakes my hand and pulls me into a man-hug. He looks cleaner, a more approachable member of society than how he looked last year in Florida. His light-colored hair is actually styled, spiked up a little in the front. He's wearing a pair of dark blue jeans and a solid black, short-sleeved shirt and a pair of biker boots. And he decided to shave the stubble, just like I did.

"Yeah, it has been a long damn time," I say and usher him and Jen inside. "Come on in."

"Oh my God, you're so gorgeous!" Jen says to Bray, and they do a sort of half hug, holding each other's elbows but not pressing their bodies together, probably not wanting to wrinkle their outfits.

"You too, girl," Bray says with a huge smile. "Look at you. Gah! I envy that long, blonde hair!"

Jen's hair does seem to have gotten longer; now it tumbles down past her waist.

"Well, I want your silky chocolate hair," Jen says with the same measure of smile. "So I say we trade."

I decide to stay out of that conversation the more it begins to veer off into chick stuff. I turn back to Tate, who's holding a six-pack of Coronas. He holds them out to me.

"You got a fridge?" he asks.

"No, I use an Igloo ice chest out back," I joke, and take the cardboard six-pack dangling from his index finger. He follows me into the kitchen.

Before long, we're all in the living room catching up.

"Yeah, Caleb is doin' hard time now," Tate says from the love seat, where he's sitting with Jen. "He was sentenced to eighteen years, but we're hopeful he'll get out on parole long before that."

"Damn, man, that's a long time," I say, and squeeze Bray's knee next to me. I glance at her, testing the waters of the topic, but she's OK with it, and I knew she would be. Because she's been doing great in just about every aspect of her life since her attempted suicide.

Her soft blue eyes smile at me, then she looks at Tate and Jen. "That is really sad. I only served about a year, so I can't imagine what's Caleb's going through."

Tate shakes his head, clearly still dejected about his brother being back in prison. He always will be. "He'll be all right. In fact, I think he's probably doing better now than his first time around." A faint smile appears.

"Why's that?" I ask.

Tate's smile gets bigger. "Well, three months after he went in, he got a visit from his ex-girlfriend, Cera."

"No shit?" Bray says, unbelieving.

Tate nods. "Yep. She visits him every week."

"They're back together?" Bray asks.

I can see the happiness in her face over this news. She had told me about the conversation she had with Caleb outside the motel that night in Baton Rouge. I think it really hurt her to know that Caleb loved this girl so much that he would do anything for her, yet she didn't seem to believe in his innocence after a five-year relationship.

Jen smiles hugely and winds her fingers through the back of Tate's short hair, her arm propped on the back of the couch. "Yeah, they're back together. I knew they would be eventually. She talked to me about him all the damn time." She rolls her eyes as if it had annoyed her, but it's obvious that it hadn't much. "I just wanted to stay out of their problems. But I'm glad she came around. A little earlier and she could've spared him the prison sentence, but I guess better late than never."

"That's awesome," Bray says, bright-eyed.

"Yeah, it is," Tate says. "I think Caleb is going to be okay. At least for now. We'll have to see how long she can keep this up with him being behind bars."

"Well, don't think about that," Bray says. "Stay positive."

Tate nods, having to agree that's the best way to go about it.

"So anything new with you two?" I ask. "No babies or engagement rings?"

Jen's nose wrinkles. "Uh, no," she points. "And no," she points again a little to the left.

Tate laughs and raises his back from the couch, resting his elbows on his knees. "We'll never get married. Already established that. Babies, on the other hand"—he grins and Jen sneers—"I'd like to have one someday."

"Well it's not gonna be by *me*," Jen comes back. "No babies are coming out of this body. *Ever.*"

Tate raises a brow and chews on the inside of his lip arrogantly and says, "Well as long as you're okay with me stickin' my dick in some other chick for the sole purpose of making a baby, then I'm good to go."

Jen presses her front teeth together and smacks him across the arm.

Bray and I just laugh under our breaths. Some things never change.

Tate throws his head back, laughing, and then mumbles to me,

"She'll give in one day," as if he was only halfway trying not to let Jen hear, but he knows she did.

Jen shakes her head and smiles.

"What about you?" Tate asks us, and I notice him glance at our hands, looking for rings.

"Someday," Bray answers. "We thought about getting married this year, but we've decided to wait. At least a couple more years."

"Well when you do, I better get an invitation," Tate says.

"Didn't take you for the wedding type," I say with laughter in my voice.

Jen pats him on the leg and purses her lips. "Anyone's wedding but his own," she says.

There's another knock at the door. I get up to answer it.

"Elias!" Grace says with her arms held out for me.

I hug her as Bray, Tate, and Jen come up behind us.

"Oh my God, Grace, I've missed the shit out of you!" Bray says, squeezing her, apparently not worried about wrinkling her clothes this time.

"Me too!" Grace says, stepping back, clasping Bray's hands with hers. She looks Bray up and down. "Damn, you are rockin' that dress."

More chick stuff. I step to the side and welcome the dark-haired guy taller than me by at least two inches with tattoos down both arms and one peeking from the collar of his shirt. He looks like a rocker guy who just walked out of an Abercrombie and Fitch store dressed in casual jeans and a light-gray collared shirt.

"Come on in," I tell him, and he and Grace move farther into the room.

Grace turns to the guy and says, "This is my boyfriend, Knox." Then she points to all of us. "Elias. Bray. Tate and Jen."

Knox nods and smiles subtly, burying his hands in his pockets.

We spend the next half hour catching up (and we talk less about Caleb, since Grace doesn't seem comfortable talking about him with Knox being here).

Finally, Bray's sister arrives at the door solo. She's dressed up much like Bray: wearing a long-sleeved knit dress and a pair of boots. And she looks nervous.

"Come in and meet everybody," Bray says, looping her arm through Rian's. Bray then introduces Rian to everyone.

"It's great to finally meet you all," Rian says. "Brayelle has talked a lot about you."

Bray and I exchange looks across the room, and we're probably thinking the same thing. These were the people we had been on the run with, so Rian doesn't exactly think of them as innocent friends who we just met at the library or someplace. But Rian, staying true to her word to always be there for Bray, treats them all with respect and even seems to be enjoying herself.

We head out around nine to a fall party going on at a local nightclub. With Halloween just a couple weeks away, the town is gearing up for the many Halloween parties that will go on. Even the streetlights are decorated in orange and black.

Life is good, and every day it proves to be more so.

Tate and Jen went back to Miami the day after they visited, but we keep in touch and will be making a trip down to Florida next summer to spend a week with them. Grace and Bray talk all the time. On the phone. E-mail. Text messages. By the time spring rolled around, they had been back and forth to Norfolk and Savannah to visit each other three times. And I've even heard them discussing something about Grace and Knox moving to Savannah. I couldn't be happier about news like that, especially since Grace is such a great friend to Bray. She knows all about the things that Bray has gone through, and while at first it made me nervous that Bray would open up to her so fast about such personal things, it didn't take me long to fully accept it. She needed a best friend like Grace.

Aside from having me and Grace in Bray's life, and even Mitchell and Bray making up and getting back to normal, Rian and Bray spend a lot of time together. Rian's all right in my book. Sometimes she'll try to be the big sister and piss Bray off, but it's all perfectly harmless, your average sisterly squabbles that I think are pretty healthy to have.

And Bray has a better relationship with her mom now, too. Her dad is still a stubborn hard-ass, but I think even he is coming around.

But Bray and her illness has been the biggest turnaround of all.

Before we left the hospital that day back in July when I pulled her from Mr. Parson's pond, I vowed to do everything in my power to help make her better. I set her up with a good psychiatrist—after I did a bit of research on the woman—whom Bray seems to love. She sees her once a week, and since I make good money at my roofing job, I pay for Bray's health insurance. She argued about it in the beginning, but I won that argument. Dr. Ashley worked with Bray to help find her a medication to manage her bipolar disorder and that doesn't make her feel catatonic or, worse, like killing herself. Bray has done really well, and I can feel it, that she's a happier person.

Come to find out—and this is hard for me to think about—but before we left the convenience store that day in Baton Rouge, Bray had it set in her mind that she was going to commit suicide eventually. For a month after she got out of the hospital, I told myself that they must've put her on some kind of medication while she was locked up, which ultimately caused the suicide attempt. Just like back in South Carolina. It tore my heart out when she finally admitted to me one day that the only reason she didn't pull that trigger was because I was sitting there. She couldn't die knowing that she would put me through something like that. And she had contemplated ending it while she was locked away. But with limited means of pulling something like that off—though she claims she still could've done it—it helped to keep her alive.

Alive long enough until she could get out and die in the one place she had always found peace in her life. Mr. Parson's land. Where we met. Where we spent our childhood.

But with my help, the love and support of her sister, and the right counseling and medication, Bray is a changed person. I see it in her every day. She's happy. When I watch her smile or hear her laugh, I know that the darkness that lives inside of her—and it will always be there—is so small, so weak now, that it can't hurt her anymore. I worried for a while if she was only better because I was with her. I couldn't stand feeling that if we were to break up someday— not that I'd ever see that happening—that she might commit sui- cide. As much as I wanted to be her crutch, her rock, I didn't want to be the only thread holding her life together.

Thankfully, I found out that I'm not.

We still fight but we always make up, and she's never reverted back to that darkness. Not that far, anyway. She still has her moments, but she loves life and every day she shows me that. But yeah, life is good. And I know it's only going to get better.

It has been a long road for Bray, but I'm helping her travel it every step of the way. And even though sometimes she still feels like she doesn't deserve someone like me, she's learning that she does.

Everyone deserves someone who loves and cares for them enough to see them through life's obstacles. *Especially* people like Bray.

# THIRTY-THREE

## Bray

*Three years later . . .*

*T*oday, I'm a very different person than I once was. It's so strange looking back on my life, wondering how I managed to get through any of it in one piece. I truly am one of the luckiest people in the world. Not only because I have Elias in my life, but because I survived two and a half suicide attempts. Not many people can say that. I'm not sure what made *me* so special, what gave me the right to live when so many others who deserved a shot at life more than I ever did, lost their battle on the first try. But whatever it was, I'll always be grateful.

I know that I never would've made it through anything if it weren't for Elias and his unconditional and unwavering love for me. He, in every sense of the word, was *everything* to me. He was my parents, my sister, my friends, and the love of my life. He was my conscience, my will, and my direction.

Today, Elias is still all of those things. Even though I have a great relationship with my sister now and my father has finally started acting like one. I have the best friend in the world, Grace, who lives less than ten minutes from Elias and me. My mother calls me twice a week and we actually spend time together, doing things that mothers and daughters do. It took most of my life to feel like I had a family other than Elias, but now that I do, I couldn't be happier.

But like I said, I really am a different person.

I wake up every morning next to Elias, thankful that the person I used to be, as damaged as she was, was never strong enough to chase him away. And when I crawl out of the bed in the mornings and stand in front of the bathroom mirror, I look at that girl staring back at me, and for the first time in my life, I *like* her. I understand her. I'm not ashamed of her.

I smile as I look at myself, then grab my toothbrush and get ready for the day. Elias has been marking the calendar for three weeks, counting down the days to something he refuses to tell me. I waltz into our tiny kitchen and spin around dramatically, modeling my new summer dress, white with little straps over my light sun-kissed shoulders.

"Overdressed? Underdressed? What do you think?" I ask, grinning at Elias, who is sitting at our small, round two-person kitchen table.

He shakes his head and gulps down the last of his orange juice. "Nope. Not gonna happen," he says. "Quit trying to get hints out of me."

"Oh come on," I whine playfully and walk toward the refrigerator. "That's not going to give anything away."

"Give up, Bray." He laughs and pushes his chair underneath the table.

"Fine," I say, surrendering. "Did you talk to Dad?"

Elias nods and rinses his plate off at the sink. "Yeah, he called while you were in the shower. He said your mom will be home about an hour after we get there. Not sure I like that."

I roll my eyes and smile at him as I close the refrigerator. "Give him a chance, babe. He can handle it."

"I dunno," Elias says, shaking his head solemnly. "He always has that nervous look in his eye. The whole time we're gone I'll be worried your dad will be hiding in the closet when we get back."

I laugh out loud and set the juice container back in the fridge. "He'll be fine," I say. "Mom will be back before it comes to that."

Elias steps up to me and fits his hands on my hips. "The dress is perfect for the occasion. Just so you know," he says with a smile in his voice.

I smile and look down at it briefly. "Really?"

He nods and then kisses my forehead.

"OK, well let's get out of here," I say, grabbing my purse from the cabinet. "Plane leaves in an hour." I drink down my juice and leave the glass on the counter.

We fly to Athens, and my sister picks us up from the airport and drives us to my parents' house. Dad is sitting in the living room watching old reruns of *Cheers*, trying to look casual, when we walk through the front door.

When he gets up from his favorite chair, I walk straight over and hug him tight. "Hi, Dad."

He kisses the top of my head and rubs my back with both hands. "It's good to see you," he says and then squeezes me a little tighter. It still feels awkward when he treats me with such fatherly kindness, but I wouldn't trade it for anything.

Rian moves through the room and heads straight into the kitchen. She had been talking about leftover homemade cheesecake that Mom had promised to save for her, on the ride here. She was worried Dad might've eaten it before she arrived.

"And it's good to see you, Elias," Dad says with a welcoming nod.

A smile breaks out on my face. They actually get along now, though in the beginning it felt like walking on eggshells every time we'd visit my parents. Gradually, the two of them shed their grudges and came to an understanding.

They exchange a few more words, and then my dad steps up to Elias and reaches out both hands. "And how's my favorite grandson doing?" he says with a big, awkward smile, looking down at our son in Elias's arms. He never was good with children.

Elijah, a year old in a few days, with dark hair and bright blue eyes just like mine and his daddy's, makes a timid face and recoils against Elias's chest.

Dad's hands drop to his sides. He makes a face, too, though it's funny to me because he seems more afraid of Elijah than Elijah is of him.

"He doesn't like me," he says, nervously fondling the thick silver watch on his right wrist. "Maybe you should wait until your mom gets here before you head back to Savannah."

I reach out for Elijah, and he practically leaps into my arms. "Oh don't be ridiculous, Dad. He's just not used to you. Only sees you once a month." I put Elijah into my dad's arms.

Dad holds Elijah, keeping his little butt (dressed in OshKosh B'Gosh blue jeans) propped in the bend of his arm. He looks nervous.

Elias glances over at me, an uneasy yet laughable look on his face.

Just when Dad thinks he might be able to pull this off, Elijah bursts into tears, reaching out his little arms to me.

Dad uses the opportunity and immediately hands him over.

Rian comes back into the living room holding a slice of cheese-cake on a small white plate. "He's walking now," she teases Dad, then takes another small bite off the end of her fork. "You think you can keep up?" She glances at me, and then Elias, trying to contain her laughter.

I pass Elijah to Elias and open the diaper bag on the couch. I explain everything Dad needs to know to hold him over until Mom gets here.

I know Dad can handle it. And Elias isn't as afraid to leave him with Dad as he pretends to be. According to Mom, Dad does a much better job with Elijah when there's no one staring at him, or teasing him about changing diapers and whatnot.

Elias and I stay for only a few minutes, then Rian drives us back to the airport so we can make our return flight to Savannah. I'm so excited. And nervous. Whatever this surprise is that Elias has for me, it must be pretty special, because he's been walking on air for the past three weeks. He was even the one who called my parents up and made the arrangements to have Elijah spend the weekend with them. Neither I nor Elias like leaving our son overnight any-where, even with family, but we know that for some occasions we just have to let go. Apparently, this was one of them.

"I miss Little Man already," Elias says on the plane.

I look at him. "Are you *really* worried?"

Elias laughs lightly and shakes his head. "Maybe only for your dad."

I laugh, too.

Silence lingers between us for a moment as we both look out in front of us.

"Elias?" I ask quietly, looking over again.

"Yeah?" He smiles softly at me with the back of his head pressed against the seat.

"Do you remember that night at Jen's house? When we talked about whether or not we'd go back in time if we could?"

"Yeah, I remember," he says. He takes my hand and laces his fingers through mine.

"Well, you were right," I say.

"About what?" He raises his head from the seat.

I squeeze his hand. "You said that when we were free to live our lives and enjoy our time together that I wouldn't feel the same way. That I wouldn't want to go back to our childhood. You were right."

His blue eyes brighten. "I'm glad that I was," he says and kisses my knuckles.

## Elias

We make it back to Savannah by early evening and drive our car from the airport to the place I've been wanting to take her for weeks. I took a risk doing this without her, especially since it's not something small and inexpensive. And a part of me is still worried that the whole idea might backfire, that instead of making her happy, it might bring back bad memories instead. But I have to go with my gut. With my heart. And my heart tells me that there were many more good memories than bad and that she'll love it.

"Are you ready?" I ask, taking Bray by the hand to help her out of the car.

She raises the other hand to her face and adjusts the blindfold over her eyes.

"Now don't try to peek," I say.

"I'm not!" she laughs. With my help, she stands up beside the car door, curling her fingers over the top of the door to have something to hold on to. "It's not even my birthday."

I shut the car door and pull her carefully beside me as we step onto the grass. "It doesn't have to be," I say and squeeze her hand.

Her lips spread into an even bigger smile. She grabs me with her free hand when her heels go over a bump in the ground. I cup her elbow in my hand to steady her walk.

"Well, you could've told me not to wear heels," she says as she struggles to stay upright.

"Sorry, I didn't think about that," I say with a hint of a grin in my voice. "But something tells me you won't need any shoes."

It's a hot summer evening, just like we like it. The night is approaching, but the light of the day is still barely holding on as the sky transitions into twilight. The fireflies are already out, twinkling off and on all around us. I walk with her hand in mine, guiding her farther out onto the land. I can feel how excited she is the way she clutches my hand. That huge, toothy smile beaming under the fabric of the blindfold. The joy in her voice.

When we get to a good distance, I stop and walk behind her, fitting my fingers on the blindfold knot.

"Oww! Be careful."

"Sorry, babe," I say and try the knot more carefully so I don't pull her hair.

Finally, the knot comes loose, and I let the blindfold drop from her eyes. She gasps and stares unblinking out at the massive field with trees on all sides. A large pond with a dock sits off to the east with a cluster of trees behind it. Her fingertips dance over her lips.

"What..." She looks over at me. "What *is* this?"

I smile. "It's *ours*. I've been saving up for a down payment since the day I started my roofing job three years ago. Got a bank loan for the rest. It's all ours. All thirty-two acres of it." I point in the distance toward the woods. "And just over there is a creek."

Her fingers begin to tremble, still resting over her lips.

"I'm going to build our house here," I add, taking her into my arms, wrapping them around her from behind.

Her tears start to flow and she makes a cute snort-choking sound when she tries to force them back. I turn her around and pull her into a hug.

"A new beginning, remember?" I say and squeeze her gently within my arms. I kiss the side of her head and rub the palms of my hands up and down her bare arms.

She sniffles and wipes the tears away from her eyes. "I can't believe you did this."

A little worried she isn't reacting the way I had hoped, I ask, "Are you...upset?"

She lifts her face away from my chest and looks into my eyes, shaking her head as a few new tears roll down her cheeks.

"No," she says with a faint hint of disbelief in her voice. "This is...it's...I just love you so much!" She jumps into my arms, wrapping her arms around the back of my neck, her thighs wrapped around my waist. Her lips kiss my face all over, even my eyelids and the little hollow under my nose. I squeeze her tight.

"You were right again," she says and breaks the hug, setting her feet back on the ground. She bends over and grins at me.

"About what this time?"

She slips off her heels. "About not needing shoes."

Then she shoves me in the chest with the palms of her hands and knocks me right on my ass in the grass, then takes off running. The sound of her laughter carries on the breeze.

For a moment I just watch her, a brief moment suspended in time that I want to cherish forever. I watch as her dark hair wafts behind her and bounces majestically against the back of her thin white dress. The way her soft, lithe legs run gracefully over the tall, prickly grass, and the brilliance of the fireflies blinking all around her. I watch how the twilight casts shadows on her smiling face when she looks back at me, and I get lost in the moment just before I take off after her.

# A LETTER FROM THE AUTHOR

Dear Reader,

Elias and Bray's story was an idea I'd been thinking about writing since long before Camryn and Andrew's in *The Edge of Never*. Elias and Bray have lived in my head for so long, that it was the most cathartic experience to be able to put pen to paper and finally see them come to life. I wanted their journey to feel real, and raw, so I did my best to hold nothing back. And in the end, I created something that I was thrilled to be able to share with you.

Since Elias and Bray grew up together, there were a lot of memories and scenes that I played out but just couldn't find the right way to add them into the novel. They had years together that I couldn't fully explore and so many moments to truly fall in love, so I wanted to give you a look at one of those moments. Growing up, Elias was always there to protect Bray and make sure she was safe and happy—even if it meant sacrificing his own happiness—and this bonus scene is just one of those times.

I hope you enjoyed reading SONG OF THE FIRE-FLIES as much as I loved writing it! Have fun getting a little glimpse into Elias and Bray's past ☺

Happy reading,

## SENIOR YEAR

### ELIAS

Mitchell, wearing the same Tool T-shirt he wore to school yesterday, stood next to the entrance of the gym, his shoulder pressed against the metal railing of the steps. His dishwater brown hair looked like he woke up with it like that, disheveled in spots and flattened against his head in others. I always wondered how he ever got laid. But he did and he did often.

"Dude, are you sure about this?" he asked. "You know Bray will be pissed if she ever finds out."

I sighed and nodded, uncrossing my arms. "Yeah," I said, though I was still conflicted about the whole thing. "Landon is a douche bag. Bray will thank me for it later." Somehow I didn't really believe that.

I started walking toward the restrooms just outside of the cafeteria. Mitchell followed alongside me.

"Seriously though," he said, trying to keep up, "why don't you just ask Bray to prom? I don't get you two. So weird. You both act like you're not into each other like that"—a burst of air left his lips making a *pffft* sound—"but you're both pretty fucking delusional, if you ask me."

"Well, I'm not asking you."

I stopped at the entrance to the restrooms, looking over Mitchell's shoulder to watch the cafeteria for the next group of seniors to emerge. In about five minutes, it'll be the Hatcher cousins, but they never go into the restroom, so this is perfect timing.

"OK, whatever, man." Mitchell laughed and shook his head.

He leaned his back against the brick wall, crossing his arms over his chest.

"Better hurry up then," he said, nodding toward the restroom. "Unless he's in there taking a shit, he'll be coming out soon."

"Just watch the door," I said and disappeared around the corner.

Landon was checking out his spiked-up jet-black hair in the mirror when I walked in, twisting pieces of it in his fingertips. He glanced at me in the mirror and nodded, but was more involved in his hair to notice the look of animosity growing on my face.

"What's up, man?" he asked, staring into the mirror.

"I heard you asked Brayelle Bates to prom," I said, stepping up closer.

"Yeah, what about it?" He readjusted a few more spikes of hair.

"I'm here to tell you to back off," I said.

Finally, he looked over at me, a trace of humor playing across his face. He laughed lightly under his breath and went back to messing with his hair.

"I asked her first," he said, sensing my jealousy, "and she said yes. Not my issue, bro. So, get over it."

I might've just threatened him with more words, but all bets were off when he looked over at me again with an even deeper grin and added, "Who better to take to prom than a girl who's a sure thing?"

I moved toward him fast, grabbing the front of his button-up black shirt in my fist and shoving his back against the dingy tile wall. His dark eyes grew wide and the humor dropped from his face in an instant.

"This is how it's gonna go," I said through gritted teeth. "You're going to tell Bray that you can't take her. Make something up. I don't care what, but you're not going to mention me." I pushed him harder against the wall, tightening my fist around the fabric of his shirt to emphasize how serious I was. "And you're gonna stay away from her, or I'll find you and I'll beat the shit out of you. Do you understand?" I glared into his shrinking face.

Landon Murphy had always been a conceited player, who toyed with girls' emotions just to get them to sleep with him, but in the face of a fight he was a coward. And I never cared much for violence—that was usually Mitchell's area of expertise—but I wasn't about to let this guy take advantage of Bray. If he had been any other guy, one who was decent and might've been good for Bray, I wouldn't have gone to such extremes. I would've hated it, seeing her with anyone, but I would've stayed out of it.

Landon put up both hands in surrender.

"All right, all right, *Jesus*! I get it." He was nervous, but not terrified. Things like this weren't worth his time, or any plastic surgery he might have to get after some angry boyfriend messed up his pretty-boy face. He was the type who'd rather just let it go and move onto the next vulnerable girl.

I held onto his shirt for a few more intense long seconds and finally released him.

He pushed his back away from the wall and began ironing out the wrinkles in his shirt with the palms of his hands.

"Hurry up, Elias!" I heard Mitchell say from outside the door. "The emo table is on their way in!"

I looked at Landon one last time, still with the same threatening glare.

"I'm good," he said, putting up his hands again. "Seriously. Point made."

I heard the water faucet squeaking on as I turned and left the restroom, stepping to the side as a small group of guys walked past.

Ten minutes later, Bray walked up with her sling bag tossed over her shoulder, to stand next to me and Mitchell on the gym wall outside.

Her smile was beautiful.

It always was.

Bray's long, dark hair lay softly against the back of her thin white top. It's the first time I'd seen her today, except in short passing in the hallways when we didn't have time to talk.

I swallowed hard as she approached Mitchell and me.

"Hey, guess what?" she asked as she took me into a hug, which was always one of the highlights of my day. I rubbed the palms of my hands against her back and held on to her a little longer than I normally do.

For a moment, I thought whatever she had to tell us had something to do with Landon Murphy, until I realized she probably wouldn't be smiling like that if it was.

"What?" Mitchell asked her before I had a chance.

I glanced over at him as Bray pulled away from me, tucking her long bangs behind her ear. He knew I wanted him to leave soon. Just before Bray walked up, Mitchell and I had been talking more about me finally giving in and asking her to prom myself.

I intended to do just that. I was nervous, us being best friends and all, but I *had* to do it.

He glanced at his watch. "Shit, I've gotta go. I was supposed to see Mr. Palmer about my makeup test."

He bowed out quickly and flashed me a knowing look just before he took off.

Bray looked at me, bright smile still intact.

I wanted to kiss her.

"I might get to go to college," she said excitedly. "My Aunt Tara who lives in Sacramento said she could help my parents pay for it."

Surprised and happy for her, I felt a smile spread across my face.

"That's awesome," I said and took her into another hug.

Like before, it took longer to pull away.

"I mean, of course I have to talk to my parents to see if they can afford the other half, but I really think they'll be happy about it."

I hated to see her like this. Well, I loved to see her happy, but I hated to see her so high on her hopes and dreams, *too* high on them. I think she knew deep down that the chances of her parents shelling out that kind of money on her education was a long shot. Bray spent most of her school life getting into trouble and not doing so well with her classes.

But I remained positive and never let my smile fade.

"Really, that's awesome, Bray."

That's all I could will myself to say for fear of getting her hopes up even higher than they already were.

"So, what's going on with you?" she asked.

I hesitated for a moment, rubbing the back of my head nervously with the palm of my hand.

"Well, I, uh...I wanted to ask you something."

Just then, she saw Landon walk by and she smiled hugely

raising her hand to call him over. But he blatantly ignored her and walked right past.

The smile dropped from her face, and her hand fell to her side. She looked at me confusedly and then put up her finger.

"Hold on," she said. Before I could stop her, she left me standing there and went after Landon.

He ignored her for the rest of the day and later that evening, Bray got the call.

I tried to console her when she called me that night, but she was so angry and hurt. And I felt like shit for it. But it was for the best, I kept telling myself.

After she hung up, I finished up my dinner and set out for her house. I was finally going to ask her to prom and I didn't want to do it over the phone. But once I got there, she wasn't as angry as she had been earlier.

"The jerk called it off," she said on her front porch, "but right after I got off the phone with you, Kyle Anthony called and asked me to prom. Apparently, when Lissa found out about it she jumped at the opportunity to play matchmaker."

Her smile began to brighten.

My heart sank.

Our timing was never going to be right—mine sucked—but her happiness was always my first priority. So, I put on a brave smile and said, "Kyle Anthony, huh?" I pursed my lips and nodded as though contemplating whether to approve or not. She might suspect something was off, if I didn't. "He's kind of a pansy"—she smacked me lightly on the arm, smiling—"but I guess he's all right."

"Damn right he is!" Bray laughed.

Then she leaned against the porch step, resting her elbows there. "What about you? Lissa told me you'd probably ask"—she looked up in thought, chewing on the inside of her bottom lip and wrinkling her cute little nose—"what's that crazy-eyed girl's name?" She shook her finger at me. "The one who—"

"Amy Tanner," I cut in, grinning because I knew what she was doing; she was playing my own game.

"Yeah!" She nudged my leg with her knee. "Well?"

"Well what?"

"Are you going to prom with her or not?"

I nodded. "Nah, I decided not to go. It's not really my thing. You should know that by now."

And then a long awkward silence filled the space between us. I wondered if she was thinking the same thing that I was, that she wished I had asked her to prom a week ago.

I know I should have.

Camryn Bennett shocks everyone when she leaves the only life she's ever known. Grabbing her purse and her cell phone, Camryn boards a Greyhound bus ready to find herself. Instead, she finds Andrew Parrish...

Please see the next page for an excerpt from

*The Edge of Never*

# ONE

*N*atalie has been twirling that same lock of hair for the past ten minutes and it's starting to drive me nuts. I shake my head and pull my iced latte toward me, placing my lips on the straw. Natalie sits across from me with her elbows propped on the little round table, chin in one hand.

"He's gorgeous," she says staring off toward the guy who just got in line. "Seriously, Cam, would you *look* at him?"

I roll my eyes and take another sip. "Nat," I say, placing my drink back on the table, "you have a boyfriend—do I need to constantly remind you?"

Natalie sneers playfully at me. "What are you, my mother?" But she can't keep her eyes on me for long, not while that walking wall of sexy is standing at the register ordering coffee and scones. "Besides, Damon doesn't care if I look—as long as I'm bending over for *him* every night, he's good with it."

I let out a spat of air, blushing.

"See! *Uh huh*," she says, smiling hugely. "I got a laugh out of you." She reaches over and thrusts her hand into her little purple purse. "I have to make note of that," and she pulls out her phone and opens her digital notebook. "Saturday. June 15th." She moves her finger across the screen. "1:54 p.m.—Camryn Bennett laughed at one of my sexual jokes." Then she shoves the phone back inside her purse and looks at me with that thoughtful sort of look she always has when she's about to go into therapy-mode. "Just look once," she says, all joking aside.

Just to appease her, I turn my chin carefully at an angle so that I can get a quick glimpse of the guy. He moves away from the register and toward the end of the counter where he slides his drink off the edge. Tall. Perfectly sculpted cheekbones. Mesmerizing model green eyes and spiked-up brown hair.

"Yes," I admit, looking back at Natalie, "he's hot, but so what?"

Natalie has to watch him leave through the double glass doors and glide past the windows before she can look back at me to respond.

"Oh. My. God," she says eyes wide and full of disbelief.

"He's just a guy, Nat." I place my lips on the straw again. "You might as well put a sign that says 'obsessed' on your forehead. You're everything obsessed short of drooling."

"Are you *kidding* me?" Her expression has twisted into pure shock. "Camryn, you have a serious problem. You know that, right?" She presses her back against her chair. "You need to up your medication. Seriously."

"I stopped taking it in April."

"What? *Why?*"

"Because it's ridiculous," I say matter-of-factly. "I'm not suicidal, so there's no reason for me to be taking it."

She shakes her head at me and crosses her arms over her chest. "You think they prescribe that stuff just for suicidal people? No. They don't." She points a finger at me briefly and hides it back in the fold of her arm. "It's a chemical imbalance thing, or some shit like that."

I smirk at her. "Oh, really? Since when did you become so educated in mental health issues and the medications they use to treat the hundreds of diagnoses?" My brow rises a little, just enough to let her see how much I know she has no idea what she's talking about.

When she wrinkles her nose at me instead of answering, I say, "I'll heal on my own time and I don't need a pill to fix it for me." My explanation had started out kind, but unexpectedly turned bitter before I could get the last sentence out. That happens a lot.

Natalie sighs and the smile completely drops from her face.

"I'm sorry," I say, feeling bad for snapping at her. "Look, I know you're right. I can't deny that I have some messed-up emotional issues and that I can be a bitch sometimes—"

"*Sometimes?*" she mumbles under her breath, but is grinning again and has already forgiven me.

That happens a lot, too.

I half-smile back at her. "I just want to find answers on my own, y'know?"

"Find *what* answers?" She's annoyed with me. "Cam," she says, cocking her head to one side to appear thoughtful. "I hate to say it, but shit really does happen. You just have to get over it. Beat the hell out of it by doing things that make you happy."

OK, so maybe she isn't so horrible at the therapy thing after all.

"I know, you're right," I say, "but..."

Natalie raises a brow, waiting. "What? Come on, out with it!"

I gaze toward the wall briefly, thinking about it. So often I sit around and think about life and wonder about every possible aspect of it. I wonder what the hell I'm doing here. Even right now. In this coffee shop with this girl I've known practically all my life. Yesterday I thought about why I felt the need to get up at exactly the same time as the day before and do everything like I did the day before.

Why? What compels any of us to do the things we do when deep down a part of us just wants to break free from it all?

I look away from the wall and right at my best friend who I know won't understand what I'm about to say, but because of the need to get it out, I say it anyway.

"Have you ever wondered what it would be like to backpack across the world?"

Natalie's face goes slack. "Uh, not really," she says. "That might...suck."

"Well, think about it for a second," I say, leaning against the table and focusing all of my attention on her. "Just you and a back-pack with a few necessities. No bills. No getting up at the same time every morning to go to a job you hate. Just you and the world out ahead of you. You never know what the next day is going to bring, who you'll meet, what you'll have for lunch or where you might sleep." I realize I've become so lost in the imagery that I might've seemed a little obsessed for a second, myself.

"You're starting to freak me out," Natalie says, eyeing me across the small table with a look of uncertainty. Her arched brow settles back even with the other one and then she says, "And there's also all the walking, the risk of getting raped, murdered and tossed on the side of a freeway somewhere. Oh, and then there's all the walking..."

Clearly, she thinks I'm borderline crazy.

"What brought this on, anyway?" she asks, taking a quick sip of her drink. "That sounds like some kind of mid-life-crisis stuff— you're only twenty." She points again as if to underline, "And you've hardly paid a bill in your life."

She takes another sip; an obnoxious slurping noise follows.

"Maybe not," I say thinking quietly to myself, "but I *will* be once I move in with you."

"So true," she says, tapping her fingertips on her cup. "Everything split down the middle—Wait, you're not backing out on me, are you?" She sort of freezes, looking warily across at me.

"No, I'm still on. Next week I'll be out of my mom's house and living with a slut."

"You bitch!" she laughs.

I half-smile and go back to my brooding, the stuff before that she wasn't relating to, but I expected as much. Even before Ian died, I always kind of thought out of the box. Instead of sitting around dreaming up new sex positions, as Natalie often does about Damon, her boyfriend of five years, I dream about things that really matter. At least in my world, they matter. What the air in other countries feels like on my skin, how the ocean smells, why the sound of rain makes me gasp. *"You're one deep chick."* That's what Damon said to me on more than one occasion.

"Geez!" Natalie says. "You're a freakin' downer, you know that right?" She shakes her head with the straw between her lips. "Come on," she says suddenly and stands up from the table. "I can't take this philosophical stuff anymore and quaint little places like this seem to make you worse—we're going to The Underground tonight."

"What?—No, I'm not going to that place."

"Yes. You. Are." She chucks her empty drink into the trash can a few feet away and grabs my wrist. "You're going with me this time because you're supposed to be my best friend and I won't take no for an answer *again*." Her close-lipped smile is spread across the entirety of her slightly tanned face.

I know she means business. She always means business when she has that look in her eyes: the one brimmed with excitement and determination. It'll probably be easiest just to go this once and get it over with, or else she'll never leave me alone about it. Such is a necessary evil when it comes to having a pushy best friend.

I get up and slip my purse strap over my shoulder.

"It's only two o'clock," I say.

I drink down the last of my latte and toss the empty cup away in the same trash can.

"Yeah, but first we've got to get you a new outfit."

"Uh, no," I say resolutely as she's walking me out the glass doors and into the breezy summer air. "Going to The Underground with you is more than good deed enough. I refuse to go shopping. I've got plenty of clothes."

Natalie slips her arm around mine as we walk down the sidewalk and past a long line of parking meters. She grins and glances over at me. "Fine. Then you'll at least let me dress you from something out of *my* closet."

"What's wrong with my own wardrobe?"

She purses her lips at me and draws her chin in as if to quietly argue why I even asked a question so ridiculous. "It's *The Underground*," she says, as if there is no answer more obvious than that.

OK, she has a point. Natalie and I may be best friends, but with us it's an opposites attract sort of thing. She's a rocker chick who's had a crush on Jared Leto since *Fight Club*. I'm more of a laid-back kind of girl who rarely wears dark-colored clothes unless I'm attending a funeral. Not that Natalie wears all black and has some kind of emo hair thing going on, but she would never be caught dead in anything from *my* closet because she says it's all just too plain. I beg to differ. I know how to dress, and guys—when I used

to pay attention to the way they eyed my ass in my favorite jeans—
have never had a problem with the clothes I choose to wear.

But The Underground was made for people like Natalie and so
I guess I'll have to endure dressing like her for one night just to fit
in. I'm not a follower. I never have been. But I'll definitely become
someone I'm not for a few hours if it'll make me blend in rather
than make me a blatant eyesore and draw attention.

# TWO

*W*e make it to The Underground just as night falls, but not before driving around in Damon's souped-up truck to various houses. He would pull into the driveway, get out and stay inside no more than three or four minutes and never say a word when he came back out. At least, not about what he went inside for, or who he talked to—the usual stuff that would make these visits normal. But not much about Damon is usual or normal. I love him to death. I've known him almost as long as I've known Natalie, but I've never been able to accept his drug habits. He grows copious amounts of weed in his basement, but he's not a pothead. In fact, no one but me and a few of his close friends would ever suspect that a hot piece of ass like Damon Winters would be a grower, because most growers look like white trash and often have hairdos that are stuck somewhere between the '70s and '90s. Damon is far from looking like white trash—he could be Alex Pettyfer's younger brother. And Damon says weed just isn't his thing. No, Damon's drug of choice is cocaine and he only grows and sells weed to pay for his cocaine habit.

Natalie pretends that what Damon does is perfectly harmless. She knows that he doesn't smoke weed and says that weed really isn't that bad and if other people want to smoke it to chill out and relax, that she sees no harm in Damon helping with that.

She refuses to believe, however, that cocaine has seen more action from his face than any part of her body has.

"OK, you're going to have a good time, right?" Natalie bumps my backseat door shut with her butt after I get out and then she looks hopelessly at me. "Just don't fight it and *try* to enjoy yourself."

I roll my eyes. "Nat, I wouldn't deliberately *try* to hate it," I say. "I *do* want to enjoy myself."

Damon comes around to our side of the truck and slips his arms around both of our waists. "I get to go in with two hot chicks on my arms."

Natalie elbows him with a pretend resentful smirk. "Shut up, baby. You'll make me jealous." Already she's grinning impishly up at him.

Damon lets his hand drop from her waist and he grabs a handful of her butt cheek. She makes a sickening moaning sound and reaches up on her toes to kiss him. I want to tell them to get a room, but I'd be wasting my breath.

The Underground is the hottest spot just outside of downtown Raleigh, North Carolina, but you won't find it listed in the phone book. Only people like us know it exists. Some guy named Rob rented out an abandoned warehouse two years ago and spent about one million of his rich daddy's money to convert it into a secret nightclub. Two years and going strong, the place has since become a spot where local rock sex gods can live the rock n' roll dream with screaming fans and groupies. But it's not a trashy joint. From the outside it might look like an abandoned building in a partial ghost town, but the inside is like any upscale hard rock nightclub equipped with colorful strobe lights that shoot continuously across the space, slutty-looking waitresses, and a stage big enough for two bands to play at the same time.

To keep The Underground private, everybody who goes has to park elsewhere in the city and walk to it because a street lined with vehicles outside an 'abandoned' warehouse is a dead giveaway.

We park in the back of a nearby Mickey D's and walk about ten minutes through spooky town.

Natalie moves from Damon's right side and gets in between us, but it's just so she can torture me before we go inside.

"OK," she says as if about to run down a list of do's and don'ts for me, "if anybody asks, you're single, all right?" She waves her hand at me. "None of that stuff you pulled like with that guy who was hitting on you at Office Depot."

"What was she doing at Office Depot?" Damon says, laughing.

"Damon, this guy was *on her*," Natalie says, totally ignoring the fact that I'm right here, "I mean like all she had to do was bat her eyes once and he would've bought her a car—you know what she said to him?"

I roll my eyes and pull my arm out of hers. "Nat, you're so stupid. It wasn't like that."

"Yeah, babe," Damon says. "If the guy works at Office Depot he's not going to be buying anybody any cars."

Natalie smacks him across the shoulder playfully. "I didn't say he worked there—anyway, the guy looked like the lovechild of... Adam Levine and..." she twirls her fingers around above her head to let another famous example materialize on her tongue, "...Jensen Ackles, and Miss *Prudeness* here told him she was a lesbian when he asked for her number."

"Oh shut up, Nat!" I say, irritated at her serious over-exaggeration illness. "He did *not* look like either one of those guys. He was just a regular guy who didn't happen to be fugly."

She waves me away and turns back to Damon. "Whatever. The point is that she'll lie to keep them away. I don't doubt for a second that she'd go as far as to tell a guy she has Chlamydia and an out of control case of crabs."

Damon laughs.

I stop on the dark sidewalk and cross my arms over my chest, chewing on the inside of my bottom lip in agitation.

Natalie, realizing I'm not walking beside her anymore, runs back toward me. "Okay! Okay! Look, I just don't want you to ruin it for yourself, that's all. I'm just asking that if someone—who isn't a total hunchback—hits on you that you not immediately push him away. Nothing wrong with talking and getting to know one another. I'm not asking you to go home with him."

I'm already hating her for this. She swore!

Damon comes up behind her and wraps his hands around her waist, nuzzling his mouth into her squirming neck.

"Maybe you should just let her do what she wants, babe. Stop being so pushy."

"Thank you, Damon," I say with a quick nod.

He winks at me.

Natalie purses her lips and says, "You're right," and then puts up her hands. "I won't say anything else. I swear."

*Yeah, I have heard that before...*

"Good," I say and we all start walking again. Already these boots are killing my feet.

The ogre at the warehouse entrance inspects us at the door with his huge arms crossed in front.

He holds out his hand.

Natalie's face twists into an offended knot. "What? Is Rob charging now?"

Damon reaches into his back pocket and pulls out his wallet, fingering the bills inside.

"Twenty bucks a pop," the ogre says with a grunt.

"Twenty? Are you fucking kidding me?!" Natalie shrieks.

Damon gently pushes her aside and slaps three twenty-dollar bills into the ogre's hand. The ogre shoves the money into his pocket and moves to let us pass. I go first and Damon puts his hand on Natalie's lower back to guide her in front of him.

She sneers at the ogre as she passes by. "Probably going to keep it for himself," she says. "I'm going to ask Rob about this."

"Come on," Damon says and we slip past the door and down one lengthy, dreary hallway with a single flickering fluorescent light until we make it to the industrial elevator at the end.

The metal jolts as the cage door closes and we're rather noisily riding to the basement floor many feet below. It's just one floor down, but the elevator rattles so much I feel like it's going to snap any second and send us plunging to our deaths. Loud, booming drums and the shouting of drunk college students, and probably a lot of drop-outs, funnel through the basement floor and into the cage elevator, louder every inch we descend into the bowels of The Underground. The elevator rumbles to a halt and another ogre opens the cage door to let us out.

Natalie stumbles into me from behind. "Hurry up!" she says, pushing me playfully in the back. "I think that's Four Collision playing!" Her voice rises over the music as we make our way into the main room.

Natalie takes Damon by the hand and then tries to grab mine, but I know what she has in mind and I'm not going into a throng of bouncing, sweaty bodies wearing these stupid boots.

"Oh, come *on*!" she urges, practically begging. Then an aggravated line deepens around her snarling nose and she thrusts my hand into hers and pulls me toward her. "Stop being a baby! If anybody knocks you over, I'll personally kick their ass, all right?"

Damon is grinning at me from the side.

"Fine!" I say and head out with them, Natalie practically pulling my fingers out of the sockets.

We hit the dance floor and after a while of Natalie doing what any best friend would do by grinding against me to make me feel included, she eases her way into Damon's world only. She might as well be having sex with him right there in front of everybody, but no one notices. I only notice because I'm probably the only girl in the entire place without a date doing the same thing. I take advantage of the opportunity and slip my way off the dance floor and head to the bar.

"What can I get'cha?" the tall blond guy behind the bar says as I push myself up on my toes and take an empty bar stool.

"Rum and Coke."

He goes to make my drink. "Hard stuff, huh?" he says, filling the glass with ice. "Going to show me your I.D.?" He grins.

I purse my lips at him. "Yeah, I'll show you my I.D. when you show me your liquor license." I grin right back at him and he smiles.

He finishes mixing the drink and slides it over to me.

"I don't really drink much anyway," I say, taking a little sip from the straw.

"Much?"

"Yeah, well, tonight I think I'll need a buzz." I set the glass down and finger the lime on the rim.

"Why's that?" he asks, wiping the bar top down with a paper towel.

"Wait a second," I hold up one finger, "before you get the wrong idea, I'm not here to spill my guts to you—bartender-customer therapy." Natalie is all the therapy I can handle.

He laughs and tosses the paper towel somewhere behind the bar.

"Well that's good to know because I'm not the advice type."

I take another small sip, leaning over this time instead of lifting the glass from the bar; my loose hair falls all around my face. I rise back up and tuck one side behind my ear. I really hate wearing my hair down; it's more trouble than it's worth.

"Well, if you must know," I say looking right at him, "I was dragged here by my relentless best friend who would probably do something embarrassing to me in my sleep and take a blackmail pic if I didn't come."

"Ah, one of those," he says, laying his arms across the bar top and folding his hands together. "I had a friend like that once. Six months after my fiancée skipped out on me, he dragged me to a nightclub just outside of Baltimore—I just wanted to sit at home and sulk in my misery, but turns out that night out was exactly what I needed."

Oh great, this guy thinks he knows me already, or, at least my "situation." But he doesn't know anything about my situation. Maybe he has the bad ex thing down—because we all have that eventually—but the rest of it, my parents' divorce, my older brother, Cole, going to jail, the death of the love of my life... I'm not about to tell this guy anything. The moment you tell someone else is the moment you become a whiner and the world's smallest violin starts to play. The truth is, we all have problems; we all go through hardships and pain, and my pain is paradise compared to a lot of people's and I really have no right to whine at all.

"I thought you weren't the advice type?" I smile sweetly.

He leans away from the bar and says, "I'm not, but if you're getting something out of my story then be grateful."

I smirk and take a fake sip this time. I don't really want a buzz and I definitely don't want to get drunk, especially since I have a feeling I'm going to be the one driving us home again.

Trying to take the spotlight off me, I prop one elbow on the bar and rest my chin on my knuckles and say, "So then what happened that night?"

The left side of his mouth lifts into a grin and he says, shaking his blond head, "I got laid for the first time since she left me and I remembered how good it felt to be unchained from one person."

I didn't expect that kind of answer. Most guys I know would've lied about their relationship phobia, especially if they were hitting on me. I kind of like this guy. Just as a guy, of course; I'm not about to, as Natalie might say, bend over for him.

"I see," I say, trying to hold in the true measure of my smile. "Well, at least you're honest."

"No other way to be," he says as he reaches for an empty glass and starts to make a rum and Coke for himself. "I've found that most girls are as much afraid of commitment as guys are these days and if you're up front in the beginning, you're more likely to come out of the one-nighter unscathed."

I nod, fitting my fingertips around my straw. There's no way I'd openly admit it to him, but I completely agree with him and even find it refreshing. I've never really given it that much thought before, but as much as I don't want a relationship within one hundred feet of me, I am still human and I wouldn't mind a one-night stand.

Just not with him. Or anyone in this place. OK, so maybe I'm too chicken for a one-night stand and this drink has already started going straight to my head. Truth is, I've never done anything like that before and even though the thought is kind of exciting, it still scares the shit out of me. I've only ever been with two guys: Ian Walsh, my first love who took my virginity and died in a car accident three months later, and then Christian Deering, my Ian rebound guy and the jerk who cheated on me with some red-haired slut.

I'm just glad I never said that poisonous three-word phrase that begins with "I" and ends with "you," back to him because I had a feeling, deep down, that when he said it to me, he didn't know what the hell he was talking about.

Then again, maybe he *did* and that's why after five months of dating, he hooked up with someone else: because I never said it back.

I look up at the bartender to notice he's smiling back at me, waiting patiently for me to say something. This guy's good; either that, or he really is just trying to be friendly. I admit, he's cute; can't be older than twenty-five and has soft brown eyes that smile before his lips do. I notice how toned his biceps and chest are underneath that tight-fitting T-shirt. And he's tanned; definitely a guy who has lived most of his life near an ocean somewhere.

I stop looking when I notice my mind wandering, thinking about how he looks in swim shorts and no shirt.

"I'm Blake," he says. "I'm Rob's brother."

*Rob? Oh yeah, the guy who owns The Underground.*

I reach out my hand and Blake gently shakes it.

"Camryn."

I hear Natalie's voice over the music before I even see her. She makes her way through a cluster of people standing around near the dance floor and pushes her way past to get to me. Immediately, she takes note of Blake and her eyes start glistening, lighting up with her huge, blatant smile. Damon, following behind her with her hand still clasped in his, notices, too, but he just locks emotionless eyes with me. I get the strangest feeling from it, but I brush it off as Natalie presses her shoulder into mine.

"What are you doing over here?" she asks with obvious accusation in her voice. She's grinning from ear to ear and glances between Blake and me several times before giving me all of her attention.

"Having a drink," I say. "Did you come over here to get one for yourself, or to check up on me?"

"Both!" she says, letting Damon's hand fall away from hers and she reaches up and taps her fingers on the bar, smiling at Blake. "Anything with vodka."

Blake nods and looks at Damon.

"I'll have rum and Coke," Damon says.

Natalie presses her lips against the side of my head and I feel the heat of her breath on my ear when she whispers, "Holy shit, Cam! Do you know who that is?"

I notice Blake's mouth spread subtly into a smile, having heard her.

Feeling my face get hot with embarrassment, I whisper back, "Yeah, his name is Blake."

"That's Rob's *brother*!" she hisses; her gaze falls back on him.

I look up at Damon, hoping he'll get the hint and drag her off somewhere, but this time he pretends not to get it. Where is the Damon I know, the one who used to have my back when it came to Natalie?

Uh oh, he must be pissed at her again. He only ever acts like this when Natalie has opened her big mouth, or done something that Damon just can't get past. We've only been here for about thirty minutes. What could she have done in such a short time? And then I realize: this is Natalie and if anyone can piss a boyfriend off in under an hour and without knowing it, it's her.

I slip off the bar stool and take her by the arm, pulling her away from the bar. Damon, probably knowing what my plan is, stays behind with Blake.

The music seems to have gotten louder as the live band ends one song and starts the next.

"What did you do?" I demand, turning her around to face me.

"What do you mean what did I do?" She's hardly even paying attention to me; her body moves subtly with the music instead.

"Nat, I'm serious."

Finally, she stops and looks right at me, searching my face for answers.

"To piss Damon off?" I say. "He was fine when we came in here."

She looks across the space briefly at Damon standing by the bar, sipping his drink, and then back at me with a confused look on her face. "I didn't do anything...I don't think." She looks up as if in thought, trying to recall what she might have said or done.

She puts her hands on her hips. "What makes you think he's pissed?"

"He's got that look," I say, glancing back at him and Blake, "and I hate it when you two fight, especially when I'm stuck with you for the night and have to listen to you both go back and forth about stupid shit that happened a year ago."

Natalie's confused expression turns into a devious smile. "Well, I think you're paranoid and maybe trying to distract me from saying anything about you and Blake." She's getting that playful look now and I hate it.

I roll my eyes. "There is no 'me and Blake,' we're just talking."

"Talking is the first step. Smiling at him—" (her grin deepens) "which I totally saw you doing when I walked up—is the next step." She crosses her arms and pops out her hip. "I bet you've already had a conversation with him without him having to pry the answers out of you—Hell, you already know his name."

"For someone who wants me to have a good time and meet a guy, you don't know how to shut up when things already appear to be going your way."

Natalie lets the music dictate her movement again, raising her hands up a little above her and moving her hips around seductively. I just stand here.

"Nothing's going to happen," I say sternly. "You got what you wanted and I'm talking to someone and have no intention of telling him I have Chlamydia, so please, don't make a scene."

She gives in with a long, deep sigh and stops dancing long enough to say, "I guess you're right. I'll leave you to him, but if he takes you up to Rob's floor, I want details." She points her finger at me firmly, one eye slitted and her lips pursed.

"Fine," I say, just to get her off my back, "but don't hold your breath because it's *not* gonna happen."

Camryn Bennett and Andrew Parrish have never been happier. After a whirlwind romance on their amazing road trip, they are engaged—and a wedding isn't the only special event in their future. They have so much to look forward to—until tragedy blindsides them...

Please see the next page for an excerpt from

*The Edge of Always*

# ONE

## *Andrew*

few months ago, when I was laid up in that hospital bed, I didn't think I'd be alive today, much less be expecting a baby and engaged to an angel with a dirty mouth. But here I am. Here *we* are, Camryn and me, taking on the world...in a different way. Things didn't quite turn out how we planned them, but then again, things rarely do. And neither of us would change the way they turned out even if we could.

I love this chair. It was my dad's favorite chair, and the one thing he left behind that I wanted. Sure, I inherited a fat check that will set Camryn and me up for a while, and of course I got the Chevelle, but the chair was equally sentimental to me. She hates it, but she won't say so out loud, because it was my dad's. I can't blame her; it's old, it stinks, and there's a hole in the cushion from my dad's cigarette smoking days. I promised her I'd get someone in here to clean it, at least. And I will. As soon as she figures out whether we're going to stay in Galveston or move to North Carolina. I'm fine with either, but something tells me she's holding back on what she really wants, because of me.

I hear the water from the shower shut off, and seconds later a loud *bang* vibrates through the wall. I jump up from the chair, letting the remote control hit the floor as I rush toward the bathroom. The edge of the coffee table clips the shit outta my shin as I pass.

I swing open the bathroom door. "What happened?"

Camryn shakes her head at me and smiles as she leans over to pick the hair dryer up from the floor beside the toilet.

I breathe a sigh of relief.

"You're more paranoid than I am," she laughs.

She glances down at my leg as I rub it with my fingertips. She sets the hair dryer back on the counter, comes up to me, and kisses the side of my mouth. "Looks like I'm not the one who needs to worry about being accident prone." She smiles.

My hands cup her shoulders and I pull her closer, letting one hand fall down to touch her little rounded belly. I can barely tell she's pregnant. At four months I thought she'd at least be emulating a baby hippo, but what do I know about this stuff?

"Maybe so," I say, trying to hide the red in my face. "You probably did that on purpose just to see how fast I could get in here."

She kisses the other side of my mouth and then goes in for the kill, kissing me fully and deeply while pressing her wet, naked body against mine. I moan against her mouth, wrapping my arms around her.

But then I pull away before I fall into her devious trap. "Dammit, woman, you've gotta stop that."

She grins back at me. "You *really* want me to stop?" she asks with that up-to-no-good smile of hers.

It scares the shit out of me when she does that. Once after a conversation laced with that smile, she stopped having sex with me for three whole days. Worst three days of my life.

"Well, no," I say nervously. "I just mean right now. We have exactly thirty minutes before we have to be at the doctor's office."

I just hope she's this horny throughout her entire pregnancy. I've heard horror stories about how some women go from wanting it all the time until they get really big and then if you touch them they turn into fire-breathing banshees.

*Thirty minutes. Damn. I could bend her over the counter real quick...*

Camryn smiles sweetly and jerks the towel from the shower curtain rod and starts drying off. "I'll be ready in ten," she says as she waves me out. "Don't forget to water Georgia. Did you find your phone?"

"Not yet," I say as I start to ease my way out the door, but then I stop and add with a sexually suggestive grin, "Ummm, we could—"

She shuts the door in my face. I just walk off laughing.

I rush around the apartment, searching under cushions and in odd places for my keys and finally find them hiding underneath a stack of junk mail on the kitchen counter. I stop for a moment and take a particular piece of mail into my fingers. Camryn won't let me throw it away, because it was the one she looked at when giving the 911 operator my address the morning I had that seizure in front of her. I guess she feels like that piece of paper helped save my life, but really what it did was help her eventually understand what was going on with me. The seizure was harmless. I've had several. Hell, I had one when we were staying in the hotel in New Orleans before we started sharing a room. When I finally told her about that later, needless to say, she was not happy with me.

She worries all the time that the tumor will come back. I think she worries about it more than I do.

If it does, it does. We'll get through it together. We'll always get through everything together.

"Time to go, babe!" I yell from the living room.

She comes out of our room dressed in a rather tight pair of jeans and an equally tight T-shirt. And heels. *Really? Heels?*

"You're going to squeeze her little head in those jeans," I say.

"No, I'm not going to squeeze her *or his* head," she counters as she grabs her purse from the couch and shoulders it. "You're so sure of yourself, but we'll see." She takes my hand and I walk her out the door, flipping the lock on the knob before I close it hard behind us.

"I know it's a girl," I say confidently.

"Care to wager?" She looks over at me and grins.

We step out into the mild November air, and I open the car door for her, gesturing inside with my palm up. "What kind of bet?" I ask. "You know I'm all for betting."

Camryn slides onto the seat, and I jog around to my side and get in. Resting my wrists on the top of the steering wheel, I look over at her and wait.

She smiles and chews gently on the inside of her bottom lip while she thinks for a moment. Her long blonde hair tumbles down over both shoulders, and her blue eyes shine with excitement.

"You're the one who seems so sure," she finally says. "So, you name the bet and I'll either agree to it or I won't." She stops abruptly and points her finger sternly at me. "But nothing sexual. I think you pretty much have that area covered. Think of something…" she whirls her hand around in front of her "…I don't know…daring or meaningful."

Hmmm. I'm officially stumped. I slide the key in the ignition, but pause before turning it.

"OK, if it's a girl, then I get to name her," I say with a soft, proud smile.

Her eyebrows twitch a little and she turns her chin at an angle.

"I don't like that bet. That's something both of us should take part in, don't you think?"

"Well, yeah, but don't you trust me?"

She hesitates. "Yes...I trust you, but—"

"—but not with a baby name." I raise an eyebrow interrogatively at her, but really I'm just messing with her head.

She can't look me in the eyes anymore, and she appears uncomfortable.

"Well?" I urge her.

Camryn crosses her arms and says, "What name did you have in mind, exactly?"

"What makes you think I already have one picked out?" I turn the key and the Chevelle purrs to life.

She smirks at me, cocking her head to one side. "Oh, please. You obviously have one picked out already, or you wouldn't be so sure it's a girl and making bets with me when we have an ultrasound to get to."

I look away, grinning, and put the car into reverse.

"Lily," I say and just barely catch Camryn's eye as we back out of the parking space. "Lily Marybeth Parrish."

A little smile tugs the corners of her lips.

"I actually like that," she says, and her smile gets bigger and bigger. "I admit, I was slightly worried—why Lily?"

"No reason. I just like it."

She doesn't seem convinced. She playfully narrows her eyes at me.

"I'm serious!" I say, laughing gently. "I've been going over names in my head since the day after you told me."

Camryn's smile warms, and if I wasn't such a guy, I'd cave to the moment and allow myself to blush like an idiot.

"You've been thinking of names all this time?" She seems happily surprised.

OK, so I blush anyway.

"Yeah," I admit. "Haven't thought of a good boy name yet, but we've got several months to think about it."

Camryn is just looking at me, beaming. I don't know what's going on inside her head, but I realize my face is getting redder the longer she stares at me like that.

*"What?"* I ask and let out a laugh.

She leans across the seat and raises her hand to my face, her fingertips pulling my chin to the side. And then she kisses me.

"God, I love you," she whispers.

It takes a second to realize I'm grinning so big my face feels stretched out. "I love you, too. Now get your seat belt on." I point to it.

She slides back over onto her side and clicks the seat belt buckle into place.

As we ride toward the doctor's office we both keep glancing at the clock in the dashboard. Eight more minutes. Five. Three. I think it hits her as hard as it does me when we pull into the building's parking lot. In no time at all we may meet our son or daughter for the very first time.

Yeah, a few months ago, I didn't think I'd be alive...

———

"The wait is killing me," Camryn leans over and whispers to me.

This is so strange, sitting in this doctor's waiting room with pregnant chicks on all sides of us. I'm kind of scared to make eye contact. Some of them look pissed. All of the magazines for guys seem to have a man on the cover in a boat holding up a fish with his thumb in its mouth. I pretend to read an article.

"We've only been sitting here for about ten minutes," I whisper back and run the palm of my hand across her thigh, letting the magazine rest on my lap.

"I know, I'm just nervous."

As I take her hand, a nurse in pink scrubs steps out from a side door and calls Camryn's name, and we follow her back.

I sit against the wall while Camryn undresses and then puts on one of those hospital gowns. I tease her about her butt being on display and she pretends to be offended, but the blush gives her away. And we sit here and wait. And wait some more until another nurse comes in and has our full attention. She washes her hands in the nearby sink.

"Did you drink enough water an hour before your appointment?" the nurse asks after the hellos.

"Yes ma'am," Camryn says.

I can tell she's afraid something might be wrong with the baby and the ultrasound will show it. I've tried to tell her that everything will be fine, but it doesn't keep her from worrying.

She looks across the room at me, and I can't help but get up and move over to her side. The nurse asks a series of questions and snaps on a pair of latex gloves. I help answer the questions that I can, because Camryn seems increasingly worried every second that goes by and she doesn't talk much. I squeeze her hand, trying to ease her mind.

After the nurse squirts that gel stuff on her belly, Camryn takes a deep breath.

"Wow, that's some tattoo you've got there," the nurse says. "It must've been pretty special to sit through one as large as that on the ribs."

"Yeah, it's definitely special," Camryn says and smiles up at me. "It's of Orpheus. Andrew has the other half. Eurydice. But it's a long story."

I proudly raise my shirt over my ribs to show the nurse my half.

"Stunning," the nurse says, looking at both of our tattoos in turns. "You don't see that in here every day."

The nurse leaves it at that and moves the probe through the gel pointing out the baby's head and elbow and other various parts. And I feel Camryn's grip on my hand slowly ease the more the nurse talks and smiles while explaining how "everything is lookin' good." I watch Camryn's face go from nervous and stiff to relieved and happy, and it makes me smile.

"So are you sure there's nothing to worry about?" Camryn asks. "Are you *positive*?"

The nurse nods and glances at me briefly. "Yes. So far I don't see anything of concern. Development is right where we want it to be. Movement and heartbeat are normal. I think you can relax."

Camryn looks up at me, and I have a feeling we're thinking the same thing.

She confirms it when the nurse says, "So, I understand you're curious about the gender?" And the two of us just pause, looking at one another. She's so damn beautiful. I can't believe she's mine. I can't believe she's carrying my baby.

"I'll take that bet," Camryn finally agrees, catching me off guard. She smiles brightly and tugs on my hand, and we both look at the nurse.

"Yes," Camryn answers. "If that's possible now."

The nurse moves the probe back to a specific area and appears to be giving her findings one last check before she announces it.

"Well, it's still kind of early, but...looks like a girl to me so far," the nurse finally says. "At about twenty weeks during your next ultrasound, we'll be able to determine the sex officially."

# TWO

## *Camryn*

*I* honestly don't think I've ever seen Andrew smile like that before. Maybe that night I sang with him the first time in New Orleans and he was so proud of me, but even still I'm not so sure anything can match his face right now. My heart is pounding against my ribs with excitement, especially over Andrew's reaction. I can tell how much he wanted a little girl, and I swear he's doing everything in his power to keep from tearing up in front of the nurse. Or me, for that matter.

It never mattered to me whether it was a boy or girl. I'm like just about every other expecting mom out there who just wants it to be healthy. Not that our baby's health doesn't take precedence over gender in Andrew's mind, though. I know better than that.

He leans over and kisses me lightly on the lips, his bright green eyes lit up with everything good.

"Lily it is," I say with complete agreement, and I kiss him once more before he pulls away, running my fingers through his short brown hair.

"Pretty name," the nurse says. "But keep a boy name handy, too, just in case." She pulls the probe back and gives us a moment.

Andrew says to the nurse suddenly, "Well, if you don't see a little package of junk already on my kid, it's definitely a girl."

I choke out a small laugh and vaguely roll my eyes as I look at the nurse. What's even funnier is that Andrew was being serious. He cocks his head to one side when he notices the amused look on my face.

We spend the rest of the day shopping. Neither of us could resist it. We've spent some time looking at baby stuff before but never bought much, because we didn't know if it should be pink or blue and we didn't want to end up with a room full of yellow. And even though there's still a chance it could be a boy, I think Andrew is more convinced than before that it's a girl, so I go along with it and let myself believe it, too. But he still won't let me buy much!

"Just wait," he insists when I go for the next girlie outfit in the newborn section. "You know my mom's planning a baby shower, right?"

"Yeah, but we can get a few more things now." I put the outfit in the cart anyway.

Andrew looks into the cart and then back at me with his lips pursed in contemplation. "I think you've surpassed a *few*, babe."

He's right. I've tossed about ninety dollars' worth of clothes in the basket already. Oh well, if anything, if it turns out to be a boy I can exchange it all later.

And that's how the rest of the day goes until we stop by his mother's house to give her the news.

"Oh, that's wonderful!" Marna says, pulling me into a hug. "I thought for sure it'd be a boy!"

My hands slide away from Marna's arms, and I sit at the kitchen table with Andrew while Marna heads to the fridge. She pulls out a tea pitcher and starts preparing us a glass.

"Baby shower will be in February," Marna says from the bar. "I've already got everything planned out. All you have to do is show up." She beams at me and puts the tea pitcher away.

"Thank you," I say.

She sets a glass down in front of each of us and then pulls out the empty chair.

I really do miss home. But I love it here, too, and Marna is like another mom to me. I haven't been able to bring myself to tell Andrew yet about how much I miss *my* mom and Natalie, just having a friend to talk to. You can be in love with the greatest guy on the planet—and in fact, I am—but it doesn't mean it won't be somewhat difficult not having other friends. I've met one girl my age here, Alana, who lives upstairs with her husband, but I just haven't been able to click with her on any kind of level. I think if I'm already making up lies to keep from going somewhere with her when she calls, then clicking with her at all might never happen.

But I really think my secret sadness and missing home and all that is because of the pregnancy. My hormones are all out of whack. And I think it also has a lot to do with worrying. I worry about everything now. I mean, I did a lot of that before I met Andrew, but now that I'm pregnant, my worries have multiplied: Will the baby be healthy? Will I be a good mother? Did I screw up my life by… I'm doing it again. Fuck. I'm a horrible person. Every time that thought crosses my mind it makes me feel so guilty. I love our baby and I wouldn't change the way things are if I could, but I can't help but wonder if I…if *we* messed up by getting pregnant too soon.

"Camryn?" I hear Andrew's voice and I snap out of my deep thoughts. "Are you all right?"

I force a believable smile. "Yeah, I'm good. Was just daydreaming—y'know, I prefer purple over pink."

"I got to name her," Andrew says, "so you can choose whatever colors you want." He encloses my hand underneath his on the table. It makes me smile just to know that he cares about any of this stuff at all.

Marna pulls her glass away from her lips and sets it on the table in front of her.

"Oh?" she asks intrigued. "You've already picked out a name?"

Andrew nods. "Lily Marybeth. Camryn's middle name is Marybeth. She should be named after her mom."

*Oh my God, he just melted my heart. I don't deserve him.*

Marna smiles over at me, her face full of happiness and every other emotion imaginable that someone like Andrew's mother could possess. Not only did her son beat his illness and come back strong from the brink of death, but now she has a granddaughter on the way.

"Well, it's a beautiful name," she says. "I thought Aidan and Michelle would be first, but life's full of surprises." Something about the way she said that seemed to have a hidden meaning and Andrew notices.

"Something going on with Aidan and Michelle?" Andrew asks, taking a quick sip of his tea.

"Just part of being married," she answers. "I've never seen a marriage without *some* kind of struggles, and they've been together for a long time."

"How long?" I ask.

"Married only five years," Marna says. "But they've been together for about nine, I believe." She nods as she thinks about it further, satisfied with her memory.

"It's probably just Aidan," Andrew says. "I wouldn't wanna be married to him." He laughs.

"Yeah, that would be weird," I say, wrinkling my nose at him.

"Well, Michelle won't be able to make the baby shower," Marna says. "She has a few conferences she has to attend, and it just doesn't fit with her schedule, especially since she's so far away. But she'll probably send the best gifts out of everyone." She smiles sweetly over at me.

I acknowledge her and take another sip, but my mind is wandering again and I can't stop it. All I can think about is what she said a few comments back, about never knowing of a marriage without struggles. And I slip right back into worry mode.

"Your birthday is December the eighth, right, Camryn?"

I blink back into the moment. "Oh...yes. The big twenty-one."

"Well, looks like I have a birthday party to plan, too, then."

"Oh, no, you don't need to do that."

She waves away my plea as if it's ridiculous, and Andrew just sits back with that dopey grin on his face.

I give in because I know with Marna there's no use trying.

We head home after an hour, and it's already dark out. I'm so tired from running around all day and from the Lily excitement.

Lily. I can't believe I'm going to be a mom. A smile spreads across my face as I step into the living room. I drop my purse on the coffee table and plop down on the center cushion of the couch, kicking my shoes off. But before too long, Andrew is sitting down next to me with that knowing look on his beautiful face.

I could fool Marna, but I should've known better than to think I could fool him.

# ABOUT THE AUTHOR

J. A. REDMERSKI, a *New York Times*, *USA Today*, and *Wall Street Journal* bestselling author, lives in North Little Rock, Arkansas, with her three children, two cats, and a Maltese. She is a lover of television and books that push boundaries, and is a huge fan of AMC's *The Walking Dead*.

Learn more at:
JessicaRedmerski.com
Twitter, @JRedmerski
Facebook.com/J.A.Redmerski